A Very Private Arrangement

E.M. Phillips

For Rachel,
For our Salad Days
and our Donkey Days,
from The Strand to Brighton,
for times remembered
and absent friends.

To Iris
with best wishes
from
Eve

A Very Private Arrangement

E.M. Phillips

A Very Private Arrangement

Published 2008 by Sagittarius Publications
62 Jacklyns Lane, Alresford, Hampshire SO24 9LH
Tel: 01962 734322

Typeset by John Owen Smith

ISBN 978-0-9555778-4-0

Printed and bound by CPI Antony Rowe, Eastbourne

Part I

'O! how this spring of love resembleth

the uncertain glory of an April day.'

W.S.

1

STRATTON PLACE, BLOOMSBURY

March 1934

The brass knocker on the blue door to the side of the gallery was fashioned into a lion's head, so polished that in the bright spring sunshine it almost hurt the eyes. Standing beside Miss Lockwood as she gave the knocker a brisk rat-tat, Anna stared at the lion's head until it became two bright discs, which with a little more concentration could be made to pass and re-pass each other. Engrossed in this diversion she was brought back to the present by the sound of unhurried footsteps descending the stairs. The door opened and a thin grey-haired man in shirtsleeves and wearing a long green baize apron stood on the threshold. He bowed, motioning them inside with an extravagant sweep of the arm.

''Afternoon madam, I'm Charlie and I'm to look after the lassie until Mr. Patrick gets back.'

Anna grinned in response to his strong Glaswegian accent and breezy smile but Miss Lockwood stood firm, resisting his inviting gesture to step over the threshold. 'Is Mr. Farrell not here?'

The man gave Anna the faintest of winks. 'He is not; he was away early this morning an' won't be back until late tonight.'

'This really is too bad; I cannot possibly wait on Mr Farrell's convenience.' Anna's jailer gave her shoulder and irritable shake; as though it's *my* fault, Anna thought, 'Anna, you will stay with this gentleman. Conduct yourself in the proper manner and remember that it is very kind of your uncle to have you at such short notice.'

'Yes, Miss Lockwood.'

'And don't forget to give Miss Harrison's letter to Mr. Farrell as soon as he returns.'

Anna sighed and rolled her eyes. 'No, Miss Lockwood.'

'Be sure you do.' She bent a deeply suspicious look on the manservant then, 'See you keep your coat on!' she admonished Anna and with this cryptic command gave her charge's shoulder a last bruising squeeze and departed.

Anna stood with the man called Charlie as together they watched

Miss Lockwood's large tweed-clad rear out of sight. 'Have y' noticed,' he asked conversationally, 'how some people look like animals? Now that one there, she's a bullfrog comin' an' a cart horse going!' Anna gave a snort of laughter and he motioned her inside the door. 'Hurry up, lassie; I've got scones in the oven and they'll be about ready – hungry, are ye?'

Without waiting for her reply he crossed the hallway and began to climb the stairs, which unlike Cousin Ruth's threadbare linoleum treads were carpeted and secured at each rise with polished brass rods. Used to strange houses and sometimes even stranger people, Anna followed him obediently but with some caution; he seemed to be quite normal, but you never knew...

'Actually I'm starving,' she offered, 'it took ages to get here and Miss Lockwood wouldn't use the dining car. She *said* it was because it was full of men, but she might have made that the excuse to hang onto the lunch money.'

'Is that so?' He gave her a considering look. 'Why could she not eat with men in the car?'

'Because she doesn't like them,' she answered reasonably.

'Good job she's not stayin' here then. There's no wimmin in this house.'

'There's nothing else *but* women at school, nor at Cousin Ruth's.'

He shook his head. 'Ach, the poor lady – to be taken sudden like that; will ye go to the funeral?'

She shrugged. 'Only if Uncle Patrick makes me'

She hoped he wouldn't. It gave her a creepy feeling to think about Cousin Ruth, cold and dead and in her coffin; she didn't at all fancy watching it lowered into the ground with all those worms and beetles and things. Poor old cousin Ruth; Anna felt a sudden pang of remorse that she hadn't really liked her all that much. She hoped the old thing had managed to get to heaven because she'd certainly made enough song and dance about it while she was alive.

She watched the man Charlie as he moved around opening cupboards and taking out cups, saucers and plates. She wondered if she could ask him about his employer. Her uncle she supposed must be well off because he owned the gallery and this house, and she knew that since she'd been orphaned he had paid her school fees. But whenever she'd questioned Cousin Ruth about this elusive benefactor she had been met with pursed lips and a disapproving 'We don't discuss Patrick Farrell in *this* house – he is an Emissary of the Devil!' so that she had eventually given up asking. Now all that was about to change and she would be able to judge matters for herself.

Looking on the bright side though, she felt an Emissary of the Devil sounded promising. However, Cousin Ruth had been given to some rather strange flights of fancy. No doubt Uncle Patrick would turn out to be like the rest of the Farrell men, old, not very interesting and on intimate terms with the more terrifying proclamations of all the Old Testament prophets.

She'd have to watch her step, she thought gloomily. If she upset him he might stop paying her fees and then she'd end up in some blooming awful orphanage, Since the age of six when she'd been unceremoniously shuffled off to boarding school, she had spent her vacations with whichever relations were willing to have her foisted upon them; the occasional appearance of the two strangers who were her parents providing the only remission in a life of mind-numbing boredom.

After both parents had, as Ruth rather censoriously put it, so inconsiderately died of yellow fever whilst spreading the Word of the Lord in darkest Africa, Anna had lived with her cousin. The past two years of school vacations spent in the cramped Victorian villa on the outskirts of Colchester hadn't been particularly happy ones and the time she was required to spend on her knees night and morning, whilst Cousin Ruth loudly bewailed her manifold sins to a wrathful and all-seeing God, something to be endured rather than enjoyed, although even that had been preferable to being passed around the family at regular intervals like an unwanted parcel; invariably ending up with someone different every holiday and most of them batty. She didn't fancy going back to never knowing in which particular household she might fetch up next.

Pulling off her hat she looked around the big blue and white painted kitchen with interest. Everything was very clean and tidy, just like Cousin Ruth's, but this one was much, much bigger and instead of being cold and austere had a warm, welcoming feel to it.

Shining copper pans hung from a ceiling beam. On the top shelf of the pine dresser that stood against one wall were ranged a biscuit barrel with a blue Chinese pattern, an ornate and gilded cheese dish and a collection of prettily decorated storage jars. Propped against the back of each of the remaining three shelves were rows of decorated plates and beneath them cups and jugs hung from hooks. All the china was decorative and beautiful, but few matching in either pattern or size. On the opposite side of the room was a long, foreign looking range, two deep porcelain sinks with shining brass taps and simply dozens of wooden cupboards. At the far end tall French Windows stood open onto a flight of stone steps leading to a long narrow garden.

Anna had never seen a kitchen like it; there were even pictures and photographs on the walls. One that caught her eye immediately was an enlarged snapshot of two men in a garden, one of them recognisably a younger Charlie, who stood with a hand on the shoulder of a dark-haired, handsome young man seated in a cane garden chair, an open book on his knees, his head half turned and smiling up at his companion. For several seconds Anna gazed at this picture, wondering who the young man was and why they both looked quite so pleased with themselves.

'If you've finished looking you'd best take off your things and make yourself comfortable.' She jumped and blushed as Charlie spoke behind her. Ignoring Miss Lockwood's mysterious injunction she hastily took off her coat and hung it with her hat behind the door then stood waiting as he removed a tray of scones from the big oven.

'Here, lassie, give them a minute or two t' cool and there's a feast fit for auld Rabbie himself.' With an expert hand Charlie turned them onto a wire rack on the table.

She gave him a sidelong glance. She hoped he wasn't going to start on about "wee sleekit cow'ring timorous beasties" she got enough of that sort of thing at school. Taking one of the four wheel-back chairs set about the central table she sat gazing hungrily at the scones. The smell of them was making her stomach hurt. 'Might I have one now please? I don't mind if I burn myself.'

He pushed plate and butter dish towards her. 'Here lassie, you eat all you want as soon as you want. The Lord knows you're skinny enough.'

*   *   *

Now what's Patrick going to think to have this young colt about the place for these weeks? Charlie watched her devouring the scone as he made a pot of tea. *Lord knows we can do without a curious female watching every move we make...*

She looked up suddenly. 'What are you thinking?' she asked her eyes sharp and wary.

He answered with some asperity, 'That there's not much of you for fourteen but what there is probably spells trouble!'

'I won't *be* any trouble,' she said quickly, then added with less certainty, 'not to you, anyway. I don't know about Uncle Patrick. If he's anything like the rest of the family I don't think I'll be all that keen on *him*!'

10

He looked at her with composed blue eyes then began to pour the tea. 'Could be he's thinkin' the same about you.' he answered.

*   *   *

Anna awoke, knowing it was late by the bar of sunlight that lay across her bed and had a moment's panic, thinking she was still at school and had slept through the rising bell.

She sat, pushing back the fat, light as thistledown French quilt that Charlie had called a *duvet* and looked around the room, marvelling again at the curved Empire bed in which she was lying, the beautiful polished chest and wardrobe and the open sash-windows with their snowy white muslin curtains. Clasping her hands behind her head and giving a sigh of contentment, she lay back against the pillows.

Tired and full of good food she had gone to bed early the previous evening, only pulling her nightdress from her case and splashing her face with water before crawling into the huge bed, there to fall asleep almost as soon as her head touched the plump feather pillows.

She'd been glad of the excuse to put off meeting the owner of all this luxury for a while longer, but now she would *have* to get up and see him. Her stomach lurched. If he wanted to pray for ages before breakfast she'd die, she really would.

She shuddered at the memory of one Christmas she'd spent with old Uncle William in his draughty Yorkshire house miles from anywhere. He'd droned an interminable grace each morning whilst the thin streaky rasher and minute pullet's egg on her plate grew ever more cold and unappetising, although, she recollected with another shudder, all his piety hadn't kept the dirty old beast from rubbing his dry, brown-blotched old hand up and down above her knee whenever he got the chance.

She looked across at the long foolscap envelope propped against the swing mirror on the bow-front chest of drawers. Grubby and creased from her pocket it contained her end of term report and a letter from the headmistress. There had been a long succession of such letters to various temporary guardians, not all of them bearing good news. She wondered what Miss Harrison had written about her this time.

She lingered in bed for a few minutes longer before stepping down onto the thick bedside rug. It felt like a flat and very dead sheep beneath her bare feet. Giving a little squeal she hopped off it quickly and padded across the polished boards into the adjoining bathroom.

Turning both bath taps on full she watched the steam rise to the ceiling then, after first carefully removing the flowered paper from the bar of rose geranium soap nestling in a blue china dish, she stepped into the unaccustomed luxury of the great claw-footed bath.

Afterward, dressed in skirt and jumper she stood before the oval swinging glass in the bedroom, twisting the stubbornly waving thick tresses of dark hair into one long plait to hang down her back. She stared at her reflection for a few moments, wishing that she was blonde and pink, with blue eyes and rounded limbs like her friend Valerie; not this skinny brown creature with sharp elbows, a wide mouth like a clown and untameable hair already fighting to escape the confining plait.

She stuck out her tongue at her image and taking up the foolscap envelope went down the stairs on legs grown suddenly unsteady, her heart beating fast. A door opposite the kitchen was open and through it she saw a table set for breakfast. Seated at the far end was a man, his head bent over a newspaper. She gave a timid knock on the door, he looked up sharply and she saw with a jolt of surprise that he was the other man in the photograph on the kitchen wall.

$$*\qquad*\qquad*$$

Reluctant to face the expected hoydenish female who was about to upset his ordered existence, Patrick Farrell afforded the newcomer one brief glance then returned to his newspaper admonishing, 'Come in, this isn't Buck House; you don't have to knock!'

'Sorry. I didn't know and it's always safest.'

Realising that conversation was unavoidable he sighed, removed his gold-framed spectacles and for a few moments studied in silence the coltish but not ungraceful figure hovering uncertainly in the doorway. Curiously the child looked startled and confused as though he had suddenly sprouted two heads, but she recovered swiftly, meeting his gaze squarely, with just a hint of bravado.

Her clothes were quite dreadful but he saw with relief that the slanted grey eyes fringed with long black lashes and the curling tendrils of dark hair about her small pointed face were in sharp and pleasing contrast to the worn grey skirt, drab jumper and clumsy shoes. His eyebrows rose fractionally. Well, well...how on earth, he wondered silently, had that pair of unprepossessing globetrotting Bible thumpers managed to produce *this* little pixie!

She came forward offering a creased and quite disgustingly dirty envelope.

'I'm Anna, Uncle Patrick. This is for you.'

'I am not your uncle.' He took the envelope gingerly in two fingers. Good God, how had she managed to get it in *that* state? 'I merely have the misfortune to be a distant, I am glad to say very distant, relative of your late father.'

The grey eyes were unblinking. 'What *do* I call you, then?'

Again he considered her for a moment in silence, then, 'Just Patrick will suffice.' Replacing the spectacles he ran a finger under the flap of the envelope and extracting the two foolscap sheets laid them on the table before him to smooth out the creases.

He did this awkwardly, almost clumsily for such a neat looking man; Anna saw he wore a dark kid glove on his left hand and wondered why. He didn't invite her to sit down so she remained standing as he read first the letter and then her report. Eventually he laid the papers on the table and looked up at her over the spectacles. 'It would appear your schoolwork is quite impressive but the letter is hardly a paean of praise, is it?'

Her heart sank to somewhere around her knees. 'I don't know,' she said in a small voice. 'I haven't seen it.'

'Your Miss Harrison says you are not very pliable; I wonder what she means by that?'

'I expect it's because I don't always do as people think I should.'

His regarded her gravely. 'She also says that you can be sullen when reprimanded.'

'Yes, well...' Anna hunched her shoulders in resignation. 'I expect that's just the way I look.'

'How do you look?'

Restless under this interrogation she shifted uneasily and gave him an oblique glance. 'Probably nothing like as respectful as Miss Harrison thinks I should.'

'Hmm.' He pointed to a chair at the opposite end of the table. 'Sit there. Charlie and I have already eaten but I daresay he will find you some breakfast.'

He turned his attention again to the *Times* and she did as she was told, her keen eyes noting the table had been laid for three. She wondered that the manservant Charlie apparently ate at the same table with them and itched to ask why, but stayed as silent as her companion obviously required, studying him covertly as she sat waiting for her breakfast.

He was very dark with a square jaw and straight brows and she thought from the way he sat that he probably wasn't very tall. His hair, thick and black and wavy was shot with silver, although the face

13

beneath the hair was quite young and almost unlined except for a network of wrinkles about the corners of eyes that were a darker shade of grey than hers. While she could see he was what Cousin Ruth would describe as being too-handsome-for-his-own-good, whatever that may mean, a deep curve either side of his long full mouth gave him a grim repressive air. Altogether, she thought, he didn't look like someone with whom she'd want to argue overmuch.

With his immaculate charcoal grey suit, snowy white linen and pale blue tie stuck with a diamond pin, he was a far cry from any other Farrell she'd ever met. She was suddenly conscious of her own shabby clothes; although they were the best she had they were ill-fitting and cheap. Expensive or fashionable garments had been frowned upon in Cousin Ruth's household, along with independent thought and anything that might be counted as having a good time.

When Charlie appeared bearing bacon and creamy scrambled eggs she stopped worrying about her clothes and concentrated on breakfast, reasoning that if all the food was going to be as good as this and the previous night's supper it would be quite a decent three weeks. Charlie too looked as though he might be fun and she'd appreciated his comments on Miss Lockwood. She was less sure about the austere and unsmiling Patrick. He had, she thought, looked much happier and less forbidding in that puzzling photograph.

When she finished breakfast she pushed her plate aside with a satisfied sigh and turned her attention back to her temporary guardian only to find that he was now watching her. Abruptly he asked, 'Why do you wear your hair in that perfectly dreadful mare's tail?'

She stared. 'It keeps it tidy. It has to be for school.'

'It would look better short.'

She shrugged her dismissal. 'It doesn't matter.'

He put his paper on one side, took off his glasses and placed them in his breast pocket. 'One's appearance always matters. One should make the most of the looks God has given one.'

'It doesn't matter how my *hair* looks if God hasn't made the rest of me beautiful, does it?' she asked with devastating logic.

'Who told you that you were not beautiful?'

'Nobody,' her guileless eyes met his. 'But then nobody ever told me I was either!'

He folded his paper with a snap and stood up tucking it under his arm and she saw she had been right, that he wasn't anything like as tall as the man Charlie.

'All the more reason to make the best of what you do have,' he answered crisply, adding, 'Charlie will cut it for you this morning.'

'*Charlie?* Cut my hair?'

'Why not, he cuts mine.' He stood looking down on her, his left hand in his pocket the other rubbing his chin. Close up he looked even less like the sort of person one argued with and she capitulated quickly, 'How short?' she asked nervously.

He held his index finger and thumb about two inches apart. '*That* short, then it will curl.'

She was stung into protest. 'I'd look like Shirley Temple.'

'No,' he said, and his mouth twitched briefly. 'Somehow I can't imagine you would ever look in the least like Shirley Temple.'

'Well, all right, but only if you tell Miss Harrison that it wasn't my idea.'

'I think I can promise that.' He rubbed his chin again. 'If you have finished breakfast would you like to see the Gallery; that is, if you think you can do so without touching or breaking anything.'

She said, 'Yes please,' and followed him down the stairs into the narrow hallway, then through a side door that led to the main room of the gallery.

*　　　*　　　*

The room they entered was large and square, papered in soft grey and white stripes, the lofty ceiling heavy with ornate mouldings around the cornices and the two sparkling chandeliers; the whole floor space filled but not cluttered with polished antique furniture. On tables and chests were arranged statuettes and trinket boxes and a plethora of small objects in porcelain and ivory and bronze; larger statues and vases stood on plinths or on the floor and the walls were hung with pictures. At the back of the gallery was a glass-fronted office and through an archway in the far wall she could glimpse another narrower room with rugs in piles on the floor, the walls hung with tapestries.

Tersely informing her that she may look but not touch, Patrick Farrell sat in a high-backed Regency chair and observed her progress around the room.

She was no mere half-interested wanderer, he noted; she took her time, studying the furniture, pictures, statues and other *objets d'art* with grave interest. He put up a hand to conceal an involuntary smile when, despite his warning she put out a delicate finger to smooth the curly head of a small ivory carving of a naked boy.

He wondered uneasily what on earth he and Charlie were to do for the next three weeks with this oddity who had been foisted upon them

15

at such short notice. It was not a household to easily adapt to some adolescent female, even one as obviously naïve and young for her age as this, but they could hardly have refused the desperate *cri de cœur* from old Ruth's solicitor.

God only knew what kind of life she'd led so far he mused, shunted from one unwilling relative to another by her possibly certifiably insane parents. He hoped the child hadn't been inculcated too deeply into the obscure and to him distasteful and completely incomprehensible religious sect embraced by her parents and most of their relatives. He really didn't think he and Charlie could keep her for the entire holiday if she was given to the sudden and loud personal communication with the Almighty that appeared to be an essential part of their faith; Charlie, he thought with a grin, would have a fit if she started on *that*! At least they could be thankful that she had managed to avoid acquiring those flat East Anglian vowels; her voice was pleasant and slightly husky with only the faintest trace of a regional accent.

Finishing her lengthy tour of the room she came to stand by his chair. She asked, 'Is everything here for sale?'

'Yes. That is how I make my living…buying and selling.'

'I don't think I couldn't bear to let *any* of them go.'

'It hurts progressively less after one has parted with the first object that one desires to keep.'

She said doubtfully, 'I suppose so,' She glanced up as a passer-by paused in front of the gallery. The wide bay window was covered with a heavy iron grill; the door secured top and bottom with iron bolts. 'Shouldn't you open the door?' she asked. 'Someone might want to come in.'

'I have to wait for Charlie.' He hesitated, ridiculous to still mind having to make the admission after more than fifteen years. Steeling himself, he touched his gloved left hand, saying brusquely, 'This is just for vanity; no use I'm afraid for dealing with all that ironmongery.'

'Gosh, what happened to it?' She was matter-of-fact, appearing neither embarrassed nor uncomfortable.

'I left it in Flanders in nineteen-seventeen.' He kept his voice clipped and unemotional. 'If it hadn't been for Charlie foolhardily charging to the rescue the rest of me might have stayed with it. As you see I've had to put up with him ever since.'

He watched the corners of her wide mouth tuck in on a smile. 'I could manage the door,' she offered, 'but perhaps Charlie might not like it after taking all that trouble.'

'Perhaps not,' he agreed.

She looked around the gallery again before laying tentative fingers on the arm of his chair. 'But I could help you in here if you'd let me, not because of your hand and the door and all that but because I'd like to be able to look after some of these things.'

He hesitated. What harm could she do and at least it would keep her busy and out from beneath Charlie's feet. He said, 'I think that might be arranged,' and was immediately rewarded by a startlingly brilliant smile lighting the small features; allowing him a sudden disturbing glimpse of an inviting beauty yet to bloom. He pulled his brows together in a frown, thinking acidly that while she may not invite much more than a second glance now, he wouldn't be at all surprised to find her causing some unwary man one hell of a load of trouble at some future date. Silently he thanked God that he'd be unlikely to be responsible for her when *that* happened.

* * *

In the days that followed Anna's appearance in Stratton Place Patrick, although remaining reserved and faintly aloof, seemed not to mind her presence in the gallery. He appeared amused by her enthusiasm and impressed by her eye for the beauty of line and colour in ceramic and porcelain and ivory, promising that he would take her to an auction before she returned to school. An honour, Charlie assured her that to his knowledge had never before been bestowed upon another living being, apart from himself.

She blossomed in this unfamiliar atmosphere of approval. Despite Patrick's austere manner she enjoyed being with him; began to see the wry, dry humour behind the reserved front he presented to the world. Watching him as he dealt with clients, noting how much money changed hands over the sale of a painting or statue or piece of furniture, she began to understand how he and Charlie lived in what to her eyes was unbelievable luxury and plenty. Impressed by his bewildering knowledge of his trade she was fired with a fierce ambition to learn all she could in the short time she would be at Stratton Place. By helping in the gallery she could show her gratitude for this sudden elevation from poverty to plenty. Pushing firmly to one side the thought of her eventual return to school, and the dreaded likelihood of next time drawing Uncle William in the sweepstake for the long summer holidays, she determined she would absorb and store for future reference everything that her benefactor said and did; just in case she was ever allowed another visit to his wonderful, exciting world.

That the benefactor himself was at first startled, then intrigued by her zeal was not missed by Charlie, who from his position on the sidelines watched with some amusement the inroads this small innocent was making on his lover's life, and wondered how and where it would all end.

*   *   *

Toward the end of her first week Patrick passed a judicious eye over her at the breakfast table one morning before stating bluntly, 'You cannot continue to give either us, or this establishment, a bad name by walking about like a *doppelganger* of Little Orphan Annie. Either we keep you under lock and key or you have something a little less drab and ill fitting to wear. This morning Charlie will take you shopping for new clothes.'

Anna looked first amazed, then doubtful. 'Will Charlie know what to get?'

'As Charlie knows even less about female attire than I do, that would appear unlikely. It will be up to you to choose what you want – I said "want", you notice, not "need".'

Perplexed she asked, 'But how will I know what I need,' she corrected herself quickly, '*want.*'

He gave his tight smile.

'Oh, you will, Anna; you will!'

*   *   *

He was quite right. Although overawed at first by the shops and disbelieving of their prices, after her first tentative venture over the thresholds of the perfumed and carpeted Junior Miss departments of Messer's John Lewis, Dickens & Jones and Liberty's she began to relax and enjoy herself.

For one who had known only the deadening environment of frugal, careful households and the austere surroundings of boarding school, it might have proved a temptation to be greedy, but even though a mischievous Charlie egged her on to extravagance, Anna was too much in awe of Patrick to be reckless with his money and took time and care over the selection of each dress and coat and pair of shoes.

'Why is he paying for me to have all these things?' she asked Charlie, as her purchases were finally loaded into a waiting taxi.

'Because he likes tae have beautiful things around him,' he answered with a wink and she blushed and stumbled and fell up the running board of the cab.

*   *   *

That night, her bed strewn with open boxes and an ocean of tissue paper, she looked hard at her reflection in the long wardrobe mirror to see if anything had changed; but even wearing her favourite dress, a soft lawn in deepest rose, the pointed collar embroidered with flowers and with her hair curling close to her head like a cherubs, she still couldn't see how any of it made her the least bit beautiful. Charlie she decided sadly must have been pulling her leg. While Patrick might find beauty in inanimate objects, he was unlikely ever to find *her* anything like as attractive or interesting as he might find some priceless painting or statue. Perhaps the reason such a good-looking man didn't have a wife she mused, was because he hadn't yet met any woman who could match or surpass the charm of a Renoir portrait or an exquisite piece of Dresden china.

She sighed. "Plain Jane" cousin Ruth had called her. Despondent Anna turned away from the mirror. It had to be faced; she was an ugly duckling and all the pretty clothes in the world would never turn her into a beautiful swan.

2

She came downstairs cautiously on her first Sunday in Stratton Place, relieved to find that Patrick wasn't lying in wait dressed in funereal black and armed with the Old Testament.

'Where is he?' she asked, when Charlie appeared bearing their breakfasts.

'Gone to church o' course; like he always does on a Sunday,' he answered and she felt a rush of disappointment and betrayal. He was like the rest of them then, even if he hadn't yet forced her to listen to great chunks of the Bible and spend an unreasonable amount of time on her knees. She pushed her bacon and tomatoes around her plate and looked at the clock on the mantelpiece. It was only nine-thirty, early to be going to chapel. Perhaps, her stomach lurched; perhaps he was a preacher like Uncle Frederick. That would be awful but it might mean he would be absent for most of the day.

'Ye won't have long to wait.' Charlie continued. 'Any minute now he'll be in an' raring for his breakfast.' He sat down and stared at her. 'Now what's put that look on your face?'

She muttered, 'Nothing.'

He grinned. 'I'm surprised at you. Telling' fibs and on a Sunday, too. Did ye want to go with him, then?'

'No, I blooming didn't!'

The force of her answer made him smile. 'Ah, well,' he said, slyly, 'it's nice to know I'm not the only heathen around here.'

As she opened her mouth to reply she saw that Patrick must have come quietly into the house and now stood in the open doorway, appearing pleasantly relaxed as though he'd spent an enjoyable hour with friends. In Anna's considerable experience no Farrell ever just popped out before breakfast to their devotions and came back looking refreshed and amiable, but took all morning and usually returned from them thoroughly irritable and worked up. She shut her mouth abruptly; how much of her conversation with Charlie had he overheard?

He gave them both a quizzical look. 'Can I hazard a guess at who might be the other heathen?' he asked, answering her unspoken question, and she blushed as Charlie uttered an audible snort and disappeared towards the kitchen. Sticking her chin in the air in a small show of defiance she admitted, 'It's me.'

The lines either side of his mouth deepened. '*Is* it?' He seated himself and shook out his table napkin. 'But then I imagine your encounters with the Almighty have been somewhat more fraught than mine!'

'It isn't that I've got anything against God personally,' she stood her ground. 'I just don't like being made to grovel all the time.'

He began to butter a slice of toast, observing mildly, 'Well, you are welcome to join Charlie in being a heathen in this house if an overdose of hell-fire and damnation have put you off enjoying for an hour the beauty and the glory of God, A pity; but there it is...'

She digested this in silence for a moment, wondering if there was a catch somewhere. 'You mean I don't have to go to chapel with you?'

'Chapel?' he looked amused. 'No. You only accompany me to *church* if you really wish to do so.'

When Charlie returned with another dish of bacon and tomatoes Patrick suggested, 'You might tell us about your lifetime of Sundays spent with the Alleluia Chorus then, if you are interested, Charlie will tell about his, which are mainly spent reading the racing papers, and I shall tell you all about mine. Afterward we can compare notes as to which of us has had the better time.'

She eyed him cautiously. 'Are you sure you want to hear? It's pretty boring.'

'Quite sure...and I am never bored.'

She hesitated, still dubious. Charlie gave her an encouraging wink and she said, 'All right then,' and launched into an unselfconscious *reprise* of Sunday's *à la* Farrell that kept both men sitting straight-faced, not daring to look at each other as she described her childhood Sundays of unrelieved East Anglian gloom, laying before them the whole weird and wonderful world of her family's own peculiar brand of religious fervour; from Cousin Ruth's frequent, loud and over zealous communications with the Almighty, to Uncle William of the wandering hands and interminable grace before breakfast. An unsuspected gift for mimicry in her depiction of the spittle-strewn utterances of hell-fire lay-preacher Uncle Frederick had Charlie biting his lip and Patrick shielding his face with his hand.

When she finished there was a short silence, broken eventually by an explosive 'Bloody *hell*!' from Charlie.

Patrick sat back in his chair and regarded her with a commendable degree of controlled mirth.

'Quite.' he said.

21

*   *   *

That evening, curiosity and the opportunity to wear some of her new clothes in public overcame her initial reluctance to be involved in any kind of church going with Patrick, even such an attractive one as he had described. Rather warily she accepted his invitation to the evening service at All Saints in St-Margaret's Street.

'You may sit outside and wait for me if you wish,' he suggested, as they left the car, which like its owner was dark and polished and handsome, to pass through the arched gateway into the paved courtyard. 'I have no intention of hauling you screaming through the door!'

Taking a sideways glance at his face she flushed at his expression of barely concealed amusement, then marched forward with all the haughty bravado of a French aristocrat to the guillotine.

*   *   *

The impact of that most charismatic bastion of Anglo-Catholicism was immediate and dramatic. Overcome by so much breath-taking beauty, spellbound by the hushed melodious words and the purity of the boy's ascending voices, Anna sat entranced and open-mouthed. Patrick, watching the changing emotions patterning her face, cynically notched one up to Anglicanism and one down to the Farrell family in general.

His at first mischievous determination to show her something so at odds with everything she had ever so far experienced appeared to have been spectacularly successful. That she had an unusual eye for and appreciation of beauty had already been made evident by her delight in the contents of the Gallery. The obvious fact that it was the beauty of the service, not it's content that held her rapt attention didn't worry him; faith may come later, or it may not.

He could not, nor did he wish, to make himself responsible for that.

*   *   *

The days passed and she settled comfortably into the ways of the household. As Charlie frequently remarked, she was no trouble and it would do them no harm to have a younger presence around the place for a while.

Patrick remained mostly silent on the subject of their young guest, although with every passing day he became more acutely aware that they were courting trouble by keeping this engaging cuckoo in the nest. That both he and Charlie were enjoying her company was undeniable, but he could see all too clearly that by allowing her to become quite such an integral part of their lives they might be putting themselves in considerable danger.

They needed that, he thought with rare vulgarity, like they needed a pain in the neck, but there was no doubt in his own mind that to turn the child over in the summer to the unhealthy attentions of Uncle William, or the deadening piety of one or other of their motley crew of relatives would be nothing short of criminal.

*   *   *

On the evening of the day she'd spent at Sotheby's with him, he waited until she was in bed and he and Charlie settled in their chairs either side of the hearth, before giving voice to his thoughts.

'How do you think we might fit that little oddity into this household, Charlie – on a permanent basis that is?'

Charlie lay back in his chair, letting go a soft whistling breath. 'Well!' His long Scots face split into a smile. 'I knew you were enjoying that lass's company, but I didn't think you'd take it that far; you must be going soft in the head to even think of such a thing.'

'My conscience bothers me when I think about her being shuffled off again with any of that sanctimonious crowd, but we both have to agree; that's always been the way we've settled matters between us. If you don't think it could work, say so.'

'She's not much trouble.' Charlie was thoughtful. 'But it could be tricky.' He looked up, eyes very straight and clear. 'When she leaves that school for good in two or three year's time and is around all the while, she'll cotton on then, if not before. I know she's fairly naïve for her age, but she's bright as a brass button and those eyes don't miss much.'

Patrick hunched his shoulders. 'We've managed our *ménage à deux* for all these years with discretion. If we make it a *ménage à trois* we shall just have to be doubly discrete, for Anna's sake as well as our own.'

'If we take this on, she'll give all that pent-up affection she's never been able to show...and she'll need it returned,' warned the older man. 'We have to be sure we can manage that – and someday she'll have to know about you and me, then what happens if she can't take it?'

'I think we'd have to cross that bridge when we came to it.'

'It would be putting a lot on her young shoulders.'

'Perhaps, but she already knows what it means to be an outsider. She could surprise us both if that time came.' Patrick leaned to pick up the decanter of brandy from the table beside his chair. 'We don't have much time to make up our minds. I wouldn't want her going back without something being settled, so I'll need to see my solicitor pretty quickly to make sure none of the damned relatives puts a spoke in the wheel. Whilst they've never minded taking my money, my religious practices have always been a sore point with them. The idea of having another Farrell teetering as they see it, on the edge of Rome, is bound to raise a storm. Then there's the school of course...' he passed Charlie his glass. 'Well, do we do it, or do we let her go?'

Slowly and in silence Charlie emptied his glass; offered it for a refill then took several more thoughtful sips before pronouncing judgement. 'I think we keep her,' he said, 'although the prospect of going through the charade of separate bedrooms every bloody holiday like we are now doesn't exactly fill me with joy!'

Patrick answered him dryly. 'We don't have to stay in them every night, do we?'

Charlie gave him a searching look. 'You'll rather enjoy being *in loco parentis*, won't you?'

He shrugged. 'How would I know? I've never been a father of any sort, have I?'

'Would you be having any regrets about that?'

'What – this late in the day?' Patrick's eyes crinkled; he leaned forward, touched Charlie's hand and smiled. 'Never; not for one moment you old fool, but I would rather like to have a hand at being a father to this one – though why the hell I imagine I'll do a better job than the rest of them I've no idea.'

'Och, laddie,' Charlie leaned back in his chair and gave his sly grin, 'with a wee spot of help from a friend I think you might manage rather well!'

*　　　*　　　*

Anna sat on the top of her trunk while Charlie snapped the locks. Staring down onto his grey head she couldn't help wondering if this would be the last time she'd ever see him.

She'd made up her mind she wasn't going show how much it hurt to leave. Every day she'd hoped Patrick might say she could come back in the summer, at least for a little while. But he had spent much of this last week away from the gallery, leaving Charlie to deal with any customers and returned each evening distant and pre-occupied. Patrick, she was beginning to realise, could be unapproachable without saying a word. Yesterday he'd left early in the morning and she'd waited and waited for him to come home; only when there was still no sign of him by midnight had she finally capitulated and gone to bed.

At breakfast that morning he'd looked drawn and tired and it had been a silent meal, even Charlie finding little to say. Now the Easter holidays were finally over; she would leave tomorrow and nothing had been said. She had a hollow sick feeling and her heart really was aching, she could feel it like a bruise deep inside her chest, but she wouldn't beg for something that neither of them had even thought to mention.

'That's it, then.' Charlie straightened and gave her a lop-sided grin. 'I suppose there'll be some peace around here now!'

'I suppose so,' she stood up, resting a hand on the trunk. 'Shouldn't this have gone yesterday? It'll never get there in time now and I shan't have any clothes to wear but these I have on.'

'You don't need to worry about that. It'll be there when you need it.' He stood looking at her for a moment, his head on one side. 'I told Patrick ye might be needing a new uniform; we should have got that while we were shopping.'

'Matron sees to all that. It saves anyone else the bother and they just add the cost to the fees.'

'That's all right, then,' he said cheerfully, apparently oblivious of her misery. 'Lunch is in half an hour but Patrick wants to see you first. Better go now. Ye never know, as you're off tomorrow he might be good for ten bob!'

She waited until he'd left before went slowly down the stairs and into the drawing room, where she found Patrick seated in his favourite wing-backed chair, apparently immersed in a Sothebys' Catalogue. Now her throat was hurting too and she had a lump in it that wouldn't go away. She hovered in the doorway, clinging to the polished brass handle. 'Charlie said you wanted me.'

'Yes.' Patrick put the catalogue aside. 'Did he say why?'

'No,' she swallowed hard at the lump, 'he went to get lunch ready.'

'How very diplomatic of him; he has a bad habit of steering clear of awkward moments.' He contemplated her in silence for several seconds before saying conversationally, 'If you are to be a permanent member of this household we had better get a few things straight before you return to that nunnery; the main one being that I don't want to be handed any more letters of complaint from your Miss Harrison each and every time you come home. Is that clear?'

She opened her mouth to speak, but no words came and she shut it again, staring at him in dumb bewilderment before his words properly registered. Then she gave a great gulp and tears began trickling down her cheeks.

He said '*Tsch!*' and took the handkerchief from his breast pocket. 'Charlie said you'd do that!' He flicked a finger at the chair opposite his. 'Sit down and wipe your face – and for God's sake blow your nose as well before it starts running – and don't *sniff.*'

She said, 'Yes, Patrick. Sorry,' took the handkerchief and wiped and blew as ordered, then sat squeezing the damp lawn into a ball between her hands. She sniffed and he winced. 'Do you mean it…that I can come again…*live* here all the time in the holidays…and when I leave school?'

'That is the general idea. But you really must stop being a tiresome child and behave yourself at school.' He drew his brows together. 'Miss Harrison says you are intelligent and good at your studies, but that you are disobedient, disregard school rules – apparently for the hell of it – and can be a perfect nuisance to the staff. That just won't do. That you should need to kick over the traces from time to time is understandable, but in future if you *must* break the rules remember to do so quietly and less obviously.' His mouth twitched. 'That only applies of course to when you are at school; the house rules here you will break at your peril!'

She said, 'Yes, Patrick!' her eyes solemn.

'Something else I must make quite clear...' momentarily he hesitated, '…is Charlie's position here; while it pleases him to call himself my major domo and to run this household, I am not his master and he is not my servant; neither is he yours. You will obey him as you would me and treat him with respect; always. Do you understand?'

She didn't, any more than she understood why Charlie shared their meals and told Patrick off if he annoyed him – or why that picture on the kitchen wall continued to puzzle her, but nodded in docile agreement. 'Yes, Patrick.'

'We will drive down to Cornwall in the morning, but this afternoon we must see about uniform clothes, which is tiresome but Charlie assures me is necessary.'

Anna ventured, 'I told Charlie: Matron always kits me out and bills the things.'

He said dryly, 'I had noticed. In future we shall save her that trouble – but one moment...' He stopped and eyed her judiciously. 'You haven't yet said if all this meets with your approval. You do not *have* to return here in the summer, you know.'

'Oh, Patrick – yes, please – I do want to – more than anything else in the whole world!' She jumped up and throwing her arms about his neck began weeping copiously. He said '*Tsch*!' again and detached her so forcibly that she sat down on the floor with a bump and was obliged to have her relieving weep against his knee.

This, Patrick found to his surprise, gave him a certain amount of proprietary pride and an even greater amount of altruistic pleasure.

3

MARLCLEW, CORNWALL

November – December. 1936

A week after school reassembled for the winter term the French mistress, Mam'zelle Richaud fell ill and departed, largely unmourned and certainly unloved, to a TB sanatorium. Her delighted pupils rejoiced when lessons were interrupted and the school thrown temporarily into chaos as charabanc loads of girls were rushed to the antiquated X-Ray machine at the local hospital. After a decent interval during which it was found that no one else had the infection, Miss Harrison appeared one morning in the Lower Sixth classroom to introduce Madame Gallimard, Mam'zelle's decade younger and considerably more attractive replacement.

Waiting until the headmistress had left the room Madame seated herself on the edge of her table and swinging an elegantly shod foot asked with a smile, 'Shall we begin with introductions? You know who I am. Now tell me your names and the things that interest you and we shall have made a good start.'

Admiring Patrick's easy command of languages, Anna had worked hard over the past two years and now sat in the back row; a position filled only by those who were a long way ahead of their peers. As the newcomer began her questioning at the front of the class she had to wait for what seemed an age before the inquiring blue eyes finally reached her. She stood up eagerly, 'Anna Farrell, Madame. I like French and Literature and Antiques!'

There was an immediate titter from the class but Madame stilled it with a brief, commanding gesture, 'Antiques; how interesting… *Farrell*, did you say? Are your parents collectors?'

'No, Madame.' Anna was disconcerted by the sudden intense regard of the pale eyes. 'My parents are dead. I live with my guardian, Patrick Farrell. He owns a gallery in London.'

'*Does* he?' Her eyes sharpened. 'You must tell me more when there is time. I too am interested in antiques.' She turned her attention again on the class. 'Now,' she said briskly, 'shall we see where you were in your studies before Mademoiselle Richaud was so sadly taken ill.'

Madame, they discovered later from cook, who kept her ear to the ground and knew everything, was not French, only married to a Frenchman. Although she had lived more than twenty years in France she had been born in Cornwall and after the recent death of her husband returned to her home county to buy a cottage on the edge of town.

Attractive and chic, she sent a breath of fresh air sweeping through the classroom and the study of French became of absorbing interest to Anna, who at first sight had tumbled headlong into the agony and ecstasy of her first adolescent crush. Of course, she admitted to Valerie, she had one of a sort on Patrick because he was so good looking, but it wasn't the same as this; *this* was different because Madame had exactly the kind of looks and soignée air that Anna dreamed of for herself.

Life assumed a rosy glow and long week-end walks past Carey Cottage in the hope of seeing her idol rapidly took the place of shopping in the village store, or an occasional visit to the town cinema.

'You've only got a pash because she takes a special interest in you,' observed Valerie crossly as they struggled along the cliff path in the teeth of a winter afternoon's rain. 'Actually, she gives me the pip. *I* don't get all the after class chit chat, although my French is almost as good as yours. If you ask me, she's a nosy old bag, always questioning you the way she does.'

'It's only because she's interested in china and porcelain like me and enjoys hearing about the gallery,' Anna defended. 'Besides, it's nice to be asked out to tea, isn't it?'

'I'd go to tea with Lucretia Borgia to avoid the fish paste sandwiches and seed cake dished up on Fridays in school!' Valerie huddled down into her coat collar. 'But honestly, Anna, I don't like her much. She's so sweet on the surface but underneath...I dunno, there's something about her...and she really does pry, you know.'

Anna said, 'Rubbish,' but she was disquieted by Valerie's shrewd observations. The teacher's questioning was flattering and seemed innocent enough, but Anna had an uneasy feeling that she frequently told her more about her life in London with Charlie and Patrick than either of them would have wished, but it was difficult to resist her interest and delicately probing questions.

*   *   *

The door of Madame's cottage was opened in response to Anna's

29

knock by a tall, brown-haired young man, who after regarding them for a moment with serious eyes the colour and shine of polished chestnuts, greeted them pleasantly.

'Please come in, Maman is expecting you.' He smiled, holding the door wide. 'I am Asa Gallimard and this...' he gestured, as a slightly shorter and altogether more handsome youth appeared behind him, '*this* is my little brother, Félix!'

'*Mon Dieu,*' the newcomer raked them both with his bold blue gaze before it came to rest on Anna. 'Move over, Asa...' he grinned, adding not quite under his breath, 'this one is for me!'

Anna's own greeting died in her throat as her erstwhile passion for Madam was rapidly transferred to the attractive and rakish Félix. So blinded was she that she scarcely noticed Asa being swiftly and expertly annexed by Valerie, who had four brothers and knew exactly how to enjoy the company of any young male while keeping him safely at arm's length – a skill Anna had yet to acquire.

Madam explained rather curtly that her sons had arrived unexpectedly; Asa from his post-graduate studies at the Sorbonne, Félix from his post as a cub reporter for a Paris newspaper. Anna thought they were oddly matched for brothers; where Asa was dark, Félix was fair; Asa's English was colloquial and almost perfect, while his brother phrased his words in the French manner and spoke with a strong accent.

'Félix wished to make sure it would not be too dull at Christmas in Maman's new home.' Asa offered with a sarcastic glance at his brother. 'I was born in Cornwall and he in Dinan; but now he is a Parisian and restless in the country. He will I am sure return to France for his Christmas dinner.'

'No.' Félix's sparkling eyes were fixed on Anna's face. 'I think after all, that I shall enjoy the scenery better here.'

Confused and suddenly shy she looked away and intercepted a look of extreme displeasure from mother to son. Startled she glanced at Félix then back at Madame, who returned her look with one of cold distaste before saying peremptorily, 'Félix, please help me in the kitchen and leave your brother to entertain our young guests.'

He answered with a compliant '*Oui, Maman,*' and followed her from the room. Asa watched him go then gave Anna a sly, sideways glance. 'Where *is* your home, Anna?'

Confused and upset by Madame's coldness she blushed and stammered, 'L-London.'

'Ah, such a pity,' he sighed. 'Now I am sure that my brother will spend Christmas in Paris.'

Her blush deepened to crimson. 'I can't imagine that where he spends Christmas is anything to do with me,' she said haughtily, turning her back on his mocking smile.

Although unaware that the first shots had been fired in what was destined to be a very long battle, she decided right there and then that she most definitely did not like Asa Gallimard. It was a mystery she thought, how anyone as charming as Félix could possibly have such a boorish brother.

Despite, or perhaps because of his mother's disapproval, on his return to the room Félix danced attendance upon both girls; paying exaggerated compliments and flirting brazenly with Anna. Warmed by all this attention she passed the afternoon wrapped in a hazy, delightful dream, only vaguely aware that Madame's cold eyes were watching her every move.

By the time they returned to school her mind and heart were overflowing with the knowledge that what she was feeling could mean only one thing: she was deliciously, deliriously in love. Shaking off the teasing Valerie, she rushed to the lavatories and locking herself in a cubicle took out and read the note Félix had dexterously tucked into her pocket as they left.

Sweet Anna,
I shall be back on December the sixteenth. You are such a clever girl that I am sure you can slip out for a little while to see me that I may wish you a Joyeux Noël...I shall be by the gates of your school at six o'clock.
Bonne nuit, chère petite Anna...meilleurs vœux,
Félix.

*   *   *

Dorothy Gallimard stood at the window and watched the two girls out of sight before turning back into the room.

Asa sat at ease by the fire his long legs outstretched and hands behind his head. Félix was at the piano, strumming slowly and singing *Vous Qui Passez San me Voer?* in an affected, lyrical tenor. For a moment she observed the two young men in silence before demanding irritably,' Félix, be quiet a moment, *if* you please!'

He stopped and looked up in simulated surprise, 'Maman?'

'I want you to understand that I will not tolerate you making calf eyes at that girl.'

'Which girl, Maman?' he was the picture of innocence.

'Anna Farrell; she is one of my pupils and as such is out of bounds to you.'

'What about me?' inquired Asa lazily, 'is she "out of bounds" to me?'

She flushed. 'Yes, to you also, but you are not such a fool as your brother to chase little girls.' She turned again to Félix. 'You understand? You are to keep away from her.'

He smiled provocatively. 'Why *should* I bother with her – she is such a plain little thing.'

'Plain?' She shook her head. 'Oh, no, not plain when one really looks, but she is barely sixteen and my pupil. I forbid you to meet with her again.'

He shrugged. 'Very well – but such a fuss about a girl. One might think she has the plague or some similar affliction.'

'Perhaps Maman knows some dark secret about her,' put in Asa mischievously, 'confess, Maman; she is really Dracula's daughter in disguise!'

'That is enough.' Her eyes blazed. 'Understand – neither of you will have anything more to do with that girl...or her *family*.' She almost spat this last before turning and swiftly leaving the room.

Asa looked thoughtfully at the door as it closed behind her. 'Now what was all that about family?'

Félix grinned and struck a resounding chord on the piano. 'As yet I have no idea, but now feel duty bound to meet again with the enchanting little Anna and perhaps find out!'

Asa warned. 'Careful; Maman angry is not someone to be taken lightly.'

'*Oh, la, la, la*, what can she do? Take a stick to me as though I am a little boy again?' Félix blew vulgarly through his lips and banged down the lid of the piano. '*You* be the good boy, Asa...me, I shall go on being the bad boy. It is much more fun.'

Asa watched him with a cynical smile, knowing that with Félix it was all bravado, Maman could still frighten him. However, Félix in pursuit of some girl or other was as crafty and devious as a fox. If he wanted to see Anna Farrell again, he would undoubtedly do so, and to hell with anything their mother might say or do.

*　　　*　　　*

In the kitchen Dorothy stared bleakly at a painting of the home in Brittany that she had left only a few months before. She should never have returned to this country after Auguste's death, she acknowledged

32

bitterly. All she had gained was anxiety and unhappiness instead of the peace she sought after so many years of her sterile and unhappy marriage.

She could see now that she had been a fool not to ignore the girl once she knew her connection to that man, but the scar on her mind she had thought closed and healed had proved to be merely a scab over an old wound. As such, one had to keep picking at it even though one knew it would bleed again.

She put down the picture, suddenly resolute; there must be no more visits by that girl to her house. Impossible to risk the boys seeing her again, she could not bear the thought that through Anna either might be drawn into the cesspool of Patrick Farrell's life.

She gave a grimace of pain. It was plain for all to see that the girl had been captivated by that man and his *servant*, and thought them both perfect human beings; but just wait, she thought with sudden vicious spite, until the little innocent either stumbled upon, or was told the truth. Then, if there were any justice in the world, the charming Patrick Farrell would suffer through his young ward's certain rejection of *him* something of what he had caused others to suffer all those years ago.

*   *   *

Félix was waiting as promised by the gate and as she stepped into the roadway reached for her hand, pulling her towards him.

'Bravo, I knew that you would manage!'

'Only for a few minutes,' she was nervous, looking over her shoulder. 'This isn't a good time…besides, I'm freezing.'

'So, where do we go for your few minutes?'

She led him along the high wall to where a narrow path had been made behind the elder bushes growing alongside the road. 'If anyone does come they won't see us here.'

When she stopped he turned her towards him, putting his arms around her. 'Do I get a Christmas kiss?'

'All right,' she pecked him swiftly on the cheek; he gave a low laugh and pulled her closer.

'Not like that…like this!' He took her chin in his hand and tilting her head closed his mouth on hers. She felt his tongue pressing against her teeth; what *was* he doing? After a few moments he leaned back, holding her by the shoulders. 'You have not done this before?'

'How did you know?' She was crestfallen. 'Am I doing it wrong?'

'No. You are not "doing it" at all!' His voice was full of laughter.

33

'Now pay attention.' He put his arms around her again. 'Do as I do...it is easy and most enjoyable when you know how!'

Being taught to kiss by Félix Gallimard was certainly enjoyable, the longer it lasted, the better it became. When he held her more tightly to him she began to go hot and prickle all over. Embarrassed by her feelings she tried to pull away but he only pulled her closer still, so that even through their thick winter clothing she could feel his heart thudding in time with her own. After what seemed a very long time he took his mouth from hers and whispered, 'That was good, yes?'

She put her shaking hands behind his head, pulling him down to her again. 'Yes, oh yes!'

'And you are warmer now?' he teased. 'I think you must be. Even an ice-maiden would melt after such a kiss!'

Melting, she thought, her head spinning as he continued to kiss her, that's what it felt like; melting into a lovely dark cave filled with fur...She was aware that his fingers were unbuttoning her coat, his hand caressing her breast and that she shouldn't let him, but she didn't care; only wanted the warmth and the feelings to go on for ever.

The faint shrilling of the school bell for supper brought her to earth with a rush and she pulled her mouth from his saying breathlessly, 'I have to go. I really have to.'

'*C'est dommage;* just when we were enjoying ourselves so much!' She could see his eyes glitter in the light from a passing car. 'Tomorrow, Anna...will you meet me tomorrow?'

'Yes, for the last time. We go home the day after.'

'Then it must be somewhere better than this dripping tree – and for longer.' He hugged her to him. 'Tell me where and when and I shall be there.'

She thought quickly. 'Do you know the path that runs alongside the creek from where the village street ends?'

'No, but I will ask Asa. He has a map and has walked much today.'

'Well, where the path passes the hedge at the bottom of the school grounds there is a boat house... but no one uses it in the winter. I'll come directly after tea; at five o'clock and that will give us more time to...to,' she stumbled over her words, glad of the darkness hiding her hot face, 'to do this again!' she finished with a rush.

He laughed, kissed her again swiftly then let her go.

'Goodnight, my sweet little Anna.'

'Goodnight, Félix.'

She ran back through the gates, buttoning her coat as she ran. At

34

the kitchen door she stopped to listen before cautiously turning the handle and peeping in. The room was empty but she could hear muted voices from the direction of the pantry. Her heart thudding painfully she slipped through the door, crept past the pantry where the housekeeper and cook were deep in conversation and fled soundlessly through into the corridor and up the worn linoleum clad stairs to her study. Still warm from Félix's embrace she curled up in a chair and smiled blissfully at Valerie, who stopped filing her nails and sat up expectantly.

'Well? Did you go through with it?'

'I did! I met him!'

'*And*?'

'We kissed…for ages and ages until I almost stopped breathing!'

'Glory, Glory!' Valerie threw the nail file into the air and caught it again. 'What else?'

Anna looked guilty. 'What d'you mean…what else?'

'You *know*…straying hands and feely-feelies.'

Anna blushed scarlet. 'Don't be disgusting.'

'He did, he did – and you let him!' Valerie crowed delightedly. 'Oh, *do* tell.'

Anna mumbled, 'Nothing happened. We just kissed. Listen,' she was suddenly wheedling, 'I've said I'll meet him after tea tomorrow in the boathouse; it's the only chance before the vac.'

'OK, but don't be too long, if Miss H discovers you're missing I don't want the old thing giving *me* the third degree.'

'Only an hour, I promise.'

'Just keep an eye on those hands,' warned Valerie darkly. 'You take my word for it he's a fast worker. I know, I've watched my brothers at it for long enough; I can spot a lecher at fifty paces!'

Anna sniffed disparagingly. 'So that's where you got your dirty mind, spying on your brothers.'

'That and fighting off their pals for the past couple of years,' she laughed. 'You listen to your Auntie Valerie, my girl, and remember what I've said when you find a pair of hot little hands creeping up your skirt!'

*   *   *

The following evening Félix leaned against side of the boathouse and watched Anna run away from him towards the shelter of the trees, then seconds later flit briefly across the lawn before disappearing into the shrubbery at the corner of the house. Tucking the rolled car rug under his arm he began to walk back along the path, treading carefully on the frosty ground, ruminating that it was not exactly the best weather for an assignation of the sort he had just enjoyed with the inexperienced but ardent Anna Farrell. Although she'd pushed his hand away when he had tried to do more than fondle her small breasts, he was confident that it wouldn't be long before she would let him do whatever he wished.

He whistled softly between his teeth. He simply must have her, but he could wait. Once back in Paris there would be other easier girls to enjoy before Anna surrendered. He smiled into the darkness, excitement stirring in him again; she must be a virgin and there weren't many of those to be found in the circles in which he habitually moved. He must have patience, not frighten her off. But it would be worth the waiting, he thought; there would be greater pleasure to be had in taking one who was not so immediately willing, than with any street *poule* he might find.

Returning to the house he slipped quietly through the door and tossing the rug onto the hall chest, mounted the stairs on silent feet. No sense in bringing maman out hard upon his heels.

Asa lay on his own bed in their shared room, his feet propped on the iron bed end and an open book on his chest. Looking up at Félix's entrance he smiled his lazy smile. 'No need to creep like that, you are quite safe. She has gone to the Abbey for Compline and to pray for your black soul.'

His brother let out a long breath. 'So there is a God in heaven!' He flung himself on his bed. 'I don't know how you can stand her for the whole vacation. Thank God I am here for only one more day, otherwise I should be tempted to commit matricide.'

Asa put down his book. 'This is rather more comfortable than that *maison close* you call a lodging; you would do better to stay here with me for Christmas, even with maman watching your every move.'

Félix sat up lacing his hands about one knee. 'She is worse, you know, since papa died...' He looked away. 'I still miss him, don't you?'

'Yes. Very much, he was always kind and understanding – but a libertine. She has always feared you would be the same, and of course you are!' Asa's mouth twisted in a satirical smile. 'But as none of papa's blood flows in my veins she doesn't worry about me quite so much.'

Félix gave his brother a cautious, sideways look. Asa's place in the family had never been a subject for discussion, indeed was a topic forbidden by their mother. Although papa had been rather more forthcoming and both he and Asa had over the years gleaned further snippets of information about his birth from various family sources, they had never openly explored their relationship and the habit of silence was hard to break. Now Félix hesitated for a moment, then curiosity getting the better of him asked, 'Do you ever think about your parents? About what happened to them?'

'Not really, although when I was small I was sometimes inquisitive and would ask about my mother,' Asa shrugged, 'but it upset maman, so I stopped asking; for as long as I can remember *she* has been my mother as much as you have been my brother and that is sufficient for me.' He gave his slight, sardonic smile. 'I remember papa once saying that apart from one obviously efficient act of copulation my father does not exist, so how could I even begin to imagine *him*!' His mouth tightened into a thin line. 'I think I should not have liked him. I rather despise men who make that kind of error. A man should not make love unless he is able to take proper care of his woman.'

Félix narrowed his eyes. 'No wonder none of yours stay around for long, they probably think you are in training for the priesthood.' He added with sudden venom, 'You're a cold fish, Asa!'

Asa was unperturbed. 'Not so; but better perhaps a cold fish than a hot little dog trying to get his paws up the skirt of a trusting schoolgirl.'

'Umm...' his brother smacked his lips. 'She is such a delicious innocent, and with the most sweet little breasts. You mustn't be jealous.'

'You little shit!' Disgusted Asa flung his book at his brother's head. 'You are only doing this because maman forbade you. Leave that child alone or I swear I'll beat some sense into you.'

Félix dodged the book and swore. 'Anna is no child and what I do with her is my business, not yours.' He retreated to the door as Asa swung his feet to the ground. 'Just keep your mouth shut and your nose out of my affairs.'

The house shook as he slammed the door. Asa raised his eyes heavenward then after a moment retrieved his book from the floor and returned to his previous comfortable position against the pillows.

If their mother should discover Félix had seen that plain little virgin again his brother might wish he'd heeded the warning to hunt elsewhere. In a fighting mood their mother was quite capable of reducing that grubby-minded adolescent Don Juan to a quivering jelly, though quite why she was so determined to keep her precious Félix away from one gauche, not particularly pretty little schoolgirl

37

was a mystery. Asa yawned and stretched and was surprised to feel a faint stirring of lust. Why was that he wondered? The skinny little Anna Farrell wasn't at all his type. Félix, he thought loftily, was welcome to his little-girl fantasies; for himself he preferred his women older, experienced and wearing something rather more *soigné* and alluring than that terrible kilt...

4

MARLCLEW, CORNWALL

February 1937

Anna lay half asleep, her eyes closed against the square of pale light around the drawn curtains. She'd been dreaming about Félix and it took a minute or two for her to be properly awake and free of his presence. Just thinking about him made her feel light-headed and breathless.

Opening her eyes at last she looked across to the other bed where Valerie still slept, rosebud mouth slightly open and fair plaits spread across the pillow either side of her pretty doll-like face.

'Val,' she called softly, 'Val...wake up.'

Valerie opened wide her china blue eyes and turned her head. 'Why? What's wrong?'

'Nothing, I just wanted to talk before the bell goes.' Anna sat up, hugging her knees, gazing with some exasperation at the picture of wide-awake pink prettiness. 'How do you *do* that?'

She looked mystified. 'Do what?'

'Wake up so quickly looking like Jean Harlow after she's put on a half pound of make-up?'

'Dunno about that.' She rolled onto her side. 'I always feel more like Boris Karloff until I've washed. What did you want to talk about?'

'I dreamed of Félix. I really thought he was here.'

'What – in *bed*? Oh, wally, wally!'

'Of course not, but he'll be back again this weekend. I expect that's what made me dream about him. He is gorgeous, isn't he?'

Valerie shrugged. 'So-so I suppose if you like those pretty looks, but Asa's nicer.'

'He's too superior and sarcastic. Like some old man.'

Valerie sniffed. 'Better than Félix, though, *he* acts as though he's about fifteen and just discovered girls. I think he's very immature and untrustworthy. You watch out, Anna. He's only after one thing.'

'I know.' She gazed dreamily at the ceiling. 'But then all chaps are, aren't they?'

'Yes, but nice girls don't let them have it!' reproved Valerie. 'Just

39

imagine if you let him – you know – and you had a *baby*! Anyway, suppose you were seen sneaking off one of these days...then where would you be?'

'Sent to la Harrison then slung out I should think.' Anna sighed and punched the pillow. 'I really hate this place. You can't think what a strain it is to work hard and behave all the time. Sometimes I wish I hadn't promised Patrick I would, but you don't promise Patrick something and then go back on it...not if you want to go on living, you don't!' She sat up abruptly and swung her feet out of bed. 'I'm going to have first go at the showers and get some hot water for a change. Coming?'

'No. It's too nice in bed.' Valerie watched as Anna pulled on her dressing gown and took her wash-bag from the hook on the door. 'Don't mess it up because of Félix, he just isn't worth it. You may be that old bag Harrison's golden girl ever since you decided to be a nice, hard working, law-abiding swot, but I'd miss you so if you were caught and got kicked out.'

'Don't worry. I'll be careful.' Anna rumpled her curly hair and gave the sudden smile that could in seconds transform her from only moderately attractive to almost pretty. 'After all these years here you and I have to see it through to the end together.'

'Oh, don't!' Valerie closed her eyes tight. 'I can't bear to think of leaving and going home to Tunbridge Wells! I'm being brought out next year and given a Season. I shall feel just like a nice fresh chicken with all the cockerels come to eye me up and strut around crowing until one of them gets me! Oh, you are lucky being an orphan...Patrick would never do such a thing to you.'

'I know I'm lucky. When I'm finished here he says he'll take me on the Grand Tour,' Anna giggled suddenly, 'to Cannes to sin, Rome to be saved and Munich to be warned!'

'I get the sin and the saving, but warned about what?'

'Herr Hitler and National Socialism of course, dopey!'

'Oh, but mummy thinks he's sweet.'

'Does she?' Anna paused at the door to look back over her shoulder. 'Then I should tell her to have another think. When I told Patrick I couldn't take seriously a man with that sort of moustache, he said, 'Forget the moustache. Just look at those eyes and you'll take him very, very seriously indeed.''

'Oh, politics...'Valerie waved a dismissive hand. 'That's even more boring than a whole roomful of chinless wonders.'

*   *   *

40

Anna slipped away after tea, knowing she had at least a clear hour to spend with Félix. When, breathless from her race down the lawn and through the concealing woodland she reached the boathouse to find him waiting for her.

Closing the heavy wooden door she stepped into the punt and sank down at his side gasping for breath. 'I nearly fell over the gardener's boy as he was cycling home...I don't know which of us got the bigger fright! I gave him a shilling and he said he'd keep quiet.'

Félix laughed and pulled her into his arms. 'A shilling was too much. He will think you rich and next time will expect more!'

He felt the rapid rise and fall of her breast and desire clenched like some giant fist around his loins. It had to be today when he had the perfect place; there may never be such a good opportunity again. He kissed her and she put her arms about his neck and kissed him back, but when he began to push her skirt up she thrust his hand away saying, 'No. You never know when to stop!'

He gave a breathless laugh. 'But I don't want to stop and neither do you. Don't pretend to be such a little prude, Anna. You like doing naughty things with me, don't you?'

She blushed. 'Yes...sometimes, but you always try to go too far.'

'But what do you expect when you make me want you so much?' He slid her down into the well of the boat, pressing her hard against him. Pulling aside her blouse he kissed the hollow at the base of her throat. 'I can't wait for ever – especially when I know you want me also... you do want me don't you, Anna?'

She wasn't yet at all sure she knew what it was she was supposed to want. Playing for time she squirmed away from his seeking mouth.

'Don't!' Cross and dishevelled, she pushed at his chest. 'You're squashing me.'

He laughed, then released her and reached for the long punt pole. 'I've found somewhere better than this miserable place where we shall go. You open the gate and give us a good push, then just a few shoves will take us to the other side.'

She said scathingly, 'You don't shove a punt, you pole it you ignorant Frenchman – and don't forget the tide's only just on the turn. We don't want to get stuck in the mud.' Expertly she leaned to release the latch on the gates, pushing them wide and allowing the punt to glide silently across the creek, the trees shielding them from any casual observer at the school.

'Where are we going?' She jumped onto the bank, hitching the rope around a tree stump and tying it firmly. 'I can't be long or I'll be missed.'

'Here, just here.' He took her hand. Ducking down under the trees they came out onto a clearing and a small clapboard cottage. She hung back, laughing nervously, whispering, 'This is old Harry Pardoe's place. I'm not passing there – he'll see us.'

'Not so, he is in the hospital in Penzance...an appendicitis Maman said. It will be more comfortable there than in the punt.'

She was aghast. 'We can't just break in!'

'No need.' He chuckled, reaching up above the lintel. 'Here he leaves his key for Bella to feed his cat while he is away. She told me so when she was cleaning our house this morning.'

She demurred. 'Félix, I don't think we should.' Larking about in the boathouse was one thing. Going into this empty cottage with him away from the safety of the school grounds quite another; but he roused such strange, exciting feelings in her...and she *was* almost seventeen.

She stepped hesitantly into the cottage her heart thumping; in the dusk he took her hand, drawing her further into the room.

'Come, Anna, trust me. You will enjoy this and I shall take care to protect you. I am no stupid boy to give you a baby.'

'I should hope not!' Her face flamed, but she followed him on legs suddenly become weak and shaking, aware that she didn't really want to be here alone with him but it seemed so rude to keep saying No. She clung more tightly to his hand.

'Here.' He pulled her down onto the floor and unresisting she allowed him to unfasten her coat as he lay beside her. She shivered and her heart began to thump as he pushed up her jersey and blouse to caress her breasts. 'Don't be afraid,' he murmured against her mouth. 'It will be all right. I will take care of you.'

She said through chattering teeth, 'What are you going to do?'

Putting his mouth close to her ear he told her. She gasped. 'Is that really what people do when they make love?'

He laughed. 'Of course, you little goose.'

Her head spun and she pleaded silently, *Please God, don't let Patrick find out because he'd be so disappointed in me and I couldn't bear that...*but she did love Félix and although what he had just told her sounded awful if he loved her then it must be all right. She clung to him, hiding her face against his chest. 'Will it hurt?'

'A little perhaps, but not for long...sit up now.' With practised hands he pulled off her jersey, blouse and skirt. She clutched her hands across her breast to cover her nakedness as he peeled off her stockings then tugged impatiently at her navy school knickers. '*Mon Dieu,* what is this – *deux du culotte!*' he peered at the white liners. 'For what do you need two pairs?'

She giggled hysterically. 'The dye comes off – Oh!' She stared as he stood to strip off his own clothes then looked away, her face scarlet. He laughed. 'Never seen a naked man before, *chérie?*'

'No,' she risked another look and her eyes widened. 'What are you doing?'

'Protecting you – and me!' he knelt, parting her legs and pressing her back down onto the rug. She began to shiver uncontrollably. 'Don't be frightened...' he lowered himself onto her, 'no virgin ever died of making love for the first time!'

*   *   *

It was almost dark when he closed the door and returned the key to its place above the lintel. She whispered, 'It's late. I must have been missed by now. I don't know what I'm going to tell Miss Harrison.'

He gave a low laugh. 'You can say you have been walking in the grounds.'

'A bit feeble considering it's almost too dark to see...and you don't have to do the lying, I do and I'm not very good at it.' She tried to sound grown up but she was still bewildered, unable to come to terms with what she had allowed him to do to her in that grubby little shack.

He kissed her. 'It will surely be worth a few lies to have gained so much pleasure.'

So that was what it was all about – pleasure! She felt confused and cheated. Félix hadn't as she'd imagined been very romantic; certainly hadn't whispered the expected loving words in her ear. She'd had only the haziest idea of what she was supposed to be feeling and what she had felt hadn't been enjoyable as he'd promised, only hot and painful. Thinking about it now she felt her insides curl with remembered hurt.

Old Pardoe's fireside rug had been hard and hairy, smelling of coal dust and cat pee and clogged with stale food; altogether the whole thing had fallen far short of her romantic expectations. Was this what all the fuss was about? She had been hurt and frightened by his hard invasion of her body, mystified and confused by his swift climax; relieved when it was over and he lay heavy and warm between her thighs, no longer moving and hurting, but breathing harshly with his heart beating hard against hers.

But despite the disillusionment and pain she loved him with all the single-minded intensity of a newly awakened adolescent, hungry for the close human contact he offered. It wasn't his fault she'd been ignorant and stupid and hadn't known what to expect or what to do, she thought miserably. She held his hand tightly saying impulsively, 'I love you terribly, Félix!'

'Do you?' He sounded amused. 'But, Anna, one does not have to love to enjoy such pleasure.'

Bewildered and feeling the first stirring of anger, she said, 'I thought people only did what you did to me when they were in love. Don't you love me, Félix?'

'What a question so soon! You are sweet and made me want you so much...but in love?' He shrugged. 'That I know nothing about. Is it not sufficient that we can enjoy this without talking of love?'

She twisted away from his arm and pushed him hard so that he almost fell. 'You're a cad, Félix Gallimard! *You* might have enjoyed yourself but I just hurt...'

'Hey, hey...' he recovered his balance and made a grab at her, but she pushed him again and ran for the creek and the safety of the punt, only to let out a wail of horror when she reached the bank and found it empty. As she stood frozen on the pathway the moon came from behind a cloud and she could see the punt in the distance, moving swiftly down stream in the tidal waters, the mooring rope trailing from the stern.

'Félix, quick...the punt...'

He reached her side and uttered a crow of laughter. 'You goose, you did not tie it – tomorrow it will be half-way to France!'

'But I did. I don't make mistakes like that. It's *miles* to the bridge and it will take an age to walk!' Cold and with her teeth chattering with fright, she stood clutching her shoulders and shivering. Her voice rose hysterically. 'Someone's untied it. Someone's been watching us and played a trick.'

There were quick footsteps and Asa came into sight on the towpath. In the light from the moon she saw his expression was a mixture of anger, shock and dismay. He looked at them both accusingly. 'I thought I heard voices! What are *you* doing here?'

Speechless, Anna stared at him with wide, frightened eyes. For a long moment he held her gaze before turning to meet his brother's mocking grin, demanding, 'Was it *you* left the punt? I thought one of those silly girls must have crossed with it earlier and walked back by the bridge. I was going to return it, but slipped on the wet grass and let go...I ran to see if I might catch it but the water flows too fast for that.'

Angrily he glared at his brother then looked again at Anna's stricken face. His voice softened. 'Do not look so frightened, Anna. We cannot now splash about in the dark but it is bound to stop in one of the pools beyond the bridge where there are many low branches. I shall fetch it in the morning for you and return it quietly. No one need know.'

Anna fought an almost overwhelming desire to weep. She knew that by the time she returned everyone *would* know; they would be out looking for her from the school and she would be in serious trouble if found with these two at this time of night. A wave of anger at them both suddenly swept over her and she sat down hard on the bank saying furiously, 'You're a bloody useless pair of nits, aren't you!'

Félix clicked his tongue reprovingly.

'*Pourriez-vous répéter, mam'zelle s'il vous plait?*' he asked and exploded into laughter.

Furious she turned on him. 'Shut up, you idiot. They'll hear you up at the house.' Close to tears again she grabbed an arm of each. 'What am I going to *do*?'

All three stood helplessly on the bank; even the irrepressible Félix for once subdued; eventually, silently and in single file and with Asa leading they walked the mile and a quarter along the uneven river path to the footbridge, where Anna left them with a terse and miserable 'Goodnight' before making her way towards the school and certain retribution.

Félix watched her out of sight then expelled a long breath. 'Well, thanks to you, brother, our little friend really *is* in trouble now!'

Asa swung round on him in sudden fury. 'You've had her tonight, haven't you, you bastard?'

'Of course, no need to look so.' He laughed. 'She proved willing ...after only the smallest persuasion!'

A second later he was lying on the riverbank, both hands clasped over his bleeding mouth. Dazed and swearing, he tried to scramble his feet, but Asa was upon him again, catching him by the collar of his coat and hauling him upright.

'You filthy, dirty, despicable, little *shit*!' He punctuated each word with a slap to either side of his brother's head before pushing him back violently against a tree.

With a roar of fury Félix recovered his senses and swinging wildly with both fists he broke away to race along the pathway towards the safety of Carey's Cottage.

Asa followed slowly, cursing beneath his breath and nursing his bruised knuckles, at the same time taking pleasure in imagining how Félix would have to think up an excuse for his appearance for Maman...that would surely tax even Félix's imagination.

But when he entered the cottage his mother was tenderly bathing her son's cut and swollen lips and gently taking him to task for being so foolish as to run into a tree in the dark.

Silently Asa mouthed *bâtard*! Félix grinned back and his brother climbed the stairs, his mouth set in disgust.

The little sod could squirm his way out of anything.

*   *   *

By the time Anna was hauled before an outraged Miss Harrison, reaction had set in and she was feeling so exhausted and overwrought that she could only weep and hang her head.

No, she admitted in a whisper, she shouldn't have taken the punt out so late on her own and without permission. Yes, she should have tied it properly. Yes, she was ashamed of herself, and No she would never *ever* do such a thing again.

'Almost every member of staff has been out looking for you...I was ready to call the police. Anna, how *could* you?' Miss Harrison's tone was icy. 'I really have no alternative but to send you home tomorrow, at least for the remainder of this term...I simply cannot imagine what your guardian will say to all this.'

'*Please,* don't send me home.' Anna pleaded desperately, 'I'll fetch the punt back tomorrow and I promise not to take it out again...Please, Miss Harrison, punish me any other way, but don't send me home.'

Miss Harrison wavered. It would do the school's reputation no good to make too much of such a silly thoughtless incident and despite having in the past been a most difficult and problematic child, Anna was now one of her star pupils. She drew in her breath. 'Very well, I will not distress Mr Farrell by informing him of your stupid and dangerous actions but you cannot go unpunished.' She took a long ruler from her drawer and stood up. 'Put up your hand, Anna.'

Anna's humiliation was complete; in a few weeks she would be *seventeen* and here she was, being treated like a disobedient junior. It was almost unbearable, but anything, even this, was better than returning home in disgrace.

Her punishment over, she squeezed her stinging hands together hard as the mistress regarded her severely over her spectacles.

'You will not be allowed out of the school grounds for any reason for the remainder of this term. I am disappointed in you, Anna, you were my choice for head girl for your last term, now you will have to work very hard indeed for the remainder of this one to win back my trust.'

Anna was fervent, 'Oh, I will, I will!' To have returned home and been forced to explain her fall from grace to Patrick and Charlie was too awful to even think about. They were both far too sharp to believe the story she had told Miss Harrison and there was simply no way that she could ever possibly tell them about Félix.

*　　*　　*

Valerie was round-eyed. 'What on earth were you *doing* on the other side of the creek anyway?' she whispered.

'Nothing, only mooching around.'

'A funny thing to be doing in the dark.'

'It was all right until that idiot Asa let the punt go.' Anna hunched down under her covers. Furtively, she wiped her eyes on the sheet. If only Félix had said he loved her it would all have been worthwhile. Now her hands stung abominably, she was sore in all her tender parts and her limbs ached. She felt miserable and appallingly wicked and went hot all over when she thought about the stain on old Pardoe's rug: 'Amid so many, it will not notice!' Félix had said and laughed.

"Beware! Your sins will find you out!" Uncle Frederick had thundered from his pulpit. She wiped her eyes again. It seemed he'd known a thing or two.

She loved Patrick and Charlie, and in return they were loving and warm towards her. But she had no memory that in her whole life anyone had ever held her really close to them before. She wished now that she hadn't let it happen, but despite her shock at the undignified and painful reality of sex and her disillusionment at Félix's lack of romance, she desperately wanted to feel his arms around her again.

But not ever, she thought with a shudder, like it had been in Pardoe's cottage. She'd *never* let him do that to her again.

47

5

STRATTON PLACE

Bloomsbury, April 1937

Félix had gone back to Paris immediately after that disastrous weekend, only returning once more before Easter. Despite the strictures imposed on her movements by Miss Harrison, when another note arrived from him via the gardener's boy, Anna slipped away to the boathouse, determined she would make him understand that she wouldn't submit to another such so-called pleasure.

When Félix felt her instinctive withdrawal from his embrace, he knew he'd been too impatient and too light-heartedly dismissive of her naïve declaration of love. If he were to be sure she'd still be there for him whenever he visited he would have to take more care. Accordingly he held her lightly until he felt her relaxing in his arms, then with gentle hands and lips coaxed and cajoled her again into final surrender, so that she clung to him, whimpering in a half-terrified agony of pleasure.

Afterwards as they lay in the cold darkness of the boathouse Anna wanted nothing more from life than to lie entwined in this close embrace forever. Tightening her arms about him as he made to leave her she begged, 'Don't move…please stay with me like this.'

He whispered, 'No, no…it is not safe,' and withdrew, leaving her feeling chilled and sad; still waiting in vain to hear him say he loved her. She tried to talk about the future and asked how they would meet when she'd left school and returned to London for good, but he stopped her mouth with kisses, 'Soon, soon, we will make plans,' he promised, 'we have plenty of time before us.'

Overwhelmed by the feelings he'd aroused in her, she wilfully closed her mind against the frightening thought that for him making love had nothing to do with loving. But clinging to the conviction that it was only a matter of time before he felt as she did, she determined to wait patiently until they could be together again when he would, he must, love her in return.

*   *   *

It was miserable to leave for the Easter holiday without seeing him again, but her spirits lightened as every turn of the wheels brought her closer to home.

As her train ground towards the buffers at Paddington she hung out of the window until she could see Charlie waiting by the gate. Swinging open the carriage door she jumped down onto the platform before the train had stopped, all the dignity of her years vanishing as she ran towards the barrier, waving and calling, 'Charlie! I'm here…I'm here!'

Thrusting her ticket into the collector's outstretched hand she reached Charlie, flinging her arms around his neck, letting the tide of travellers swirl around them as she hugged him. 'There's my bonnie lassie!' he said and giving her shoulders a last welcoming squeeze took up her case. 'Come along with you now, I've the car outside.'

'Where's Patrick?'

'Gone to see some paintings on the Brompton Road; we'll to fetch him on the way back.'

She laughed, hugging his arm as they crossed the station hall. 'Four whole weeks, Charlie…what shall we do with all that time?'

He grinned. 'Same as we always do: work, eat and talk; although Patrick thought he might take you to Paris for a few days first, for a birthday treat and to buy some clothes. Would you like that?'

She said, 'Yes, that would be lovely,' thinking that while she was there that beast Félix would most likely be back in Cornwall again and continuing his running battle with Madame, who was still trying to make him leave his job at the newspaper and follow Asa to the university, so far without success.

She would miss him for the next four weeks. His fleeting visits had been little islands of warmth in the cold grey sea of school in winter, and now she could think of little else but the burning, all consuming desire he'd aroused in her. She gave an involuntary sigh and Charlie paused in the act of opening the car door.

'Now what's was that for?'

She forced a smile, 'Nothing.' She slid onto the back seat and pulled the door closed. 'Let's go and find Patrick.'

*   *   *

Patrick came to where she waited by the car; he kissed her on both cheeks then held her at arm's length for a long scrutiny. Noting the brightness of her eyes; the little telltale flush that stained her skin, he asked, 'What have you been doing with yourself since Christmas?'

Anna's heart gave a thump and she laughed nervously. 'Nothing,' she repeated.

'Yes you have.' Patrick's smile held a hint of puzzled speculation. 'Perhaps it's that you've almost, but not quite, grown up.'

Charlie gave a derisive snort, 'Its called being almost seventeen!'

'Is it?' Patrick's gaze was still on her face. 'I wouldn't know. I don't remember what it felt like to be that young. How does it feel, Anna?'

She avoided his eyes. 'Uncomfortable,' she said and began hastily to chatter about the awfulness of school, her hoped for future elevation to Head Girl and how her French had progressed under Madame Gallimard.

Patrick nodded approval then almost immediately pulled his brows together in a frown. 'Did you say *Gallimard*? Is she an English-woman?'

'Yes. Why, do you know her?'

'No, but it isn't a common name and I've done business in Paris with an Auguste Gallimard, who is married to an Englishwoman, but his home is in Dinard and I've never visited him there or met his wife. I believe she is a teacher so it is possible that she is your Madame, though why she should be teaching in England I can't think, unless they've separated.' He gave a short, humourless laugh. 'That wouldn't surprise me...he's a nice man, an expert on French porcelain, but a great charmer with more mistresses than I imagine even a French wife, let alone an English one, could tolerate for ever!'

'Well he hasn't any mistresses now.' Anna dismissed Auguste airily with the callousness of youth. 'He died last year; now she lives in a cottage in Rosstennan village, but she is very interested in porcelain so he must be the one...'

She explained Madame Gallimard's appearance as a teacher of French, skirting carefully around any mention of her sons; relieved when they arrived back at the Gallery and Patrick let the subject drop. She was torn, feeling she should tell him about all the probing questions and Madame's cooling interest in her since that memorable invitation to the cottage when she had met Félix for the first time. But as he didn't raise the subject again, she prudently decided not to mention all the questions about the Bloomsbury house and it's occupants, reasoning that Madame's curiosity had most likely been because Patrick was in the same business as her late husband and she had probably just enjoyed talking to someone who shared her interests. All the same, Anna hoped Auguste Gallimard's widow would continue to remain in ignorance of her own involvement with

Félix. The glimpse she'd had of her cold disapproval at the cottage that day had been quite enough. Altogether it was a great relief to have been spared any more visits. The only conversation she and Madame had now was as pupil and teacher and confined to work within the classroom.

What Madame needed, she thought, was a really nice husband who didn't chase other women and then she might stop bothering so much about what Félix was doing!

Later that afternoon when Patrick had retreated to the walled rear garden with his paper, leaving her to help Charlie prepare the evening meal she said mischievously, 'Wouldn't it be fun to fix Patrick up with the widow Gallimard? She's very attractive and chic – I think I'll lure him down to Cornwall next term and leave them to talk antiques together.'

Charlie lost for a moment the rhythm of his knife slicing through carrots and shot her an enigmatic look, commenting dryly, 'I doubt he'd take all that kindly to such an arrangement.'

She took a piece of carrot and chewed reflectively, looking at him slant-eyed. 'Why wouldn't he? Hasn't he ever had a girlfriend?'

'I wouldn't know; possibly – mebbe in his salad days.' His tone was flat and disinterested.

She persisted. 'I wonder why he isn't married. It can't just be because of his hand. *I* think he's terribly attractive in a brooding sort of way…you should see how some women look at him!'

'I've been seein' it for years,' he interrupted shortly and pushed a cabbage across the table towards her. 'Just stop your chattering will you an' wash an' shred that or they'll be no meal tonight.'

'All right, keep your hair on!' She bowled the cabbage under-arm into the sink. 'I was only asking. Anyone would think you were his mother the way you carry on sometimes.'

He flared into sudden temper and leaning across the table shouted, 'You'll be thinking I'm *your* mother if I lay the flat of my hand across your backside, you impudent, bad-mouthed brat!'

She backed up against the sink and gave vent to a nervous snort. 'Crikey, take it easy, Charlie. I only said…'

His eyes glittered and he flourished the knife, 'I heard fine well what you said!'

'What the hell is all the yelling about?' Patrick appeared suddenly at the top of the steps leading down into the garden and stood frowning, a hand resting each side of the iron balustrade. He looked from one to the other. 'Charlie, kindly put down that knife and Anna, stop trying to climb into the sink and tell me what is going on!'

51

Charlie swung his arm, stuck his knife in the table and leaned on it, his knuckles showing white and his face like stone. Anna glared at Patrick indignantly.

'*Me*? I'm not the one doing the all the shouting! I teased him and he lost his rag that's all. It's not my fault if he can't take a joke.'

Charlie's face was still tight with anger; Patrick looked at him in silence for a moment then raised an enquiring eyebrow. 'Charlie?'

He growled, 'Leave it. It doesn't matter,' and jerking the knife from the table he turned a dismissive shoulder. 'Anna, get that cabbage washed, will you? Or must I do everything myself?'

'Do this, do that – certainly, m'lord!' Upset at being the focus of his anger she wrenched the cold tap then leapt back as a jet of water hit the cabbage, drenching her dress and sending a liberal spray of icy water across the kitchen. She screamed and Charlie blasphemed loudly.

'Christ *Almighty* – will ye get out o' my bloody sight before I brain ye!'

Patrick ordered coldly, 'One of you turn that damned tap *off* – and whatever the problem is, sort it out between the pair of you p.d.q or I shall be dining out!' Turning abruptly he retreated back down the steps, shutting the door firmly behind him.

Anna turned off the tap and slumped against the sink while Charlie stood at the splattered table and wiped his hands down his face. For a long moment she stared into his eyes in silence and he stared back impassively. Biting her lip she said in a small voice. 'I'm sorry I was rude, Charlie, and I didn't do that on purpose.'

'Are you sure about that?'

'Quite sure…and I'm sorry I told you to keep your hair on!'

He picked up a towel and threw it at her. 'Anything else you're sorry about while you're at it?'

She caught the towel and began to dab at her wet dress. 'Being born?' she ventured.

He scowled, but the anger had gone from his eyes. 'Get on an' see to that cabbage,' he ordered tersely and after a moment's hesitation she took a knife from the block and began to hack thoughtfully into the cabbage. Charlie recommended slicing carrots and slowly the tension left the air as everything apparently returned to normal.

Neither Charlie nor Patrick ever referred to the incident again, but the whole silly squabble stayed in Anna's mind. Why on earth, she wondered, should her lovely even-tempered Charlie get into such a flaming temper because she'd said women found Patrick attractive?

6

PARIS

April, 1937

'I refuse absolutely to go up that wretched Tower again,' Patrick was adamant. 'Twice is more than enough.' He regarded her distantly. 'How even you can possibly gain pleasure by standing at the top of that monstrosity in a rainstorm I simply cannot imagine.'

'You have no soul.' Anna lifted her face to the weather. 'Paris rain isn't like London rain. It even tastes different.'

'But *I* prefer to shelter from it, not drink it.' He took her arm and crossing the road guided her towards a café. 'Cognac for me, coffee for you I think.'

'No, *please* Patrick – I'm seventeen and this is *Paris*; cognac for you and cognac for me too!'

He made his familiar '*Tsch!*' and ordered the drinks. When they came she sipped cautiously; then smiled 'It's nice...lovely and warm.' She toasted him shyly. 'Thank you for Paris, for the clothes and all the lovely places we've been. I feel at least ten years older.'

He cast his eye approvingly over the narrow dark green suit and honey coloured silk scarf she wore with such style. Once out of her young girl dresses and into the understated elegance of Parisian couture, she had blossomed into a remarkably attractive young woman. He half-closed his eyes and smiled. 'Oh, I think not. Certainly no more than five and it's not quite over yet. We have two more days before I have to be back in London. Where would you like to go tomorrow?'

'Oh, perhaps the Louvre again and save Fontainebleau for our last day, or we could – '

'Forget about the sightseeing and go dancing,' suggested an all too familiar voice from behind and she spun around on her chair to find Asa looking down on her with his saturnine grin. They hadn't met again since that night at Pardoe's cottage and it was something of a shock to see that without Félix for comparison he appeared much more attractive than she remembered. He bowed. 'Everyone dances in Paris in the spring. Only tourists exhaust themselves walking around galleries.'

Recovering herself quickly she made a disdainful face. 'Trust you to bob up and give a lecture; save it for your future students, poor things!' Turning back to Patrick who was surveying the newcomer with polite interest she said formally. 'Patrick, this is Asa Gallimard, Madame's eldest son. Asa, this is my guardian, Patrick Farrell.'

The two men shook hands, Patrick saying smoothly, 'Please, won't you join us?'

Anna scowled, her irritation spilling over as Asa sat beside her. 'What are *you* doing here?' she demanded. 'I thought you and...' she stumbled, '...that you and your brother would both be at home by now.'

His face darkened. 'Félix has gone to Spain.'

'*Spain*? What on earth for?'

Patrick saw the colour drain from her face and was suddenly alert. Intrigued he thought, Now what is going on here?

Asa shrugged. 'He is not fighting – only trying his hand at reporting the war from a safe distance. He will keep well away from any Fascist guns.'

'Well, I think he's incredibly brave to go there at all.' Anna's lip trembled at his denigration of her beloved.

Asa looked at her with something like compassion. 'Anna, I know Félix; he is no hero. He will just do the minimum of work then get out as quickly as possible.'

'I don't believe that; he could be in terrible danger, and all for a newspaper story.'

Asa remained unrepentant. He said with a calm reasonableness that made her want to slap him. 'People need to know what is going on in the world.'

She wailed despairingly, 'Why on earth does anyone, idealist or otherwise, want to go to Spain just to fight a load of Fascist thugs?'

'We shall all be doing that sooner or later – and rather nearer to home than Spain.' His voice was very dry, 'but I wish with Maman that Félix had continued his studies and not thrown everything up to put himself in the firing line for the sake of a newspaper story.'

She flushed and snapped, 'I suppose you're bound to get your *Doctorat d'état* and find yourself a nice safe job well away from trouble, you swot!'

'But naturally.'

Patrick hid his amusement at her rapid change from poised young woman to quarrelsome schoolgirl. Putting aside for the moment his curiosity about why his ward should be in such a state over the absent Félix he intervened quickly. 'What are you going to do once you have your degree?'

'I already have a post offered...a Junior Lectureship in European Political History becomes vacant in October this year at London University. As I was born in England of an English mother I have dual nationality, which has made it easier to gain employment there.'

'You must come and see us when you are settled. Anna finishes school this summer and can take you sightseeing.' Patrick's expression was apparently devoid of mischief, but Anna gave him as poisonous a look as she dared and lapsed into silence, letting the tide of their conversation pass over her head.

Asa's news had spoiled her lovely holiday and she was washed with misery. How could Félix just go like that, without a word? And suppose Asa let slip to Patrick something about their meetings? She felt her stomach knot with apprehension; she wouldn't put it past him to deliberately start dropping hints right here and now...She became aware that Patrick was speaking to her and looked up blankly. 'I'm sorry. Did you say something?'

'Yes, that you might like to finish your day-dreaming and make up your mind where you would like to go next.'

She answered absently, 'I don't mind. You choose.' She saw Patrick's brows pull together in annoyance, but the thought of Félix in danger had robbed her of all caution about showing the misery that now filled her.

'Very well, but first finish the drink you insisted that I buy you.'

She picked up her glass to gulp the rest of her cognac; choking as the unfamiliar fiery liquid hit her throat she wheezed and spluttered helplessly, furiously conscious of Asa's ironic grin as Patrick impatiently patted her back and offered his handkerchief.

'It's unlike you to be so careless, Anna,' Patrick's expression was distinctly questioning. 'Perhaps you were having more of a nightmare than a day dream?'

'I have a headache. I think I'd like to go back to the hotel and lie down.' She avoided looking at him. 'Excuse me, Patrick...you carry on without me. I'll see you later.'

Without waiting for a reply, she stood and walked away, horribly conscious of the two pairs of eyes watching her undignified retreat.

*   *   *

After taking his leave of Patrick, Asa returned to his apartment, striding heedless through another shower of rain, not entirely sure whether Fate had played into his hands, or just delivered one of her

55

favourite dirty tricks. On the one hand was the undoubted bonus of seeing Anna without Félix on tow, on the other the inescapable fact that she felt no more sweetly towards him in Paris than she had in Cornwall. However, the opportunity had been too good to miss; here in Paris he could speak to her without the risk of either Félix or *maman* popping up at any moment.

Recalling the scene in his mother's house after Anna's visit he wondered again why she had been so adamant that neither of them should have anything to do with either the girl or her family. Now that he had met the principle member of that family her behaviour seemed even less reasonable. What could she possibly have against the charming Patrick Farrell?

Asa had instantly warmed to Anna's quietly perceptive companion, but all the same, there *was* something a little odd about him...he frowned, recalling the guarded eyes and air of reserve beneath the charm, and wondered if Patrick Farrell might be homosexual. He'd met several such attractive and faintly elusive men who almost invariably were, so perhaps that was their mother's objection to Anna and her family.

Despite all the years in France his mother was still very British... and old-fashioned British at that. He remembered he had once brought home for the weekend a slightly effeminate fellow student from university. She had been icily polite during his stay, but afterwards made it clear that any other such male friends would not be welcome again. At first he'd been irritated by her intolerance, then later amused by her eagerness to welcome any of his girlfriends to the house.

'She can't help it,' Auguste had said when he complained, 'She's not that keen on men in general, and even less kindly disposed towards those like your friend. Just let her see you kissing a few girls and she'll be happy!'

Asa smiled as he opened the door to his apartment. It had been good advice. His mother's suspicions had soon been put to rest and he was able to mix unhindered with whom he pleased when away from home. Hetero or homosexual, it made no difference to him. First and foremost, a friend was a friend.

Reaching his room he stripped off his wet clothing and sat on the edge of the bath waiting for it to fill, thinking about the abrasive Anna and wondering why he should concern himself so much over her. She meant nothing to him and what she did was none of his business, but it still seemed a great pity to have her so in love with a rascal such as Félix. At least, he thought, he seemed to have got M'sieur Farrell on his side and the betting was her guardian would make sure she at least met him if he invited her out tomorrow evening. He would ring their hotel first thing in the morning, he decided, and ask her guardian if she may dine with him.

I must try not to annoy her, he thought, I'll take her dancing then for a quiet meal and when I'm sure she is ready to listen, tell her the truth: that Félix is a thoughtless perpetual adolescent, heedless of any needs other than his own; one who will never love her, only take all she has to give and just walk away when he is tired of her. It will hurt for a little while, he reasoned, but at least she'll not go on waiting for the love that will never come, and it will free her to find someone more worthy when she is older and more ready for love.

*   *   *

For the rest of that day Anna kept to her room, using her mythical headache as the excuse to avoid having dinner with Patrick, then suffered a guilt-ridden, restless and extremely hungry night. Félix's thoughtless departure for Spain without sending her a word was almost more than she could bear. Now she heaped all her unhappiness upon Asa as the bearer of bad news. He was like some malignant spirit, she thought angrily; sent by fate to cause her trouble.

When she came to breakfast the next morning Patrick contemplated her pink-rimmed eyes in silence for a while then asked, 'Since when did you begin having such long-lasting headaches?'

'Since people like Asa turn up to ruin my holiday!'

'Not, I fear a strictly honest answer and certainly lacking in charity.' He looked on with disapproval as she began savagely to butter her toast. 'You will need to behave better than that if the young man is to take you dancing tonight.'

'I wouldn't dance with Asa Gallimard if he could do it better than Fred Astaire!' she answered him tersely and he raised an eyebrow in mock surprise.

'Better not tell him that when he turns up in his glad rags this evening.'

She put down her knife and glared at him defiantly. 'Patrick, I won't go.'

'Anna, I think you will.' He was calm and reasonable. 'It is only good manners, of which you seem to be rather bereft since yesterday.'

She flushed. 'Please…'

'I'll make a bargain with you…you tell me what caused yesterday's sudden and remarkably long lasting headache, and I will telephone to say you are still too unwell to go out this evening.'

Anna gave him an imploring look. 'It's private. Can't I have a private place?'

'My dear Anna, is it that bad?'

At his the sudden concern in his tone she struggled against her tears. 'Yes, no…it's nothing, really. We've only really met twice but we just don't get on, that's all.'

'I wonder why.'

'Just incompatible, I suppose. Some people are, aren't they?'

'Then wouldn't tonight provide the opportunity to call a truce, even for a few hours – give you the opportunity of enjoying a pleasant evening with a handsome young man and perhaps get to know him better?'

She muttered, 'He's only being polite and he's not *that* handsome.'

'He was very insistent – in the nicest possible way. I really think you should go.'

She was mulish. 'You have an unfair advantage over me.'

'I do?'

'Yes. I have to go because you're in *loco parentis* and still use that to make me do as you ask.' She took a bite out of her toast and gave him a sideways look, adding boldly. 'Better make the most of it though; it won't work for much longer!'

He laughed outright. 'Anna, you are beginning to cross swords with me.' He leaned forward and kissed her cheek, for him an unusual spontaneous expression of affection. 'Thank you for giving in so easily.'

'That seems to be one of my gifts,' she answered, then added quickly, 'and please don't ask what I mean by that!'

'I won't. You're quite right. Everyone should have a private place. I should know. I've had one for years.'

She gave a sly smile. 'You tell me about yours and I'll tell you about mine.'

He accorded her a long, very level look.

'Some day perhaps; but not yet.'

*   *   *

When Asa reached the Hotel promptly at eight o'clock, immaculate in evening dress she was waiting for him and they exchanged a brief and impersonal greeting before he took her arm and escorted her to a waiting taxi. Once seated in the closed intimacy of the cab he regarded her stony profile for a few minutes in silence before

58

admitting, 'I did not expect you to come with me tonight.'

'I'm not doing it for you but for Patrick, so don't get any ideas!' Anna was waspish and hostile. 'You might have taken your lily-liver in hand and asked me yourself instead of going through him.'

'Yesterday you did not give me the chance,' he looked down, not quite concealing his smile, 'your, er, sudden headache...most convenient for you, but awkward for me.'

'Yes, well, you shouldn't have been such a pig.'

'I know.' He spread his hands, saying humbly, *'Je regret; je suis absolument désolé; je vous présente toutes mes excuses...'*

She gave an explosive snort of laughter. 'Oh, do shut up, once is enough!'

'OK.' He grinned. 'A truce then – at least for tonight.'

She smiled and began to relax. Gazing out of the window at the passing nightlife of Paris she was unaware of Asa studying her profile and reviewing his dismissal of her as a naïve, not particularly pretty schoolgirl. Taken separately her features were unremarkable, but put together they added up to something that although not beautiful in the conventional sense was arrestingly attractive. Yesterday she had looked what she was: a seventeen-year old girl wearing fashionable clothes. Now, in a smoky-blue evening gown that was elegant and discreetly expensive, she'd acquired an unexpected poise and the appearance, at least, of maturity.

Made suddenly and uncomfortably aware of the figure revealed by the sleekly fitting satin, he wondered how he could ever have imagined her plain and uninteresting...or made the error of still thinking of her as a child.

The long-lashed eyes were suddenly turned on him; glinting with amusement as though reading his thoughts, but she only gave a demure smile agreeing, 'I think I can manage a truce, Asa...just for tonight!'

*   *   *

They went to a dance hall near the Tuileries. At first she was wary of him, keeping him at arm's length, but he danced beautifully and his firm hand on her back held her close. As one dance followed swiftly upon another, she began to enjoy herself, moving smoothly where he led as though she'd always danced with him in this way.

It was the closest she had been to any man other than Félix and after a time she was disturbed to find the nearness of his tall broad-shouldered body arousing in her some very familiar sensations. All at

59

once her knees were unsteady and she felt the heat rise, colouring her face. She began to panic, knowing the situation was rapidly getting out of hand...at least for herself if not her companion. She risked a glance at his face, but his expression appeared closed and impersonal. It would be too stupid and gauche to stop suddenly, she thought, but she couldn't stay this close and have these feeling for a man she didn't even like – and she felt she would die on the spot if he were to notice...

Then in the midst of her confusion came the startling realisation that she was not the only one experiencing a problem.

The blush spread to every part of her body as he stopped abruptly in the middle of the dance to move her away from him, making her even more aware of just how close they had been by the sudden chill she felt from shoulders to knees. He said tersely, 'It's becoming too crowded. I think we should go elsewhere.'

Unable to prevent her startled 'Oh!' and shaken by his unexpected arousal she struggled for composure. Breathlessly she asked, 'Do you mind if we find somewhere to eat? I'm starving.'

'Of course,' he began to walk through the other couples his fingers barely touching her elbow as he steered her towards the doorway. 'There is a club I know nearby...mostly gaming and cabaret, but the food is good,' his voice was clipped and abrupt, 'unless perhaps, M'sieur Farrell would disapprove?'

'I shouldn't think so.' Now they were no longer so close she quickly recovered her poise, 'I think he's something of a gambling man himself, or was before I arrived to blight his life. At least, that's what Charlie says.'

'Who is Charlie?' He was distant, only politely interested.

'You know I'm not quite sure how to describe him, except to say that he's a shrewd old Scotsman who is very good at keeping both Patrick and me in order. He saved Patrick's life during the war and seems to have been taking care of him ever since.'

'I *see*...a useful man to have around, *n'est-ce pas?*'

Glancing at his profile Anna saw that he had pulled his mouth into a straight tight line, either in amusement or disparagement. She had a sudden desire to rattle him and wipe that irritating look off his face. She asked bluntly, 'Why did you suddenly stop dancing?'

He gave her an oblique look.

'Why do you think?'

'That's no answer to the question.'

'All right,' he pursed his lips for a moment. 'I stopped because we were both beginning to enjoy ourselves too much.'

With innocent malice she queried, 'Is that a crime?'

'Anna, you know perfectly well what was happening back there. I am twenty-two, you are seventeen. I do not allow myself to get into difficulties with such a *jeune fille* as yourself, nor allow you to dance so close.'

Stung into retaliation she snapped, 'Don't worry, if you were the last man on earth I wouldn't fancy *you*.'

'If I were that then you would perhaps have some fierce competition.' He was dryly sarcastic. 'So we shall now go to *La Faisson d'Or* and not fancy each other for the remainder of the evening…but in a civilised manner.'

'Suits me.'

She was stiff with anger. Just who did he think he was to be so disgustingly superior? How could she have allowed him, even for a moment, to arouse those feelings in her?

She pulled her elbow away, walking beside him with as much dignity as her five foot four allowed. Unable, despite her anger, to forego enjoying the heady enjoyment of most certainly having aroused equally unwelcome feelings in the supercilious Asa Gallimard, and shaken his irritating *sang froid* to its seemingly impregnable depths. It was, she thought, turning out to be a much more entertaining evening than she had had anticipated. From somewhere around her chest arose a bubble of anticipation.

She felt attractive, excited and ripe for mischief…

*   *   *

When they reached *Le Faisson d'Or* the cabaret had just ended. While Asa was exchanging greetings of the Patrone, Anna was swept from his side by a contingent of boisterous longhaired students, each vying with the other for a dance. Controlling an urge to snatch her back and possibly slap her hard, Asa was forced to watch a suddenly sparkling Anna quickstepping lightly across the floor in another man's arms.

Earlier, dancing so close and with her body moving in rhythm with his he had found her inviting, disturbing and alarmingly sexy. Not for a king's ransom, he brooded, would he risk that again, but felt an unreasonable resentment that any other man should enjoy having his libido aroused in the same way. For a while he stood watching her as she passed from partner to partner, then in an uncharacteristic mood of anger and recklessness, seated himself at a table and beckoning to the barman, commenced working his way steadily through the list of cocktails on offer.

*   *   *

Pointedly ignoring him and enjoying so much other male attention, Anna allowed herself to be swept along on a tide of admiration, wine and several light-hearted propositions to ascend to *une chambre* and view the French equivalent of interesting etchings, so that it was at least an hour before her attention was drawn again to Asa by her current dancing partner, a lanky youth whose eyes were partially obscured by a curtain of artistically long hair, who nudged her with a bony elbow commenting, 'That one you came with will be sorry in the morning!'

Following the direction of his gaze Anna stopped abruptly, riveted to the spot at the sight of Asa wrestling drunkenly and ineffectually with a peroxide blonde, who was taking vociferous and coarse objection to what appeared to be his attempt at Apache dancing.

Galvanised into sudden action Anna crossed the floor and grabbing his arm with fingers of steel hissed, 'Put her *down*, Asa. At once, and come home!'

She was amazed at the authority in her voice and even more amazed when he immediately relinquished the blonde to drape himself across her own shoulders, belching loudly and replying fondly, 'Without a doubt. Take me to your bed, *ma petite* Anna and let me *ravir* you!' then wafting fumes of gin, sank slowly to the floor and lay comatose, his long legs out straight and arms draped across his chest.

Like a corpse waiting for a coffin, she thought uncharitably and stirred him with a disdainful foot, thinking mutinously that it wasn't her fault Asa was pissed as a newt, it was Patrick's; if he hadn't insisted she came out with the bloody man tonight she wouldn't now be standing in some low dive with a drunken sot at her feet.... She looked questioningly at her dancing partner who had followed her. 'Is there a telephone?'

'Yes…at the bar.' He took Asa beneath the arms and hauled him onto a chair. 'Leave him to me.' He clicked imperious fingers at a passing waiter. 'Coffee, black, a basin of ice water and a towel, quickly, if you please!'

She waited impatiently as Patrick was paged around the George Cinq. When he finally came to the phone he listened in silence to her explanations then asked tersely, 'Where are you?'

'On the left bank; at club called *Le Faisson d'Or.*'

'I know it. Wait there for me. You do pick your time and place, don't you? You have interrupted a game of Baccarat and I am winning.'

'Sorry, Patrick, but it was your idea – and it's not *me* who's pissed and out for the count!'

Returning to where Asa was slumped across the table, his head on his arms she said spitefully, 'Another gallon of coffee and you might actually resemble a human being, you boozy swine...' She almost stamped her foot. 'Wake up, damn you – I've just had a flea in my ear from Patrick over you!'

He groaned, protesting thickly, 'There was no need to teferlone your old man. I am pershufly captleble...capapul...canabul...' he belched loudly. '...perfushly ABLE to get myshelf home!'

Aggravated, she kicked his ankle viciously hard so that he yelped and spilled his coffee. 'He is *not* my old man,' she hissed. 'My God, If only your mother could see you now!'

Asa dabbed with the wet tablecloth at the stain spreading across his dress shirt. *'Mon Dieu, mon Dieu...j'ai envie de vomir!'* he moaned, looking piteously at Anna who glared back in hostile silence. Be sick then, she thought meanly, and see if I'll lift a finger to clean you up.

When a steely-eyed Patrick finally appeared almost an hour later her loud and unfeeling, 'Crikey – the cavalry's here at last, Gallimard, so finish your coffee and get on your horse!' earned her a reproachful look from the recovering Asa and an icily censorious one from Patrick. After that one freezing glance he ignored her and concentrated on guiding the limping invalid to a waiting taxi.

They rode in silence to Asa's apartment, where Anna stayed in the taxi while Patrick helped an apologetic and embarrassed Asa to bed. When they resumed the journey to their own hotel Anna sat hunched in her corner, her head against the window, only too aware of Patrick's cold grey gaze. She was tired, hungry, and seething with righteous indignation. If he was waiting for an apology she thought rebelliously, then he was going to wait a bloody long time...

'You could have called a cab and seen him home without so much fuss.' Patrick finally broke the silence, his voice icily accusing. 'Why involve me?'

She continued to stare out of the window. 'When I 'phoned you he was falling-down drunk and I certainly wasn't going to risk getting him to bed on my own. I'd rather wrestle with an anaconda. It's not my fault it took you hours to get to that low dive; what did you do – finish your game of cards first?' '

He ignored her question. 'A man such as that does not get drunk without a reason. What did you do to make him end up in that state?'

'What did *I* do?' She turned on him indignantly. 'I did nothing, absolutely *nothing*; we were dancing when he stopped suddenly and dragged me off the floor as though he'd just discovered I'd got the Black Death. After that I'd nothing to do with him again until he got ratted and started trying to throw some tart around that low night club – allow me to point out that it was *me* who rescued the ruddy idiot from making a bigger fool of himself than he already had!'

He pulled at his lower lip with thumb and forefinger, looking at her with narrowed eyes. 'You're a terribly bad liar, Anna. What really happened?'

Suddenly she felt deflated. All the anger and defiance left her and she reverted with a bump to being seventeen and in hot water again.

'Oh, it wasn't anybody's fault.' She pulled her wrap tightly about her and looked away, shielding herself from his questioning look. 'We were getting on fine, then he – then I – well, we were dancing and I suppose we got a bit too close. It was nothing, really, just one of those silly flare-ups. I shouldn't have dragged you into it.'

'That doesn't particularly matter. I'm more interested now in why you never mentioned knowing either of the Gallimard brothers, nor why the tiresome Félix having departed to Spain should have concerned you so much.'

She felt her heartbeat quicken. She might have known he had been saving that little broadside for one of her more vulnerable moments. "Nobody likes to think a friend is in danger,' she answered lamely.

'True, but why all the secrecy?'

'Oh, for goodness sake!' her temper flared again. 'There is no secret. I just didn't think to mention either of them. That's all.'

'After – what is it? Four, five months of squabbling with Asa?' he was relentless and disbelieving, 'and of doing *what* with the fly-by-night Félix? Do you squabble with him?'

'Sometimes, but he's not a sanctimonious prig like Asa.'

He sat back, folding his arms, disapproval emanating from him in waves. 'For some reason of which I am becoming increasingly curious Asa appears to think you need rescuing from his brother.'

'That's typical of Asa to go tattling to you behind my back. I suppose he talked a load of rubbish about Félix and me while he was pissed. He knows absolutely nothing – '

He cut smoothly across her vehement denial. 'You are telling me far more than Asa did; be careful, Anna, you are much too young to become involved with the Félix Gallimard's of this world. He'll run like a stag should you try to corner him and want more than he's willing to give.'

'I haven't the faintest idea what you mean and I wish you wouldn't lecture me.' She stuck her nose in the air, adding recklessly, 'I've had all that. You sound just like Uncle Frederick in full flight on one of his bloody useless cliché-ridden sermons!'

He sucked in an exasperated breath. 'If you were a few years younger I'd be tempted to give you a good hard spanking! However, as you are now old enough and apparently foolish enough to make a mess of your life...' he was caustic, his voice thin with suppressed anger, 'by all means continue to ignore those who care for you and your future. But when you fall flat on your face, as you surely will, don't expect *me* to rush forward and pick you up.'

*　　　*　　　*

As she took off her new gown and got ready for bed, she cursed herself liberally with words that would have shocked Miss Harrison to the soles of her sensible shoes. Because Patrick had been astute enough to see through her she'd fought back. Waging a war she knew she couldn't win she'd completely lost her head and broken all his unwritten rules. After he'd dismissed the cab, infuriated by his continued cold, measured sarcasm, she'd rounded on him in the busy hotel foyer and sworn at him; then frightened by the look in his eyes had fled ignominiously to her room to lock the door and lean back against it, shaking uncontrollably and with angry tears scalding her cheeks.

Now, lost and indecisive, she prowled back and forth in her dressing gown, beating her hands together and moaning, 'What have I done? Oh, what have I done! Blast you, Asa – this is the second time you've landed me in it!'

She glanced at her watch. One o'clock, there was no way she could face Patrick again tonight. In fact, she didn't feel she'd ever be able face him again, tonight or any other. It was the first time she'd seen him so close to losing his temper and most fervently hoped it would be the last.

Suddenly resolute, she took a sheet of notepaper from the table draw, found pen and a bottle of ink and with a shaking hand wrote 'SORRY' in large letters. Crossing the room she slipped it under their communicating door then crept into bed to lie for an hour with burning eyes and aching head before eventually falling into an exhausted sleep.

When she awoke the next morning there was a corresponding note on her side of the door in Patrick's neat script:

'So you should be. Asa will be here later to make his apologies to you. Treat him kindly, or believe me I shall take the greatest pleasure in wringing your charmless little neck.'

Difficult, she thought, reading it for the third time to know if he meant it or not. Splashing through a shallow bath then dressing quickly she went downstairs, steeling herself for the inevitable confrontation. After a short hunt she ran Patrick to earth in the almost deserted breakfast room, hidden behind a copy of *La Figaro,* a half-eaten croissant and a cup of coffee at his elbow.

Without lowering the paper he said, 'You've missed breakfast,' and in silence she pulled out a chair and sat down. She was dreadfully hungry, but was sure the lump in her throat would probably make it impossible ever to eat again.

Eventually, she gave an embarrassed cough. 'Are you still angry with me?' His hands tightened on the paper and she cleared her throat, adding morosely, 'Because if you are I think I'd rather be somewhere else…like the bottom of the Seine, for instance!'

'Don't be ridiculous – and Notre Dame to atone for your sins would be more appropriate.' He lowered his paper and gave her an exasperated look over his glasses, 'You do that to me just once more and I promise you will wish yourself back with Uncle Frederick and his bloody useless, cliché-ridden sermons!' He snapped his paper onto the next page. 'Don't you *ever* dare to swear at me again like that, in public or private, whatever sort of corner you've got yourself into; is that quite clear?'

'Yes, Patrick; I'm very sorry. Truly I am.' She eyed the half-eaten croissant hungrily. 'Might I have that? I didn't get supper last night.' She looked at him limped-eyed. 'The drunk I was with didn't stay on his feet long enough to buy me any.'

He pushed the plate towards her. 'You are an undisciplined brat.' He was terse and unsmiling. 'I blame Charlie. I shall have to speak to him about it.'

She was suddenly desolate, wishing she were safely at home in Bloomsbury with Charlie to fight her corner. She looked down at the plate and a tear slid slowly down one cheek and plopped on the croissant

He watched her for a moment in silence then stood up. 'I'll order you a proper breakfast.' As he passed her chair he paused, his hand on her shoulder. 'Perhaps you'd rather skip the rest of our holiday and go home to the old hen?'

'Not really.' She rubbed her cheek against his hand. 'If you'll just stop being horrible to me I'd like to stay here with you.'

'I cannot imagine why.'

'Nor me.' She recovered quickly and gave him her ingenuous grin. 'Two eggs, please, Patrick, some mushrooms and lots of bacon!'

'I said breakfast, not a banquet.' Abruptly he turned away, but not before she'd seen his smile. Over his shoulder he said, 'I'll bill it to Asa!'

*   *   *

Asa arrived an hour later, pale, limping and visibly hung-over. Under Patrick's satirical gaze Anna was forced to make an abject apology. Her companion of the previous night's debacle responded by doing the same and kissing her on both cheeks, after which they sat a wary foot apart and engaged in polite conversation about museums and art galleries.

A cynically perceptive onlooker, Patrick was not deceived. Reading between the lines he deduced that it hadn't only been alcohol making Asa's world go around the previous night, nor, he guessed shrewdly, had he been the only one to be taken by surprise. If Anna ever got her mind off the elusive Félix long enough to analyse her own feelings Asa might be in for one hell of a rough ride – enjoyable, but definitely rough. He hoped she wasn't in too deep with Félix, but feared she was. He may not know much about women, he acknowledged wryly, but he knew the light of young love when he saw it, and about all the pain and complexity it could bring when one was too young to resist temptation, but not yet old enough to deal with the possible consequences.

He wished he could have protected her from that.

7

MARLCLEW, CORNWALL

May 1937

The storm when it broke was set in motion by a most unlikely catalyst and no one could have been less prepared for the consequences than Anna.

Discounting the evening with Asa and the ensuing bruising row with Patrick Paris had been wonderful, but returning home to Charlie and working again in the Gallery put the seal on her happiness.

Patrick had apparently forgiven, although she doubted he'd forgotten, her fall from grace. He had taken her to auctions, letting her for the first time bid for pieces of china and porcelain. They'd discussed her future when she should leave school that summer, with Patrick agreeing that if she did well in her final exams and still wished to make her career in the antiques business, she could either seek an apprenticeship to one of the big auction houses before University, or study straight away for a degree in Fine Arts.

She would really buckle down to work, she determined, even if it was too ghastly to still be at school and obliged to wear that ridiculous kilt. After all the lovely clothes she had worn in Paris and London, it would be hard to revert to school uniform again. Four weeks of being treated as an adult had accelerated the metamorphosis from schoolgirl into young woman and she returned for her last term full of confidence.

*   *   *

She was making spasmodic efforts to arrange her possessions in the prized number ten study when the door was pushed open and Sophie Soames, known predictably as Soapy, put her pale face and unfashionably shingled head around the door.

'A letter for you – I brought it up. Who do you know in Spain?'

Anna jumped and reached for the envelope but Soapy held it tauntingly above her head. 'Come on, tell.' She danced away across the room, saying gleefully, 'Crikey, look there's a name and address on the back: F. Gallimard, 10 – '

'Hand it over, *now* – and in future don't come in here without knocking.' At the look on Anna's face Soapy gave in hastily.

'All right, no need to be like that.' She tossed the letter onto the bed and retreated to the safety of the open door before firing her parting shot. 'Stuck-up cow – I bet old Gallipots doesn't know her precious son's writing to you. You could be the *ex*-head of house if Harrison finds out about this!'

Anna took a threatening step forward. '*Out!*'

Soapy squealed and ran. Anna banged the door shut behind her and sat on the bed, tearing open the envelope with shaking fingers.

Dear Anna,

We are shortly to leave Spain. I have had enough of the madhouse of war and shall not again be anxious to leave Paris.

Asa wrote to say that he met you there but didn't tell me anything you did or how you were. I think he is trying to make me jealous.

I look forward to when we can meet in the boathouse and be again together.

  A bientôt   *Félix*

She folded the single sheet of paper back into the envelope then turned it over and stared at the telltale name and address on the back. Only Félix could be so blithely unthinking as to do such a thing! A good job it was dopey Soapy and not her housemistress that had got to it first or she really would have been in trouble. But she was safe enough: even Soapy wouldn't risk the subsequent unpopularity she'd suffer if she opened her mouth to anyone on the staff, much as she might enjoy doing so.

*   *

Anna finished her French composition and stared out of the classroom window, thinking of Félix, conscious of his letter warm in her blazer pocket. She turned irritably as her elbow was nudged and a slip of paper slid onto her desk.

It was from Soapy, who was hopeless at French, begging for Anna's help. At any other time she might have answered her plea, but remembering Soapy's pantomime with Félix's letter the previous week, she barely glanced at the note before contemptuously screwing it into a ball and flicking it back.

Soapy shot her a spiteful look before turning away and waving her hand in the air.

'*Madame!*'

'Yes, what is it, Sophie?'

'I was wondering if you spoke Spanish, Madame!'

Anna's stomach gave an uncomfortable sideways lurch; she sent one agonised glance towards Valerie before turning her gaze on Dorothy Gallimard, who was smiling indulgently at Sophie

'A little; why do you ask?'

Soapy's eyes were wide and ingenious, 'Oh, it's just that Anna got a letter from Spain and I thought she might want someone to translate it for her!'

Anna felt the blood drain from her face as every head turned towards her, some mildly interested and other slyly knowing. Beside her Valerie hissed an audible '*Bitch!*' and grabbed Anna's hand under their shared desk.

Madame stood as though transfixed, her pale eyes fixed on Anna's white face. There was a long, tense silence in which the proverbial dropped pin would have sounded like a thunderclap.

'How interesting,' her words when they came were cool and measured, '*would* you like me to translate it for you?'

Anna gripped Valerie's hand tightly and licked her dry lips. 'No thank you, Madame. There is no need. It's in English.'

Smirking triumphantly Soapy turned to her again and delivered the *tour de force*. 'Can I have the stamp for my collection, Anna? It has such a lovely clear Madrid postmark!'

Madame drew a deep breath. 'I think that is enough chat for this morning; continue with your work, everyone. Anna, please wait and see me after class.'

*   *   *

As the door closed behind the last girl she gave a tight, unpleasant smile. 'Now Anna, please come here and tell me your letter. Naturally I am interested as I also have someone who writes to me from Madrid.'

Anna's throat dried. *She's enjoying this – like some horrible sleek cat waiting to pounce, but why? Why should it matter to her so much that Félix has written to me? He's a grown man and by the summer I'll have left here and able to write to and receive letters from whom I please.*

She felt her courage surge back. Lifting her head she looked straight into the cold, accusing eyes.

'There's nothing to tell. It's just a letter from a friend.'

'And would that 'friend' be my son?'

Cow, she thought; aloud she asked innocently, 'Which one,

70

Madame?'

'Don't fence with me, Anna. Is the letter from Félix?'

For a moment Anna stared her out. 'Yes Madame.'

'You know the school rule about girls corresponding with men other than close relatives?'

Anna shrugged. '*I* haven't corresponded with anyone, only just received a letter from someone who obviously hadn't been told the rules!'

'Do not be insolent. Before you come with me to Miss Harrison I should like to see this letter.' She held out her hand. 'Now, Anna, if you please.'

Anna thought rapidly. There was no point in refusing. She only had to keep her nerve. Any threat of reporting her to la Harrison was unlikely to be carried out once the bloody woman had read the thing. She'd hardly want that lady to know one of her sons was arranging a secret assignation with a pupil. Silently, she took the envelope from her pocket and placed it on the outstretched palm.

Madame read it, her lip curling before tossing it contemptuously on the desk. 'Very touching…I can imagine what he means by "being together again" Félix always did have a taste for adolescent sluts! But I blame him as much as you. I forbade him to see you again.'

Anna flushed at the insult but kept her temper. 'Why?'

'I doubt that you would want to know that.' Her eyes sharpened. 'How did you come to meet Asa in Paris?'

Anna was tempted to give her a blow-by-blow account of her evening with Asa then deciding discretion was the better option, shrugged again. 'Patrick and I were in a café and he came to speak to us…' She almost leapt back at the expression on Madame's face, stammering. 'W-We, t-talked for a while…'

'Asa talked to *him*?' Her face was ugly with rage; her beautifully modulated voice rising to a harsh screech. 'I told him…I forbade either of them to have anything to do with that man. How dare he…how *dare* he!'

Spittle flew from her lips. Gasping as though she had been running she gripped the sides of her desk with both hands so tightly that the knuckles showed white.

The hairs rose on the back of Anna's neck and for a moment she was paralysed with fright, then suddenly galvanised into action she made for the door but her adversary was there before her, baring the way. 'No. You do not leave until I am finished.' She leaned back against the closed door her eyes wild. 'Understand; for my sons there will be no more meetings – not with you, nor that disgusting, depraved creature that you are pleased to call your guardian.'

At this attack on Patrick Anna flushed with anger. 'You have no right to say such things. I suppose you think you can insult me because of Félix, but I won't allow you to call Patrick filthy names; he's done nothing to deserve them and you don't even know him.'

'Oh, but I do; and he knows me,' she was triumphant, baring her small even teeth in the travesty of a smile, 'although it has perhaps suited him to forget.'

Anna shook her head decisively. 'You're mistaken, Madame. He told me he knew your husband but that you'd never met – and Patrick doesn't tell lies.'

'No? I would challenge you on that.' She was calmer now, confident enough to leave the door and return to sit at her desk, bracing her hands against the edge. 'When you next return home I suggest you ask Mr. Farrell if he remembers Cecelia Osborne and when he last saw *her* – and me. I think you will find that will jog his memory.'

She was in control again now. Drumming her fingers on the desktop and watching Anna's face closely, she added silkily, 'You could also ask him to tell you all about his so-called manservant Charles Caulder.'

'*Charlie?*' Anna almost laughed. 'I *know* all about Charlie; he isn't a so-called anything. He cooks and looks after Patrick and me...and he's a good friend.'

'I can believe that's what you think. You really are a little ignoramus, aren't you?' Giving her cat-like smile again she picked up Félix's letter. Tearing it methodically into small fragments she dropped them into the waste paper basket then contemptuously dusted her fingers. She said calmly, 'If you ever mention one word about the contents of that missive to anyone here I will immediately inform Miss Harrison what kind of little slut she has contaminating her school.'

She walked towards the door, opened it, then turning added, 'And should you or any member of your degenerate household again see, speak or correspond with either of my sons, I shall not rest until I've seen Patrick Farrell and his *friend* hounded out of London.'

*　　　*　　　*

Anna stared at the closed door then let out a shaky pent-up breath. She sat on the nearest desk and putting her feet on the seat, propped her chin on her hands and tried to make sense of Madame's hysterical and menacing outburst. But her brain refused to co-operate, unable to comprehend why one short letter from Félix should have prompted such invective...and against Patrick and Charlie of all people.

'Who the hell,' she wondered frantically, 'is Cecelia Osborne? And how can that crazy old bird know Patrick when he doesn't know her?

Somehow she would have to get home and talk to him.

Although angry and confused and frightened by witnessing Madame apparently going off her rocker, Anna was confident that all she had to do was get back to Stratton place, tell Patrick and he would make sense of it all for her.

She jumped as the door opened again, but it was Valerie, wide-eyed with concern.

'Are you all right? I hung around in case you needed rescuing... God, when she let out that screech, I nearly peed myself!'

Anna began to laugh unsteadily. 'Me too.'

'How did Soapy know the letter was from Félix?' Valerie demanded. 'She didn't steam it open, did she?'

'She didn't have to; the idiot put his name and address on the back.'

Valerie's eyes glittered. 'If that old loony Gallimard reports you to Harrison I'll ruddy murder dopey Soapy,'

'It's all right. She won't do that, not yet, anyway – and you can leave Soapy to me.' Anna ran her fingers through her hair. 'Val, I've got to get home. *Now.*'

'Why?'

'Oh, don't ask, please. I just have to talk to Patrick.'

'You can't. We've only just come back; you'll never get permission.'

'But I *must* see him and I can't ask him to come here.'

Valerie looked gloomy. 'They won't let you. Not unless it's for a family crisis like a funeral.'

They looked blankly at each other for a moment then Anna started to grin. 'Uncle William!' she said. 'I can knock off Uncle William!'

Valerie giggled. 'It'll have to be a telegram; from London and as though it's come from your guardian, otherwise Harrison will smell a rat.' Her brow creased in thought. She tugged at her plait then her face cleared. 'I know: Archie, my eldest brother, has a flat in Islington. We'll go into the village when lessons finish and send a letter. He should get it Thursday morning at the latest and can telegraph the Head straight away. Can you bear to wait two or three more days?'

'Not really, but I shall have to.'

'What about *Patrick* – what on earth's he going to say when he sees you turn up out of the blue?'

Anna was starting to get a queasy feeling in the pit of her stomach. She didn't even want to think about how he might view her arrival on the doorstep confessing she'd not only taken his name in vain but had killed off Uncle William to boot. But she had to go. It would be bad enough waiting a couple of days; she couldn't possibly go through the whole term with Madame watching and gloating, while she worried herself sick.

And all this because of Félix and his wretched letter...

'I don't know,' she said miserably. 'That's a chance I'll have to take. I just can't go on facing that woman until I've asked him about something she said.'

'Cheer up.' Valerie gave her a quick hug. 'We don't have another lesson with her until Thursday afternoon and by then you'll be on your way to London.'

Anna pushed aside the thought of being a target for Patrick's displeasure and narrowed her eyes thoughtfully. 'I'll make sure I catch that creep Soapy when she's on her own tonight. Cutting her throat with our fruit knife would be too messy and I don't have a gun, but I'll to think of something else I can do to show just how displeased I am with her!'

*   *   *

She kept watch that evening until she saw Soapy's room mate come down the stairs and disappear into the bowels of the building to fetch the evening cocoa, then sprinted silently up to the room above her own.

Her quarry was at the table, munching on a chocolate biscuit from the tin at her elbow and pouring over her stamp album; at the sight of her visitor she gave a terrified squawk and dropped the biscuit.

'Hello, Sophie dear!' Anna showed all her teeth in a fulsome smile. 'I *am* pleased to see you have your album out. I've come to help you with your stamp collection.'

Sophie shrank back into her chair. 'If you touch me I'll report you!'

'Of course I won't touch you,' Anna purred. Looking around the study her eyes lit on an enamel bowl of green, pungently smelling, turgid and decomposing frog's spawn on the windowsill and she smiled beatifically. 'How could you be so neglectful, Miss Soames?' she clicked her tongue reproachfully. 'Those poor little things are deader than your own brain cells!' she took a deep sniff, 'and getting whiffier by the minute!'

Like a rabbit mesmerised by a stoat Soapy watched helplessly as the bowl was lifted and its contents poured with slow ceremony: first over the stamp album, then into the biscuit tin and finally trailed over the table, the last globules sliding to the floorboards with an obscene squelch.

Tenderly, Anna placed the empty reeking bowl upside down on her shrinking victim's head. 'Honestly, Sophie *dear*,' she cooed, 'whatever made you think I'd touch you – as if I'd do any such thing without wearing gloves!'

On the stairs she met Soapy's study mate bearing two steaming mugs. Anna relieved her of one. 'I'd better have this. I don't think dear Sophie will want to spend any time drinking cocoa tonight.' She smiled sweetly. 'If I were you I wouldn't go in there just yet – she has an *awful* lot of cleaning up to do before bed time and she really doesn't smell very nice at all!'

8

STRATTON PLACE, BLOOMSBURY

May 1937

Anna looked at her watch. Seven-thirty; another twenty-minutes and she would be at Paddington. She'd have a cup of tea in the station buffet before getting a taxi to the Gallery but that would be about all she could manage. She was hungry but felt nauseous at the thought of the sandwiches in her pocket. Her stomach went into a hard knot as it had been doing spasmodically since she'd left Cornwall.

It had gone almost too well. At the end of morning lessons Miss Harrison had received the telegram bearing the news of Uncle William's sudden demise. Anna, summoned to her study to hear the sad news had mercifully managed to squeeze a tear or two. Travelling money had then been pressed into her hand, a packet of sandwiches provided for the journey and the gardener summoned to drive her to the station.

The train had barely left Liskeard before she'd begun to panic.

Patrick wouldn't be pleased. In fact Patrick would most likely be extremely displeased to see her back again in less than a fortnight. After all, what did she really have to say that would justify her sudden re-appearance?

I've just shot myself in the foot, she thought miserably as the train ate up the miles. Rushing off like this to ask him to explain the outpourings of some woman who's obviously as mad as a hatter; he would want to know what started it all then she'd have to tell him about the letter... She blanched and wiped her palms on her knees. Oh, God! How was she going to explain *that* and still keep secret her meetings with Félix? Cursing Asa, who had been responsible for bringing up his name in front of Patrick, she sat back and closed her eyes. She fingered the ticket in her coat pocket and wondered should she give up the whole thing, stay on the train at Paddington and return to school? *No, you fool* she admonished herself silently. Trying to explain her rapid return to Miss Harrison would take far more courage even than she'd need to face Patrick. At least when she got home there would be her friend Charlie to act as a buffer.

An elderly woman seated opposite her leaned forward her face filled with kindly concern. 'Are you feeling all right, my dear?'

'Thank you, yes. I'm just a bit travel-sick, that's all.' Anna summoned a smile. 'I'll be fine as soon as I get off the train.' Then added silently, that's if Patrick doesn't throttle me and bury my body in the garden!

*   *   *

She paid off the taxi then stood, suitcase in hand in the gathering dusk, looking up at the first-floor windows. There was only one light and that in the small study where Patrick usually did the accounts. Her heart sank. If Charlie were in the whole front of the house would be lit, not just that one window.

She put down her case and stood indecisive, chewing her lip. If Charlie was out at this time in the evening he was probably at the dog track. As Patrick had once observed somewhat caustically, Kempton Park may be more Charlie's style and betting on greyhounds a poor second to doing so on horses, but an occasional spot of slumming at the White City didn't go amiss now and again.

Oh, well. She couldn't stand around on the pavement waiting. She'd just have to risk it. Picking up her case she took her key from her pocket and cautiously opened the door. Reasoning that if she could reach the kitchen without being heard she could wait there until Charlie came home, she took off her shoes and with these in one hand and her case in the other, crossed the hallway in the dark and climbed the stairs on her toes. Once at the top she tiptoed towards the kitchen and had almost reached it when Patrick called 'Charlie?' and opened the study door.

Anna stood blinking at the sudden shaft of light. 'No. It's me.'

She heard him mutter something, then the landing light was clicked on and he was staring at her with startled eyes.

'Anna? What on earth are you doing here?' He looked at the suitcase then at the shoes in her hand and his gaze sharpened. 'Are you in some kind of trouble?'

'No-o...not exactly,' she clutched her attaché case to her chest, holding it like a shield before her. 'Well, that is...yes, in a sort of way!'

'Make up your mind.' He took the case from her and gestured back towards the open door of the study. 'In there, if you please...and you can put those shoes back on now.'

She preceded him silently and sitting in his swivel chair bent to replace and fasten her shoes. Aware that he was leaning back against

77

the cluttered, roll-topped desk with his arms folded, waiting for her to finish, she delayed as long as she dared before reluctantly straightening to meet his eyes.

He began without preamble. 'Does the school know where you are?'

She whispered. 'Yes.'

'Have you been sacked?'

'No.'

'Well, thank God for that.' He sighed. 'By that I assume you furnished the inestimable Miss Harrison with some urgent reason for your return. If you think you can explain without tying yourself in knots, I'd like to know what it was.'

Anna drew a deep breath. 'It was to go to a funeral.'

His expression remained unchanged except the lines either side of his mouth deepened fractionally. 'Not mine, I hope!'

She suppressed a nervous snigger. 'No Uncle William's.'

'A reasonable choice although unfortunately rather premature; however,' he took a cigarette from the box on his desk, stroked the wheel on his lighter and eyed her over the flame. 'I really think you should begin at the beginning and explain why you felt a sudden need to come home again so soon.'

She looked at him beseechingly. 'Please don't be angry, Patrick. I know I shouldn't have done it like this but I couldn't wait. It's about Madame Gallimard.'

'Go on.'

'She, well she went for me a few days ago. She said some awful things about you…and Charlie.' She faltered at his suddenly drawn brows. 'Patrick, she says she knows you – and that you know her. It isn't true, is it?'

'Not so far as I'm aware.' He watched her through the smoke of his cigarette, rubbing his right hand slowly over its gloved fellow. 'Did she say where we might have met?'

'No. Actually I think she's batty. You should have heard her when I said we'd met Asa in Paris!' She frowned and looked up to meet his intent gaze. 'She said if you remembered someone called Cecelia Osborne, you'd remember her too.'

Very slowly and deliberately he took the cigarette from his mouth and stubbed it out in the brass ashtray. He asked quietly 'Do you know this Madame Gallimard's Christian name?'

'Dorothy, I think. Yes, I'm pretty sure that's the name in some of her books at school.'

There was a long uncomfortable silence. Patrick's face was like carved granite. Ana looked away from him and stared down at the carpet, aware that she may have done something quite dreadful in repeating Madame's ludicrous remarks. Her heart began to jump unevenly as the silence built until it became unbearable. She was so distressed that she didn't notice the tears beginning to trickle down her face until he placed a handkerchief into her hand. 'Use this,' he said through tight lips. 'What else did she have to say?'

'A lot of stupid things,' she wiped her eyes. 'She called you some disgusting names and said this was a degenerate household and that Charlie was your so-called servant. When I said he wasn't a so-called anything; that he was our friend the old bitch sneered and called me an ignoramus.'

She faltered at the expression on his face. 'I'm sorry, but she is, you know!'

'Possibly.' There was another long silence before he squatted down on his heels, clasping her hands in both of his. It was the first time she'd ever felt his false hand; it was hard and smooth beneath the soft kid glove and she gave an involuntary shiver.

He said dryly, 'It's all right. It won't drop off!' For a few moments he looked steadily into her eyes then moved his shoulders in a wry, defeated gesture. He said quietly, 'In a way she was right, although a kinder person would have called you innocent, rather than ignorant. You see, to everyone outside these four walls, a servant is just how Charlie chooses to appear – has to appear. To be seen as anything else would be dangerous for us both.' He spoke soberly, every word clear and concise. 'Society is not kind to men who live together as we do, Anna, and the law even less so. The fact that Charlie and I share our lives in the way that other, perhaps more fortunate men and women share theirs, could land us both in prison.'

She gazed back at him blankly. His good hand tightened on hers. 'Anna, do you understand what I am saying?'

Suddenly, the answers to all the puzzling questions that had been at the back of her consciousness since she came to this house slotted into place: that tantalising picture on the kitchen wall; the strange master/servant relationship that wasn't anything of the kind: *he is not your servant, neither is he mine*; the looks she had seen them sometime exchange: private and intimate, as in the photograph. The few close friends who came to the house while she was there were almost all male, she realised now; quietly diffident men who treated her courteously, but were all without exception, guarded and faintly aloof, like Patrick himself...

Heat rushed to her face and her heart raced wildly. What a fool she'd been! It wasn't as if she'd not heard about such things. No wonder that cow had called her an ignoramus! A host of confused emotions raced through her. How *could* he and Charlie do such things, things too awful and disgusting to even think about? Why couldn't they be like ordinary people and live properly, not have foul horrible secrets and tell lies...and that bitch Madame must have known all along...

An overwhelming desire to hurt him swept over her and she looked up to meet his steady gaze. 'You mean you *sleep* together – in the same bed?' Her voice was filled with loathing and disgust.

If he was distressed by the blunt questions, he didn't show it. 'Yes. That's what people do who love each other.'

She stared accusingly into the still grey eyes, demanding bitterly, 'Why bother to have separate rooms when I come home then? Why hide what you do from me?'

'It seemed the right thing to do. Even if in the beginning we had felt you were sufficiently mature to be told, there was no guarantee that you wouldn't at some time, albeit unwittingly, be indiscrete.'

'Well if you'd been honest from the start you would have saved yourself a lot of trouble because I'd never have wanted to live with either of you.' She turned her head away in revulsion, 'and if I had I wouldn't have been daft enough to tell anyone, would I? Why on earth should I *want* anyone else to know about you? It isn't exactly the sort of thing to shout from the rooftop, is it? Not the kind of thing to chat about with my friends. In fact, I'd die rather then tell anyone anything so disgusting.'

She was shaking with anger and tried to pull away from him, but he held fast with his good hand.

'Darling Anna, when you first arrived, you were much too young to be told, let alone understand – '

'And you think I understand now? How did you expect me to feel when you *did* get around to telling me? That I'd think, "Oh, goody, I'm living with a couple of - of *freaks*. I quite understand – everybody's doing it, aren't they? It's the most natural thing in the world!"' She battled furiously with the threatened tears. 'Well, have a bloody good laugh. Madame was right. I *am* an ignoramus...or I was until five minutes ago.' Her voice began to shake uncontrollably. 'You know something? I hate you – I really *hate* you, both of you. I wish I'd gone to live with Uncle William. I'd rather have that dirty old man putting his hand up my skirt than be with either of you.'

Wrenching herself away from him she raced up to her room. Banging the door shut behind her she fell across her bed in a storm of

80

weeping. Everything was spoiled – soiled; nothing in her life would ever be the same again. She raged against Madame, against Félix, against Asa and Patrick and Charlie; against God, or whoever else might have been responsible for sending her to this house in the first place. She even raged at poor old cousin Ruth for dying so inopportunely...and all the while the scorching tears cascaded down her face.

She would have to leave, tonight. Just pack a case and go. She was old enough now to find some sort of work. Her head began to throb and the pounding at her temples threatened to split her skull. But if she left, she thought desperately, where would she live until she found employment, and even if she found work would she be able to earn enough money to support herself?

She was overtaken by a fresh storm of weeping. There was no way out; no way out at all. She was in a horrible big black pit from which there was no escape...

*   *   *

The long case clock on the landing was chiming ten o'clock when she heard the door open and the sound of Patrick's feet on the polished boards. Exhausted and spent, she lay limp and passive, curled on her side. He drew up a chair beside the bed. 'Is there anything I can say or do that will make it possible for you to go on living under this roof without feeling distress and shame?' he asked gently, 'Any way that I can make you understand that love, whatever form it takes, is always precious to the lovers, whoever they are.'

At his words so quietly spoken she felt her eyes, sore and painful from so much weeping, fill again with tears; she tried to summon the anger she had felt hours before and failed. It had been easy to lash out in temper and fright but how could she really hate either of them? This was Patrick, who had given her so much and asked so little in return; when Charlie came back he'd be the same funny, loving friend he'd always been. She thought about Madame's vicious words; her threat to 'hound them out of London'; perhaps see them in prison. How could she bear the thought of either of them being treated so.

'I *don't* understand; I don't know if I ever can, but I will try because I love you and I don't think I could bear not to be with you.' She sat up; grabbing for his hand and curling her fingers tightly about his she began to rock backward and forward. 'Oh, why did I let that horrible woman send me bolting up here?'

'I'm sorry; it was a rotten way for you to find out. I blame myself that we've left it so long, but we wanted to be sure you were really

81

ready to understand before we told you – and were both so terribly afraid that you'd want to leave us when we did.'

'It's just been so awful waiting to come home...then when I got here I thought you'd be angry with me and say I was making a fuss about nothing, but I didn't expect all this...Oh, Patrick, of course I can't go away now, not after all this time. Where would I go; what would I do?' Now she was hot with shame. 'I'm so sorry I said all those things about hating you. I was angry and frightened and I didn't really mean it. I couldn't. Please forgive me, *please*.'

'I was surprised, not angry at your coming and there is nothing *to* forgive. I am the one to ask forgiveness for having so shocked and frightened you.'

She up, gulping and wiping the heel of her hand across her face, 'Valerie's brother lent her a book about Oscar Wilde last term and we read it twice before the penny dropped! It all seemed so weird...but as neither you nor Charlie is the very least like Oscar or the Darling Boy, I'd never, *ever* have thought about you that way!'

His long mouth curved. 'Perhaps we should take that as a compliment.'

She was silent a moment, sitting with bent head. She asked tentatively, 'Patrick, do you...you know...do you really *love* Charlie?

'Yes I do, very much.'

'Does he love you?'

'I should hope so; I can't think why else he would have put up with me for the past seventeen years!'

She rubbed her fingers over the gloved hand lying on hers, asking inconsequentially, 'Does your hand hurt?'

'Sometimes, but it's my conscience that's giving me hell right now.' He rose to his feet and stood looking down on her. 'I hope the change of subject doesn't mean you don't want to talk any more.'

She hesitated. Oh, what a mess. She'd have to tell him. She hunched her shoulders. 'I think all this trouble at school is my fault, Patrick. At first I thought Madame Gallimard was just interested in this place, and you, because of her husband. She asked a lot of questions and I told her about everything – you, me, Charlie, the Gallery. I stopped when Valerie said she was being too nosy but by then I'd probably already said too much.'

'Then what caused such a fracas all of a sudden?'

'You would ask that, wouldn't you?' she picked at the hem of her skirt. 'I think you are going to be very angry if I tell you.'

'All the same, I think you must...' he paused as the front door banged and Charlie's step was heard on the stairs. He raised one

82

eyebrow. 'Saved by the bell,' he said, 'here's your champion come to see fair play!'

Charlie had obviously had a good evening. He was whistling the roistering Chancellor's song from *Iolanthe* as he climbed. Pausing half-way he called, 'Patrick, where are you?'

'Up here – in Anna's room,' Patrick gave Anna a wry smile. 'Brace yourself.' he said.

'What the hell are you doing there?'

They heard him take the last stairs with a bound and appear in the doorway, only to stop dead at the sight of Anna, sitting cross-legged on the bed, her face streaked with tears. His eyebrows shot up into his hairline.

'God *Almighty,* what are *you* doing here?' He glanced from her to Patrick, who looked back at him, his countenance sphinx like and inscrutable. Charlie's own expression was suddenly thunderous. 'Patrick, you bastard, I know that look!' He swung back again to Anna, demanding, 'What's this bloody man been doing to upset you so?'

She stared at him in amazement, her eyes huge at hearing his speech suddenly devoid of the glottal stops and Glaswegian twang. The cultured tones she was hearing now owed rather more to the influence of Edinburgh and Morningside than Glasgow and the Gorbals. A hysterical giggle began bubbling in her throat. She asked, 'Charlie…why are you talking like that?'

He recovered himself quickly. 'Like what, lassie?'

'Like a, like a…' She hunted round for a suitable description. 'Like a Burlington Bertie!'

'The game is up, Charlie…all of it, so you can just drop the faithful old retainer act.' Patrick passed a weary hand over his forehead. 'Anna, I think I'd better introduce Major Charles Caulder, late of the Duke of Killoran's Own Infantry Brigade…Now, can we all please go down into the drawing room because I'm in desperate need of a very large drink.' He paused at the door to give the open-mouthed Anna a blandly inquiring look. 'After which I expect *you* will be anxious to tell us both exactly what you did that's set all three of us hurtling towards disaster like three witless idiots on an out of control express train.'

*   *   *

It all had to come out: her incautious talks about Stratton Place then the visit to Dorothy Gallimard's house and the meeting with both of madam's sons. When she tried to by-pass her subsequent meetings with Félix, Patrick wouldn't let her and again she cursed that chance encounter with Asa in Paris. Haltingly she confessed to the rendezvous with Félix in the boathouse; paused, struggled, then prompted by a suddenly hard and merciless Patrick, admitted to going alone with him into Pardoe's cottage...

At this last she felt, rather than heard, his in-drawn breath; keeping her eyes down, faltering and stumbling, she rushed on to the safer ground of Félix's letter, Madame's terrifying outburst and the telegram summoning her home sent in Patrick's name, but mercilessly Patrick went back over her story until he had drawn out every detail of the pursuit by Félix that ended with her seduction in the grubby environs of Pardoe's cottage. Once or twice she glanced at his face but it was wiped clean of any expression so that she couldn't judge what he was thinking, or how angry he might be. She seemed to have been talking for hours, her voice became rough and hoarse and quite suddenly she ran out of steam and sat mute, her aching head propped on one hand, her imploring eyes fixed on Charlie.

'That's enough, Patrick.' Charlie, who had so far kept silence, intervened angrily. 'Leave her alone.' He put a protective arm about her shoulders. 'I don't think she needs to have her nose rubbed in it any further.'

'We get it straight, and we do that *now*.' Patrick's mouth was a thin line.

'Well you've got it as straight as you're getting tonight. Anna should have been in bed long before this. She needs a good night's sleep, in the morning it will be *her* turn to ask both of *us* the questions. Let's hope she shows a little more compassion than you have this past hour or more.'

Anna turned her face into Charlie's chest, burrowing into him like a hunted thing seeking shelter. She felt his big hand patting her shoulder and began to weep again, the tears sliding silently down her cheeks to lose themselves in the rough tweed of his jacket.

With an effort Patrick pulled himself out of his chair. 'No, being angry doesn't help.' His voice was weary and strained. 'What's happened can't be undone. I'm sorry, Anna.' He touched her shoulder gently then looked at Charlie, who glared back furiously. 'I think a bath, a warm drink and a quiet word in the Almighty's ear might be a good idea for all of us tonight, don't you?'

Brusquely Charlie shook his head. 'You go. I'll stay here for a while...Just another dram or two will put *me* in the right frame of mind to sleep, but as a life-long heathen I think I must leave God to you!'

Patrick answered mildly, 'I don't mind at all there just being God and me, but I'd rather you didn't wake either of us when you finally decide to stagger up the stairs.' He stooped to ruffle Anna's hair then drawing her to her feet put his arm around her shoulders. 'Come along, little one.' His mouth twitched. 'Remember, tomorrow you have to be up early for Uncle William's funeral!'

*   *   *

When he had seen her to her room he stood for some moments on the landing, drumming his fingers on the banister rail, then squaring his shoulders and taking a deep breath went swiftly down the stairs to where a grim faced Charlie stood waiting. He said wearily, 'All right, Charlie, let's get it over...'

'You bastard,' Charlie followed him into the long drawing room. 'What the *fuck* did you think you were at – bullying the child like that?'

'I have no idea.' Patrick sat down, resting his head against the chair back. 'Perhaps I just lashed out at her in much the same way, and for the same reasons as you are about to lash out at me: disappointment and impotent fury because someone I loved had been diminished, albeit even very briefly, in my eyes.'

'Well, you made a bloody good job of it, you shit.'

'Tell me something I don't know.' He closed his eyes. 'I'm sorry. I'll make it up to her – somehow.'

'You'd better; and you'd better damned well come clean about everything to do with us – '

'I'd already started – and taken the fall-out whilst you were out enjoying yourself.' He opened his eyes and grimaced in distaste. 'Sorry, that was uncalled for: and yes, you are quite right; I am a shit.' He leaned forward, hunching his shoulders. 'Christ, Charlie, I thought I'd put the past behind me: that I could forget all the pain and the misery before I met you. Now it's all back and right now I feel like slitting my own bloody throat...'

For a few moments Charlie sat silent, then getting heavily to his feet took up the decanter and poured a long measure of brandy into each of two glasses. He held one out to his companion. 'Here. You need this.'

Patrick took the glass and sat warming it between his palms. 'A fine substitute for a parent I've turned out to be!'

'You haven't done too badly up till now; and nobody said it

would be easy.'

Patrick smiled faintly. 'She trusts you.'

'Aye; but she loves *you* – she doesn't know it, mind, and right now it's only puppy love, but it's your approval, your affection she wants now, that makes her very vulnerable. So let go a little more and let her know she has those things.'

'What a wise old bird you are.' Patrick put down his glass and leaned forward, resting his hand on Charlie's where it lay on the arm of his chair. 'Forgive me?'

Charlie gave a wry smile. 'Nothing to forgive: I quite liked seeing you lose your rag for once. Just don't lose it again with Anna, there's a good chap.' He finished his drink. 'Bed, I think, or I may be tempted to stay here and get drunk as a skunk!'

Later, on the edge of sleep, Patrick asked, 'Think Dorothy will come after us?'

'No.' Charlie shook his head. 'What could she say? Who would she tell?'

'Sometimes I feel we've been too lucky all these years. That someday, *someone* will burst the balloon – and on tonight's showing it might just be Dorothy holding the pin!'

Laughter rumbled in Charlie's chest. 'Not very likely; after all, who's going to bother about hassling a couple of boring old farts like us, when they've the Prince of Wales and Wallis Simpson to gossip about?'

*   *   *

Worn out by the anxiety and exertions of the day Anna slept deeply, awakening to the shrill squabbling of birds in the tree outside her window. For a long time she lay watching them hop from branch to branch, each trying to claim one particular territory as their own, while turning over and over in her mind all that had happened since leaving the school yesterday. If she closed her eyes she could still see Patrick's stricken face, feel Charlie's arms holding her safely. They hadn't changed, weren't really any different than they had been before she'd discovered the truth. Everybody, she thought sadly, had something to hide and in her own way she'd been just as secretive and deceitful. Perhaps, she thought hopefully, she might understand more about Patrick and Charlie when she was older; had discovered more about that grown-up world beyond the schoolroom.

Washing and dressing quickly, she left her room and stood for a moment on the landing, listening to the familiar sounds of Charlie moving around in the kitchen below. Descending the stairs quietly she pushed open the kitchen door to watch him in silence for a few seconds before saying humbly, 'Hello...I suppose coffee is out of the question for a delinquent sinner?'

He looked around, smiling. 'If it is then we'll all be going short! Come in. I was just making a pot.'

'Where's Patrick?' She sat down, resting her chin on her hands as he placed cups, sugar and cream jug on the table. 'Still zonked out, or is he already in the gallery?'

'Neither.' He spooned coffee into a cafetière and filled it from the kettle. 'I heard him go out while I was shaving. I imagine he went to early Mass.'

He sat down opposite her; tentatively she put out her hand.

'I'm truly sorry about causing all the trouble last night. I hope you and Patrick didn't have a row once he'd got me out of the way: I heard you start on him when he went back downstairs.'

'No, we didn't row. He was still feeling much too guilty to defend himself against what I had to say!' He covered her hand with his, watching her with his direct blue gaze. 'Anna, this Félix; do you love him?'

'Yes.' She felt the blood creeping up her face. 'At least, I think so. I've never been in love before but I've felt this way from the first moment I saw him.'

'And does he feel the same?'

She shook her head dumbly. She couldn't to lie to herself, or Charlie. Last night, after Patrick had forced her to confront every aspect of her relationship with Félix, she'd faced squarely for the first time the painful knowledge that what ever it was he felt for her, it was something very different from that which she felt for him.

Now she looked up with an attempt at a smile. 'At least he's never lied and said he did – and I couldn't *make* him love me, could I?'

'Then why did you go on seeing him?'

'I suppose it's because I hoped that one day he *would* love me.' She pushed the hair back from her flushed forehead. 'I feel so guilty over starting all this, Charlie. Could Madame really cause trouble for you and Patrick? "Hound you out of London", as she said?'

'I shouldn't think so – it's unlikely that anyone would believe her, even if she tried. We've lived here for the past ten years and to all but a few of our closest friends I'm simply manservant to a fairly affluent bachelor. There are hundreds of other such households, most of them precisely what they seem.' He grinned and drawled, 'Like Jeeves and Bertie Wooster, don't you know!'

'Where did you get that accent?'

'It came naturally.' He began to pour the coffee. 'I'm just a poor boy from the Glasgow slums, clever enough, and ruthless enough to claw my way out of poverty and leave the Gorbals and my feckless, boozing family behind. First, with a philanthropic Headmaster, who saw me through a scholarship to a prestigious Edinburgh high school and paid for my uniform and keep. Another scholarship and a lot of hard work in the vacations saw me through to University and an eventual commission in a Highland regiment, where I might have stayed if Patrick and I had never met. A snotty-nosed slum kid can't do much better than that!'

She took the coffee he offered. 'How did a snotty-nosed slum kid meet up with Patrick then?'

'On the firing step of a trench in Flanders: he was a Brigade Bombing Officer, which at that time was certainly one of the most dangerous jobs on the Western Front. We were waiting to go over the top and all of us were pretty jittery; I think I noticed him particularly because he was leaning against the wall of the trench, smoking a Turkish cigarette and reading Proust, apparently quite oblivious of what was going on around him!' He dropped sugar into his coffee, stirring it slowly. 'Jerry had brought up a bloody great gun and held us pinned down under heavy bombardment for days. Patrick's orders were to lead his chaps over and get near enough for them to blow it to pieces. All we had to do was go over with them and give covering fire as they went forward.'

He paused for a moment, staring over her shoulder as though seeing pictures on the wall. He picked up his cup and took a careful contemplative swallow.

'He and I chatted a while; perhaps half and hour, before we got the order to move. Unfortunately Fritz was ready and waiting...machine guns, field guns the lot. They just mowed his bombers down and within minutes there weren't even enough of *us* left to give any kind of covering fire.'

He paused and rubbed a hand across his eyes. 'At first it looked as though Patrick had a charmed life. I could see him away out front, charging forward through the smoke, blowing his whistle and bowling his bloody bombs over-arm as though he was playing in a school cricket match. He'd almost reached the gun when he went down. Hours afterwards when it was almost dark and we'd left the shell crater we'd sheltered in and were making our way back to the trenches, my sergeant thought he heard a faint 'peep'. I crawled across to have a recce and found Patrick lying in a crater, just about alive and with his whistle still stuck between his teeth. His left hand was completely gone and I could see he'd lost a hell of a lot of blood. I couldn't leave him there for the stretcher-bearers to fetch later because by then he'd have been dead, so I dragged the silly bugger back to the trench with me and carried him back along the line to the field hospital.' He gave a sudden grunt of laughter. 'When I looked in at the place next day he was giving the nurses hell over his missing hand, yelling he wanted it back to give it a decent Christian burial with the rest of him!' He cocked an eye at her and grinned. 'Of course he was delirious at the time.'

'What happened then? How did you come to be here together?'

'Just pure chance, really; Patrick was sent back to Blighty a few days after my visit and I stayed in Flanders with my lot until well after the Armistice. Although we'd only met quite briefly before he went over it was enough for us to recognise ourselves in each other. I thought a lot about him and wondered if he'd made it or not.'

He paused and smiled reminiscently. 'God, Anna, you've no idea what he was like at twenty-three; he was certainly the best-looking thing in khaki *I'd* ever seen! In the hospital the nurses couldn't leave him alone – not that it did them any good...' he grinned. 'Then early in nineteen-twenty I was on leave in London, walked into a bar for a beer and there he was.' He broke off to give her a shrewd challenging look. 'Are you really not still shocked to the back teeth about us, or are you just a very good actress?'

Anna shook her head. 'I'm a rotten actress; what you see is all there is. At first, when Patrick told me, I was angry, really angry and I said some awful things to him of which I'll always be ashamed...' she rubbed her finger around the rim of her cup, shaking her head as if to clear her thoughts. 'I'm still not quite sure what I feel, or think. I did get such a shock, you know, but now I realise I wasn't really *shocked*, if you see what I mean, only furiously angry and I didn't, still don't properly understand.' She hunched her shoulders. 'Sometimes I think I must be really stupid; eighteen my next birthday and I couldn't see what was right under my nose!'

She stared down into her coffee and he watched her bent head, a faint smile hovering around his mouth. He said. 'You're very like Patrick, you know. When he was young he was constantly at war with himself and nothing like as astute as he now is; generally he ended up making a fine old mess of everything. I have a suspicion that you are the same, but like him you're fine as you are and like him, as time passes you'll find the best way to deal with whatever life throws at you is to accept, to try to understand, then finally forgive...yourself, as well as others.'

Putting down her cup she stood up and leaned across the table to lay her hand against his cheek. 'Thank you for rescuing me last night when he gave me such a rotten time; I felt about six years old and you were just what I needed to get me back to seventeen again.'

'Always happy to oblige…and for the record, he's riddled with guilt, so treat him carefully when he returns.'

She blew him a kiss. 'I can't wait; I'm going to look for him now. Keep the coffee warm, Major!'

*   *   *

She left the bus at Oxford Circus and walked through Portland Place to Margaret Street. All was quiet as she passed under the archway and into the courtyard. Only an old man sat on the bench by the porch, his face lifted to the sun. 'You're too late,' he said querulously as Anna approached and looked at her with cross, rheumy eyes, 'it's all over.'

She thought, not by a long chalk it isn't chum, it's only just started, but smiled at him, answering, 'Yes, I know,' and passed through the open door into the hushed quiet of the church.

Inside the air was heavy with incense and a shaft of sunlight pierced the stained glass of the great window, spilling a splash of bright colour onto the floor of the nave. For a moment she thought the church empty and stood hesitating on the threshold until a slight movement drew her attention to a lone figure half way down the nave, hunched forward on a chair, elbows on knees and head bowed.

Walking quietly to where he was she slid into a seat behind him. She said softly, '"Oh, what can ail thee knight at arms, alone and palely loitering!"'

He sat up and turned to face her, laying an arm along the chair back. 'Have you come as *La Belle Dame sans Merci* to hold me in thrall for my sins?'

'I wouldn't know how to hold anyone in thrall,' she answered and he smiled.

'I doubt that. But how are *you* feeling this morning?'

'Still embarrassed and rather bruised, but better for having told you all *my* sordid secrets.'

'Confession is good for the soul. What are you doing here? Did that old hen send you to fetch me home?'

'No. I just wanted to see you; perhaps make sure you still wanted to see me.' She looked around the familiar building. 'Has it helped?'

'It always does.' He stared up at the soaring arch of the roof.

90

'There are only two places I feel safe and at home; here, and back at the Gallery with Charlie.'

'I've mucked everything up for you, haven't I?' She rested her forehead against his arm. 'Opening my ruddy great mouth like that!'

He gave a reproving shake of his head. 'I don't pay Miss Harrison's astronomical fees to have you use expressions like that in the House of God.' He smiled again and stood up. 'Come along. We have to talk: I promised Charlie, and now would seem as good a time as any other. We can sit outside and enjoy this lovely morning.'

She made a face. 'There's a rather grumpy old man on the seat. We may have to go elsewhere.'

But when they left the church the old man had gone. Patrick sat on the wooden bench and drew her down beside him. 'I think that if I go back to the beginning; explain how I felt and some of the things that happened to set me on this particular path through life, it may help you understand a little better; make it easier for you to go on feeling comfortable with Charlie and me.' His eyes twinkled. 'Now that there is only God and us,' he said, 'perhaps I can match your courage of last night and tell all.'

9

OXFORD INTERLUDE

1912 – 1914

It was as quiet as an early Sunday morning in the little courtyard as he began to speak, his voice even and low-pitched.

'The important part, the part that concerns all of us, began at Oxford in nineteen-twelve when I was a very naïve very shy nineteen year old starting my first term at St Johns. Oxford then was full of rich young men who weren't necessarily there to work but because it was the right and accepted place to go when they left school. My parents were only moderately well-off and I really couldn't afford to move in those circles but did so anyway. I was young, not bad looking and it was fun to go to dances and take girls to the theatre or the flicks; sometimes give tea or supper parties in my rooms to the undergrad's from Somerville and Lady Margaret Hall…and more often than not also give them a leg-up over the wall after lock-up!' He saw Anna's involuntary smile and raised a warning finger. 'If you are going to do that, I shall stop!'

'Sorry. It was just the thought of you waltzing around with a bevy of town beauties and feeding tea and cake to a load of blue stocking women!' She composed her face. 'I won't do it again – promise.'

He said dryly. 'Giving tea or supper parties was the done thing in those more innocent times; I also gave them for my fellows without having any ulterior motive, my sexual inclinations being at that time somewhat ambivalent. I liked the company of women, I still do. Conversely, there were, and still are, plenty of men whose company I do not like. However, I digress…'

'I read Classics and did moderately well, but ended my first year rather heavily in debt. So I moved out of my college rooms to share some cheap lodgings on the Woodstock Road with a very likeable, easy-going chap named George Osborne. George was a Theology student I'd become friendly with and he introduced me to Anglo-Catholicism, which one might say was endemic in the colleges at that time. It was all rather heady stuff to an idealistically minded young chap like me from a pious, but very Low Church background. Embracing it gave me a sense of crusading and possible martyrdom, of marching to a different drum. It was through George's influence that I eventually shed my non-conformist upbringing and converted, but that was later and after I'd left Oxford, when confession and absolution offered mitigation for some of the mess my life had become.'

He stopped to take his cigarette case and lighter from his pocket and Anna waited patiently until he had selected and lighted a cigarette before asking, 'Did *you* have to put up with the Alleluia Chorus when you were a child then?'

'Not to the same degree as you, but yes, there was Chapel twice on Sundays and a fair amount of weeping and wailing and gnashing of teeth!' He paused then and contemplated his cigarette in silence for a moment before continuing. 'At one time I had aspirations towards the Anglo Catholic priesthood but getting religion at twenty meant facing all kinds of problems that I'd never allowed myself to think about before in any depth, most of which were hardly commensurate with becoming a priest.'

He hesitated and stopped again, then let out a long breath, complaining ruefully. 'I had no idea this was going to be so difficult!' He rubbed a hand over his hair. 'You see, back in nineteen-thirteen nobody talked about sex so one went on being ignorant for a great deal longer than your generation.'

'Well, most people, girls anyway, I wouldn't know about boys...talk about it now all right, but I don't know that we're any less ignorant,' observed Anna honestly, with a sudden vivid recollection of events in Pardoe's cottage that made her blush.

'Hmm.' He gave a faint smile. 'Perhaps there isn't all that much difference! However, the problem for me then was that whilst Oxford was full of clever and beautiful young women it was home also to a number of rather beautiful young men. I became very confused indeed during my second year about which I found the most attractive. George was kind enough to be concerned about me and suggested that I spent part of the Easter vacation with his family in Falmouth, saying he had two beautiful sisters who would soon help to clear my mind!' He smiled reminiscently and drawing on his cigarette blew a smoke ring into the still air adding, 'He turned out to be quite right, at least in the short-term!'

'The sisters were Cecelia and Dorothy!' Anna exclaimed and he nodded.

'Yes. Until you dropped your bombshell last night I hadn't any idea that Dorothy was your Madame Gallimard...how could I? We hadn't spoken for more than twenty years; I had no idea she'd married a Frenchman and moved to Paris, and we never met during the time she was married to Auguste.' He rubbed a hand over his face and expelled another long breath. 'I behaved very badly towards her and her sister and she has obviously held that against me for all these years.'

Anna gave a puzzled frown. 'But why should it matter to her how you live? I still don't see why she's got it in for you and Charlie.'

He hunched forward, resting his forearms on his knees. He said, 'You will when you've heard the rest of the story.'

*   *   *

'After we'd spent a few days with my parents George and I travelled down to Cornwall together. At that time my father was auctioneer for a large gallery in Chichester that dealt mainly in pictures. As George shared a mutual passion for paintings they got along famously, leaving me to browse the junk shops and markets with my mother in search of interesting pieces of bric-a-brac. My father had hopes of a post in the auction house for me, but I was always much more inclined towards my mother's interest in antiques.

'When George and I arrived in Cornwall the two girls met us at the station. Cecelia was a small, sweet young girl barely out of the schoolroom and within minutes of our meeting I knew I was attracted to her, although I didn't particularly care for her older sister, Dorothy. At twenty-one *she* was a very handsome young woman with a rather forceful character. George had told me their mother died when they were quite young and the girls had little in common with their father, who was a rather remote academic; consequently Dorothy was very over-protective of Cecelia and made it difficult for us to spend much time together...' He broke off to contemplate the glowing end of his cigarette again and Anna saw with some amusement that the urbane Patrick was looking distinctly uncomfortable and self-conscious.

'Unfortunately,' he continued, after a pause, 'as the days passed I became aware that Dorothy had developed a passion for me. Each time I tried to see the younger sister alone, up would pop the elder like an unwanted jack-in-the-box!''

Anna was having a problem with her mouth again and he broke off to give her an embarrassed glance. 'Look, I know this is all very funny in retrospect, but if you want to hear it all you'll have to exercise a modicum of self-control for a just little longer!'

She widened her eyes and sat up straight. 'I'm sorry. I know I said I wouldn't – it's just that I can't imagine Madame as a lovesick girl, but go on, I won't laugh, truly!'

'Very well; to continue...when Dorothy took to tracking me around the house and grounds and inviting me on long solitary walks I didn't know what to do. For George's sake I didn't want to risk offending her and perhaps create an awkward situation, so in the end I decided that a walk or two and few chaste brotherly kisses would keep her happy and have her less jealous of any time I spent with her sister. How little I knew about women.'

'Oh, Patrick, I do feel for you!' Anna smothered another resurgence of mirth. 'She still isn't the sort of person to be easily distracted!'

'I imagine not. Then she was like a rather overwhelming and devoted puppy, but one I didn't wish to own.' He shared her amusement for a moment before his face clouded. 'I very much *wanted* to be in love with Cecilia. She was pretty and charming and I was genuinely attracted to her. I knew that the feelings I'd experienced towards the beautiful young men in Oxford were dangerous and forbidden.' He made a wry face. 'The unwritten eleventh Commandment in fact, and I thought Cecelia could be my saviour; that she was young and innocent and wouldn't expect, or even want, more passion and commitment than I was able to give. It was not an unusual situation, at that time many basically homosexual young men, including the notorious Oscar, opted for the safety of marriage, even if that marriage eventually became something of a sham.

'When the vacation was at an end we promised we would write and see each other whenever we could, when she kissed me goodbye I told her I loved her and wanted to marry her.' He shook his head. 'It was a terrible thing to do and I have no defence. What I remember most about that parting wasn't Cecelia's kisses but the look on Dorothy's face as the train left the station. I think she was probably feeling horribly let down and angry, and as the train pulled away she gave me a really terrifying look of the purest loathing.'

Anna said feelingly 'You don't have to tell me. I've been on the end of one of those myself.'

'Then she obviously hasn't changed much.' He dropped his cigarette onto the ground, rubbing it into the paving with his shoe. 'After that I didn't go down to Cornwall again. With George's help Cecelia and I met several times in Oxford during the remainder of my last year. By the time I'd taken Greats the war had started and along with George and most of my friends I volunteered for the Army. Cecelia came to see me on the last weekend before I was due to leave for Sussex to join my regiment. Everything and everyone seemed in turmoil, all of us rushing around in our new uniforms, high on mixed emotions of excitement and fear. I borrowed a friend's rooms in college so that we could have somewhere to say our good-byes in private.

'You may find it hard to believe, but at just twenty-one I'd never been alone in a room with a woman before, never done more than exchange some fairly innocent kisses and there was absolutely no thought of seduction in my mind. But being together in that atmosphere of "this may be the last time" with its inevitable heightening of our senses...'

He paused and rubbed his face again. 'Remembering what happened that afternoon I still feel the same shame and despair I felt then. Because after we'd made love I knew with absolute conviction that I couldn't fool myself any longer; that I should never be able to marry any woman and live with her for the rest of my life as a normal, loving husband. The fact that Cecelia once aroused proved to be a passionate young woman made it even more impossible. Had George still been in Oxford I would have told him and asked his help to end it all with at least a semblance of honour. Although he would undoubtedly have been angry I'm sure he'd have understood. Unfortunately, he'd already left for France and was killed a month later. So I took the coward's way out: I wrote telling her the truth, went overseas almost immediately and never saw her again. On my first leave home I took my guilt to the Church, which welcomed me, forgave me and eventually taught me to live with my past and present, more or less in peace.'

He paused again and she prompted, 'And then you met Charlie.'

'And then I met Charlie.' He lit another cigarette. 'As you know we first met very briefly in the trenches. I heard he'd visited me when I was in the field hospital and that he'd won the M.C. and been mentioned in dispatches for bringing me back under fire...I bet he didn't tell *you* that! Within a few days I was sent home, and in the way of things in wartime we lost touch for two or three years.'

'He told me this morning you met again a year or two after the war.'

'Yes. He was just back from Europe and at the time I had a temporary job teaching French and German at a prep school in Hampstead. We had several meetings while he was on leave and I knew then that the initial feelings I'd had for him in France were real – and that they were reciprocated.'

He sat staring into space for several moments in silence, rather as Charlie had done that morning. When he again spoke his voice was quiet and intense.

'Standing on a firing step in the trenches, waiting to go over the top, even an hour in a man's company can begin to forge bonds. I knew almost as soon as we spoke to each other that if we survived he would become important to me. I have no doubt that had I not been injured that morning our relationship would have begun then and continued, much as it has to the present day.' He shook his head. 'I wish it had, because in the years between I had to learn some very hard lessons about the difference between love and lust. Without Charlie I don't know what kind of mess I might have made of my life.

'However, after his leave was up he had to return to Scotland and rejoin his regiment. Shortly after that my mother died suddenly and I went home to stay with my father.' He was silent for some time again, drawing deeply on his cigarette and staring at the traffic moving past the archway. 'He was utterly devastated by my mother's death,' he continued eventually. 'I don't think they'd ever spent so much as a day apart since they were married. Six weeks after she died he went out for a walk one morning and never returned. A boatman found him later that day in the water at Chichester harbour. The coroner's court decided it was accidental death, but I wasn't so sure, I'm still not. I think perhaps he just found that he couldn't go on without her.'

'Oh, Patrick,' Anna's eyes filled with tears. 'How awful; what did you do?'

'The only thing I could think of, I wrote to Charlie. He sent back a telegram by return with just two words: 'I'm here.' The day after my father's funeral I caught the night sleeper to Killoran and that was that. Three months later he resigned his Commission, I sold the Sussex house and we went to live in France where we were less likely to fall foul of the law. I studied fine arts in Paris and Charlie fulfilled a latent ambition to train as a chef – it was his idea to play the servant and master game when we finally returned to this country. There's something pretty comical about the idea of a regular Army Major playing servant to a war time commissioned Captain…he thought it was hilarious and it's certainly had its amusing moments!' He gave her a sidelong glance. 'It fooled you all right, didn't it?'

'Um…' She was thoughtful. 'Although right from the beginning I remember thinking it a bit odd that he always ate with us and told you off when you annoyed him. Then after you said he was neither your servant not mine, I just thought of him as my friend Charlie. I always will; that's why I was so furious when Madame was so foul about him. I still don't see why she still has it in for you both after all these years. It doesn't make sense. She got married and had her own life, didn't she?'

'Oh, I can understand.' He sighed. 'After all, as she would see it I'd led her on, which I suppose I had, even if only through an ignorance of women in general and her in particular. I had secret meetings for a year with her seventeen-year-old sister and ended by seducing *her*! After which I sent a bald letter to say sorry, but I'd made a mistake; I couldn't marry her because I was homosexual. For a woman like Dorothy I could hardly have delivered a more devastating insult if I'd tried. Given her sheltered upbringing Cecelia probably didn't even know what a homosexual *was*, but I've no doubt Dorothy damned soon enlightened her! No wonder she never tried to find me.'

'Well, yes. Put like that I can see why Madame would have been less than pleased.'

'I *did* see Dorothy once more, you know: in Paris.' He pulled his mouth down. 'It was the Christmas before we came back to England. I was at the midnight Mass in Notre Dame when I suddenly had the feeling that someone was watching; I looked around and there she was, staring at me from a few feet away. It gave me a hell of a turn, I can tell you! Then just as I thought she was coming at me she stood up, gave a last vicious glare and walked away. It was the first time I knew what was meant by a Basilisk like stare!'

'I bet she wouldn't have left in such a hurry if you'd been anywhere else but in a church.' Anna commented feelingly. 'You can count yourself lucky – she frightened the life out of me when she lost her rag.'

'Poor Anna, how you've suffered for my sins,' he smiled a little uncertainly. 'Now you know everything; do you understand a little more?'

'Yes, I think so; but it's a lot to take in all at once.'

'I know; one doesn't expect miracles. Just promise you won't pack your bags and leave the old hen and me for a more respectable member of the Farrell family.'

'No, I won't pack my bags,' she promised, then added honestly, 'I wouldn't want to live with any of them – and no one else would have me anyway!'

He laughed and stood up, holding out his hand. 'So that's settled. Now I think we must get back to the gallery, have some breakfast and open up shop or I shall be losing customers.'

*   *   *

'Did you buy all this straight away when you came back?' she asked

98

as they reached Stratton Place.

'Yes. My parents left me a useful inheritance; Charlie and I pooled our resources and bought the house and gallery in nineteen twenty-seven. It was a good investment and one that neither of us has ever regretted.'

She gave a mischievous grin. 'At least he can now stop wearing his apron and talking with that ridiculous accent when I'm around.'

'I think it's given him quite a lot of amusement over the past couple of years to do that.' He put his key in the lock and swung the door wide, then stood aside for her to enter. 'All you have to do to keep him happy, Anna, is to still treat him as your friend Charlie and continue letting him spoil you and defend you against me whenever he deems it necessary.'

'Thank you, I think I can manage that.'

'And try not to think too badly of me…we all make mistakes when we are young. I just made some rather devastating ones and the repercussions still seem to be going on.'

'How could I think badly of you after what I've done?' She turned impulsively and kissed him and his arms went around her in a warm, loving hug. When he released her she looked at him with tears in her eyes.

'You can do that again, Patrick, as often as you like!' she said and kissed him once more before climbing the stairs to where Charlie was making breakfast.

10

MARLCLEW, CORNWALL

May 1937

Anna returned to Cornwall and school wearing a suitably sad and grief-stricken expression for the premature demise of Uncle William. Miss Harrison and her staff were most sympathetic, all that is but Dorothy Gallimard, who quite clearly disbelieved the reason given for her pupil's abrupt departure and greeted her return with a barely restrained anger and a caustic tongue.

From the first moment of Anna's reappearance in the classroom both knew that a state of war existed between them; the possibility that one or other could inflict a wound that might prove fatal only serving to heighten the tension. It was uncomfortable for Anna but she bore it stoically as the price to be paid for being, however unwittingly, the cause of the trouble she had stirred in Stratton Place.

But her air of quiet, but triumphant confidence showed Dorothy Gallimard clearly that far from being broken and disgusted with the result of her visit home, if it came to a battle Anna would defend Patrick Farrell vigorously and to the death if necessary. So she constrained her anger, letting it seethe silently in her breast, contenting herself by treating her recalcitrant pupil with cold disdain.

One Saturday morning shortly after her return, Anna and Valerie were lazing under the willow, supposedly engaged in revision for a History examination, when the gardener's boy sidled up to them. Pushing an envelope into Anna's hand he muttered from the side of his mouth: 'From the Froggie bloke, miss…that should be wurth a tanner!'

Anna snatched the letter and glared at him so that he quailed slightly.

'And how much were you given to deliver it?' she demanded.

'Cross me 'eart and 'ope ter die I didn't get nuthin'!'

'Liar, shove off, Albert or I'll tell your mother and she'll soon have your ill-gotten gains for a pint of gin!'

He retreated across the lawn until he was out of reach before blowing a raspberry. As Anna made a rush at him he stuck two derisive fingers in the air and shouting 'Stuck-up tart!' took to his heels. She looked after him thoughtfully. "D'you think he'll tell anyone?'

'Not he – he'd be too scared of having to cough up the cash!'

Anna pulled at the flap of the envelope and drew out the single sheet.

Félix began without preamble:

Anna...What have you done to Maman? I have returned to a hornet's nest. Better, I think to have stayed and been bombed by Franco than come back to this. I must talk with you; the boathouse at five o'clock today. I have missed you.
Félix'

She went hot and cold by turns and her knees shook. Although neither Patrick nor Charlie had forbidden her to meet with Félix again, she knew it would hurt and disappoint them both if she did. "I trust you will not see that young man again," Patrick had said. "Not for my sake, but for yours. You have to get through the rest of your schooling without any more interruptions or difficulties."

But at the sight of Félix's name every good resolve she had made never to see him again fled. 'He's back!' she turned a radiant face on Valerie. 'Oh, Val...he's back and he says he's missed me!'

*   *   *

He pounced as she slid through the door and half-laughing, half-crying she went into his arms.

Félix kissed her thoroughly and thought how good she was to come back to, how sweet and fresh she tasted after so many aggressively unwashed female comrades. He drew her towards the punt saying, 'Come, sit down and tell me what you have done to Maman...she is like a tigress. *Sacre nom de Dieu,* I thought she would have my ears off, she scorched them so!'

'It's not my fault. I did nothing to her – it's all to do with something that happened years ago.' Anna was cautious. She didn't imagine for one moment that Madame had given him the real reason for her fury and she wasn't about to tell him.

She sat down in the punt, keeping a distance between them. 'Don't let's talk about that now. Tell me about Spain. Was it dreadful? Did anyone shoot at you? Were you scared? ...I would have been!'

'It was vile, and yes, I was frightened, many times. Boisson was supposed to write for the paper about the heroic freedom fighters and there were many courageous ones, but some did such terrible things…in the end I left Boisson and came back. My *rédacteur en chef* has sacked me for not remaining, so now I have no job. I must then come here because… *Je suis fauché*…' he rapped his knuckles against his head, 'How do you say it?'

'You're broke!' she supplied and giggled at his expression.

'Yes? It is not funny – I could not pay for my rooms and come for help, only to be savaged by Maman as I step through the door!'

'Heavens – you didn't tell her you were seeing me?'

'Are you mad? I would rather go back to Spain and watch nuns being raped and priests butchered. She is a *très grande folle*, I tell you, *a hystérique*.' He shrugged helplessly. 'I shall give her some time to calm down then shall try again to discover what has caused all this. If she does not regain her senses I shall be forced to come and sleep in this place…'

Reverting quickly to his usual amorous and practical self he caught her suddenly about the waist and pulled her down into the bottom of the punt. 'Come Anna. There is just time. We shall enjoy each other now and leave my Maman to rage alone!'

'Félix, no – I'm supposed to be seeing that everyone else is behaving as they should.' She pushed her hands against his chest.

Breathing hard he threatened. 'Then come down tomorrow. If you are not here I shall come and find you, so beware!'

She felt her resolutions weakening. 'All right, but only to talk,' she scrambled away from his restraining arms and climbed out of the punt. 'I'll come the same time tomorrow.'

Slipping back to the school with her heart hammering against her ribs, she tried not to think about Patrick, how disappointed he would be that she'd so easily let Félix back into her life. But I can't help it, really I can't…and I won't let him do anything, she promised. I can keep him in order, I know I can; I just want to be with him again for a little while, that's all.

*   *   *

Dorothy waited for Félix to come back, aware that she had made a grave error in trying to browbeat her son. Usually she could intimidate him, but this time he'd been unexpectedly resistant to her rage, only waved despairing hands and gone, leaving the house with the echo of the slammed door sounding loud in her ears.

She paced the living room from end to end. What should she do?

102

It was bad enough that Asa would soon be in London and close to the Farrell household, although surely there would be no reason for *him* to see either Anna or her guardian again, but it was impossible to have Félix here with that girl at hand...Suppose he had gone to see her? She put her hands to her throbbing head. There was only one answer to her dilemma: she must return to France. It had been a terrible, costly mistake ever to leave. Perhaps she could even persuade Asa, anglophile though he was, to secure a post in a French University. Félix she would deal with now by financing him provided he returned to Paris immediately. That would at least buy her a little time.

Trembling and clasping her shaking hands tightly together she sat down. She must compose herself and be ready for him. It should not be a problem. Félix was not like Asa. He was a Frenchman and loved France. He would have no difficulty in leaving both England and Anna Farrell behind.

*   *   *

Félix walked home slowly, in no hurry to resume the battle with his mother. Seeing Anna again had stirred and unsettled him, and he couldn't understand why. Other girls he coupled with he could leave and go on to the next, so why did he return to this unsophisticated schoolgirl who could be both compliant and rejecting by turns. Who all too clearly loved him but was sufficiently clever not to keep telling him so. *Merde,* but he had even fought with Asa over her; something that he would never have done for any other young girl.

But he must not stay too close to her for long because there was no way in which he would become entangled in a long *affaire* with Anna Farrell. She was the kind that ultimately one married, and marriage was not for him. No force on earth would have him live such a life as Maman and papa...always eternally warring and scoring off each other. He sighed. *Asa was right I am like papa, but I won't make his mistake. A mistress is fine and can be changed, but a wife...Oh, la, la, la...not for me. Not for Félix Gallimard!*

He walked on, deep in thought. How was he to soothe Maman and keep her from castigating him again? First he must apologise and then...his stomach lurched slightly. He took a deep breath and squared his shoulders. Then he must be firm, respectful but firm.

*   *   *

Dorothy stared at him impassively as he came to where she sat by the

103

window, noting the heightened colour and air of excitement that underlay a subdued and contrite manner. She resisted the impulse to touch him, to push back the wing of silky hair that flopped over his forehead, only said steadily. 'I trust you will not choose to disappear again when I am speaking to you.'

'*Non, Maman,*' He bowed and spread his hands in humble apology. '*Je suis désolé!*'

'Very pretty, and easily said!' Expertly she searched the blue eyes. 'Have you been to see that girl – and don't ask 'what girl?' You know whom I mean.'

He suppressed the temptation to lie; it could only delay the inevitable row. He said, 'Yes, Maman. I have seen her; for a few moments only.'

She drew in a sharp breath. 'Why are you defying me like this?'

He sat down in an easy chair and lighted a cigarette, noting with interest that his fingers scarcely trembled at all. His mother's temper had always terrified him; his instinct when trouble threatened was always to run. But if he didn't face up to her now, get for himself a little of Asa's courage, he would never be free and would continue to run. He said, 'Maman, if you wish me not to see her, I think you must give me a reason.'

'Do you? The only reason I can, or will give, is that she comes from a most objectionable and distasteful background and is a brazen and insolent child. One with whom you have no business to be having any kind of relationship, however appealing a little slut she may be.'

He flushed but kept his temper.

'Maman, I think you should understand that it was I who seduced Anna, not the other way about. She is not a slut and I do not see why her background, however unpleasant, should make her one. I think you must have reasons other than those you have given me.'

She turned away from him.

'Her guardian once did me and someone very dear to me, a terrible unforgivable wrong, so great that I cannot speak of it. Sufficient that I now feel it is impossible for me to stay here and teach in the school while she is a pupil. I should like you to return to Paris in the morning – for good, and begin looking for a suitable house or apartment for me...and if you wish for yourself also. I will finance you until you either return to university or secure another position.' She turned back to face him again. 'You understand?'

'Oh, yes, maman. I understand.'

'You agree to this?'

'Do I have a choice?'

'Not if you wish to eat and have clothes on your back.'

He shrugged and grimaced his distaste, 'Very well, but I go in two days, not one.'

'Why?'

'That, Maman is my business. Just as your past is yours, my present is mine. I shall not question you, if you will not question me...*n'est-ce pas?*'

'You are becoming as difficult as Asa.' She answered coldly and he gave a mocking smile.

'Asa was born difficult, Maman. I have had to learn...but I am catching up with him quickly!' he said.

*   *   *

Anna sat back in the punt. 'You mean Madame is *leaving*?' She was stunned. 'She is going back to France?'

'Yes, but you must say nothing at the school. It would not be right until she is ready.'

'Of course I shan't tell anyone, not even Valerie. But Félix, if she goes, when will I ever see you again?'

'This I do not yet know for certain, but until you are finished at the school it would be foolish for me to show myself once Maman is no longer here – ah, do not look so sad.' He put his arms about her. 'It is not the end of the world.'

'It feels like the end of my world.' Despite her resolution, she struggled against tears. 'I know you don't feel for me as I do for you Félix and I'm not going to make a fuss. Come back to see me if you can. Write to me sometimes, but *don't* put your name and address on the back!' She smiled shakily. 'I would hate never to see you again.'

He felt his decision not to make love to her, to leave her now and make an end of it, weakening. 'I'm sure we shall see each other again sometime and I shall never forget you, Anna; never.'

She leaned her head against his chest whispering. 'And I shall never forget you. Not as long as I live.'

The feel of her dissolved all his resolutions and in an uncontrollable upsurge of passion he drew her down onto the rug. Cupping her face in his hands he looked down into the slanted grey eyes. 'There is sufficient time for us to make a good farewell,' he said huskily. 'If one must say goodbye it should be like this...always like this.'

Impossible not to respond, to pull away from him now, as she knew she should. With his hands and lips on her it was already too late. With trembling fingers she began to unfasten his shirt. 'Once more, Félix, only once more…'

Closing her eyes she gave herself up to the pain and the pleasure of loving Félix.

Part II

If you can look into the seeds of time,

and say which grain will grow, and

which will not, speak then to me.

W.S.

11

LONDON

Autumn 1938

Asa was at the corner of Northumberland Avenue when he saw her. The walk and the carriage of her head were unmistakable, even at this distance. Without pausing to think, he sprinted across the road and along the Embankment.

'Anna!'

She turned at his call, her face breaking into a smile of recognition. 'Asa!' she held out her hands, 'the times I've meant to discover if you were still in England.'

Catching her hands in his he laughed, 'And the times I've meant to screw up my courage and visit your gallery.'

'I thought you would have gone back to France – after Madame left.'

'No. I prefer it here. I am British by birth you know.' He still held her hands, now he raised them to his lips and kissed her fingers. 'Hello, again, Anna!'

She smiled up into his eyes. 'Where were you going on this fine evening?'

'Nowhere much; I thought, a long walk by the river then later back to the Strand where I know of a perfect place to take a lady to dine, except that I have – had, no lady to take.' His dark eyes snapped with laughter. He asked, 'Have you been to Le Bagatelle?'

'No. Is it another of your low dives?'

'Certainly not, this is London, not the Left Bank in Paris; it is most respectable.' He took her arm and they began to walk along the Embankment together. 'Would you care to dine there with me tonight?'

She laughed and squeezed his arm. 'If we can walk as far as Waterloo Bridge without fighting, you're on,' she said. 'Patrick is away at Long Melford in Suffolk, haggling over a half-dozen James the First chairs. Charlie's betting on the gee-gee's at Goodwood and not due back before midnight, so I have time to do just as I wish.'

He shortened his long stride to hers as they walked. It was a hot evening and he had rolled up his shirtsleeves and carried his jacket slung over one shoulder. She wore a slim navy linen skirt, with a cream blouse unbuttoned at the throat. The hollow showing between the revers of her blouse and the silk sleeve moving against his skin sent a familiar sensation snaking through him; sternly he repressed it and shifted to take her hand, a move that brought only temporary relief, the feel of those slim fingers in his only serving to conjure memories of holding her close on a far-off Parisian night. Hastily, he asked: 'So what have you been doing all these many months since I last saw you in Paris?'

'I'm a student now, of a sort. I *was* going straight to University, but then an opportunity came up that I couldn't miss. An old friend of Patrick's offered to teach me the 'Tools of the Trade' in his Auction House for a year, so that's what I'm doing now. I have a place at Cambridge for next autumn.'

'I should have imagined Patrick could have taught you as well, or better, than any other man.'

She smiled up at him. 'He could, and has, but thought, quite rightly, that it was better for me to take an apprenticeship elsewhere for a while.'

'And before that – did you go to Europe as planned?'

'Yes…but I lost an awful lot of money on the tables in Cannes; Patrick couldn't seem to understand and got rather cross when I tried to explain it was the playing, not necessarily the winning, that counted.'

'Ah, there you made a very expensive discovery!'

She gave a gurgle of laughter. 'That's what he said. He made me leave after only a week. After that we spent three weeks in Rome and Florence, although even then I didn't see all I wanted to.' Her face clouded suddenly. 'Afterwards we went to Germany, to Munich and Berlin.' She looked up at him with sober eyes. 'There's a war coming, Asa. Over there, you can *smell* it. Why can't people here see what's happening? First Austria, then Czechoslovakia…after that, how can they just watch complacently while Mosley's Blackshirt thugs strut through the East End like Hitler's gangsters through Berlin?'

'Here is an island and people feel safe cut off from the barbarians. They don't think they will be hammering at *their* gates.'

'If I was a Jew, even living here I wouldn't feel safe…and they *will* be hammering at our gates, won't they?'

'I fear so, and soon.'

She paced on in silence for a while. He flexed his fingers around hers and gave them a comforting squeeze. 'Tonight is not for talking about war. Soon we shall turn around and walk to our dinner in the

Strand. I should like to make up for the one that in Paris I did not buy for you!'

She gave him the remembered sideways glance.

'The accent is almost *too* perfect,' she said, 'but you'll still have to work on the syntax to pass muster as a true born Englishman!'

* * *

They quarrelled later that evening. About Félix, of course, when they were wandering through the streets after an evening of talk and laughter. Asa had said incautiously: 'Félix is back with his paper, you know...all is apparently forgiven and forgotten. I think perhaps he is very good at his job.'

'Um, I know.'

'You do?'

'Yes.' She glanced around at him as they climbed the steps of the National Gallery to lean on the balcony. 'He comes from time to time. He has a friend with a 'plane at Le Tourquet, who has a girl friend near Biggin Hill. If I have a free weekend when they fly over, we meet.'

'And is he your lover still?'

She said, 'Now why is that question so offensive, coming from you?'

He watched the flush rise to her hairline then looked down at his clasped hands. 'I'm sorry. I shouldn't have asked that.'

'Damn' right, you shouldn't!'

He sighed. 'Now that I've brought up the subject and annoyed you, I might as well go on...Do you know why I wanted to see you alone when we met in Paris?'

'No. But I can't imagine it was because you were desperate for my company – not the way the evening worked out,' she added with biting sarcasm, 'however, do go on because I can't wait to know.'

'When Félix first started chasing you, I warned him off.' He turned, keeping his gaze on her face. 'Being Félix, he took no notice. The night he seduced you I did my best to put his teeth down his throat...'

She blazed, 'How dared you! What business was it of yours what he did?'

'I thought I should make it my business,' he said deliberately, 'because Félix is an amoral lecherous little sod, who will have anything in a skirt. He is constitutionally incapable of being satisfied by one woman. I cannot imagine that he will ever marry – you, or

111

anyone else, because to be responsible for another person's happiness and well-being is totally beyond his comprehension.'

Furiously, she interrupted him. 'You are jealous – he said you were; you are a destroyer, Asa, like Madame. You can't bear to see others happy!'

'A destroyer? Perhaps, but only of dishonesty and deceit,' he remained unmoved by this outburst. 'Jealous? No. I wanted only to see your innocence left unspoiled until you were properly grown up. Not to have him take it then leave you and go blithely on to his next conquest.'

'But he hasn't left me, has he?' she asked triumphantly. 'He still comes, doesn't he?'

'How often?' he asked quietly, 'and what do you imagine he does for companionship in his bed in the times between?'

She froze, as though he had slapped her in the face. He could see her struggle as his words sunk in and longed to put his arms around her; to comfort her and heal the wounds he'd inflicted.

Eventually she leaned her elbows on the parapet, pushing her fingers through her short curls, 'Asa, I *know* what he is, and of course he'll never love me as I do him. In many ways Félix is the least romantic and most practical man in the world. He comes for sex and when we're together we have fun and are very, very happy. When he goes, I think for him it ends painlessly at the bedroom door, whereas I die a little, then recover and go on until the next time.' Again she looked sideways at him, cocking her head and giving the ghost of a smile. 'You and Patrick should get together and try to solve the mystery of Félix and me; he thinks much as you do.'

'I can't believe that you, of all people, can just sit around, waiting for a man who doesn't love you to condescend, now and again to walk in and take you to bed when he can find the time.' He was bitter, moving his shoulders in an angry, dismissive shrug.

'I don't sit around waiting. I get on with my life.' For a few moments she stared across the square at home-going lovers, walking with linked arms and contented faces then turned to look at him again. 'Don't think I haven't tried to finish it, I have. It just doesn't work.'

He was silent, leaning beside her, his bare arm touching hers, and once again she felt a remembered stirring of her senses. His face was taut, his mouth set in uncompromising lines and he flinched when she touched his arm gently, asking, '*Pax*, Asa? After having wrung *that* admission from me, I think a taxi home would be a very good idea.'

He said quietly. 'You are not alone in your foolishness. One can romanticise even the most unsatisfactory of relationships,' then led the

112

way back down the steps.

They were both silent on the way back to Stratton Place. When the cab stopped outside the Gallery, he got out with her, keeping the cab waiting while she found her key. 'I suppose,' he said, 'you wouldn't have a theory to cover why *I* now want to keep coming back?'

She smiled a little sadly. 'I never speculate about other people's motives...how could I, when I don't understand my own?'

He sighed. 'No one can say we're not consistent, you and I. We've run true to form and ended the evening with a quarrel; how about dinner next week when the wounds have healed a little?'

She gave him a long considering look before agreeing primly. 'That would be very nice, M'sieur Gallimard!'

He bowed and clicked his heels. 'Saturday evening at seven then...I will call for you. *Au revoir, Mam'zelle Farrell!*'

He turned to re-enter the cab, but she stopped him with a hand on his arm. 'Just one thing, Asa...what have *you* been doing for companionship over the past eighteen months?'

He raised his brows. 'I? Nothing much, nothing that mattered,' he gave his ironic smile. 'I think,' he said, 'that I've been rather busy trying not to notice that *I* might have fallen in love!'

*　　*　　*

She was in the kitchen making a pot of tea when Charlie returned; she looked up, her lips curved in a smile. 'Hi, Charlie; isn't it a lovely evening?'

'So-so; it's starting to rain!' He slipped his jacket over a chair back and sat down.' You look like the cat that found the cream!'

She took a biscuit from the Victorian biscuit barrel, 'No, just a very good dinner.'

'Ah-ha,' He folded his arms on the table. 'You've never given in and gone out again with Valerie's brother, have you? I thought better of you than that.'

'You jest, of course,' she grinned. 'Archie has all the finesse of Attila the Hun and the hottest pair of hands this side of Hades...The last time we went dancing I needed a crowbar to prize him off! Try again.'

'Not Félix, I hope...'

'Getting warmer...'

He narrowed his eyes. 'Not his *brother*?'

'The very one,' she put out their mugs and began to pour the tea.

113

'We met on the Victoria Embankment by chance, ate at Le Bagatelle, then walked for hours...*don't* expect to see me before nine tomorrow morning, will you? I'm exhausted.'

'From walking?'

'Yes you sweet old fuddy-duddy; *only* from walking!'

His eyes crinkled. 'How nice to know there's at least one gentleman left in town.'

'Don't hang out the flags yet. With Asa, I don't think that what one at first sees is necessarily what one ultimately gets!' She was thoughtful. 'You know, Charlie, he's the only person I *always* cross swords with every single time we meet, but he still manages to keep me liking him, no matter how much he gets into my hair. I find that just a little unsettling. He has to have some flaws lurking in there somewhere!'

Charlie sipped his tea and gave a significant 'Hmm!' He found the subject of Anna's men of abiding interest and amusement. She was seldom found without an escort, but none seemed to have the necessary staying power to weather her amused indifference. They appeared to be of little significance and came and went like so many pieces of paper in the wind. He said 'Hmm,' again and she gave him a withering look.

'Don't start getting ideas, he's a friend, that's all, and from previous experience of Asa I can tell you that I'm unlikely ever to need a crowbar to prize *him* away from my person!'

*   *   *

She found it difficult to sleep that night as *vignettes* of the evening passed rapidly before her closed eyes: Asa's strong, precise hands as he cracked walnuts, passing the kernels to her across the restaurant table. The way his gaze had held hers when he talked and how he'd thrown back his head and laughed like a boy at something she'd said. How he had first angered her, then deflected her anger without apology or withdrawing a word and still left her able to like and trust him.

Which one of us has changed, Asa or me? Or is it both of us? Perhaps we haven't changed at all, only allowed ourselves to make time to be friends.

But it wasn't just friendship she'd experienced all that time ago in Paris, nor was it friendship alone she'd felt for him this evening. She could feel again his hand in hers as they'd walked, and the warmth of his arm against her sleeve as they'd leaned together on the Gallery steps.

Cloudily, before her senses were lost in sleep, she puzzled over his parting words and the enigmatic smile that had accompanied them, wondering with whom he might have fallen in love and how he came to be so different from other members of his family, because he wasn't a bit like Félix...nor Madame.

Auguste, she thought drowsily, must have been a very nice man to have had such a son.

* * *

They met several times that autumn, as war clouds gathered and an uneasy feeling of *déjà vu* settled over the land.

While Hitler bullied and Chamberlain vacillated and that old war-horse Churchill stood mocked and alone, warning in sombre tones of coming disaster, they walked together in London's parks, where workmen and students dug trenches in the short turf under the azure blue skies of a fading summer; while in cupboards across the land gas masks lay waiting for the remembered horrors of Passchendale and the Somme.

'All the waving of every piece of paper in the world won't stop that paranoid little corporal,' Patrick commented, on the evening of the day that a smiling Chamberlain returned from Munich promising "Peace in our Time." 'A few months from now and we'll be in the thick of it.'

It was after dinner and they were all in the garden at Stratton Place, Patrick, Charlie, Anna and Asa. The evening sun slanted down through the trees, sparking off their wineglasses and turning the beech hedge behind them into burnished gold.

Asa looked at the glowing tip of his cigarette then up at the branches above his head. 'Yesterday, I volunteered for the Army. They tell me I shall be commissioned and could be called to report for training at any time over the next few weeks.'

'So you'll stay over here...with our lot?' asked Patrick.

He answered quietly, 'They are my lot, too. I was born here.'

'You won't go back to France?'

'Eventually, I imagine, but not wearing these clothes,' he grinned, then sobered at Anna's expression. 'You must have known I would, Anna. I just prefer to go earlier, rather than wait to be called-up. At least then I shall be better prepared.'

She shook her head but stayed silent, leaning back in her wicker chair, closing her ears to the talk of war ranging back and forth between the three of them.

Asa, she thought, fitted so perfectly into this household, in a way that Félix never would. Since their casual meeting after so long, he had picked up the tenuous threads of friendship and become a part of all their lives with seemingly effortless ease. Patrick and Charlie had accepted him warmly and without question and he now spent most of his free time at Stratton Place.

Now he would be going. Off to some camp, then to a regiment, then to God knew where...and what of Patrick? Would he be content to sit back this time or would he somehow, with the same calm and balanced acceptance of what was right and honourable, squirm his way back into the Army?

Through half-closed eyes she watched them: Asa, long and dark and lean, with hawkish face and those polished brown eyes; Charlie, tall and thin, sparse grey hair and eyes like twin sapphires in his lined face; and her dearest Patrick: shorter, slightly stocky; with handsome sculptured features, dark smooth skin and eyes like night. She repressed a sigh: Asa would go; so might Patrick. Thank God, Charlie at least was a bit too long in the tooth to be used as cannon fodder...

*   *   *

When Asa rose to leave that night, she walked with him to the door. He took her hand then bent to kiss her cheek.

'Don't worry too much just yet. It seems we have a little breathing space, but soon I must go over to see Maman. In time France, I fear, may be no place for her and I think she should come back to England.'

'Just don't mention you hob-nob with Patrick and Charlie,' she half-joked and he laughed.

'No. But it is time, I think, that she stopped being so very English and straight-laced about those two...It's quite absurd that she should still harbour such feelings.' He looked hard at Anna's carefully guileless expression and asked accusingly. 'Why do I feel that you know a great deal more than you ever say about my Maman and why she hates Patrick with such zeal?'

'Don't ask me; ask her, if you dare!'

He shook his head. 'I think not.'

'Very wise of you,' she said, straight-faced, then kissed him and watched until he was out of sight. She went in, closing the door behind her, thinking that this was one of those times when the past hung over her like a dark cloud and the future was even less inviting.

116

Twenty-four years ago Patrick had given out all the wrong signals to Dorothy Gallimard before proceeding to seduce her sister, and still the repercussions of *that* far-off summer rumbled on.

She hoped no such lasting problems would arise from her not entirely dissimilar relationship with that lady's sons.

12

LONDON

February 1939

Asa arrived in Stratton Place to find Charlie supervising the delivery of the sheets of corrugated iron that were, according to the booklet he held at arms length and in disdainful fingers, destined to be turned into an air-raid shelter.

'Getting ready to start digging, are you, Charlie?' Asa grinned and drew an unwilling smile in return. 'I've the whole week-end free so if you like I'll roll up my sleeves and do my bit with a shovel.'

Charlie looked him up and down then shook his head. 'Not in that outfit...I'll find you something a little less splendid. Go on in, Anna's taken over cooking lunch and Patrick will be through from the gallery any minute now – careful there!' he admonished testily as a sheet of iron was rammed into the side entry gate. 'Not much point in you fellows knocking the place down before Goering gets here, is there?' Grumbling, he followed the men down the path as Asa beat a hasty retreat up the stairs.

'Any chance of a crust of bread to spare for a starving soldier?' he asked from the open kitchen door and Anna spun around, dropping the spoon she held with a clatter.

'Oh, God; you've really done it!'

'I certainly have, and God had nothing to do with it!' He advanced into the room, stooped to pick up the spoon then placed his cap on her head. 'Shall I grow a moustache? Everyone at Camberley seemed to have one...I felt quite naked amongst so many hirsute English gentlemen!' he stroked his upper lip. 'Perhaps a thin one – like the so English Ronald Coleman?'

'Idiot,' she held his arms and stood him back from her, 'I thought you were still in France.'

'No. My orders to report followed me there on the next steamer and I only just managed to return in time...then there was *no* time.' He gave a wry grin. 'Now I come to you with sore feet and pains in joints I never knew I had. Cosset me, Anna, for I am a broken man.'

'Anyone less...' she smiled and let him go. Taking off the cap she tossed it onto the dresser. 'Sit down, you'll feel better after a good meal.' Turning back to the stove she busied herself with the bubbling pans. 'Did you manage to persuade your mother to return to England?'

'No. She will not budge an inch. She say's that even if war comes the German army will be stopped at the Maginot Line and never reach Paris.'

'Then let's hope she's right...she usually is!' Anna sent him a sarcastic look over her shoulder and he laughed.

'I took my courage in both hands and told her how welcome I was in this house, which made her so angry that she was indiscreet...Anna, did you know that she and Patrick were acquainted?'

He watched her back stiffen. She lifted a pan lid and replaced it again slowly.

'Yes, I've known for some time, but it was a long time ago.'

'You don't have to keep secrets from me, you know. I thought the reason she was so determined to keep Félix away from you was just Mama being her usual manipulative and jealous self. Now I suspect it goes a great deal deeper than that.'

She left the stove and came to perch on the table next to where he sat. 'If you are that curious you'll either have to brave your mother's wrath again or ask Patrick. If you ask *him* I don't know what his reaction might be...I think perhaps you should leave matters as they are.'

'Not an easy thing to do.' He looked at her intently. 'Especially, as in some strange way, Maman appears to be even more upset now by *my* perfectly innocent relationship with everyone in this house than she was by Félix's much more reprehensible one with *you*. However, I should not like to hurt Patrick in any way...nor lose his friendship, so I shall not ask.'

She smiled, 'There are many more things to worry over than any problems there may have been between Patrick and your mother; as I said, all that's in the past and should stay there.' She laid her hand on his where it rested on the table. 'How long is your leave?'

'I must return on Sunday morning to a new camp where I shall learn how to kill people quickly and efficiently before they get the chance to do the same to me.' He shrugged. 'Sooner or later I imagine I shall find myself back in France, but not in such a pretty uniform as I have no doubt my brother will manage!'

'What is he reckoning on doing then?'

'He is already *en réserve militaire* and says he will try to become *aide-de-camp* to some General and hope to spend the war well behind the lines!' He smiled without mirth. 'Knowing Félix, that's just what he'll do.'

She was thoughtful. 'Did you know Patrick has already been invited to an interview at the War Office? I gather Army Intelligence is on the cards...all those languages he has, I suppose.'

'He should be able to rest on his laurels...one hand is surely enough to have given!'

'We might say that,' she smiled, 'but I think Charlie has his measure when he says that Patrick's a natural born Don Quixote...and the Third Reich is an awfully tempting windmill. Given the chance he'll go all right.'

He covered her hand with his. 'And you?'

'Goodness knows. Make munitions, go into the Army...something, whatever seems the best thing to do. What is quite certain is that no one will make use of my eye for china and porcelain, nor be interested that I can spot a fake Ming vase at twenty feet,' she gave a rueful laugh and hunched her shoulders. 'When this war comes we shall all immediately stop doing the things we do well and start doing others a great deal less efficiently. Crazy, isn't it?'

'Completely,' he curled his fingers over hers. 'I might not be back for some time after this weekend, so will you come dancing at the Café de Paris tonight?'

She grinned. 'I'll sort out some glad rags. With you looking all so shiny and new I shall have to find something special to do you credit.' She glanced up as Patrick entered the room. 'Look who's come for lunch, Patrick...doesn't he look splendid?'

'Quite amazingly so,' Patrick's gaze flickered briefly over their joined hands. 'Charlie said you'd arrived. Can you stay for the weekend or must you rush off elsewhere?'

'No. I should like to stay, but only until Sunday. I've volunteered to help put in your shelter.'

'I can't see those pieces of tin withstanding much, but I suppose it might possibly give the illusion of safety if one had nowhere else to hide.' Patrick gave a dismissive wave of the hand. 'Personally, I think I'd rather take my chance lying in my own bed...not that any of us are likely to be here if and when the Luftwaffe decide to call.' He smiled at Anna's inquiringly raised brows. 'Yes...I've managed to rent the house I've been after at Tring, so at least we have somewhere to send Charlie with the contents of the gallery should it becomes necessary. We can just leave some basic furniture, food and pots and pans here for when any of us are in town, otherwise everything else can go.'

'Will you all move down there with Charlie?' queried Asa

innocently.

'Anna may if she wishes, but I have a feeling I shall be busy elsewhere. I gather that experienced not-so-old buffers who survived the last lot might be quite useful the second time around, so I imagine I shall not be allowed to moulder on the shelf for long.'

'Anyone who mentions the war in my hearing for the remainder of this weekend will be heavily fined,' announced Charlie, coming in on the end of Patrick's words. He lifted Anna away bodily from where she'd returned to the stove and took command. '*Spaghetti al Pomodoro* now, my friends then coffee and a nice rest before we start digging up the lawn!'

*   *   *

They toiled all afternoon digging the foundations for the shelter, Asa, unusually tousled and grubby in old jersey and corduroy trousers loaned by Charlie laboured uncomplainingly, matching Charlie's apparently effortless spadework. Anna stacked a mountain of turf and Patrick supplied beer and encouragement in generous quantities.

Later, after Charlie had called a halt to their labours, Anna lay relaxed in a gently steaming bath and listened to Asa singing under the shower in Patrick's bathroom. She stared unblinking at the wall, wondering if it was such a good idea to spend the evening in his arms, albeit only on the dance floor.

It was no use trying to fool herself, nor pretend that she didn't find him attractive. Memories of Félix were at last beginning to fade. He had not returned to England in months and managing life more or less successfully without him was something at which she'd had plenty of practice, enjoying a fair amount of light-hearted fun with others along the way. But the possibility that she might transfer her repressed emotions and physical needs to his brother had to be faced.

Sex, she thought honestly, was almost bound to rear its head. It always did. She had become good at dealing with that, but had a sneaking suspicion that with Asa it might prove a little more difficult than most; even thinking about him caused a disturbingly familiar stirring inside.

Lazily, she slid down to rinse off then reached for a towel, thinking that as he'd never made a pass in all these months, all she had to do was keep from dancing too close to those shining buttons and she'd be unlikely to make a fool of herself with the almost too much of a gentleman, Asa Gallimard.

*   *   *

The band was playing 'Goodnight Sweetheart' for the last dance; she was in Asa's arms and they couldn't have danced closer without risking arrest. At the vocalist's last "Goodnight" the music faded slowly, the lights dimmed and Anna found herself subjected to the most thorough, twenty-four-carat kiss she had ever received.

It was no Félix-style, frankly predatory preface to the swift removal of her clothes but a deeply sensuous and exploratory caress. One which said quite unmistakably, "This is nice, and I'm not going to pounce, but sooner or later I'm going to try a lot harder and expect a great deal more in return...if that's all right with you!

The lights came up and for a long moment they gazed into each other's eyes, then he bent his head, 'It's all right, worried grey eyes,' he whispered and chuckled softly, 'Ce n'est pas encore l'heure!'

*   *   *

It was past midnight; Patrick and Charlie had long since retired and the old house was settling into itself with a series of audible creaks and rustles.

They came in quietly, stealing up the stairs with their shoes in their hands, suppressing their giggles like a couple of errant children. Asa was merry and slightly tipsy, Anna a little more so. They were warm and comfortable and easy now in each other's company. There had been a few more undemanding kisses on the way home in the taxi and now Anna was enjoying the feeling that comes when one is playing with fire at a distance, knowing one is unlikely to get burned; at least, not just yet.

'Why did you call me 'worried grey eyes'?' she asked as he sat watching her make their coffee, his arms folded on the kitchen table.

He yawned, rubbed a lazy hand over his hair. 'Oh, you know – in the ladies journals. Shy girls asking questions about love: should they/shouldn't they sleep with their boyfriends? Then signing themselves worried blue/brown/grey/green eyes!' He smiled. 'Such questions from shy girls.'

'You shouldn't be reading the back pages of ladies journals. They are sinks of iniquity, full of thinly veiled references to sex!' Anna brought the two coffees to the table then seated herself opposite him. For a moment she regarded him with sober eyes then said softly. 'Thank you for tonight, and for not doing what you know quite well I would have let you do, given the right circumstances...'

His mouth twitched. 'The night isn't yet over and my room is close yours. It would be flattering to know that worries you.'

'Feel flattered,' she said dryly, 'because it does, but not enough to make me break the resolution I've just made to stay your friend.'

'Feel safe,' he answered, 'because I care about you...and tomorrow I shall leave without breaking either your resolution...or mine.' He smiled and raised his cup, 'to us and our joint resolutions!'

She looked at him over the rim of her own cup.

'Funny,' she observed innocently, 'How one's New Year resolutions are always broken within the month. What chance d'you think they have if made in February?'

He pursed his lips and eyed her speculatively.

'I guess we'll just have to wait and see about that, shan't we?' he said.

*   *   *

The next morning they walked together to the station, close, but not touching; Anna, acutely aware of his long body moving beside hers, knew that she would very much have liked to make love with him the previous night, and that had he made any move towards coming into her bed she might well have let him.

But that wouldn't have been good enough, because Félix was there in the background, and however hard she tried to keep him from her thoughts he was still a persistent wanted presence: one she was sure would have to be exorcised before Asa might make love to her, even if he wanted to. For all she knew of him, she thought, with sudden unease, Asa may well kiss every girl he danced with like that as a matter of course. They had hardly been the kisses of a novice.

When they reached the station he drew her into an alcove and put his hands on her shoulders, saying gravely. 'I have a problem...I have learned to march, to lead a parade without falling over those ridiculous ceremonial swords and how to salute properly, but...no one instructed me as to whether I should kiss a lady goodbye with or without the cap!'

She nodded across the booking hall. 'You could ask that Naval type over there.'

He shook his head. 'I think not. He's too handsome and might offer to demonstrate and I should not like that!' Still holding her a few inches away from him he bent his capped head and kissed her mouth. ''Till the next time,' he said and was gone, as always, without a backward glance.

123

13

BIGGIN HILL, SUSSEX

June 1939

Anna paced the hotel room, trying to convince herself that the sole reason she had agreed to this meeting was to tell Félix that she wouldn't meet again like this. In all these months he'd written no more than a half-dozen letters, unlike Asa, who since his posting to Hampshire had come to see her several times and written each week without fail.

She stopped her pacing and sat on the cushioned window seat to look out over the downs towards the sea, the familiar headache beginning to throb at her temples. It was a farcical situation in which she now found herself. For three years she'd been in love with Félix, who didn't love her, but appeared unable, or unwilling, to get out of her life. Now there was Asa, who may or may not be ever so slightly in love with her, and in whom she certainly had more than a passing interest.

But how could it be love she felt for Asa, she fretted. They still seemed destined to squabble each time they met; mostly, she had to admit, over Félix. He could irritate her almost beyond bearing then charm her back into good-humour and laughter in seconds. She loved being in his arms when they danced, the warmth of his slim and supple body close to hers. Asa, she thought, had the most beautifully flowing easy movements and even walked with an effortless grace that reminded her of Patrick. Certainly she wanted to be near him and frequently wakened from dreams of being again in his arms, but despite her feelings she was still undecided, unable to break the ties, however tenuous they may now be that bound her to Félix.

'You should give him the push.' Valerie had advised only last week, secure in her new position as wife of the handsome, wealthy and madly in love Naval Commander, who had swept her off her feet within weeks of her leaving school. 'I was telling Guy about him and he said he sounded a typical Froggie lecher and that you shouldn't trust him further than you could throw a grand piano.'

Anna had been amused at Valerie's earnest advice. 'I don't *have* a grand piano to throw – and I don't trust him, but that doesn't stop me thinking about bed when I'm in the same room with him...'

'For goodness sake...anyone would think he's the Sheik of Araby. Why don't you go to bed with Asa then perhaps you'll discover Félix is only a run-of-the-mill lover after all.'

'It's not that simple. I don't even know if Asa *wants* to go to bed with me...anyway, I'm pretty sure it isn't even a possibility while Félix is around.'

'Well then, as I said...give Félix the shove...'

Anna leaned her head against the hotel window now and sighed, thinking it was easy it was for Valerie to give advice; she'd never had to make choices but had apparently got it right the first time.

The telephone rang, startling her out of her reverie.

'*Allo, allo, bonjour, Anna...comment vas-tu?*'

She gave an exasperated sigh, 'Hanging around waiting for you, as usual. Where are you?'

'On my way,' he chuckled. 'I thought I would give you time to warm the bed!'

'I give you ten more minutes to get here before I leave to catch a train home, you cad.'

She slammed down the receiver then returned to the window seat unable, despite her words, to stop her heart leaping and turning in her breast.

'How does he do it?' she marvelled, 'After all these months with only a handful of frankly lousy letters, he's back with only one thing on his mind. So why am I such an idiot as to be just waiting for him to come through that door and rush me into bed?'

*   *   *

'Why were you so horrible to me on the telephone?'

She looked around from where she sat on the edge of the bed, dressing again to go down to dinner.

'Because sometimes it would be nice if you had the subtlety to at least pretend that you'd come for something beside sex.'

'Perhaps if you were scraggy and ugly I would!' He pulled on his trousers then leaned to kiss her shoulder. 'But what else would we do but fuck after so long?'

'You could take me dancing.'

'A waste of time, but I will if you wish after dinner, but not for too long. I have other plans for you and me.'

She was sarcastic. 'If you're sure you can spare the time,'

'How can you be so cruel...this may be our last meeting before I

125

go to war!'

'What, with a nice cushy job trotting around behind some brass hat?'

He was instantly suspicious. 'Who told you that?'

'Asa, of course, who else; not your Mama, that's for sure.'

He began to laugh. 'Did you know that Asa and maman had the most tremendous row just before he returned to this country?'

'Yes. He said.'

'Maman was cataleptic with rage and smashed some crockery against the wall.' He waved a sock dramatically above his head. 'I think she was trying to hit Asa. But he is very light on his feet so only the wallpaper was scarred!'

'He didn't tell *me* that.'

'She cannot bear the idea that he is so friendly with your family because of what happened years ago with that Patrick of yours...she is like an elephant; she never forgets a wrong...or forgives one.'

Anna stopped in the act of pulling her jersey over her head.

'How on earth do you know about your mother and Patrick?'

'Oh...another one of her rages...a long time ago when she was angry because I had seen you, she told me that he had done her family a great wrong.' He tapped the side of his nose. 'She would not say more but *I* suspect it is to do with an *affaire* she had with him.'

'Well I *know* what happened, and it has nothing to do with your mother having an affair with anyone.'

'Tell me.' His eyes were full of mischievous inquiry.

'I shall do no such thing.'

He gave a yelp of laughter. 'Your Patrick seduced my mama, didn't he? Come Anna, you can tell me!'

'Of course he didn't,' she was scathing. 'Don't be so ridiculous, Félix.'

'Well, *something* went on, or she would not fly into such rages.' He began to button his shirt, giving a slow, irritating grin. 'Perhaps Asa knows. You must ask him the next time he comes visiting.'

'No. I'll leave being a nosy bastard to you.'

'Such language!'

She looked at him crossly. 'It describes you pretty accurately... Asa is a gentleman, whereas you are, and always will be, a cad.'

'Such a very English word – cad!' he mocked, then caught her hand and pulled her into his arms. 'But having this *cad* make love to you is better than walking and talking with the dull and so-proper Asa, *n'est-ce pas?*'

He felt her involuntary response to his embrace and grinned again in a particularly self-satisfied way that made her push him back onto the bed in sudden irritation. 'No one would ever guess that you two were brothers,' she snapped, 'you couldn't be less alike.'

'That is because we are not brothers...' he stopped at her startled look. 'You didn't know that?'

'No, how could I? I'm not exactly *au fait* with the Gallimard family history!' She sat on the edge of the bed beside him, her irritation fading rapidly to be replaced by curiosity. 'Explain...'

'I do not know any details. An aunt of my father told me many years ago that Asa and I were not brothers. Asa knows more but we've only spoken of it once. It is not a thing my mother would ever allow to be discussed,' He shrugged. 'His father deserted his mother before he was born.'

'The louse!'

'Yes, that is how Asa feels also. He said he despised a man who couldn't control his impulses, nor face up to his responsibilities.'

She thought, Oh ho, did he! 'How intriguing,' she said then frowned. 'I just can't imagine Madame adopting a baby; she's not exactly the maternal type is she? And why should she when she was obviously capable of having her own – she had you, didn't she?'

'It wasn't like that. Asa is the child of maman's little sister.' Félix shrugged. 'She was barely out of the schoolroom and not married... there was a big scandal. Perhaps it was just as well that she died giving birth.'

Anna's stomach gave a great lurch and she clutched at the bed rail as the room began to spin around her. She was aware that Félix was holding her; could see his startled face and hear his voice coming as though from a great distance. She tried to speak, then there was a roaring in her ears and she went spinning down a long dark tunnel towards oblivion.

*   *   *

When she came to again she was lying on the bed with Félix bending over her, pressing a cold damp towel to her forehead.

'Anna...Anna...are you all right? *Sacre nom de Dieu* but you gave me a fright!' He sat her up, supporting her on his arm. 'What made you do that?'

'I don't know.' Her head was clearing and she thought rapidly, hunting around for a plausible excuse that would satisfy him. 'I've had a cold...' she put her hand to her throbbing head. 'I just fainted, that's all; nothing to worry about.'

'Are you well enough to dine? Perhaps you should lie down again.'

'No!'

Suddenly it was a matter of urgency to get away from this room and Félix's questioning. She must have time and space to think. Perhaps she had just jumped to the wrong conclusions...She took a deep breath, steadying herself.

'We'll have dinner. I'm sorry but after that I think I'd rather get the train back home. I'm not feeling strong enough to cope with you tonight!' She tried to soften her words with a smile. 'I'm afraid you'd be dodging the landlord to creep in after dark for very little reward for your trouble.'

He looked as disappointed as a child deprived of candy. 'Very well if you think it best, I will see you to your train then go back to the airfield and find Louis and drink away my sorrows.' He looked into her eyes with a sudden grin. 'Was it not fortunate that we managed to warm the bed *before* dinner?'

* * *

In the train she began to put her thoughts in some kind of order.

It could, she reasoned, be one of those strange coincidences, but if Cecelia had been a young and innocent girl of seventeen and Patrick her first lover, would she then have found someone else and conceived a child in such a short space of time? No, it all fitted a little too conveniently for comfort. August, nineteen-fourteen to May, nineteen fifteen when Asa was born, left no realistic time lapse. He *had* to be Patrick's son.

She sat back, feeling the prickle of sweat begin on her scalp. No wonder Dorothy Gallimard had been so incensed; so determined to keep both Félix and Asa from any contact with the Farrell family.

She thought about the repercussions this could have for them all if the truth was ever to become known. How would it affect the relationship between Patrick and Charlie? – Patrick and Asa? – Asa and her?

Her head began to spin again.

She would have to keep what she knew to herself, if that were possible, but it wouldn't be easy. Patrick had a sixth sense for when she was upset or troubled and Charlie was equally shrewd and sharp. She tried without success to imagine Asa's reaction to such news. For his mother to die at his birth after having been deserted by his father was bad enough. To discover that he'd unwittingly made a friend of

128

the father he must despise could be simply devastating, and however broad-minded he may be, his awareness of that father's sexuality would be an additional burden to bear. As for Patrick, that most honest of men, whose integrity was the cornerstone of his life, the knowledge that he had quite literally destroyed the life of an innocent human being would be devastating.

She was overwhelmed by her dilemma. To keep the truth from all three of them would be fiendishly difficult, but to let slip any hint of what she knew could lay to waste the lives of all those she most loved.

She raged inwardly. *To hell with you Félix...why did you have to say it? Why, with your typical, insouciant bloody gossiping have you just managed to threaten to blow my world apart?*

*   *   *

'Why are you back quite so soon?' Charlie's tone was carefully neutral. Anna's resumption of her occasional meetings with Félix was a constant irritation, but he worked hard at trying not to show his disapproval. 'Didn't he turn up after all?'

She said evasively, 'He arrived, yes. But I felt a bit groggy so I thought I'd come home.'

'Have you had dinner?' She nodded, he looked at her keenly and she shifted her gaze from his. 'What's up?' he asked.

'Nothing I can't deal with, Charlie. I'll just go and say hello to Patrick then I think I'm for bed...I presume he's in the gallery doing something or other.'

'Uh, huh; oh, and Asa 'phoned just after you left to say he'll be up next week-end.'

She halted in the doorway and forced a smile. 'Better kill the fatted calf then; keep feeding him up the way you do Charlie, and he'll be bursting out of that uniform!'

She went into the gallery, where she found Patrick absorbed in brushing dust out of the intricate carving on a Japanese screen. He grunted a greeting as she took up another brush and joined him at his task.

She said, 'You're working late...and before you ask, I just decided to return tonight, that's all!'

'Good.' Unlike Charlie, he never made the slightest attempt to be tactful about Félix. 'I was hoping perhaps the Army had caught up with him at last.'

'No. You'll have to hope on.'

They worked in silence for several minutes then without looking up he asked, 'Want to talk?'

She hedged, 'About what?'

'Whatever it might be that's on your mind.' He straightened and put aside his brush. 'I can practically hear the cogs turning!'

She concentrated on the task in hand. 'I'm still trying to sort it out myself.' She looked up thoughtfully. 'Patrick, tell me about confession ...when you go does it make everything come right for you...solve your problems, that sort of thing?'

He smiled thinly. 'Not necessarily. The telling helps, and so does the advice and absolution, but one still has to put in a lot of hard work sorting out the difficulties one has made for oneself...or others. Why? Have *you* something you need to confess?'

'Haven't we all?' she asked, obliquely, 'but I'm afraid I'd never find the courage to wash my dirty linen in front of anyone, even a priest...come to think of it especially a priest, my dirty linen being the way it is.'

'Are you in some kind of trouble?'

'No. You may set your mind at rest on that point. Rather, it's someone else's trouble.'

'Then don't try to sort it for them. It's almost always a mistake. Let sleeping dogs lie; an old and somewhat trite maxim, but true none-the-less.'

'That's your considered advice then, is it?'

'Yes, but you'd undoubtedly get better in the confessional.'

'Thank you kindly, but I think I'll stick with yours.' She bent her head over the screen, hiding her face from his direct gaze. 'It's what I wanted to hear, anyway.'

'Good.' He leaned and took the brush from her hand. 'Leave that for tonight. Come up and have a night cap with Charlie and me and leave any problems until the morning. Everything looks better in the morning light, you know.'

Undoubtedly it does, she thought as she followed him, but she had a nasty feeling that an awful lot of unsettling thoughts would continue to haunt her nights well into the future. She just hoped she could deal with them when they came and still keep her secret safe.

14

HALLESBURY CAMP, DORSET

May 27th, 1940 – 13.00 hrs.

Anna sat at her desk in the Platoon-hut, making heavy weather of the pay returns while keeping an ear half-cocked for the news coming in over the radio in the next room. When a sudden burst of laughter from a group of girls passing the window drowned the announcer's words, she swore loudly and raised her voice. 'Davis, either bring that damned thing in here or turn it up! I can't work on this bumph when I'm only hearing half of what's going on...'

'Sorry Corp.' Davis' untamed hair and lugubrious face appeared around the door. 'It won't go any louder – the batteries are fading. As we can't all fit into your office to listen why don't you leave that and come out here?'

'All right...just keep your eyes peeled for the Adjutant. She wants these returns by 15.00.'

Anna joined the crowd in the outer office in time to hear Alvar Liddel's calm and beautifully modulated tones announcing that the German Army had taken Boulogne, thus effectively cutting off the British and French troops and sealing the fate of those caught between the rapidly advancing enemy and the sea.

There was a silence. Somebody said: 'Reckon Adolf will be in Brighton next, girls...' and Anna turned back into her office to hide the sudden moisture that sprung to her eyes.

Sitting at her desk she stared at the blurred figures dancing across the pages before her. Somewhere out there, amongst the hundreds of thousands of troops now being crowded back towards the sea, were Asa and Félix. Suddenly, she felt sick with the longing to be again at Stratton Place; to be back with Patrick and Charlie and done with the business of war...

Aeons ago it seemed she had stood with Patrick on a chill September morning, viewing the criss-crossed brown tape now marring the elegant curved windows of the Gallery. 'Have you made your mind up yet what you are going to do?' he'd asked her. 'Will you camp out here or go down to Tring with Charlie and guard the treasures?'

131

'Neither. Did you think I would?'

He'd smiled 'Not really.'

'I'm following your example: On Monday I shall take the King's shilling. A frightfully efficient woman in khaki told me at the recruiting office that if I'm a very good girl in time they may even teach me to be an officer and gentlewoman!'

'I don't see it.' He'd smiled again and shaken his head. 'All that "my women" lark; the army just isn't you.'

'It just isn't any of us,' she'd replied soberly, and then the vans had arrived to take to the safety of the country all the crated pictures, the tapestries, statues and beautiful *objets d'art* that had been their world...

She passed an unsteady hand across her face and picked up her pen. Tonight she'd find the time to 'phone Charlie; just to hear his familiar voice and gain some comfort in this mad and dangerous world that had taken those she loved, tossing them heedlessly into the maelstrom of war.

'Corp!' She looked up. Davis was at the door again. 'Better take a look at the notice board; Archer's just come over – your OCTU course is posted. Lucky you to be getting out of this dump...wish I was.'

*   *   *

Anna put up her white tabs, moved to a dingy hutted camp in Hampshire identical to the one she'd just left, and settled down with twenty-three other women of varying ages, shapes and sizes, to concentrate on becoming an officer and temporary gentlewoman.

She had sailed more or less effortlessly from private through lance corporal and corporal and thought that she might in time become a reasonably efficient Subaltern. She was not particularly well suited to Army life, but had quickly grasped that all she needed to keep her head above water was to simply accept whichever role was allotted her by the great Producer at WAAC Headquarters then play it according to the best of her ability.

The necessary drills, tests and exercises of the OCTU course caused her no difficulties, but in those first days of June her mind was constantly on the reports coming through from France. After the evacuations from Dunkirk began she spent every spare moment hanging over the radio, listening to the dismal news filtering through from the beaches. Then as the evacuation gathered pace and the little boats set out in their hundreds to join the big ships steaming across the

English Channel, the impossible looked as though it may indeed become possible.

Eight days after the evacuation began she was called to the Company office.

'There is an urgent telephone call for you, Farrell...a Major Caulder.'

Anna kept her elation firmly under control. Good old Charlie...who was to know he was now Major Caulder of the Local Volunteer Reserve!

'You really should not be receiving telephone calls here,' the Adjutant continued, 'but as Major Caulder say's it is about your immediate family and of the utmost importance you may take it.'

'Thank you, ma'am,' she lifted the receiver, holding it tight against her ear to keep Charlie's clear tones from ringing across the office. 'Cadet Farrell speaking, sir.'

'Who the hell was that old Gorgon?' he snorted, 'just thought you'd like to know: Asa's back in one piece.'

Anna closed her eyes briefly and steadied herself with a hand on the desk. 'Thank you, sir...is there news of anyone else?'

'You didn't think *he'd* get his arse singed, did you?' He was sarcastic. 'I gather he flew from Paris headquarters with his Colonel as the Germans marched in. He's still being de-briefed and Patrick's nosing around to find out what's happening to the pair of them. I'll let you know more by letter.'

'Thank you, sir. That's very kind of you.'

'Not at all, Cadet Farrell; kiss that old Gorgon for me!'

'Yes, sir.'

She put down the receiver, met the Adjutant's eyes and without a flicker of her own lied shamelessly. 'That was to tell me some members of my family have landed safely from France, ma'am.'

'I'm very glad it was good news.' Her face contorted in what Anna recognised as a smile. 'You may return to your platoon.'

'Ma'am,' she saluted and left. Outside the door she leaned against the wall of the hut, suddenly weak as the tension of these last few days left her body. They were safe, both of them. *Oh, God*... For a moment she closed her eyes again, *if you're up there and you've time to listen...Thank you...Oh, thank you!*

*   *   *

Some fell by the wayside, but Anna completed OCTU, came out top of her platoon, put up her well-earned pips, tucked her leave pass and travel warrant into the breast pocket of her crisp new uniform and headed for Tring and a lot of cosseting from Charlie.

*   *   *

DOVE HOUSE, TRING

August 10th, 1940

'Your little Flittermouse,' Charlie informed her as they sat over their coffee on the first evening, 'has fallen on his feet again all right...*aide de camp* to some French Military *Attaché* in Alexandria. God knows what either of them is supposed to do out there to help the war effort. Patrick says that particular posting should be named the jammy-bastard's war!' He looked at her sharply. 'But Félix has probably told you all this.'

'No,' she was non-committal, 'wars aren't best arranged for continuing the sort of relationship that Félix and I have...or any relationship anyone might have, come to that.'

'I thought that all might have died down by now.'

'So it has, to a degree. I'm perfectly all right while he is at a distance.' She gave a wry smile. 'Don't ask me to explain because I can't. I don't even understand it myself. Putting it all in perspective I think what keeps me from the final break is my aesthetic pleasure and enjoyment of his physical beauty and the frankly amoral honesty of his intentions! He is peculiarly endearing in his outright opportunism and there has to be something in me that responds to that.' She smiled again. 'You see, I really can be very grown-up about it now. I'm no longer crying for the moon.'

'I'm sure that's a relief. Asa said you spoke on the 'phone to *him* for fifteen minutes without getting into an argument. That must be a record!'

'Yes. He was in London and it cost him a fortune. I can't think what he's doing hanging around for so long. Patrick said he's given him a key to Stratton Place and the pair of them are playing Box and Cox; each half-living there but scarcely ever at the same time.'

'It's odd, isn't it...' he leaned to reach for his cigarettes, 'how alike those two are sometimes? Not in looks but just the way they are.'

'How do you mean?' She was immediately wary, taking out her own cigarette packet, selecting one carefully then fiddling longer than necessary with her recalcitrant lighter.

134

'Hadn't you noticed?' He knit his brows in thought. 'The way they speak and move... I've never seen either of them make an extravagant gesture.'

'You should see Asa pissed!' she returned lightly. 'I can assure you that extravagant doesn't even begin to describe him.'

They laughed together then. The uncomfortable moment passed and Anna subtly, she hoped, steered their talk to other matters.

She thought about the conversation later as she got ready for bed and wondered whether Charlie's remarks were quite as innocent as they appeared, or if he had perhaps seen something more than a surface likeness between the two? Because ever since Félix had dropped his bombshell over a year ago, *she* had been reminded, again and again of their undoubted relationship...The way, as Charlie had observed that they moved, the twist of austerity in speech, the calm, steady eyes that missed nothing...No immediate likeness in their features, only just those shared and teasingly similar mannerisms unlikely to be noticed by the casual observer, and not really apparent unless one looked for them. But Charlie was not a casual observer: rather, a highly intelligent, very keen-eyed onlooker, who missed very little in the ways and idiosyncrasies of his fellow human beings.

* * *

Asa came the following day, on a glorious early evening, when the trees were heavy with blossom and a carpet of flowers fringed the lawn at Dove House.

Anna was setting the supper things on the long iron table under the trees when a pair of arms came around her waist and a familiar voice asked, 'How's worried grey eyes then?'

'Not worried any more.' She turned in his arms, putting up her mouth to his as though it were the most natural thing in the world, and he kissed her with great thoroughness before releasing her again.

She was startled at how thin and tired-looking he was, with a new hardness about his face. Then he touched her cheek, his mouth lifting in the familiar smile and the laughter was back in the brown eyes. He said, 'That was worth waiting for!' and stroked a finger over the sleeve of her blouse. 'I was afraid you would still be in khaki, wearing one of those quite dreadful hats and feeling duty bound to salute me.' He stood her back, his dark eyes inspecting her minutely, his eyes lingering on the row of tiny pearl buttons from waist to neck. 'Umm – I remember that blouse from Paris...Charlie will need to lend me something for this evening so that I can match your pre-war elegance.'

'That would be nice…we can pretend it's nineteen-thirty-something and the long summer vacation has just begun. We'll raid Charlie's wardrobe now.' She regarded him thoughtfully then grinned. 'You can have anything but his kilt; you don't have the knees for that.'

'How would you know?' he teased, 'you've never seen my knees, although I'll be happy to oblige.'

'That won't be necessary; at an educated guess I'd say they're nowhere near braw' enough!' She laughed and took his arm to lead him back into the house. 'Come along, get changed, then we can all relax and catch up on our news while we eat.'

*   *   *

He was reticent and not forthcoming about what he was doing in London. Anna noticed he'd still worn the same regimental badges, but was obviously not in barracks, or taking part in any army manoeuvres. Studying him covertly, she tried to imagine him behind a desk in Whitehall, but failed. Whatever it was that kept him in the capital, she was sure it was unlikely to be a mundane desk job.

'How much leave have you left?' he asked her as the three of them sat at ease beneath the trees, to smoke and empty the bottle of wine Charlie had dredged from the cellar. 'I'm on indefinite at the moment and thought if Charlie could put up with me I'd spend most of it here; just walking and relaxing while I wait for my recall.'

'Stay as long as you like.' Charlie offered. 'But Anna goes back on Sunday…' He turned to her, 'That's right, isn't it?'

'Unfortunately yes. Just five more days before I report to my new unit in the depths of Essex.'

'Then we shall make the most of them.' Asa's dark eyes held hers for moment then he smiled. 'Perhaps we can walk and relax together, that's if Charlie doesn't mind.'

'Leave me out of it,' he said comfortably. 'Between this place and the Home Guard, as we are now known, I get precious little free time to spend with anyone…Which reminds me,' he groaned and pushed himself out of his chair. 'Got to go and get into the glad rags. I'm on duty tonight and have to get my lot out and ready to repel any German paratroopers attempting to land in his Lordship's cabbage fields!'

After he had left they remained sitting in the gathering dusk, chatting and telling their news, Asa passing lightly over the shambles in France, Anna describing her progression from private to subaltern, making him laugh uproariously at her experiences in the ranks of the

136

ATS.

'Now I shall go back and sit in another dusty platoon-hut in Essex and worry about the cooks turning good food into inedible swill, inspect outbreaks of athlete's foot and try to decide who's grandmother is *really* dying so that they need immediate leave, etc, etc.,' She said gloomily. 'I'm sure male officers in a similar job have exactly the same problems, except that *their* OR's are unlikely to fall weeping on the floor as mine undoubtedly will when told to get lost!'

He looked up reflectively into the blossom above his head. 'I did have a Welsh batman in France who got tears in his eyes over the blisters from his Army boots, but then he was an emotional Celt and an exhibition ballroom dancer before the war, so I suppose that was to be expected.'

'Let's hope his feet get back to normal and he'll be able to resume his occupation.'

'I don't think so.' He blew a smoke ring into the still air. 'The last time I saw him he was minus both of them and most of one leg.'

She was silent for a moment then sighed. 'It's a shit war, isn't it?'

'Every war's a shit war.' Abruptly, he uncoiled his long length and stood up. 'Better clear these things before we start getting maudlin...'

*   *   *

Anna finished stacking the dishes in the sink and reached for a tea towel. 'You wash, I'll dry, men don't dry crockery properly; they think a quick wipe is all that's required. Come to think of it, they don't wash-up very well, either!'

Asa grinned and flicked soapy water. She called him a rude name and snapped the tea towel at his legs. Catching it he pulled her towards him joking: 'Don't you know, Subaltern Farrell, that you face disciplinary action for cursing, let alone striking, a superior officer?'

For a moment they stood close, then he pulled her into a tight embrace and his mouth, hard and demanding now found hers. They swayed, locked in each other's arms for what seemed an eternity. Anna was intensely conscious of the hushed house around them and the fact that they were alone in its silence. Asa's heart thudded against her own and she shuddered involuntarily as the fire began to run through her. He moved one hand to slowly unbutton her blouse. Sliding his palm beneath her brassiere and cupping her breast he breathed, 'I had absolutely no intention of doing this tonight. It isn't right, it certainly isn't sensible, but I have to say that I'm in love with

137

you and I want you more than I've ever wanted anything in my life.'

When he pushed the blouse from her shoulders she looked up into his eyes. 'Asa...?'

He smiled, answering her unspoken question. 'It is all right, worried grey eyes,' he murmured. 'Only virgins and saints go unprepared, and I am neither!'

*　　*　　*

Drowsily he asked, 'I hope that was the genuine article and not just done because you were too polite to tell me to sod off?'

She put her fingers over his mouth and murmured, 'Shut up, Asa,' then almost at once fell asleep with her head buried in his shoulder.

He looked down on the dark curls, then closing his eyes fitted his long body to hers, holding her close as the night air began to cool his shoulders. 'Whatever you say, Anna, *je t'aime*, whatever you say.'

*　　*　　*

Charlie surveyed first the dishes still reposing in the sink then turned his eyes to where two shirts lay discarded on the floor. Smiling, he bent to pick them up then rolling his sleeves began to run the hot tap. 'Just *stay* in Alexandria with your brass hat, will you, Mr. Félix bloody Gallimard,' he muttered under his breath, 'and let those two get on with their lives in peace!'

*　　*　　*

Anna woke with the feel of Asa's naked body warm beside her and his breath light on her forehead. Propping herself on one elbow she kissed his closed eyelids and ran a finger across his chest.

'Did we actually do what I think we did?'

He stirred, his mouth curving into a grin. 'We did, and more than once!'

'So we did.' She prodded him gently. 'It's morning. If Charlie isn't back already he soon will be, and he'll not expect you to be in my bed. You should get up *now*.'

He kept his eyes closed. 'If you want me to leave, you might have phrased that better!'

She smothered a giggle. 'Don't try to teach me my own language, Gallimard.'

'Come here.' He rolled and pulled her to him again. 'There are

138

better things to teach. Much better also, to work up an appetite for one of Charlie's breakfasts.'

He began slowly to move his mouth down over her neck and throat; she caught his head between her hands. 'I like *that...*'

'And this?' he trailed his lips lower murmuring, '*Nom de Dieu,* but that is sweet...'

Under the caressing mouth she felt as though her very bones were melting. Half agonised, half laughing she twisted her fingers in his hair. 'Now,' she begged, 'Asa, for pity's sake *now!*' He lifted his head and stared into her eyes for a moment then chuckled softly and slid swiftly up her body. 'Now it is then – *et avec le plus grand plaisir!*' he said and filled her again.

         *   *   *

Pink-faced and wearing an air of bravado like a shield she left Asa dressing in his own room and went in search of breakfast.

'Had a good night?' Charlie asked from the stove, turning bubble-and-squeak with a practised hand. She cleared her throat.

'Sorry about leaving all the washing-up – we did start, but...'

'You just couldn't manage to finish it, eh?'

'Something like that,' she smiled uncertainly, 'are you cross with me?'

'No.'

'No lecture?'

'No, but,' he gave her a straight look, 'don't play about with him, Anna.'

'That is the very last thing...' She touched his cheek. 'Stop being a mother hen, Charlie. Save that for Patrick.'

'Well, you can tell *him* what you've been up to if you wish. I won't.'

She looked gloomy. 'Knowing Patrick, I doubt I'll need to. Sometimes I think he just plucks things out of the air,' she looked at him sideways, 'any chance of his appearing while I'm here?'

'I think not. He's kept pretty busy.'

''Morning, Charlie,' Asa came into the kitchen with his usual smooth tread and none of Anna's embarrassment. 'I thought of climbing the hill up to Little Tring this morning.' He gave a theatrical leer, 'Providing I can find the energy, of course.'

She pointed at a chair, 'Just take that Cheshire cat grin off your face and sit down before Charlie takes a horse whip to you!'

Charlie flipped the bubble and squeak onto a hot plate then broke three of his precious fresh eggs into the pan. He gave an audible sigh. 'If I give you a packet of sandwiches, Asa, will you keep madam out of my hair for a few hours while I make up for the sleep I didn't get last night? I'd forgotten how quickly peace flies out of the window whenever she shows her face...I blame Patrick. I shall speak to him about it.'

She looked at him over the rim of her cup. 'Funny,' she answered, 'that's exactly what he said about *you* that time I got up his nose in Paris!'

*   *   *

They stopped to eat their picnic under the spreading arms of an ancient oak. Asa unbuttoned his shirt, flapping it slowly in an effort to cool his chest. He eyed Anna's brief cotton shorts and blouse enviously.

'In that outfit you look nothing like an officer and gentlewoman.'

'I don't look much like one in uniform, either...or at least, I don't *feel* it, and I'm told that's half the battle towards actually being one.' She grinned back at him over her shoulder as she bent to unpack the basket. 'I don't know that I'll be very good at this lark. I'll probably end the war as the only subaltern that never put anyone on a charge. Having been one of the great unwashed for the best part of a year I don't think I could bring myself to do it.'

'Do as I do. If you spot any wrongdoing, look the other way and just walk!'

She laughed. 'What a trial we must be to all those hide-bound regulars. I suspect even Charlie would look somewhat askance if you admitted as much to him.' She peered closely at the sandwiches. 'You have a choice of bully beef or bully beef.'

'I'll have the bully beef...but first...' He sat up, propping his elbows on his knees. 'I'm afraid I've been wrestling with my conscience since I arrived yesterday. I almost made up my mind I wouldn't tell you then decided I would have to be my usual honest self.'

She looked at him through narrowed eyes. 'You've seen Félix.'

'Good God,' he jumped. 'I thought it was only Patrick who did that; do you two share a crystal ball?'

'No, your eyes give you away every time.'

'That's bad news. I shall have to work on that.' He was silent for a moment, putting down a hand and plucking absently at the grass. 'He came to tell me that before he left Paris he'd gone to maman's

140

apartment to try and make her return to this country, but she'd already gone. A neighbour said she'd left almost a week before with a woman friend who has a chalet somewhere in the Pyrenees, quite close to the Spanish border. I suppose they felt they would be as safe there as anywhere.'

'Where did you meet with him?'

He couldn't bear to look at her face, knowing she'd be unable to hide her disappointment. 'In London; shortly after we both got back from France.'

'I see.'

He took her hand. 'Isn't it time to let go?' His voice held a mixture of anger and compassion. 'Four years of living in hope is surely enough?'

She gave a shaky smile. 'It isn't quite like that anymore, but it still hurts.'

He was silent a moment, then said quietly. 'I want you to know and understand that I love you very much; I think I have done so for years. Last night was not just a pleasant interlude but an expression of that love. When, or if, you can leave Félix out of your life, I give you fair warning that I shall ask you to marry me...and keep on asking until you say Yes!'

She looked at him expressionlessly. 'What makes you think *Félix* hasn't already decided to stay out of my life? After all, he couldn't be bothered to travel a handful of miles to see me when he came back from France, could he?'

He shook his head. 'Don't fool yourself, Anna...I've watched you with Félix since you first set eyes on him. I've lived with him most of my life and I *know* what he can do. It may not be love he gives, but it's a pretty powerful substitute and appears to work as well at a distance as it does close up.' He put his palm against her own, curling and twining his fingers with hers. 'I told myself I wouldn't make love to you until he was out of the way; wouldn't ever put myself in the position where I caught the crumbs that fell from his table...and now I find I've done just that.' For a moment his mouth went down at the corners. 'It seems we both have the same problem, do we not? You wait for Félix to love you, and I for you to love me. What are the odds think you, on one or the other of us getting what we want?'

Anna was silent. What *did* she really want: the casual, manipulative and ultimately bruising relationship with Félix, or Asa's tender and infinitely subtler passion?

Last night all the romance and loving she had yearned for from Félix she had found in Asa's arms. In contrast to Félix's swift and

141

well-practised approach, his lovemaking had been unhurried and deeply sensuous. With rare sensitivity he had led her, and allowed her to lead him, in an exploration of each other that was tender and intensely erotic, firing in her a deep and passionate response. It was as though he drew from her all that was intimate and ardently loving, while Félix was the Puck-like spirit who could in minutes sweep her with him into a shallow and wanton sexual excess, then afterwards walk away without the slightest sign of regret at leaving her.

Eventually she looked up and met Asa's intent gaze.

'Last night was quite the most beautiful thing that has ever happened to me,' she said honestly. 'I loved your body and everything it did to mine, and I love *you*. But I can't just forget what Félix has meant to me in the past. If the bastard turns up on my doorstep in a month, or even in twelve month's time, although I promise I'll keep him at arm's length it won't be easy and I can give no guarantee I'll be totally immune. So…' she tightened her hand on his, 'can you bear to go on taking me as I am right now, and trust me to break free of him? Or are you going to be all uptight and moral and say: 'Goodbye, Anna, it was nice knowing you, *but*…''

'It *is* nice knowing you, and I am happy to go on knowing you, and yes I can trust you and take you as you are. *But*,' he gave a bemused, half-sad smile, 'I may well be "all uptight and moral" should you ever find yourself back in bed with Félix. Because, my very dear Anna, I will not willingly share you with anyone, least of all my own brother.'

He saw the sudden flicker in her eyes before she slid her gaze from his and he tilted his head to peer at her intently, asking, 'Why do I have the feeling that you've just thought of something you'd rather I didn't know?'

She looked at him straight-faced and said reasonably, 'Well if I had would I tell you?'

He let go his hold on her hand and reached to take a sandwich from the basket, observing with equal reasonableness, 'You know Anna, there are times when I really would like to slap you rather hard!'

'I know.' She grinned. 'And if you didn't think I'd slap you right back, you'd damned well do it, wouldn't you?'

15

LONDON

July 20th, 1940 – 12.00 hrs

Asa ran up the staircase, paused before the anonymous oak door to rub his sleeve over his Sam Browne and straighten his cap, then knocked and entered. Closing the door behind him he turned and saluted.

Over his spectacles Patrick gave him an austere look. 'You don't have to stand there doing your impersonation of a tailor's dummy when we're alone!' He took off his glasses, gesturing to the chair beside his desk. 'Sit down, you idiot.'

'When you 'phoned I thought it might be a message recalling me to that bloody awful training camp.' Asa sat, taking off his cap and flexing his shoulders. 'That ape of an instructor almost broke my arm and I ended up on the sick list.'

'Well, you can go forth and break someone else's now if necessary, although it might be more politic to keep a lower profile.' Patrick fiddled with his letter opener for a moment. 'I'm sorry to get you up here in the middle of your leave but I wanted a talk. I'm off again myself in the morning and a damned good job too. I'm beginning to get desk-bound.'

He's nervous about this... Asa took a covert look at Patrick, who was now staring at his blotter, his mouth drawn into a tight line. He puzzled over a conversation overheard at the camp between the Colonel-in-charge and his Adjutant. *He* did *try to stop me going there,* he mused silently, *it's not like him, he thinks everyone should do anything they're asked to do in this war, regardless of consequence, so why worry about me in particular?*

'For the past week the buggers have been using the airfields along the French Coast to target our Channel shipping,' Patrick began abruptly, 'now they've started raiding along our south coast as well. We all know that something very nasty is building, but as yet we've nothing like the firepower needed to hit back effectively. The most we can hope for is some organised information gathering and a spot of well targeted sabotage by the French underground.' He looked up then and gave a faint smile. 'Just the sort of thing your fledgling SOE are dying to cut their teeth on. One of their chaps is already there getting the various groups together and is in urgent need of help. That's where you'll come in.'

Asa cleared his throat. 'Any idea how long I might be away?'

'I can't say; I don't run that particular show, thank God. I shouldn't be telling you as much as I have and I wouldn't if I didn't know you could keep your mouth shut.' He stood up and reached for his cap. 'Now I think there's just time for us to talk of other things over a civilised lunch before you become swallowed up by those Special Forces chaps.'

*   *   *

Asa watched Patrick fetch their drinks from the bar and when he was seated opposite him said quietly. 'If it's not breaching any confidences, I'd like to ask you a question.'

Patrick gave him a straight but reserved look. 'Ask away.'

'I think...no, I'm sure, that someone tried to keep me out of this outfit. Was it you?'

'What makes you so sure *anyone* tried to keep you out?'

'That's an old trick...answering one question with another. I overheard something I wasn't supposed to on my course...it was you, wasn't it? Why? You know I'm anxious to go.'

'Because it's much too soon: you've hardly been back above a month, and the majority of that spent in pretty intensive training.'

'I'm fit enough; they wouldn't have passed me otherwise.'

'They're grabbing everyone they can who'll be of use. An enthusiastic Anglo-French national already in the army and familiar with the terrain is a gift to them.' He was caustic. 'You need longer to recover from fighting your way across France and a more lengthy period of training – for God's sake, most agents get months to prepare – and let's face it; you look more like an Eytie than a Frenchman and I'm told your Morse code is a disaster!'

Asa was half-amused, half-exasperated. 'Oh, come *on*, there has to be more to it than that.'

Patrick answered coldly. 'Well, that's all you're getting. *I* can tell you things, but *you* may not ask.'

'I know. I'm sorry.' Asa took a drink then sat swirling the liquid around his glass. 'That was not very tactful of me, particularly as I've something I ought to tell you before I go. After all, there's no guarantee that I'll be coming back, is there?'

'I imagine not.'

144

'A pity,' he was ironic, 'because I've recently told the woman I want to marry that I'm in love with her.'

'Oh,' his companion's face was impassive. 'And what did Anna say?'

Asa gave him a cryptic look. 'Not a lot, sir, however, at least some of my feelings appear to be returned...I think.'

He answered dryly. 'There *are* easier women.'

'Unfortunately, I happen to be in love with one of the awkward ones.'

'She'll give you one hell of a rough ride from time to time. Just try to remember that she's nothing like as tough as she appears.'

'I'm discovering that quite quickly.' Asa rubbed his chin, hesitated a moment, then owned, 'Before she went back we agreed that whichever of us saw you first would tell you we've been sleeping together down at Tring, because neither of us felt it was fair to leave Charlie holding the can.' He kept his eyes firmly on the desk, unsure of what the enigmatic Patrick's reaction might be to the news that a second Gallimard had made love to Anna. 'I hope you're not furious, but if you are I'd rather you let me have it in the neck and not come down too hard on Anna...or include Charlie in any of the fall-out.'

There was a silence. He looked up to see Patrick give his rare full smile. 'You can put your mind at ease on that score. The only thing likely to make me furious is if you don't come back from your little jaunt – and in one piece. I think *one* absent Gallimard brother is quite enough for any woman to have to put up with, don't you?'

'Put that way, yes, sir!' hugely relieved Asa relaxed back into his chair.

Patrick's eyes were suddenly hooded; he looked down at his desk. 'Take care of her – no mistakes. You understand?'

'I understand; I'd never do anything to hurt Anna.'

'Few of us ever intend to do harm, but lack of intent doesn't lessen the consequences if we fail.' Abruptly Patrick stood. 'Come along. I'll treat you to a decent meal and a probably vastly inferior bottle of wine.'

*   *   *

An hour later he stood outside Simpson's and watched Asa walk away from him along the Strand, a sick hollow feeling invading his gut. Well, he'd done his damnedest to keep him from becoming involved with Special Operations, but men like Asa were desperately needed and not easily found, and he'd been fighting a losing battle from the

145

first with that crowd of cloak and dagger merchants in Baker Street.

It was burden enough, he thought savagely, not to be able to acknowledge his own son, without the added torment of knowing he might have seen and talked with him for the last time.

*   *   *

It had grown on him gradually, the conviction that Asa must be his. First with the dawning realisation that Auguste, like Dorothy, had been blue-eyed, so between them they couldn't possibly have produced a dark-eyed son. Then that Asa's features and colouring were very like Cecelia's, who had favoured her own father's dark, fine-boned looks and those peculiarly glossy brown eyes. But his unsubstantiated suspicions had only been proved shortly before Asa went to France: when the boy had been laughing with Charlie over his horoscope in the Sunday papers. The discovery then of his birth date had been ample confirmation to Patrick that his lovemaking with Cecelia had resulted in her bearing his son.

That he might have fathered a child in that brief, wartime encounter had never once entered his mind. Since his discovery he had struggled between the need to keep the truth from Charlie and Anna, and Asa himself, and his desire to right an old wrong by bringing everything out into the open.

During many sleepless nights he had wrestled with the same problem: whether he should speak, or keep silence. Without stirring some very muddy waters it would be impossible to discover what had happened to Cecelia: why her son had been adopted by Dorothy and Auguste or if Asa was even aware of whom his real mother was. Altogether too many people might be hurt if he followed his own desires and openly acknowledged Asa as his son.

Although at this time of emotional turmoil he needed more than ever the security of Charlie and his own home, paradoxically he was relieved that he was alone with his guilt. He would not, *could* not, have changed the course of his life, nor regret for one moment the one he had found with Charlie, but he would have seen that Cecelia never wanted for anything; would perhaps have been able to watch his son grow up, even if only from a distance. Why he wondered despairingly, had she never tried to find him? Where was she now and why had she handed her son over to Dorothy, of all people?

He felt the familiar stressful headache begin and wrenched his thoughts away from his private dilemma. He, like everyone else had a job to do: one that made his own conflict very small and insignificant

146

indeed beside the greater battle which was yet to come.

He turned towards Whitehall and his office and quickening his pace tried to concentrate his mind on his own coming mission.

*   *   *

HARDINGLY CAMP, ESSEX

September 10th, 1940 – 16.30hrs

The sirens began their stomach-churning wail. 'Here they come again, ma'am!' Sergeant Finnegan grabbed her tin hat and ducked under the desk.

'Holy *shit*!' Abandoning the dignity of rank Anna followed suit and they crouched side by side beneath the flimsy desk as the drone of heavy aircraft came steadily nearer. Suddenly, there was an ear-splitting crash, the wooden building shook and the sticky-taped glass cracked as though struck with a giant hammer.

'Jesus, Mary and Joseph!' the sergeant crossed herself and Anna clasped her hands over her head and prayed with her.

When the thumping drone of the Dorniers faded they crawled from under the desk sneezing and brushing grey dust from their shoulders. Anna commented shakily, 'It looks as though Harwich is about to get it again, so we could be altruistic and say that at least that's one less they'll have to put up with!'

The sergeant grinned. 'I think they only drop the odd one on the way so that we won't feel left out.'

Anna said, 'A nice thought on their part, but one I could do without.' They crunched over broken glass to the door. 'That was bloody close. We'd better have a look around and make sure everyone's all right.'

They stepped out of the company office into chaos. Smoke billowed across the camp and the air was full of the metallic taste and gritty aftermath of explosion. As an ambulance and the unit crash truck roared past, Anna, with one shocked glance took in the gaping ruin of a Nissan hut on the far side of the asphalt square. She started to run, the plump Finnegan pounding alongside her panting, 'That's the mess hall gone, ma'am…Christ, I hope the orderlies had finished laying tea…'

But when they arrived it was all too obvious that they hadn't. Shocked and appalled, they joined the crash crew and growing crowd of 'C' Company in heaving and pulling at the wreckage to reach the owners of the horribly still limbs glimpsed beneath the twisted iron sheets and splintered furniture.

Seven were pulled out injured but alive, placed on stretchers and taken away by ambulance, while three remained, hastily covered with blankets and laid on the ground to await their last journey from the camp that had so recently become their substitute for home and family; where, on a warm August afternoon a stray German bomb had robbed them of even that.

Anna stood beside the Junior Commander, mechanically brushing at her filthy uniform and controlling an overwhelming urge to weep, raging silently as she looked down on the still forms clearly outlined beneath the blankets.

What did they ever do to you, you bastards that you needed to loose off your frigging bomb on a few bowls of Spam and salad and blow a hut full of women apart?

She had been first cold with horror, then swept with a blind rage at the casual, wanton barbarism; going through the motions of being in control of herself and others in a swirling cloud of fear and fury. Now she could see a protruding foot, shoeless and dirty and dusty in a torn stocking. Bending to pull the blanket over it, tucking it in carefully as one might tuck in a sleeping child she murmured, 'That will keep you nice and warm...' then stood back in embarrassed silence.

'I'll stay with them, Farrell.' The Junior Commander, who'd arrived from a meeting some half hour after the carnage, put a hand on her shoulder. 'You go and get cleaned up.' She gave a wan smile. 'We can't let the rest of them down, can we?'

'No, ma'am, we can't do that.'

Anna brushed a hand across her face and walked towards her quarters, passing on the way groups of silent red-eyed girls bunched together, all looking terribly young and frightened and vulnerable. Although no older than most of them, she wanted to gather them into her arms to reassure them, say, 'It's all right, it was just a fluke. It won't happen again.'

But she knew that nothing she might say or do would comfort any of them. For the first time the war really had arrived on their own doorstep...not just to smash a few windows, but to maim and kill those of their own, who only a short hour ago had been laying out those bowls of salad and the plates of Spam. Joking as they worked, popping the odd piece of tomato or sliver of meat into their laughing mouths as Anna had so often seen them do before, as Asa had advised, turning a blind eye then walking on...

That night as she lay sleepless on her bed she longed for his arms, remembering their lovemaking and the way he held her afterwards: stroking her hair, caressing her quietening body, murmuring endearments until she was drowsy and slipped away into sleep.

He had written to her on the night he'd returned to London from Tring. A hauntingly tender letter; the kind a lover writes after first making love, full of gently carnal reference to the nights he'd spent in her bed, and dwelling on pleasures yet to come when they would be together again. He had ended: *You are not to worry if you do not hear from me for a while. I shall be very busy and too far away to visit and steal you from under your commander's nose and take you away to make love to you under the stars – why did we not do that at Tring? Something for us to look forward to perhaps, before the summer ends.*

Miss me, as I miss you, Anna, je t'aime...Asa.

Where was he now, she wondered, staring at the pale square of her window...how far was 'too far away' and when might the summer end?

Despite her feelings and the longing to be with him again, she couldn't quite let herself believe that she was really in love. When she had soared and known at once with Félix, how could it be the same love that she had gone so slowly and unwittingly towards with Asa?

* * *

FLETCHLEY, KENT

November 25th, 1940

Still haunted by the memory of the dead girls and bored with the endless paper work, she applied for a transfer, passing a selection board a few weeks later to become a platoon commander at an OCTU on the Kent border.

Day after day she watched as the sky filled with massed formations of enemy bombers making for London; laying waste the capital by day and night and turning the city's docks into a flaming beacon seen clearly from the old mansion in which they were all housed, making the lives of those who had families in that city into a nightmare of fear and dread.

She carried out her duties automatically, thankful that no one now was living at Stratton Place, but filled with anxiety for Patrick and Asa, both of whom had a distressing habit of vanishing without warning for anything from a few days to several weeks. The only bright spot in all this time of waiting for news was that at least she didn't have constantly to be on guard against letting fall any indiscreet words that might link Asa to Patrick or *vice versa*.

At the beginning of November, and with no explanation for his long silence, a letter on flimsy foreign paper arrived from Félix, ending with the cryptic message that he might be collecting comforts for the troops before Christmas. Hoping that didn't mean what she thought it meant, Anna penned a brief and non-committal reply then pushed to the back of her mind the uneasy feeling that her strength to resist him might soon be put to the test, a prospect she could only view with dread.

One evening she left her platoon at the end of a long and tiring afternoon in search of a needed whisky. As she paused to remove her belt outside the anteroom the hall telephone began to ring. Lifting the receiver she said brusquely, 'D Company, Subaltern Farrell speaking,' then almost dropped it as a familiar voice asked, 'Isn't that rather shameless, Subaltern Farrell, to be hanging over the 'phone and waiting for it to ring?'

'*Asa!*' She leaned her forehead against the wall and began to laugh.

'Is that all you can manage? And why are you down there teaching all those little girls to be like you?'

'I got tired of pay returns, athletes' foot and dying grandmothers.' She gulped. 'You shouldn't take me by surprise like this...'

'Charlie said you were coming on leave. Will you meet me in London first, before going to Tring?'

'Try and stop me!' She answered him without even a show of maidenly modesty, and heard him laugh. She said breathlessly, 'My leave starts on Friday. I can be at Stratton Place by nineteen hundred...will you be there then? Have you a key? – If there's a raid we can use the shelter.'

'Very romantic!' She heard a voice in the background calling his name and he became suddenly brisk. 'Stratton Place then, *à vendredi.*' Then the line went dead and she was left staring at the receiver in her hand and wondering if she'd dreamed the whole thing.

*   *   *

STRATTON PLACE

November 29th, 1940.

At the sound of his key in the lock she started down the stairs and for a moment stood transfixed, shocked into silence at the gaunt face looking up at her, the mouth and forehead creased with deep lines of exhaustion, the eyes looking into hers like hard black pebbles.

She felt the breath catch in the back of her throat, then her fear and fright turned into a spurt of angry relief and she demanded, 'How the *hell* did you get to look like *that*? And where have you been all this time, you bastard?'

He came to where she stood and took her in his arms. 'Now I know I'm really home,' he said, and kissed her and she clung to him, crying and shaking with mingled excitement and fright.

'Hush.' He wiped her tears away with his fingers and lied for her. 'I've been horribly seasick, that's all. Come along...Patrick has told me where to find his brandy. Only *he* would be so generous as not to lock it away!'

She gave a shaky laugh and climbed the stairs, his arm around her shoulders. 'I don't need brandy,' she said, 'I only need you,' aware as she spoke the words that she was telling the simple truth.

Right now, at this time and in this place, he *was* all she needed to start treading the long road back from Félix. If only he could stay, and not leave her again, she really thought she might be cured.

*　　　*　　　*

Hungry and needy, she would have rushed their lovemaking but he had other ideas on how to manage the night before them: soothing her with hands and lips, his clever fingers touching and coaxing and exploring her body until they were again in harmony.

Much later when they lay still and quiet in each others arms he cupped her face between his hands and kissed her eyes, murmuring, 'I do love you so...'

Anna pushed her fingers through the thick, waving hair, breathing in the warm, masculine smell of him and felt the tears begin to gather in her eyes. 'I'm not sure you should have made me love *you* so much, because how can I bear to let you go again?'

He moved his lips over hers. 'I know. I feel that too.'

'Come back to me Asa. Please say you'll come back.'

'I'll damned well come back: from hell if necessary,' he

murmured against her mouth, 'just to make sure that there is no place in your mind, or body, for that brother of mine to fill!'

16

DOVE HOUSE, TRING

20th December, 1940

Charlie cleared the supper dishes and made coffee from his hidden store, only brought from the back of the kitchen cupboard and brewed when Patrick or Anna came home. Waiting for the coffee to percolate, he stood looking out over the long walled garden, stark and cold and glittering eerily in the moonlight. The tree under which in summer he had sat with Asa and Anna was now heavy with frozen snow, the table and grass covered with a thick blanket of white. In this bitter winter of rationed fuel, only the kitchen and small living room could be heated to a reasonable though far from luxurious warmth. On Sunday he decided, they must put aside an hour or two to forage for wood, so that they might have a proper blazing fire on Christmas morning.

It would be a strange way to spend the festive season. Just Patrick and him, as it had been in the days before Anna. 'A pair of old codgers,' he mused, 'with this old codger at least feeling his age!'

He thought about Anna, still in Kent with her gaggle of women. Poor Anna, she'd drawn the short straw and was on duty in the almost deserted mansion until her forty-eight-hour pass began after Boxing Day. Deciding not to make the inevitably delayed and involved train journey to Tring in the ice and snow, she'd said she would spend it in Kent, doing quite what he had tactfully refrained from inquiring. Although since the event of Asa into her life Félix seemed to have faded into the background, he shared with Patrick an uneasy feeling that he was still out there somewhere.

He sighed and turned the gas down under the percolator. And what *about* Asa – where was he that he couldn't even 'phone or send a message? He didn't like to think what that young man might be doing, or how long it might be before he returned.

When he went into the sitting room with his tray Patrick was at the table, his head propped on one hand, an open book before him. His spectacles had slipped down his nose and he was quite clearly fast asleep. Charlie rattled the cups and in an instant he was awake, his head coming up, the sharp eyes alert and watchful. Charlie gave him a meaningful look.

'Since when did you start cap-napping?' he asked as Patrick took off his glasses, yawning then stretching his arms.

'It was a long journey.'

Charlie grunted, 'From Whitehall?'

'No, from before that.' Patrick gave him one of his ambiguous glances. 'Can't a man go away on holiday without you prying into his affairs?'

Charlie snorted derisively. 'Some holiday! Come over to the fire and drink your coffee, you'll freeze to death in this house if you sit a foot away from the fender for more than five minutes.'

'Um, its hellish cold isn't it? I hope Anna's keeping warmer than this.'

'She said she'll get a week-end pass sometime in the next month or so...any chance you'll see her then?'

'It's possible. I shall be around for a while now.'

Charlie stretched out his legs to the fire and sipped his coffee. 'And Asa, might he "be around" by then?'

He watched Patrick's mouth tighten momentarily before he hunched his shoulders, answering obliquely and in a tone that precluded any further questions, 'Why ask me, how would I know?'

Charlie wasn't easily deflected. He knew his man and he knew he needed to talk. He said smoothly, 'I had the impression you've made sure that you *do* know, and worry, a great deal about him. If I was the inquisitive type I might take the time to wonder why.'

There was a long and pregnant silence. Patrick eventually broke it, putting down his coffee and reaching for his cigarette case he asked flatly. 'You've guessed something, haven't you, you sharp-witted, sharp-eyed old sod? So why don't you come right out with it and stop waiting for me to open up?'

His companion smiled. 'Because you might quite rightly, tell me to mind my own business.'

'When did I ever do that? Hasn't my business always been yours?'

'I've wondered for months...you are not unlike, you know, and you have been rather over concerned about him ever since he came back from Dunkirk.'

Patrick lit his cigarette; drawing deeply and half-closing his eyes against the smoke he admitted, 'It took me a long time to face it and believe anything so preposterous, longer still to *want* to believe. But I'm as sure as it is possible for a man to be that he's my son. I'm also just as sure that Asa has not the faintest suspicion about our relationship.'

'What about Anna?'

Patrick frowned. 'I don't see how she could know anything.'

'Didn't her manner seem a bit odd when she came back from seeing that little shite Félix all that time ago? We both noticed she had something on her mind then, didn't we?'

'I can't think *he'd* be able to tell her more about Asa than she already knew.'

'Maybe,' Charlie was cynical, 'but it would be difficult to keep that sort of secret in any family without someone dropping a hint at sometime, and Félix sounds just the type to ferret around and come up with an idea or two.'

'God, it gets worse, doesn't it?' Patrick put his head in his hands. 'You could be right, I suppose. I remember that evening – she wanted to know if confession helped me to sort out my problems. I asked her then if she was in any trouble and she said no, it was someone else's...'

He trailed off acutely aware that for once his sensitive ear had deserted him and that he'd handed out the wrong advice. Poor Anna, if she had guessed what a struggle she must have had to keep quiet!

Charlie gave a wry smile at his expression of dawning embarrassment.

'It looks to me,' he observed succinctly, 'as though the only one who doesn't know *something* is Asa...who is perhaps, the one who should know everything.'

Patrick's face was wrenched with a spasm of pain. 'I can't tell him, Charlie. What on earth would I say? I've no idea why his mother handed him over to Dorothy, or where she is now...he speaks openly about being born in Cornwall, but he may not even know who his real mother is.'

'Well, he must know Dorothy isn't...his birth certificate would tell him that and no doubt it also gives his natural mother's name. He should be told his father's as well.' Charlie was stubborn and persistent. 'Perhaps in peace time there might be some justification for keeping all this to yourself, but not during a war when anything could happen at any time,' he gave an exasperated snort. 'He's no more a Gallimard than you or I and he should know that.'

Patrick shook his head wearily. 'What right have I to intrude into his world? Perhaps make him despise the mother who, for whatever reason apparently gave him away, and resent the adoptive one who fought tooth and nail to keep him from even seeing his real father? No wonder Dorothy was incandescent with fury when she discovered we'd met in Paris! And just what do you imagine would be his reaction to *me*?' He rubbed despairing hands over his face. 'What young man would want to acknowledge he has a middle-aged queer for a father? One moreover, who'd seduced his seventeen-year-old mother then conveniently disappeared from the scene? Jesus Christ, Charlie, it doesn't even bear thinking about.'

'No, put like that, it doesn't.' Charlie said slowly and stared thoughtfully into the fire. 'You couldn't have woven a more tangled web if you'd tried, could you?' He pursed his lips thoughtfully. 'I think that in this case discretion may very well be the better part of valour, for the time at least. Although if you ever decide the time is right to tell him he may show more compassion than you give him credit for. I'm sure that if he knew all the circumstances he wouldn't find it difficult to understand and forgive.'

'Perhaps,' Patrick shook his head wearily, 'but I shall have to have it out with Anna sometime; although I'll feel such a complete idiot if she's in happy ignorance of it all.'

Charlie bent to pick up the poker and stir the small fire into life. 'Keep your secret then, until you feel you can speak with Asa: Anna may not know – only guess.'

'I didn't keep it a secret from you, though, did I?'

'No – but then you never could...'

Patrick laughed. 'Enough talk of secrets and my guilty past. We have five whole days together. Let's make the most of them...'

* * *

The morning before Christmas Eve the snow fell, thawed a little the following day, then fell again and froze and stayed: a thick, crisp white covering over village, hills and woods. Willingly marooned in the old house they read and dozed and listened to music and at night in the hushed, snow-blanketed stillness of their room under the eves, they talked: reminiscing of earlier times and days when there were no sorrows, no partings.

'Just like old times: so much snow at Christmas.' Patrick said as he laid back, an arm behind his head.

Charlie said reminiscently, 'Last time we saw so much snow was in Dinard, nineteen twenty-six. It was over our boots and you got tight and fell in a snowdrift!' He gave a half laugh, then groaned, 'Oh, sod this war...I've missed you, Patrick. God, but I've missed you...'

Patrick stretched his mutilated arm across his lover's chest. 'Forget about missing: I'm here now...and don't worry; we'll do Dinard again some day; with or without the snow.'

156

Soon they slept, while the old rafters creaked under the heavy mantle of snow and a bomber's moon shone bright over the sculptured snowdrifts of a peaceful silent world.

*   *   *

ALEXANDRIA

December 27th, 1940 – 06.30hrs

Félix's be-tasselled jacket and braided *kepi* received a contemptuous glance from the American pilot as he boarded the 'plane. 'Jee*zuss*!' the pilot exclaimed aloud, 'It's the fuckin' Bolshoi Ballet come to town!'

'If we run into trouble and some Kraut starts shooting just keep your head down, stay outta my way and pray!' the air gunner ordered laconically from his turret, leaving Félix to conclude that a military aide in a fancy French uniform cut no ice with him either.

What a time of year to be dragged from the warmth of North Africa and return to England, he thought morosely. Spending several boring days with his Colonel in London might be bearable if Anna was likely to be around, although after his meeting with Asa in the charged and emotional weeks following his own escape from Paris and Asa's less comfortable one from Dunkirk, he'd stayed well away from her. He was no fool, and Asa's repeated threatening and forceful warning when they'd met in London, had at that time fuelled his own determination to end the affair. In any case, now that he had the enchanting daughter of the Spanish vice-consul so interested in him, risking Asa's wrath for a night or two with Anna simply wasn't on the cards. He wished he hadn't sent that silly letter about Christmas comforts for the troops when he knew he was coming back to London for the meetings. She would have known what he meant and was now most likely eagerly anticipating his return to her bed.

Back in Alexandria he mused sadly, Maria Dolores Venchello was demanding of his time but gave no such favours as Anna. Unused to such resistance to his charms he was feeling more than a little frustrated. His pulse quickened at the remembrance of all the times he'd held Anna in his arms. Perhaps he would see her just once more – the conferences due to take place would not begin for a few days yet so there would be time…

Falling into a restless sleep he awakened wretchedly cold, roused by a none-too tuneful rendering of *The White Cliffs of Dover* by the navigator. He sat up, easing the cramp from his back and thighs. Through the small window he could see the English coastline, indistinct and almost obliterated by falling snow. The thought of spending the night in a mess full of strangers or in some anonymous and no doubt freezing cold hotel room was distinctly unappealing; Anna's camp he remembered from her short and rather cool reply to his letter, was only a mile or so from the airstrip.

Imagining her again, warm and compliant and opening like a flower to his caresses was sufficient to stifle any immediate thought of Asa's displeasure and his own earlier resolve to give her a miss: just thinking about her was getting him randy. He smoothed down the jacket of what his brother had so rudely called his toy soldier uniform and ran a hand through his hair. After he'd thawed out with a drink and perhaps scrounged a bath, dinner with Anna then an hour or two in a hotel bed would be welcome. If she could manage to wangle a pass, all night would be even better...

'Pennyhampton an' Farthingmile Field, friggin' Fletchly, friggin' England comin' up!' bellowed the pilot. 'Jeeze, but these Limey's think up some crazy names!'

'Indeed.' Félix flicked specs of dust from his uniform with fastidious fingers. 'One simply cannot understand why they do not choose more sensible ones...such as Tallahassee or Topeka – or even Cincinnati!'

'Sure thing...' the irony had passed the pilot by, or perhaps it hadn't, as he then inquired with a grin, 'Where *you* headed for then Frenchie – Bedfordshire?'

'Lieutenant Gallimard.' Félix corrected him politely, 'and I'm heading for the sexiest female subaltern in the British Army. I shall most probably have fucked her twice by the time that *you* are eating your pork and beans!'

The pilot muttered 'Fuckin' Frogs!' under his breath and turned his 'plane into the descent towards Farthingmile field and a mess full of fuckin' Limey's...all male.

*　　*　　*

STRATTON PLACE

28th December, 1940.

Anna let herself into the side door, checked that the blackout curtains were drawn across the side window, then switched on the blue-painted hall light and climbed the stairs to the kitchen. Shivering and without stopping to remove her greatcoat or gloves, she filled and lit the gas under the kettle. There was no milk, not even dried, but in her present frozen state hot tea would be welcome, with or without milk.

She was already regretting the whim that had brought her to London. When her Commander had offered a week-end lift to Hampstead she'd accepted, without actually registering the fact that Stratton Place would in this weather be about as welcoming as a graveyard mausoleum in Siberia. Waiting half an hour for an underground train at Hampstead, then sliding her way from Russell Square over icy pavements had only added to her depression. Warmth, she decided on viewing her Spartan bedroom, was a priority.

Within an hour a wood fire blazed in the grate and the water had heated enough to bathe and wash her hair. A long soak in hot water regrettably deeper than the proscribed five inches warmed and revived her, and she had just tied the belt of her wool housecoat and begun towelling her hair dry when the doorbell rang. Swearing and wrapping the towel around her head she padded down the cold stairs, shivering as droplets of water trickled down her neck.

'All *right*!' she yelled as the unknown caller apparently jammed a finger on the bell and kept it there. 'I'm coming, I'm coming...' Leaping down the remaining stairs she flung open the door. '*Will* you shut that bloody racket?'

Félix recoiled dramatically at the sight of her cross face peering from beneath her towelling turban. '*Mon Dieu!* Is that what women are wearing in London this season?'

For a moment she stared at him in frozen disbelief, then snarled, 'I might have known!' and stepping back slammed the door shut on his startled face. He yelled, '*Salope!* 'and jammed his finger back on the bell. '

'Oh for God's *sake*!' Anna wrenched the door open again. 'Come in before the neighbours start hanging out of their windows. If they catch sight of that get up they'll think I'm running a Ruritanian brothel!'

He stepped in, taking off his *kepi* and shivering against the cold of the hallway, grumbling, 'You must entertain many men that they should think that – and why the hell did you shut me out?'

'Because you scared the bloody life out of me; turning up at this hour looking like something out of the Prisoner of Zenda!' She backed, keeping a distance between them. 'Why didn't you warn me you were coming?'

'No time.' He ignored both the insult and her palpable wish to

159

keep him at arm's length. 'I have had one hell of a job to find you. I walked across a mile of frozen snow to that tomb you call a camp, only for that old *lesbienne* adjutant to tell me you had gone …vamoosed…got the hell out of it…'

Despite her annoyance at having been taken off guard, his accurate description of the adjutant and the juxtaposition of his strong French accent and comical use of slang made her smile. 'You can come up and thaw out and when I've dried my hair I'll get you something to eat.'

He scowled. 'I do not want to eat. I want to make love to a woman with wet hair!'

'That's tough, because I'm the only woman with wet hair around here and I haven't invited you into my bed.'

'What is this?'' he complained, following her up the stairs. 'Are you hiding under the bed that Valerie's fool of a brother …what is his name?'

'Archie and he's no fool. He's a major now and has never even been within spitting distance of my bed…even if he has tried rather hard from time to time.' She paused and looked back at him over her shoulder. 'You can't just turn up out of the blue after all this time and take up where you left off, you smug bastard. I'll find you something to eat and a bed of your own. That's all.'

'Do not be tiresome, Anna…you cannot have changed so much in the time I have been away that you are going to withhold a few comforts for the troops.'

'If you want *those* try the nearest Forces Canteen.'

'Don't say that. You cannot be such a cruel Anna to refuse your *petit garçon la bien-être!*'

As they reached the top of the stairs he caught at her and pulling her back hard against him wrenched open the front of her housecoat, covering her bare breasts with both hands. Immediately and humiliatingly her body betrayed her with a rush of desire. He felt it and still fondling her breast with one hand slid the other down between her legs, parting them and deepening his caress. With his lips pressed into the hollow of her throat he murmured, 'You cannot send me away when I need you so much.'

She quickened with pleasure then in sudden panic tried to pull away but he held her fast, saying mockingly, *'Je suis venu pour une baise...'* He pulled her around to face him. '...and a fuck is just what I'm going to get.'

'Sod you, Félix…' she drew a shuddering breath, 'always the bad boy, aren't you?'

'No boy!' he hissed and ground his mouth on hers. Pushing her back against the wall he loosed his belt. 'I know you too well, Anna – well enough to know when you are ready for me,' he said then laughed and ignoring her diminishing protests, took her swiftly and impatiently against the cold stairway.

* * *

An hour later she left him sleeping and walked down the moonlit stairway into the kitchen, appalled at her surrender on the stairs, and that she had allowed him to take her again in her own bed.

'You're nothing but a tart!' She railed against herself, spooning tea into the pot. 'You let that *louche*, inconsequential bastard take Asa's place. Now he's happy as a pig that found the truffle he'd been rooting for...and you couldn't bloody wait to help him find it, could you, you immoral bitch!'

She rested her hands on the warm wooden handle of the kettle and leaned to stare at her reflection in the mirror.

How could you have been so weak after all you had found with Asa? Asa, who is a decent, honourable man and a million miles away from that unprincipled louse who, sod him, can still light that fire inside you...

She made the tea and drank it slowly, then returned to her room. Standing beside the bed she watched his sleeping face. Even in repose, with his mouth a little slack, the lines beneath his eyes showing clearly the excesses of his life to date, he was beautiful, with that soft, boyish, Rupert Brook-ish beauty that belonged to a more romantic era than this. Sadly, she acknowledged that in time the beauty would fade and that romance may never bloom for the amoral awfulness that was the essential Félix.

But even now, watching his features softened and vulnerable in sleep she felt her heart begin the familiar slow thud. Resisting the impulse to kiss his closed eyelids and stroke the silky hair, she took a spare eiderdown from the wardrobe and went silently downstairs in the dark; there to lie sleepless on the *chaise longue* in the cold drawing room until morning came and she rose early, determined that today she would end once and for all the dominance of Félix Gallimard over Anna Farrell.

* * *

He appeared in the kitchen looking cross and tousled, demanding,

'Why did you have to get up so early so that we could not again make love?'

She answered him without turning round. 'We didn't make love, Félix, we never did. We only had sex.'

He stayed lounging against the doorframe, watching her back through narrow suspicious eyes. He said abruptly, 'Has Asa been here?'

'Not for some time.' She concentrated on measuring dried egg into the basin. 'Why do you ask?'

He frowned, 'I mistrust you, Anna, when you answer with your back to me, because I think you have something to hide.'

'And I mistrust you *all* the time, Félix.'

'*Touché*,' he came to stand behind her and put his hands on her waist, kneading her hips with his fingers. 'Where is he now?'

She moved away from him. 'Your guess is as good as mine.' Over her shoulder she gave him a veiled look. 'In this country, Félix, you don't ask that sort of question.'

'To save you the trouble of answering?' there was anger in his voice. 'I am not a complete fool, Anna. Last night you tried to refuse me, now this morning you leave the bed too quickly …Now I think I know why Asa is so anxious to keep me away from you.' He gave a short, humourless laugh. 'Does he fuck better than me Anna? Screw you harder; stay there longer; make you call his name louder?'

She rounded on him then and smacked his face hard. She said with biting sarcasm, 'Keep going. You're getting there, darling.'

'*Petite chatte*!' He was more astounded than angry, then to her humiliation he began to laugh. 'This is like a French Farce is it not? I came thinking you would be eager for the pleasure I can give you, when all the time my big brother has been keeping you satisfied! How much do you love *him*, Anna…is it as much as you love me? I think not, or you would not have given in to me last night.'

She said bitterly, 'I told you: that wasn't *love*. All *you* gave me last night was relief from the need to have Asa inside me. What you don't give, you don't get, Félix. I might have loved you once but I'm over you now.'

She moved away from the stove and he stepped back, holding up his hands, warning, 'Do not risk hitting me again, Anna.'

She brushed past him to take plates from the dresser. 'I wouldn't even think of it,' she was contemptuous; 'you aren't worth the effort.'

'But I was worth the effort last night, wasn't I?' he grinned maliciously. 'I'm sure Asa would be most interested to know that it was no problem for me again to get between his woman's legs.' He

162

grinned again. 'Our little session was most timely, as unlike you, the lady I have set my heart on in Alexandria is very proper…I fear I may even have to propose marriage before she lets me fuck *her*!'

Anna stood immobile, white-faced but calm. She thought: if he doesn't go right now, I'm going to kill him. With an effort she kept control over her hands and voice, saying with cool contempt, 'Better get back to her then…and do give her my congratulations. She must be the only woman who's managed to keep you from dropping your trousers round your ankles before you've even said hello!' She gave him an ironic smile and turned back to the stove. 'Goodbye, Félix, it's been nice knowing you, *but…*'

Long after he'd left, stung by her contempt into sudden temper, swearing and slamming the door, she sat dry-eyed at the kitchen table, wishing she hadn't played his game by delivering that last scornful and mocking wound. After a time she put her head down on her folded arms, not sure if the pain she felt was for the loss of Félix or the betrayal of Asa's love. Why, she asked despairingly, hadn't she worked out before the basic unalienable difference between those two, the reason why she never would have found what she needed with Félix?

Asa was a giver, Félix a taker; it was as simple and as humiliating as that. Asa had given his unconditional love, Félix had taken without thought her innocence, accepted as his right her devotion and screwed her whenever he could spare the time.

Aloud she said, 'Anna Farrell, you stupid cow. You hadn't the faintest idea of what the word love really meant before Asa.' She raised her head and propping it on her hand wept silently, her tears splashing down onto Charlie's scrubbed kitchen table.

Rubbing her finger over the deep cut his knife had made all those years ago, she remembered with pain how a silly girl who knew nothing then of real love and commitment, had teased a strong and honourable man who knew more about both than she could ever have imagined.

17

MARLCLEW, CORNWALL
April 2nd, 1941 – 20.00 hrs

Anna leaned her forehead against the car window as they passed
through the lodge gates, staring out through the rain drenched glass to
where a battered board hung askew, still proclaiming valiantly but
inaccurately that this was The Lady Elizabeth Fairfax School for
Girls. She felt her scalp prickling with perspiration beneath the rim of
her cap. Since the shock of yesterday's briefing and the discovery that
they were leaving Kent for this most familiar place she had existed in
a state of suspended animation. Dreading the moment of return she
had passed a restless night and was now the proud owner of an
incipient headache and a very queasy stomach.

Of all the places she might want to fetch up, she thought
gloomily, this had to be the least desirable. Anywhere, even the
middle of London in a perpetual air raid would be marginally more
welcoming than this particular corner of old England; holding as it did
too many of those memories she had more or less successfully
relegated to the far recesses of her mind. Above all, it would be a
nagging reminder of Félix.

As the heavy car laboured up the long drive she glimpsed familiar
landmarks through the scuds of rain: the willow tree by the shallow
pond now whipped into a frenzied dance by the wind; the tennis
pavilion, a tattered notice flapping wetly against the door, and the pale
form of Diana, a wisp of drapery modestly concealing her bosom as
was only suitable for a statue in the grounds of a girls school. When
the graceful turrets and mullion windows of the mellow old Jacobean
building finally came into sight the driver sucked in her breath then
leaned to wipe a sleeve across the steamed-up windscreen.

'A bit of a gloomy, pile, ma'am. D'you suppose it's heated at
all?'

Anna almost said, 'It never was,' but bit back the words in time.
'Shouldn't think so, Corporal,' she summoned up a smile. 'Places like
this were built long before efficient central heating, so don't get your
hopes too high. It will no doubt have the addition of radiators the size
of tank traps that *may* begin to give off some faint warmth when the

temperature falls below zero, but more than that I wouldn't bet on.'

Corporal Owen muttered beneath her breath and drove on through the avenue of trees. When they reached the oval of lawn before the house Anna saw the Founder's statue in the centre was shrouded in a wooden casing, presumably against vandalism from either the Luftwaffe or the ATS. Owen drew up before the flight of shallow stone steps inquiring, "Will this do, ma'am?'

'Yes. Don't get out here.' Anna leant forward, her hand on the door handle. 'I'll make a run for it. If you drive around to the rear there's a lean-to where you can park under cover...turn left at the end of the house and drive to the end. It brings you up to the west wing. You can get into the house that way. Do it at the gallop and you shouldn't get too wet!'

The corporal grinned. 'You must have done a recce, ma'am.'

'Something like that,' stepping out and slamming the car door behind her she took the steps at a run. Shooting through the open front door into the lofty hall she took off her cap, shaking it and sending a shower of droplets onto the wooden floor. She caught her breath. Bloody hell, she thought, her depression deepening, the place still smelled the same: a lingering miasma of puberty, plimsolls and repressed female sexuality. Anna's heart sank and she stood with slumped shoulders until the click of an opening door roused her. Replacing her cap quickly she saluted as the Adjutant came briskly towards her. 'Good evening, ma'am. I'm sorry we're late. We had a burst tyre the other side of Plymouth.'

'I was beginning to think you'd got lost, Farrell.'

The greeting was frosty. Expressionless, Anna said, 'No, ma'am, my map-reading skills are unimpaired by wind or weather!' and in return received an even more glacial look.

'Well now you have arrived, you'll see Orders are posted on the board over there. You are O/C Accommodation. Detail a couple of clerks to help you allocate rooms. Officers in the west wing, Sergeant's Mess and sleeping quarters in the east, the dormitories and common rooms you'll somehow have to share out between O/R's and Cadets; report to me when your arrangements are completed.'

'Yes ma'am.'

Anna muttered 'Old cow!' under her breath and watched the Adjutant's skinny legs disappear in the direction of what had once been the library, but was no doubt now the anteroom, with the booze securely under lock and key. She took off her cap again to ruffle her short curls and indulge in a more leisurely appraisal of her old *alma mater*.

It wasn't nearly as spick and span as she remembered. There were brown paper strips stuck over the large panes of the leaded windows and the floor could do with old Aggie giving it a good polish. The pale patches on the staircase walls bore mute testimony to portraits of past headmistresses, the canvasses now no doubt languishing in the cellars, while the red damask curtains that once hung from ceiling to floor had been replaced by cheap blackout material.

She hung her greatcoat; respirator and cap on one of the hooks alongside the door, musing that she'd better get a move on and requisition her old room before some unappreciative subaltern took a fancy to it. Cat Morris came up behind her with a cheerful, 'Hi, got here at last then have you? This place is like Dotherboy's Hall, just wait until you see the kitchens; Victorian, my dear – and the ovens! You'd need half a dozen skivvies to keep *those* in firewood.' She rolled her eyes heavenward. 'Just guess which poor bloody sub has drawn the short straw for getting the cookhouse organised.'

'Piece of cake,' Anna was derisive. 'I've got to fit bodies into holes and you can bet your life everyone will want the one I've just shoved someone else into.' She scowled. 'If that cow Durrant wasn't already in the ante-room keeping an eagle eye on the booze I'd brace myself with a large scotch.'

Cat sniggered. 'You could always get your own back by allocating the old bat the draughtiest room in the house.'

Before Anna could reply her driver reappeared, dripping all over the floor and lugging a suitcase, 'You left your bag, ma'am. I remembered and went back for it.'

'God, I'm sorry.' Anna was instantly contrite. 'For goodness sake, Owen, get down to the kitchens, dry yourself off and see if you can scrounge a cup of tea. Hang around here too long and someone will find you something else to do.'

Cat pointed. 'Down those stairs, Corporal and keep going, and whilst you're at it, brew a bloody great pot: I'm going to need it to keep my strength up.' She grinned, giving Anna a farewell wave. 'See you at dinner; you'll be thrilled to know the Big Chief is dinning in mess tonight so it's best bib and tucker!'

'Hell's teeth…' Muttering beneath her breath Anna picked up her case and set off across the hall toward the notice board. Spotting an unlucky orderly lurking in a doorway she crooked a beckoning forefinger.

'Stacy. On the second floor of the west wing you'll find a corridor marked one to ten. Take my case up and put it in number ten. If anyone else is already in there kick them out.'

166

'Suppose it's the Chief Commissioner, ma'am?'

'It won't be. She'll already have found the Headmistress's suite.' She stood for a moment watching Stacy labour with exaggerated exertion up the wide central staircase then turned back to the board muttering, 'Now let me see, which two clerks might I nab who have the necessary brain power to help me sort out this little lot.'

* * *

Three hours later she flopped onto her iron bedstead to lie supine and exhausted on the lumpy mattress. Any minute now, she thought, Valerie would arrive hoping to scrounge a bar of chocolate, or Soapy Soames oil her way around the door and offer a shilling to do her a crib for tomorrow's French test...

She crooked her neck to stare at the ceiling. Yes, it was still there, the yellowing outline from where she'd upset Soapy's bowl of frogs-spawn all those years ago. It wasn't a dream. She really was back in her old room...Anna Farrell, Upper Sixth and Head of House with a study bedroom all to herself. All those scrubbed and shinning cadets due to arrive in the morning would be very like a start-of-term's new girls she thought despondently, and she would be expected to be all brisk and welcoming and jolly hockey sticks...She sighed and closed her eyes, unutterably depressed to think that after five years she'd somehow managed to exchange one uniform for another and fetch up under the same old roof.

She groaned and with an effort rolled off the bed. 'Get moving, ducky,' she admonished herself aloud, 'time to get tarted up for dinner. Now where the hell did I put my clean collars?'

Five minutes later she stood before the mirror of the dark wood dressing table, giving her buttons a final once over with a duster. Fastening her belt she gave her reflection a wry smile: it was impossible to keep memory at bay in this place, the best she could hope to do was exorcise it a little.

April 3rd, 1941 – 07.30 hrs

Anna passed the dinning room and the smell of kippers and walked out onto the flagged terrace, sniffing appreciatively at the morning-fresh smell of newly washed grass. Overnight the rain clouds had cleared, a light breeze aiding the sun to break through the heavy curtain of early morning mist, while in the dip of the valley the tops of trees floated like green islands on a milky sea. It was so quiet that she could hear the rhythmic slap, slap of oars as someone on the far side

167

of the river rowed home from the village with the morning milk and papers.

She paused at the edge of the shrubbery and felt for the packet of Players in her battle dress pocket. After the usual struggle with the wheel of her brass lighter she drew deeply on her cigarette then began to walk down past the neglected flowerbeds, across the sloping lawn and through the patch of woodland to the boathouse.

Brushing aside the trailing grey cobwebs, she pushed open the creaking door and at once the smell of dank river and sodden wood came up to meet her. By the misty light struggling through the palings of the water gate she could see the punt, pulled up onto the planking: thick with dust and dry as a bone. An old grey shirt lay crumpled in the bottom and she picked it up, flicking it over the dusty stern board before seating herself. … *Not your colour, Félix; too sober altogether*… Dropping the shirt back into the well she propped her elbows on her knees and resting her chin on her hands stared sombrely at the water gate, while the wall of mist became insubstantial wisps and the sun shone palely through the bars.

It hasn't changed, has it, Félix? If I'd known then what I do now you wouldn't have found me such a push-over you bastard!

She sat for an hour or more, smoking and thinking until the distant sound of wheels crunching on gravel roused her from her reverie. Stubbing out her last cigarette she glanced at her watch then leapt to her feet and scrambled from the punt.

'Oh *bugger!*' Frantically she brushed at her battledress trousers, 'Oh, shit – that's torn it!'

She pulled the door tight shut behind her and took the path through the trees at a run, then at the sight of the lorries spilling their nervous passengers onto the drive, slowed to a brisk walk.

The adjutant stood majestically on the steps above the common herd, watching her platoon commanders as they sorted out the latest in a long line of OCTU hopefuls; Anna, trying to slide unobserved around one of the vehicles caught her baleful glance. Realising too late that she had left her cap in the boathouse she smiled weakly and plunged into the heaving throng.

Another black mark, Farrell; you may have made Head of House here five years ago, but if you don't stop getting up La Durrant's nose with quite such monotonous regularity you'll never get any higher than a subaltern in this outfit…

22.30 hrs.

Wearing her dressing gown and carrying two mugs Cat edged through the door. 'Cocoa,' she said, 'what a dump; can I do my hair at your mirror? My glass has more spots than a Dalmatian with the pox.'

'Help yourself.' Anna climbed into bed and took the proffered mug. 'Thanks. I knew something good had to come out of today: the Chief going raving mad and demoting Durrant to being our batwoman springs to mind as one of my pleasanter fantasies, but cocoa will do.'

'Bawl you out, did she?'

'Umm,' she sipped her cocoa. 'Incorrect dress; poor discipline; bad example to cadets and O/R's etc. etc., bloody good job she couldn't see my pink cami-knickers.'

Cat began to unpin her long hair. 'It *was* funny, though. All those young hopefuls with shinning buttons and beautifully pressed uniforms and you rolling up in battle dress minus your cap and with dust all over your arse!'

'It was cold first thing and I needed the trousers. I meant to be back in time to change.'

'What's got into you, anyway: late on duty twice in less than twenty-four hours – never mind about the undress.'

Anna was defensive. 'Yesterday wasn't my fault. We had a flat when Owen was doing one of her famous trust-me-I-know-where-I'm-going short cuts down some country lane. As some twerp appeared to have fixed the wheel nuts on with a monkey wrench we couldn't move them. It took a hell of a lot more leg than I care to remember before I got a pimply fifteen year old on a tractor to stop and help.'

Cat looked at her over her shoulder.

'I saw you go from my window this morning. What were you doing for all that time?'

'Walking, sitting, thinking,' Anna reached for a cigarette. Cat was a good listener and she needed to talk or go crazy. 'Can you keep a secret, Cat?'

She giggled. 'Does the Pope speak Italian?'

'Don't spread it around, but I know this place. It's my old school and this was my room years ago.' She sipped gloomily at her cocoa. 'I guess nostalgia got me by the throat this morning.'

Her companion made a disbelieving snort. 'Cobblers, I don't believe you've gone all gaga over reliving your schooldays. There must be more to it than that. What happened? Did you have it off in the stationary cupboard with the art master?'

Anna grinned. 'We didn't have art masters, but there was this chap...'

Hair brushing and cocoa temporarily forgotten Cat listened raptly to the chronicling of the sins of Félix.

'Je-*sus*!' she breathed when Anna finished. 'Talk about extra-curricular activities – wish *I'd* been here instead of walled up in Yorkshire with a bunch of nuns.'

Anna said, 'Nuns are icky – but safer; much, much safer!'

*   *   *

After Cat had left for her own room Anna lay back on her pillows. Peeling the skin off her cooling cocoa she wondered why on earth she had told Cat, of all people. Her ebullient friend would never manage to keep it to herself and Anna had a nasty feeling that the youthful indiscretions she'd just confided to her would most likely be all around Headquarters in twenty-four hours – or less.

The cocoa was lukewarm; she made a face and drank it quickly before turning out the bedside lamp and sliding beneath the coarse sheets and Army blankets.

Too cold and damp to be sleeping alone she thought and was suddenly flooded with an aching longing for the touch of Asa's hands, the feel of his strong body covering hers. Shivering she pulled the blankets up to her chin and closed her eyes. Listening to the guttering outside her window overflowing and splashing down the wall she willed her body to be quiet.

If she could pray as Patrick did to his benevolent and omnipotent God she would ask: wherever Asa is now bring him back safe and sound – and soon; look after Patrick and Charlie for me because they are my anchor, the two beings in my life who give without taking, who are wise and loving and the sanest, most grown up people I know.

She hunched under the bedclothes, closing her mind to the memory of the last time Asa had made love to her. Somehow she had to live without him – and without Patrick to pick her up and Charlie to dust her down each and every time that she bit the dust.

14th April, 1942

Anna walked swiftly into the empty anteroom and poured herself a whisky, signed for it then left quickly before anyone else appeared.

As the months had passed and no word came from Asa, she had found it increasingly difficult to join in the familiar chat and complaints of her fellows; their tired, repetitive army grumbles and jokes merely adding to the painful, sometimes unbearably sad burden of being back on old territory. She found Cat and her questions and

170

eager interest in Félix *et al* a bore and an intrusion into her privacy. She avoided the boathouse and the lane to Carey Cottage; even managed to evade the easy camaraderie of the anteroom where her companions gathered to drink and unwind before the evening meal. However often she told herself that she was not unique, that at least half of the company had husbands and lovers they had not seen for a year or more, the fact remained that they at least could write and receive letters to alleviate the pain of separation. Not have to worry and guess at whether their men were alive or dead.

'Can't you tell me?' she had begged Patrick in a moment of despair. 'I don't want to know where Asa is, or what he's doing. Only that he's alive and will be coming back…'

But he'd only looked at her with eyes full of pain and answered, 'I don't know any of those things, darling, and couldn't tell you even if I did.'

In that look she'd recognised something of her own suffering and with sudden insight wondered if he could possibly have at least a suspicion of Asa's relationship to him. All her instincts then had been to tell him what she knew, but her courage had failed her, the moment passed and neither had mentioned Asa's name again.

Once in her room she took off her belt and tie and kicked off her shoes before taking the letters from her locker, where they had lain since early morning; waiting for when she could be alone. For a moment she turned them in her hands. One was typed, the other addressed in Patrick's neat script. She stretched out on the bed and propping herself against the pillows, lifted her glass in salute.

'Peace at last! Here's to you, Patrick!' She drank half the whisky in one swallow and putting the typed envelope on one side opened the one from Patrick.

Dear Young One, he wrote. *By the time this reaches you I may already be on my long leave. I hope you have some owing you so that we may meet up at Tring. Charlie tells me the Gallery is in not too bad shape, apart from losing one second story window and the side gate when a stray bomb demolished the corner off-license, (where will he get his under-the-counter whisky when he is in town now, I wonder?).*

You sound more than a little depressed with life in your Alma Mater in far-flung Cornwall. My Brigadier has suggested that you might put your excellent French and reasonably fluent German to use doing a proper *job (his italics, not mine) instead of prostituting your talents at OCTU, and asks how would you like a War Office Board and a nice, cushy job in Whitehall? Or even no Board at all and a not*

so cushy job elsewhere?
I think you'd like my Brigadier.
I hear through the grapevine that Asa will soon be back in our part of the world. He has been in hospital for some weeks but should be home and on sick leave quite soon. I'm told he is well and in one piece.

Always your
Patrick

For several moments she was faint and giddy. Just seeing Asa's name after all this time made her head spin and her heart beat wildly. She held the letter in trembling hands, reading the last paragraph over and over again.

A sob caught in her throat; she sat cross-legged, the letter gripped between her hands. Asa was in hospital, but why and where, and for how long? She gulped again, and taking up the second envelope examined the typed address for a few moments before sliding her finger along the flap and drawing out a single sheet of paper torn from an exercise book.

Dear Worried Grey Eyes...the words blurred and she read on through her tears. *This is all the paper I can find but it beats writing on lavatory paper. I know...I've tried. I leave this place tomorrow for a week or so of convalescence and Sister Constansa has promised to address and send this. Nothing to worry about –just that my hair now has a wider parting but I am sure will eventually be a great improvement when it is properly grown again.*

Lying here in hospital gave me the unusual luxury of having time to think, so I thought of you, as I do anyway, night and day, wherever I am. Please be there for me when I get back...is that an arrogant thing to ask when I have not seen you for so long? But that I cannot help and although we don't meet, you are always and ever in my thoughts and in my heart.

Soon it will be just a short trip on a pleasure steamer and then I shall see you, and hold you, and love you again.

All my love, and all my heart
Asa

For a long time she sat with bowed head, her hands clasped before her, weeping uncontrollably, the sobs harsh and rasping, torn from deep within. Eventually she raised drowned eyes to stare at the wall.

Just where have you been for almost eighteen months? She questioned silently. What am I going to do about you coming back into my life after so long...and will it all be the same? I can see your

172

face; remember how it is to wake with you beside me, and how we made love. But I'm frightened that after all this time you will be different and not so patient and understanding.

Although there is no Félix to come between us now, I know that I'm never going to find the courage to tell you what happened before he left me. Because I am a coward and so afraid that your eyes would show your hurt and contempt at being betrayed so soon after you had gone...

She ran a finger over Patrick's letter, thinking sadly that there was another one with whom she was being less than honest. She longed to break through his barrier of reserve; ask him outright if he suspected that Asa was his son. If he did, then his suffering must be as great, if not greater than hers.

With a sudden fury she thought that the only one who floated through life apparently untouched by a troubled conscience or torn in half by conflicting loyalties, was that bastard Félix. She wondered if he was continuing to swan around Alexandria in his flashy uniform and if he'd managed to get his leg over his virtuous Spanish maiden. She hoped he was still trying and that she was still holding out. It would be a salutary and much needed lesson in patience if she'd kept him waiting all this long time.

*   *   *

DOVE HOUSE, TRING

19th April 1942

Anna sat on the hard bench on the station platform, reading a 'Dig for Victory' poster over and over as she waited for Patrick's train, which was predictably late.

We shall tell each other all our news, she thought, and talk as though nothing unusual has happened. If I don't speak about Asa they will know, both of them, that if they say his name too soon I shall make a complete ass of myself...

The train came slowly into sight, clanking along the rails and pulling into the station with grinding brakes and a sudden gush of steam. She looked for the familiar figure through the smoke eddying along the platform then jumped to her feet as she saw him walking towards her. He gave his faint sardonic grin and dropping the case he carried returned her salute before putting his good arm about her shoulders.

173

She said quickly, 'I rang Charlie when I arrived an hour ago. He says he's wangled some petrol so if we give him another call he'll come and meet us.'

Patrick looked at her keenly; at the over-bright eyes that pleaded: *Please don't talk about Asa yet...I'm not ready...* Hugging her shoulder briefly he said, 'Charlie could wangle an iced cold beer in a volcano, but I'll be glad not to do that long walk back to Dove House today.'

There was a weariness about his eyes that was new; she smiled carefully and said, 'It isn't fair. You shouldn't be in that uniform; you've already done your bit. Your Brigadier should tell you to go home and put on your carpet slippers.'

'Fortunately Army Intelligence doesn't insist on youth and a full compliment of hands...sometimes it doesn't even insist on intelligence,' he returned amiably, 'and speaking of my brigadier, he has a proposition for you.'

'Nice,' she tucked her arm in his as they began to walk down the platform towards the ticket collector. 'Do tell – I haven't been propositioned for simply ages.'

He grunted. 'My lips are sealed. You'll have to wait for him to elaborate, but it will, I guarantee, be better than wearing yourself into a decline in Cornwall. You are so thin I can almost see through you.'

She glanced sideways at his face. 'Well, you're *not* thin and I can see right through *you*! You wangled for him to see me, didn't you?'

'Whatever makes you think that?'

'I'm not so dim, Patrick, that I imagine your brigadier would out of the blue suggest a job for someone he doesn't even know.'

He smiled. 'Who did what doesn't matter, getting you away from that blasted place does. So don't look a gift horse in the mouth, darling. Just say "yes, please; thank you very much, sir" to whatever he offers.'

She squeezed his arm. 'Thank *you* very much, sir, and while we are into metaphors: I know which side my bread is buttered – *and* who is doing the buttering!'

*   *   *

Charlie when he arrived seemed little changed from her last long leave. Perhaps his hair was thinner, his features sharper than before and he was beginning to look his fifty-eight years. He lived a lonely life at Dove House and she worried that the ancient market town of Tring must seem horribly dull after the bustle and vitality of London, but at least he had Frankie for company now. She put her arm around the rough brown body of the dog as he sat close to her on the back seat. A homeless hairy mongrel of indeterminate breed, he had been adopted by Charlie when he'd gone to view the damage to the gallery. From wandering half-starved among the bombed and rubble-strewn streets, Frankie now resided in luxury at Dove House and was his rescuer's constant companion.

*   *   *

'What's that wonderful smell?' she asked as Charlie opened the panelled front door and ushered them inside. 'I haven't smelt food that delicious for months.'

He winked. 'Better not ask questions, although I didn't go into his Lordship's beech woods for it...it walked out and straight into the car.'

'A Rothschild pheasant,' Patrick tutted, then grinned. 'Just let me get out of this uniform and I'll be right down to do it justice.'

'Me too; I swear we've been eating horse in Cornwall, not to mention porridge or kippers for breakfast every single day,' Anna beat him to the stairs. 'Down in ten minutes, Charlie,' and she flew on winged feet to her room under the eaves, to the Empire bed, the bow-fronted chest, rose geranium soap and everything that felt and smelled of Stratton Place and home...

She changed into a cream linen dress and standing before the oval swing mirror carefully repaired her make-up. Only when she was satisfied that her eyes were clear and her mascara intact, did she go downstairs and follow the smell of roasting pheasant to the kitchen. Later, after their meal she made coffee and they sat in the garden to talk, with Frankie laid out before them on the grass, his pink belly towards a sky studded with stars.

Slowly she felt herself relaxing completely, all the tensions and worries slipping from her mind. This was what she had longed for through all these last months, to be here in this quiet house surrounded by familiar objects and the people she loved. Even the painful memory of her last meeting with Félix, stirred by her unwilling return to Cornwall, was beginning to fade. Here, there was nothing to remind her of him, only the remembered presence of Asa walked with her through this place.

Tactful as ever, neither Patrick nor Charlie mentioned Asa; with ears fine-tuned to her every mood they waited patiently for her to make the first move. But by the time the grandfather clock in the hall

175

struck midnight, fearful still of unleashing on them what she felt would be an unstoppable torrent of emotion, she still hadn't managed to say his name.

Eventually, she saw Patrick glance at Charlie before leaning to push his finished cigarette into the earth. 'This is getting to seem a very long war, isn't it?' he observed in a neutral voice. 'Remember Paris in 'thirty-seven, Anna, with all the lights and the music and the feeling that really, whatever happened, nothing could ever change all that?'

Anna's eyes were on the stars. 'The Louvre and Notre Dame; Fireworks on the left bank, the *Tour Eiffel* in the pouring rain...' She took a deep breath and plunged on, 'Asa getting totally ratted and doing that embarrassing dance with a tart in that low night-club...' her voice broke slightly. 'You were so cross with me that night.'

'You deserved it,' he smiled and asked, 'Have you ever let him live that down?'

'Not likely, I haven't.' It was better now. The tight, painful band that had been around her throat all evening was beginning to ease. She risked a smile in return. 'That was the one and only time I'd ever felt superior to the previously unsurpassed Asa.'

Patrick took out his cigarette case then changed his mind and put it back in his pocket. Without looking at her he asked. 'When and where are you meeting?'

In control now and getting back into her stride Anna picked up her own cigarettes from the table. 'In London next Friday, when I go back to see your Brigadier; after that we shall have a few days together before I have to return to OCTU. However, that will still leave time for you to have him to yourself for a while, won't it?'

'Yes.' His tone was so dry she could almost hear it rustle. 'That's very thoughtful of you, darling. Is there anything else you'd like to suggest I might do apropos of Asa?'

She looked down at her hands. *You do know or at least suspect something...if only you'd say...* She longed to ask him, but years of living with Patrick had taught her when to stop asking questions and she gave in, answering lightly, 'No, no suggestions about Asa, but if your brigadier comes up with a good one as to how I can avoid spending the rest of this war doing a multitude of things for which I am entirely unsuited, I shall be very grateful.'

Charlie scowled. 'I'd rather be with the two of you doing some kind of decent job than stuck here in the sticks with yon hairy mutt,' and he glared ferociously at Frankie, who showed his teeth in a whiskered canine grin and panted adoringly.

176

'You've the Home Guard, Charlie.' Anna reminded, adding mischievously, 'I can't wait to hear you doing your stuff again with your chaps on Church parade.'

'And *I* can't wait to hear him once more in the kitchen at Stratton Place and know for certain that something civilised will be arriving on the dinner table.' Patrick yawned and stretched, rubbing his foot over the comatose Frankie, 'Time for bed, children.'

Crossing the hallway Anna paused with her foot on the first stair and smiled at them both. 'See you at breakfast. Not porridge, Charlie dear, or kippers...I couldn't bear it!'

They stood together watching her climb the stairs and waited to hear the door of her room close, then turned and smiled and put their arms about each other. 'Welcome home,' Charlie smoothed his hand over his lover's crisp greying hair. 'Come along;' he led the way into the small sitting room, 'I've been saving a fine single malt for just this moment.'

Patrick sat twisting his glass, watching the amber liquid swirl up the side of the glass, 'I don't think it's a good thing that she's able to keep quite such a hold on her feelings, do you?'

'No, but you have to admire her courage, and in her own way she managed it rather well, didn't she?' Charlie took a thoughtful pull at his whisky. 'After that little exchange tonight, do you still think she doesn't suspect about Asa?'

'She knows *something* ... I should have spoken when she gave me the opening, but I was taken off guard...somehow the time never seems right.' He sighed. 'I hope she treats him gently when they meet in London because he's having a particularly bloody war'

Charlie scratched his chin. 'What about Félix? She never mentions him now but I've a feeling he's still around.'

Patrick closed his eyes as though in sudden pain. 'I damned well hope not. I never even met the little sod, and I'm very grateful for that.'

'That makes two of us.' Charlie gave him a searching look. 'You look all in. I reckon you've been having a pretty bloody war, too.'

'I've known better days,' he smiled bleakly. 'I should have liked Asa to have been with all of us this week, but he had a slight set back and they kept him longer in the convalescent home than expected... I'll see him in London, but I daresay he'll want to come here later to recharge his batteries. Look after him well, Charlie if he manages to snatch a few days with you. I don't suppose it will be long before he's off again.'

'I'll feed him up and he can sleep 'till noon...Stop worrying about him, will you, and think about yourself for a change,' Charlie gave him a smile compounded of affection and mild irritation. 'Remember, *I'm* supposed to be the old hen around here, not you.'

Patrick reached out and took his hand, weighing it in his own for a moment.

'Old friend,' he said softly. 'It's so good to be back and I've missed you like hell.'

Later, just before sleep overtook his tired mind he said, 'So how does life still go on being so good for you and me, Charlie, now that we are getting old and grey?'

'It doesn't matter about getting older, only that we are together, although the times we are apart become more and more difficult.' For a moment Charlie was silent. 'Out there, when I don't hear from you, you are not stupid enough be getting yourself into any danger, are you?' he asked.

'No.' Patrick smiled into the darkness. 'I'm just a boring old desk-bound fart!'

'You're also a lousy liar; you always were'

'Stop worrying,' he murmured, 'and go to sleep, you old fool.'

*   *   *

Anna lay awake listening to the creaking of the old house. The pipes gurgling as Charlie ran a bath and the murmur of voices as they prepared for bed; worrying about them both and wondering if anything happened to the other how either would manage alone after all these years. It had to come sometime, but not yet she prayed, not yet.

She was just drifting off to sleep when she felt a hairy body insinuate itself onto the end of her bed and creep towards her pillow. She put out a hand to fondle a rough head. 'Shut the door on you tonight has he, Frankie? Never mind. *I* can do with some company.'

The dog licked her hand and groaning with pleasure stretched out on the covers, belly up and front paws limply dangling, the rear ones straight.

'God,' Anna propped herself on one elbow and peered down on the flattened and comatose body. Her voice shook. 'Damned if you don't look just like Asa when he's pissed!'

Frankie slept on unaware of the salty wetness that dripped down onto his unprotected belly and gradually trickled down his ribs to invade his wiry coat.

18

LONDON

April 26th, 1942

Anna saluted as the orderly closed the office door behind her then took a good look at Patrick's legendary Brigadier.

He was tall and loose-limbed, with thinning blonde hair and a face as creased and craggy as a relief map of the Pyrenees. At her entrance he looked up, unleashing a smile that must have been devastating in his youth and still packed enough power to make Anna blink.

He said in perfect French, 'Come in, lieutenant. Sit down and take off your cap. We won't be too formal.' He studied her for a moment in silence before asking, 'Has Major Farrell told you what this is all about?'

As it appeared that their mother tongue was going to play little or no part in this conversation she answered him in the same language, 'No, sir, only that you might have a job for me.'

'Possibly, but it would mean moving you to London. After the peace and quiet of Cornwall you might find that rather a tall order.'

'I don't mind, sir. I lived here before the war.'

'Yes, of course; you helped run that Gallery of his...some sort of relative...a niece, is it?'

She thought, As if you didn't know, but answered him composedly. 'Not quite, sir, rather more a second cousin several times removed!'

'Hmm,' she saw his eyes flick to the single pip on each shoulder. 'The Major did say you'd been in that outfit since 'thirty-nine, so how is it you haven't more of those?'

'I think I'm often out of step, sir.'

'Not the best thing to be in the army, is it? Why choose service life?'

'It just seemed a useful way to fight a war.'

'What do you know about Military Intelligence?'

She was quick-witted enough not to be rattled by this abrupt jumping from one subject to another and answered blandly, 'About as much as any other army subaltern, sir...which isn't a lot.'

'You're not supposed to know *anything*!' he reproved, but his eyes twinkled.

'No, sir,' her mouth twitched. 'I've forgotten already.'

'I can see why you're still a subaltern...' He tilted back on his chair and reverted to English, 'All right, as I'm informed your German is more than adequate...mine is rather less than that so I won't inflict it on you... I think you'll probably do. It would be a good idea if you start here at H.Q., where we can use fluent foreign language staff for all kinds of work...Do you drive, by the way?'

She said cautiously, 'After a fashion, sir...that is, I do, but I was learning on a Bedford truck with a crash gearbox, then got moved to Pay before I had the chance to progress to a car!'

'In theory, if you can drive a truck you can drive anything!' He was amused. 'Some officers prefer to do without a third ear in the car for security reasons, so you may be called upon to be both driver and aide. However, staff cars and red tabs not being expendable, I think we'll send you on a short course before letting you loose with any of our more valuable senior officers.'

She repressed a grin, 'Yes, sir.'

'Right,' he was suddenly brisk, 'I'll see your Chief Commander is informed of your transfer. Better not return to OCTU...I see you've a few days leave still to run. Just hold yourself in readiness to be called at any time after that ends. Is that clear?'

'Quite clear, sir,' she hesitated then asked, 'shall I be called for a Board, sir?

'No, I don't think you'll need another one of those.' The amused look was back. 'That's all for now.'

As she rose to her feet and put on her cap he stood and held out his hand.

'Goodbye – and good luck. You'll sign the Official Secrets Act before you leave today. Nothing said in this building or any other, ever goes beyond the four walls, including this afternoon's conversation.'

'Yes, sir.'

He walked with her to the door. He said, 'It *could* get to be a tough job; are you tough, Subaltern Farrell?'

She smiled. 'I can be, sir if called upon. Or so I'm told!'

*　　　*　　　*

She walked quickly along Whitehall in the early evening drizzle. She'd forgotten how dirty and grimy London was now, with its gritty bomb damaged streets and perpetual smell of wet sandbags. She

180

thought longingly of how good it would feel to get out of uniform, but all her decent clothes were at Tring. Still, if she hurried she could light the geyser at Stratton Place and have time for a quick splash through the regulation five inches of water before joining Asa.

She sped down the steps into the underground just in time to fall into a Circle Line train as the doors were closing. Despite the dirty floor and windows and the gloomy blue light bulbs, she was hard put not to shout aloud with relief. No more OCTU! Some other poor bloody section officer would have to take on her latest shower of cadets. For now she could camp out in Stratton Place and have a few precious days to spend with Asa.

She felt a sudden rush of guilt, remembering how she had combed meticulously through the house after Félix had been there; cleaning specks of shaving soap from the mirror, emptying into the dustbin the ashtray with its half-smoked French cigarettes and the paper folder of foreign matches, removing every sign that he had ever been there.

The news that Asa had been wounded had reinforced her decision not to tell of that visit from Félix and her own shameful weakness. He had gone, never again to be a part of her life, and she wouldn't allow the memory of that night to spoil the love and passion that she and Asa had found in each other's arms.

Tremors of excitement and anticipation began to run through her and she gripped the canvas strap of her respirator bag so tightly that her finger's ached. *Give us time to know each other before he leaves me again...let him still want me as he did before he went away...*

*   *   *

As if on cue Asa looked up as she entered the bar, felt the familiar kick inside and thought, 'Oh, dear God, here we go again!'

Suddenly he wished he hadn't chosen this public place for such a fraught and emotionally charged meeting. At the time it had seemed a good idea to have an hour or two to settle again with each other after so long apart, somewhere where he at least would have to control his emotions. Now all he wanted was to be alone with her at Stratton Place; to hold her close in his arms, see the invitation in those deep grey eyes and feel her beautiful sensuous body moving against his.

She didn't see him at first, but stood looking around the room, scanning the tables. He could sense her nervousness; see the little anxious pucker between her brows, and his heart went out to her. Then she saw him and as he rose to his feet she came across the room, pulling off her cap, shaking her hair free, eyeing the empty glasses before him and saying breathlessly, 'I see you've been keeping the barman busy while you've been waiting. I do hope that remaining large gin is for me!'

She sat down and he saw how her hands shook as she pushed them through her hair with the old familiar gesture. She was rushing her words and a feverish excitement emanated from her in waves. He wanted to put his fingers on her lips, say, 'Hush, don't worry, my love. I understand: it's *all right...*'

Her gaze darted over him. She blinked quickly at the long wound on his head, unprepared for the cicatrix that ran, red and smooth, from his centre hairline to the top of his left ear. Quite without conscious thought a vision of Félix, sleek, well fed and unharmed rose before her, and her face flooded with colour at the memory of that last meeting and how, even against her will her body had obeyed him.

Beneath her breath she said '*Shit!*' and forced herself to meet Asa's eyes. Conscious that she was babbling but unable to stop, she said in a rush, 'Asa darling, you simply can't imagine what I've gone through to get here. Have you *tried* to get a taxi in Bloomsbury these days? I thought I'd got lucky on the corner of Russell Square until a bloody Colonel appeared; then while I was saluting him the bugger pinched my cab!'

Asa moved the full glass towards her saying placidly, 'Yes, sweetheart, very trying. Don't bother to say hello...' but his own hands were shaking, giving the lie to his outward calm.

'Sorry Asa. I'm just horribly nervous; nobody said...I didn't realise how bad it was...' she gave up and spread her hands in apology. '*Je vous présente toutes mes excuses pour le langage grossier!*'

He said, 'So you bloody well should!'

For a moment, she stared at him solemnly, then she gave a cautious grin, her eyes shifted infinitesimally from his and he thought now I'm not entirely sure whether I want to kiss your lovely mouth or break your ruddy neck, you aggravating, enchanting bitch. Because I know just by that look in your eye and the way you grin that you're not only jittery as hell but hiding something! Aloud he said, 'I thought we could eat as soon as you've downed that gin. I've booked a table at Ley Ons.'

'Chinese...lovely,' she looked at him over the rim of her glass. 'But you can't spend more than five bob, you know; Lord Woolton says so. Then what – dancing, theatre, cinema, pub crawl?'

He studied her for a moment in silence then offered, 'I was rather hoping that a fuck wouldn't be out of the question!'

Her eyes sparkled. 'How very diplomatically you put things, Asa!'

'Of course, if you are tired we could romp briefly then I could creep away and leave you to your beauty sleep.' he suggested.

'Since when did you have the will power to do that?'

'Oh,' he waved an airy hand. 'I've managed so to do with all the *other* women I've slept with...especially if their husbands home are coming!'

'I love it when your beautiful English comes out French...and you're a lying bastard aren't you?'

'It could happen soon unless the right woman takes charge of me.' She said. 'I don't think I'm ready to take charge of anyone right now. I think I need someone to take charge of *me*.'

'I'm happy to volunteer...'

She sat twisting her glass in her hand for a moment, watching him openly, then met his eyes and flushed again, this time at the naked desire in them. No, she definitely wouldn't tell him about Félix. She fiddled with her cigarettes. 'Where did girls carry these things in peacetime? Whenever I'm in civvies I find myself groping my bosom to fetch them from my top pocket. I get the strangest looks.'

He put a reassuring hand over hers, smiled and said, 'Yes, darling you would.'

She relaxed a little and returned his smile. 'I think I may be in London for a while; I have a new job, did you know?'

His eyes flickered briefly. 'No, why should I?'

'Liar,' she challenged, 'who told you – Patrick?'

'Let's say I just heard that you were in line for one.'

'Hmm, no doubt in the same way Patrick "just heard" that you were on your way home.'

He said, 'I think you are prying – hasn't he cured you of that yet?'

'No. It's all right; I'm only teasing.' She turned his hand in hers and gave him her sudden luminous smile. 'I'm sorry I'm jumpy. It's been so long...I don't know what to say...all I want to do is make love. Oh, Asa, I worry about you so much...'

'As much as you worry about Félix?'

She said swiftly, 'I don't. He does nothing to cause me worry now.'

'No?' The old sarcastic twist was back on his mouth. 'Don't fret, darling, he will when he gets back.'

'Don't spoil it. Please don't spoil it.'

The sad eyes and the droop of her mouth halted his sudden, painful jealousy. He said, 'Now *I'm* sorry.'

She finished her drink, then lifting her chin in a show of bravado that stabbed him with a swift pain, stood her empty glass alongside his four. 'Better take me away and feed me, Asa. Stay here and drink one more of those and you'll be too ratted to stand up!'

He released her hand. 'I'll only do *that* if you dance too close to me again.'

He stood, tucking his cap under his arm, giving her a not quite sober grin. She looked back at him solemnly then gave her sudden husky giggle.

'You don't really want to go dancing, do you?'

'No, not really,' he put out his hand and pulled her to her feet.

'What would you rather do?' At his involuntary smile she steadied herself with a hand against his chest and gave a laugh that made his back goose-pimple. 'I know; you've already told me! But I'm sorry, Asa, I *must* have dinner, the larder is bare at Stratton Place and I'm starving.'

'When were you not? Come, we shall eat, but after that...' dropping his voice he asked, 'but after that, bed, I think, don't you?'

As they stepped out into the dark streets the sirens began to wail. 'Bugger,' Asa took her hand and began to run towards the Underground. 'Who told those sods I was back in town?'

*   *   *

He lay half-asleep, watching a pale moon laying a faint pathway across the bed, mulling over the evening in his mind. Once the All Clear had sounded and they had left the shelter to gain the haven of Stratton Place, it had been one of the best, an oasis of pleasure and sensual delight in his life of darkness and fear and death, and he'd cherished every moment as though it were his last. Stretching his feet to the end of the bed he felt her move beside him and smiled into the darkness. Turning he kissed the crown of her head. 'I thought you were asleep.'

'I thought *you* were; I was trying not to wake you.' Anna settled her cheek onto his shoulder. 'I must say I'm impressed. Perhaps you should convalesce more often!'

He felt the breath of her laughter on his skin and said, 'I don't need a bullet in my head to make that sort of love to you. I can manage that at anytime.'

'I had noticed.' She moved to sit up against the pillows. 'Do you know what I like most about you?'

'If it's rude I don't think you should tell me.' He closed his eyes

184

and laid his lips against her breast.

'It isn't.' She looked down, cradling him against her, stroking the long scar gently. 'The thing I like most is that you go on touching me and talking to me afterwards. You never just turn away, or start looking for a cigarette or say, "I'd better be going."'

He murmured rashly, 'Manners never were Félix's strong point!'

'Oh, is that what it is...manners?' She was caustic.

'No.' He raised his head. 'It's because I love you and I want you to myself without having to think about that greedy little shit.'

She gave him a tense, searching look. 'Why are you talking about Félix when we are together like this?'

'Because we always do; because he's always in the bloody way,' he turned his head aside, suddenly impatient. 'I can't even *foutre* you in peace!'

He felt her breast heave and closed his eyes again. 'If you are laughing, I really shall slap you!'

She slid a hand along his thigh and leaned down to whisper. 'You can, if you let me *foutre* you first!'

He opened his eyes and looked at her with simulated outrage.

'I beg your pardon? You will do no such thing – ' his thigh jumped under her caress. 'Well, not for another five minutes at least.'

*　　*　　*

The next morning they walked down through Torrington Place, then along Tottenham Court Road until they found a steamy café full of breakfasting Fire Watchers from the nearby ARP post.

Asa tried to retreat but Anna complained: 'I'm *dying* of hunger!' and dragged him firmly to a table before ordering sausages and fried potatoes from the unshaven Greek cook.

'Haven't you ever heard of food poisoning – and these things are eighty per cent bread and twenty per cent very old cow gristle!' Asa prodded gloomily at a pale sausage and watched it gush watery fat and shrink to half its size.

She waved her fork. 'Don't think about it, just eat!' and attacked her own with gusto. He winced visibly.

'Do they starve you in Cornwall?'

'No, but we have horrible little ATS cooks who don't care and reduce anything resembling meat or vegetable matter to a kind of greasy fibrous stew. If anyone finds anything recognisable on their plate they shout "House!"' She raised guileless eyes to his face, 'honestly, Asa. I'm not making it up.'

185

He was sceptical. 'Honestly, Anna, you are!'

'Well, maybe…a bit.' She was silent a moment, then observed, '*You're* revoltingly thin. Don't "they" feed you?'

'Mostly, and thank you for the compliment.'

She sighed and put down her knife and fork. 'I'm trying not to pry, but I *worry*…'

'Then don't. Knowing that Patrick worries himself sick about me is enough, without having you join in.' He watched the colour rush to her face. 'Why *does* he worry about me, Anna – do you know?'

She was confused and unprepared. What else am I going to discover she thought in sudden panic? If Patrick worries about you so much that it shows, I can only think of one good reason why he should…Oh, God! I believe he really *has* worked it out. Aloud she said, 'He worries about all of us. He's that sort of man.'

'Perhaps,' Asa's eyes were still on her face, 'but all the same, I'm irritated by this air of mystery about your family and mine. Félix thinks it's because Maman and Patrick were lovers, but you and I know that couldn't be true, don't we?'

'Yes.' Her blush continued to rise. She concentrated on her plate, chopping viciously at her sausage. 'We've discussed before her objections to men like Patrick. I just wish you'd drop the whole subject of your mother and the past. My conscience tells me that if I hadn't been such a triumphant, unfeeling little bitch that last term at school, she might not have gone back to France and got caught up in this bloody war.' She looked at him, anger sparking in her eyes. 'I feel guilty enough about that without having you keep dragging up her reasons for hating my family.'

'For God's sake don't blame yourself for anything that my mother did,' he was startled by her outburst. He crossed his arms and leaned across the table. 'I don't think she could help being as she was. Life hadn't been kind to her, you know. My father once said that she married him on the rebound because the man she wanted didn't want her. They were not happy together; he always had a mistress and not often the same one for long, and there were endless rows. When he died I think she returned to Cornwall to try and find the peace that she'd known as a girl – '

'– And walked straight into me!'

'Exactly,' he hunched his shoulders helplessly. 'Why she should have reacted so violently over your relationship to Patrick I still have no idea, but I can't believe it is a simple and straightforward as you make it sound. I don't want to hurt or make you angry, Anna, any more than I want to pry into Patrick or Maman's past. I love you and I value his and Charlie's friendship too much to upset or cause any of you unhappiness, but I don't like this barrier that talking about them always seems to raise between us.'

She pushed her plate away and leaned her head on one hand. 'I'm sorry. It's not your fault.'

He forced a smile. 'This is a terrible place for this sort of conversation.'

'This is a terrible place, full stop...and you were right about the sausages, but before we try to think of something else to talk about...'

She paused for a moment and he knew she was going to ask him one of those questions that always had more behind the words than appeared on the surface. Sometimes when she did this he felt he was on the brink of finding what lay behind that secretive curtain that she had become so adept at drawing between them.

When she spoke, it was in a carefully neutral tone.

'I've never asked you before but I've always wanted to know... When did *you* know for certain about Patrick? And why did you stand up for him against Madame?'

'I think I guessed the first time that we met, although it wasn't that obvious.' He returned her inquiring gaze with no sign of discomfiture. 'I stood up for him because I felt he was a good man leading a good life and shouldn't be pilloried for having the courage to be as God made him.'

'And the way God made him didn't bother you?'

'No. Not in the least.'

'Are you sure that you didn't, like Madame, feel disgusted or repulsed?'

'No,' he repeated. 'Why should I? He wasn't the first such man I'd met and liked.'

She watched him in silence for a moment then smiled. 'You always say the right thing, don't you, Asa Gallimard?'

'I'm glad I passed the test.' He watched her eyes widen innocently and added with a satirical look. 'No wonder you've been recruited into that rouge's gallery. You're a natural!'

She fluttered her lashes. 'Why, Captain Gallimard, What do you mean?'

'That you'll make a damned good side-kick for some dodgy old War Office fox,' he stood. 'I have to leave you for a while. I have a Medical Board today which will tell me when I am to re-start my war...' He leaned down to kiss her mouth. 'I'll be back this afternoon and then for our remaining time together we shall find better things to do than talk about the past.' He looked down at her plate and grimaced. '*Bon appétit*, Anna!'

When he had left she sat on for a few minutes, prodding the remains of her meal around, reflecting that no one ever exited a room more swiftly than Asa, nor left it feeling so empty as when he'd gone.

*   *   *

He came into her room and stood leaning against the bed rail, watching as she finished her packing. Without looking up she asked, 'Have you 'phoned Patrick?'

'Yes. We will meet for lunch then I shall go to stay with Charlie until I'm posted.'

He continued to watch her in silence until she clicked the hasps on the leather case and straightened to look at him. He held out his hand. 'Come. Before you leave I want to ask you something.'

She stood before him and he held her shoulders, looking at her in silence for a few seconds then asked, 'Why didn't you tell me Félix had been here?'

For a split second she was taken off guard but recovered and countered swiftly, 'What makes you think he has?'

He smiled as if at some private joke and took a crumpled blue cigarette packet from his pocket. 'This was in the pocket of the bathrobe I used this morning.'

Inwardly cursing that she'd missed that damming twist of paper, she took the Gitane packet in steady fingers and lied unflinchingly.

'It must be Patrick's…perhaps from one of his many jaunts?'

'Of course; maybe he just got tired of smoking his usual Turkish!' He was still smiling and she narrowed her eyes.

'What's so funny?'

'You…answering a question with a question to give you time to think; Patrick does that.'

'So do you…on occasions.' She screwed the packet into a ball and flipped it towards the waste basket. 'Come along or I shall be late for my interview, then I shan't know where I'm supposed to be going today.'

'There is plenty of time.' He held her with his hands about her waist. 'Anna, I don't know when I shall see you again and I want…need, to know if you will still be here for me when I return.'

'Of course, don't you know that by now?'

'And Félix? What if he comes back?'

'He won't. It's over. Finished.'

His gaze held hers so that she couldn't look away. 'Truthfully?'

188

'Cross my heart.'

He took a deep breath then smiled again. 'In that case, Anna Farrell, I really think you should marry me.'

Straight faced she said, 'No time...there is another man in my life and he's waiting at the War Office.'

'Don't play that game with me!' His hands tightened. 'When this war is over will you marry me -Yes or No?'

She looked up into the brown eyes, at the lean dark face that had become so dear to her then pulled his head down to hers. 'Yes, Asa, I will marry you whenever you wish – tomorrow if you like.'

'No. That would not be fair to either of us. We both have our jobs to do and for me...' he shrugged. 'I must do mine without worrying if I have left a pregnant wife behind!'

'Married or unmarried I don't somehow think that would be on the agenda. That can wait; in the meantime I don't need a piece of paper to give me leave to love.' She laid her cheek against his, her eyes bright with tears. 'Even if this is all there is to life, all I'll ever have, I'll always be glad I've had it with you. Just remember that and come back to me.'

'I'll do my best.'

'Don't come with me now. I don't think I could bear to leave you in a crowd of people.'

Cupping her face in his hands he kissed her deeply, '*Au revoir*, Anna.'

'*Bonne chance*, Asa,' she gave him a last smile then picking up her case left the room.

He listened to the opening and closing of the front door and her footsteps fading away along the street before he stooped to pick up the cigarette packet from the floor.

*All right, Félix, you've had your chance...*He dropped it into the waste paper basket then looked out of the window along the street down which she had just walked. He shook his head. *You are the most terrible, unconvincing liar, Anna...when are you going to understand that you need never lie to me? That despite everything I said all those months ago, I should forgive you whatever you did, and who ever you did it with, even Félix. Because you are my love and my life, my heart and my soul; you are in my very bones, and I can't even begin to imagine a future that doesn't have you at my side.*

PART III

There is nothing either good or bad,

but thinking makes it so

W.S.

19

POOLE HARBOUR, DORSET

November 6th, 1943 – 20.30 hrs

Patrick sat on the bed watching his batman pack his kit. He wondered how long they would be in Lisbon, ruminating that at least there it should be reasonably warm, even in November. His last mission in the snow-covered mountains of Yugoslavia, as a neutral mediator in the simmering antipathy between hardened Partisans and Communist guerrillas half his age, had been more than enough to make him appreciate a move even to Lisbon; that hot bed of spies, intrigue and double-dealing.

He lay back, resting his head against the cold iron of the bed end and lit a cigarette. It was a pity that he was off again so soon though, he would have liked more time in London with Anna before she left for Gibraltar with that confounded wolf Travers…he gave an inward smile, thinking that even Travers' considerable, if middle-aged charm, was unlikely to get him far with Anna; not when all available space in her heart and mind was so taken up with Asa.

'Ostensibly you'll be British Liaison Officer to the Italian top brass for your sins.' The Brigadier had grinned at his briefing. 'They're giving you a very decent Italian bloke, Captain Delgardo, for your aide. Now that Italy's turned on Adolf, Spain is packed tight with more spies and double agents than ever, and of every nationality under the sun; many of whom are just a load of thugs trying to turn an easy penny, so watch your back. You'll have one hell of a job sifting through all the information coming in, but you should be used to that by now.'

'All ready for the off sir.' Pettigrew drew the zip on the canvas holdall.

'No man ever got more gear into one bag,' Patrick observed appreciatively, 'better get an early night – five a.m. will be here all too soon for both of us.'

'Anything else I can do for you, sir?' Pettigrew inquired with delicate diplomacy. When and if his charge needed help with his belts and buckles had to be judged to a nicety; if Pettigrew sounded more nanny than batman he was liable to get a terse rejoinder to sod off.

But tonight his charge shook his head amiably. 'Thank you, no. I've some letters to write yet. I'll manage by myself tonight.'

Patrick watched him go then left the bed to sit at his table. Drawing a sheet of notepaper towards him and uncapping his fountain pen he began to write: first to Charlie, then Anna, the letters he always wrote at such times and hoped would never be delivered.

He had always harboured a deep, irrational hatred and mistrust of flying, expecting each moment to be his last; spending every journey rigid with a fear he had schooled himself not to show. The Lisbon run was particularly nerve-wracking in view of the occasional 'accidents' that had befallen the slow moving flying boats over the years. Each time he returned from any mission he enacted a little ceremony of burning the letters in the waste bin, while offering a prayer of thanks for having made one more safe homecoming.

I'm galloping towards fifty, he thought as he sealed the second envelope and wrote Anna's name. So what the hell am I doing either risking getting my arse shot off, or playing about at bloody Embassy parties rotting my gut with cocktails in place of good Highland malt?

He sat for a while, turning his pen over in his fingers then pulled another sheet of paper onto the blotter. After further hesitation he began to write again.

Asa,

I pray that you will never see this letter, but if you should I hope when you have finished reading what I have to tell you, that you will perhaps be able to understand and forgive...

*   *   *

Later, lying in bed he let his thoughts range back to the gallery and the years before war came, wondering if and when he and Charlie would ever get back to their old life. He thought about Asa and offered up a prayer for his safety; that he might soon return, marry their lovely and much loved Anna, and not carry her too far away from her home.

He tried to ignore the irritation in the stump of his left forearm. It always twitched and itched when he was anxious or tired, but if he rubbed it too much now, in the morning when he strapped on the leather harness and cup it would be sore. He closed his eyes, blotting out the thought of the take-off in the cold black silence of early morning and the long run above the water before the Short-Sunderland lifted and rose over the sea to begin its journey into the dark

20

INTELLIGENCE HEADQUARTERS, LEEMING, HAMPSHIRE

March 12th, 1944

The sentry scanned their identity papers; their driver waiting patiently until the barrier was lifted and he could turn the camouflaged Humber into the gravelled drive.

A slight case of *déjà vu* thought Anna, except that this drive led not to Lady Elizabeth's vast Jacobean mansion, but a pleasantly modest Georgian country house, the broad terrace surrounded by a stone veranda. Above the main door a gracious pillared porch was overhung with a wisteria that in summer would festoon the building with great swags of blossom, but now hung as a brown and brittle tracery against the white stone.

'Better get ourselves settled in then see if someone can rustle up some food.' Colonel St-John Travers climbed out of the car and stood looking up at the elegant sash windows still disfigured with masking tape. 'Rather better than quarters over that boarding house-come-knocking shop our first night in Gib, eh, Farrell?'

She grinned. 'Let's hope it's a little less noisy, sir.'

'We'll eat, get some of the paper work cleared, then when the rest of them arrive tomorrow we'll be able to set up H.Q. proper and get down to the real work.'

'Do you want me to see about lunch, sir?'

'No. We'll leave that to Lane...' He turned to the driver, 'See what you can do about that will you Lane? And don't forget your own grub – for the past hour your stomach's been gurgling like a bloody submerging sub!'

'Sorry about that, sir.' Lane closed the car door with a flourish then saluted with all the flowery grace of a chorus boy in an Ivor Novello musical. 'I'll see it doesn't offend your ears again, sir!'

'Cheeky sod, isn't he?' Travers began to climb the steps. 'I don't know why I put up with the little squirt.'

She said, 'Probably *because* he's a cheeky sod!'

The room she'd been allocated was small but cheerful, with an adjacent bathroom and a fine view over the extensive grounds at the back of the house. Standing on tiptoe and craning slightly to the left she caught a glimpse of the grey-green Channel lying calm under a watery sun; feeling a *frisson* of excitement at the thought of the momentous happenings that would soon be taking place along this coast.

Standing in front of the wall mirror to fix the celluloid battens into her collar points she mused that if Asa wasn't back within the next few weeks then it was unlikely she'd see him until well after Overlord was launched. She did up her top buttons and began to tie her tie, smiling as she remembered the one rushed leave they'd had together since she had said she'd marry him. Only four days at Stratton Place and they'd spent practically the whole time in bed.

This time it had been Asa who'd initially lost control, throwing restraint to the winds and rushing her out of her clothes and into bed with reckless abandon. Intoxicated at being together again after so many months, both had shown an unrestrained passion and a fine disregard for consequences.

'Do you realise that if I'm pregnant they'll probably Court-martial me for wasting all that time and money on my training – and aren't you rather locking the stable door after the horse has bolted?' she'd asked, when they woke early on their first day and Asa began rather more circumspectly to resume operations where he'd left off the night before.

He'd laughed and kissed her. 'That's all right; I'll come and visit you both in the glasshouse!'

'What happened to that upright and moral man who took me to bed aeons ago and wanted to marry me?'

'He still wants to, but you know you would never feel properly married without Patrick to give you away and Charlie to bake a cake.'

She'd added, 'And Félix as bridesmaid!'

'Wash your mouth out!' He had pounced on her, pinning her down and kissing her until she begged for mercy, after which surrender he'd continued, firmly and expertly, to making very athletic, very erotic, and blissfully satisfying love.

Now, although she still worried endlessly about his safety, since she'd been with the brigadier's 'lot' she at least knew within reason what he was doing, if not where he was doing it. Holding firmly and faithfully to the conviction that he would always return; that when the war ended they would be married then spend the rest of their lives together, she had come to accept more philosophically his long absences. Although frequently plagued by a physical need of him that caused her to have the kind of night thoughts that might possibly send Patrick straight to the confessional, she somehow managed to shrug them away with the morning light and bring her customary sharp, professional mind to each working day.

Now she firmly repressed all licentious imaginings of being in bed with Asa, ran a comb through her hair, checked her stocking seams were straight and went to join her Colonel for lunch.

*   *   *

They worked on into the early evening. It was warm for March and a bright, strengthening sun shone through the tall windows and they soon dispensed with jackets and rolled their sleeves to the elbow.

An orderly, coming in with tea and finding Travers' hand on her shoulder, their heads close together as they bent over a map, returned to the kitchen offering his opinion that the Colonel had got himself a nice bit of stuff on the side with his sexy-looking Junior Commander. Legs like hers, he opined loudly, would get old Hitler himself going.

He couldn't have been more wrong about the nice bit of stuff on the side.

Anna had been with St-John Travers for over a year now as his personal aide. It was an alliance founded on mutual respect and trust. That he was a handsome charmer on the right side of middle age and something of a flirt had at first caused one or two hiccups in their relationship. Deprived of Asa's arms she might have been tempted, albeit only briefly, by a charismatic charm that was hard to resist. But resist it she did and their association had eventually settled down into a mildly flirtatious and companionable one in private and a disciplined and impeccably correct one in public.

When six months under a Mediterranean sun had again threatened to pose a problem or two, Anna, with good-humoured diplomacy had managed still to keep their association on the right side of respectability. Now that they were back from Gibraltar and enduring the full rigors of an English spring, they had settled back into a familiar and comfortable groove, with each able to enjoy the kind of verbal sparing and physical contact that never went further than literal flirtation and an occasional decorous closeness on the dance floor.

Eventually Travers put down his pencil and rubbed his hands over his eyes.

'A lot of this is going to be simply a matter of everyone having an ear to the ground and keeping their eyes wide open...bloody boring job – I can think of a great many more exciting things to do than spend one's time on permanent watch for spies under the beds!'

'There are spiders under mine, but no spies…I've looked.' Anna began to fold the maps and place them back into their cases, adding, 'Rather a disappointment, actually, as I fully expected to find a daintily be-flowered chamber pot nestling beneath the sagging springs.'

'I'll let you know later what I find under mine. With a bit of luck, it might be a chamber*maid* – or more likely, the family ghost. I'm sure there is one.' He stretched his back and suggested, 'If lunch was anything to judge the cook by, I think we'll give the food here a miss for tonight and see what's available in this one-horse town.'

'I was stationed nearby a couple of years ago, sir. The White Harte was doing some pretty amazing things with Spam then. We could see if they still are.'

He sighed. 'I'd rather someone did something pretty amazing with a large steak but Spam will have to do, I suppose.'

In the event the White Harte came up with some very passable chicken curry, although Travers poked around suspiciously in his, remarking *sotto voce* that it was rather dark and sinewy for chicken and had she noticed a distinct dearth of cats in the town?

Later they walked the quiet streets for a while then wandered into the Abbey, to the barely concealed and somewhat unchristian irritation of the sacristan, who was attempting to lock up early when they appeared and spoiled his chances of a quick getaway. Travers gave him an urbane smile, poured a handful of silver into the offertory box with an ostentatious flourish and the sacristan melted away into the shadows.

Anna paused from examining the carved pew ends and marble monuments commemorating the town's departed citizens. Looking up at the faded and tattered Regimental banners of past wars hanging either side of the altar she said, 'You're a full-time soldier, sir, so tell me: why do men want to go to war?'

'Better to ask why do men start them. Chaps like me are only here to deal with the results.'

'But why be a soldier in the first place?'

'Someone has to do the dirty work…' He gave wry smile. 'Why are *you* in this army?'

'Not to shoot or bayonet anyone, that's for sure.' Anna returned crisply. 'I suppose it had marginally more allure for me than working in a factory or wearing those frightful breeches and picking Brussels sprouts in some frozen field in December!' She turned to walk back down the nave, adding not quite under her breath, 'Although God knows *this* uniform's bad enough, being as it is much the same colour as wartime lavatory paper and cookhouse gravy.'

'Sometimes, Miss Farrell I wonder who taught you always to have quite such a trenchant answer for everything!'

They had reached the door and as he stood aside to let her pass, she gave him a sideways glance, saying guilelessly, 'Actually, sir, it was someone not entirely unlike you, but without the bedroom eyes!'

For a moment Colonel St John Travers hung back, allowing himself the pleasure of watching her walk ahead of him. He had a wife and two sons at home in Gloucestershire and was a devoted father and reasonably faithful husband, but Anna Farrell was a constant temptation and there was something about her *derrière* that always made his palm itch, especially after an answer like that...

*　　*　　*

Headquarters settled smoothly into a familiar routine of work and within the month Anna felt she could draw a map in her sleep of each marshalling area in their particular part of Hampshire. She knew every camp and workshop, depot and petrol dump; every airfield, hospital and first aid post from Southampton to Portsmouth and Romsey to Poole.

With vast amounts of troops and equipment expected over a large area during the next weeks and months, security would be a continuing nightmare. A keen eye kept on the Colonel's subordinate and often young, not very experienced Intelligence Officers was only one of Anna's many duties, and she found her days split fairly equally between the office and the field. Also the increasing numbers of U.S. and Allied top brass arriving during the weeks since she and Travers had settled into their own HQ had created an exhausting addition to her workload.

She longed for the chance to go down to Tring; sit under the trees with a glass of Charlie's home-made and frequently lethal wine, and sleep in her own bed again. But whenever she alluded to her accumulation of unused leave Travers would brush such hints aside, launch into his own version of *Once more, unto the breach, dear friends* and send her off on yet another exercise in cementing Anglo/ French/ American relations.

'What happened to the spies under the beds?' she demanded of him after one particularly trying evening of conviviality, to which he replied that he had any amount of under-worked officers who could look for *them*, but only one bi-lingual sex-pot to hand who could keep a mess full of licentious Allied brass hats at arm's length but happy.

* * *

DOVE HOUSE, TRING

April 1944

There had been no letters from Asa since her own return from Gibraltar, but Anna heard frequently from Patrick, who seemed to slip between London and Lisbon with occasional visits to other unspecified places, while Charlie sent her regular parcels containing anything from bed socks to pickled onions.

Towards the end of April she managed to convince Travers that a break from social duties was vital to her sanity, and snatched a short leave at Tring, after extracting a promise that she would be back to more sober and important duties on her return. It was on her second morning at Dove house just as they were sitting down to breakfast that a letter came for Charlie from Patrick

She watched him out of the corner of her eye as he read and saw a nerve begin to jump in his temple. She asked curiously 'Is everything all right, Charlie?'

'I don't know; I haven't read it all yet...but just listen to this: "'Should Asa return before me could you tell him news is filtering through that a few airmen who've landed on hostile ground have found shelter on their way into Spain via the Pyrenees. Interestingly there appear to be two female birds nesting where they sheltered. Only this week a returning American pilot identified one of them as a Gallimard, an unusual specimen to be reported in those parts..."' He turned to the last page, '"Although no ornithologist, Asa is bound to be interested. Tell him also that I *must* see and speak to him on his next leave; I can't let this charade continue – "'

Abruptly he stopped reading and gave Anna a look so blank that she could have written messages on it. There was an electric silence before he cleared his throat and said, 'That's about all...'

Anna put down her knife and fork and took a deep breath. 'Charlie, you don't have to hide anything else that Patrick's written about Asa...I *know*. I've known since the summer of 'thirty-nine.'

For only the second time in her life she saw him totally out of countenance. He looked utterly stunned and his jaw dropped. 'Know what – and since *when*?' he demanded, his voice rising.

'Don't you dare yell at me, Charlie Caulter!'

His eyes glittered. 'Just how much *do* you know and why the hell have you watched the pair of us walking around the subject for the past year or more and said nothing, you devious little tyke?'

'That's bloody rich, coming from *you!*' She flared at him in a mixture of guilt and anger. 'I'm not a flaming half-wit you know...I can put two and two together. *Félix* told me that they weren't brothers but cousins and that after Cecelia died – ' She flushed scarlet and put her hand up to her mouth. 'Oh, *shit!*' She met his accusing blue gaze and set her jaw. 'That's it Charlie. It's your turn now.'

He said sharply, 'I don't think you can leave it there.'

'No? Well sod that, pal. Just don't hold your breath...' For a moment there was silence. She avoided his eyes then said, 'Sorry, Charlie. Put it down to fright...'

More gently he asked, 'Tell me, Anna. Patrick and I no longer have secrets about Asa; I'd like to feel I could say the same for you and I.'

'All right...' She sighed and pushed her plate to one side. 'You've obviously always known about Patrick's little indiscretion in nineteen-fourteen with Dorothy Gallimard's sister, and I guess he's also told you he somewhat tardily discovered that Asa was the result. I'm also guessing that neither you nor Patrick knew Cecilia died shortly after his birth.' She spread her hands helplessly. 'Charlie, you must see why I kept quiet – how could I possibly tell Patrick that?'

He sighed. 'Well, you'd better tell me now – and make it everything this time, will you?'

'I don't know *everything* only that after her sister died Dorothy found a nursemaid for the baby and went to work with the Red Cross at an army sanatorium in Essex. That was where she met Auguste, who had been shell shocked and sent over here for treatment. After the war they married and went to live in France, where they officially adopted Asa when he was as about five.' She lit a cigarette and eyed him cautiously. 'That's about it; honestly.'

'Well, you've managed to dig out most of the details, haven't you?'

'I didn't have to dig far. Once I'd got over the shock of knowing about Cecelia it was easy. Félix is always ready to talk...his mother never allowed any discussion about it, but Auguste made sure that Asa knew he was adopted and who his real mother was. He *might* have known about Patrick but if so he never told him.'

Charlie was thoughtful. 'Are you sure? Asa's deep. He may know.'

She raised both hands, pushing back her hair and rubbing at her temples. 'I'm absolutely sure he doesn't; hell, he's never said more than a half dozen words about his background. But he's no fool; he knew Patrick tried to keep him out of the SOE and that he worries about him and Asa wonders why. He keeps probing and I keep fobbing him off with a whole string of whopping half-truths. One day he's going to find out and when that happens I've absolutely no idea what his reaction would be...to me, and perhaps even more disastrously, to Patrick. I've never seen him lose his temper, but I have a strong sense of self-preservation telling me if he were to hear it from anyone else *but* Patrick, I wouldn't want to be around when it happened!'

Charlie gave a faint, wry smile. 'You could be right.' He was silent again, tipping back on his chair and looking at her with sombre eyes, before observing, 'If you won't tell Patrick the whole truth about Asa's mother, I will. I must.'

'But why? – think what it will do to him to know how Cecelia died,' she pleaded, 'doesn't he carry a big enough burden of guilt, why make it worse?'

He gave her a dry, sarcastic look.

'My dear Anna, you say you don't want to be around Asa when he discovers you've been somewhat economical with the truth. Well, I can assure you that you'd want even less to be within a mile of Patrick if he accidentally stumbles upon *all* the little secrets that you and darling Félix have been sharing behind his back since nineteen thirty-nine!'

She blenched. 'Don't for God's sake tell him in a letter. Wait until he comes on leave.'

'Umm...' He prodded the letter with a gentle forefinger. 'That will be next week.'

She shuddered. 'Then just keep him away from me, will you? I have enough problems as it is.'

'I'll do my best, but I won't make any guarantees.' He set his chair back on four legs and reached a hand across the table to take hers. 'In future, my very dearest Anna,' he said earnestly, 'will you please stop trying to keep everyone in happy ignorance, because when the effluent starts flying *you* are the one liable to catch most of it...right between the eyes!'

'Tell me something I don't know; I've been catching it there for most of my life.' Gloomily she rubbed her fingers over his. 'I bet it *is* Madame in them thar hills, you know; I knew she'd turn up again one day, just to spite me. Félix said she'd left Paris with a friend heading for the Pyrenees.'

'What a positive mine of information that gentleman is.'

She grinned. 'Yes. But he's got one thing spectacularly wrong…he thinks she's the one who went to bed with Patrick!'

She sat back and watched him for a moment in silence, before saying reprovingly. 'Keep laughing like that, Charlie and at your age you'll very likely do yourself a mischief.'

21

For some reason Anna had felt restless and uneasy all day. Never prone to headaches, from when she'd awakened that morning she'd been aware of one lurking threateningly behind her eyes. Travers had noticed and asked if she was "coming down with something and if so, get rid of it p.d.q because this is no time for anyone to be ill."

She'd recovered her spirits sufficiently to answer with some asperity that if she was likely to die she would do so quietly so as not to inconvenience *him* at all, then taken herself haughtily off to Evensong hoping that might dispel her gloom.

And it had been soothing. The Abbey had been dim with a lingering smell of incense and she could almost imagine Patrick was with her and feel the strength and calm he wore about him like a comforting invisible shield.

So powerful was the sense of his presence that when the service was over she left the Abbey, and on impulse turned to walk along the gravel path through the deserted cemetery, hugging the feeling to her and gaining some comfort from the illusion that he was there.

Deep in thought, it was a moment or two before she became aware that she was no longer alone; that someone was keeping pace beside her. Irritably she glanced sideways, saw a familiar kid-gloved hand beneath a khaki sleeve and felt her already faintly queasy stomach glissade to around her knees.

Without looking at him she asked, 'Were you in there?'

'I was; right behind you!'

She gave a secretive smile. 'That accounts for it then.'

'Getting holy, are we in our old age...or perhaps examining our guilty conscience?'

Her stomach lurched again. 'Charlie told you?'

'He did.'

She stopped walking. 'It wasn't entirely my fault,' she defended. She moved the gravel around with her foot. 'You wouldn't let me near you...'

'I know. Sit down.' He indicated a nearby bench, and when they were seated said, 'Talking to you in churchyards could get to be a habit.'

'Yes, well…you didn't have to come all this way to tell me off.'

'That isn't why I've come.'

His voice was suddenly brittle and unsteady. For the first time she turned to look fully at his face, and saw the muscles around his mouth were pulled tight, the lines either side like deep slashes in the taut skin. Drawn and grey, he suddenly looked his age. She met his still eyes and gave an involuntary shiver.

'Why *are* you here?'

He said compassionately, 'If the pubs were open I'd buy you a good stiff drink – I think you should know I've already had several…It took me a couple of goes to follow the directions Travers gave me!' His words were very faintly slurred. The first time, she thought, that she'd ever seen any sign in him that he had been drinking.

She shivered again. 'I've been feeling like shit all day – sorry, but I have. Something's wrong, isn't it? If it's bad news, please tell me and get it over with.'

He said baldly, 'Asa didn't make the rendezvous with the gunboat on his last mission. He apparently left the safe house outside St-Lunaire on time but never showed at the cove. They waited until the tide turned then had to leave without him.' His hand closed over hers. 'It's been over a week and there's been no news at all.'

A sob caught in her throat, but was quickly stifled. 'What will happen if he's been captured?' He didn't answer. Icy cold and calm she said, 'they have pills don't they – in case? Someone told me. Would he take them?'

'I don't know. I don't think so.' He cleared his throat. 'It wouldn't be the first time he's been close to disaster. He's been in some very tight corners before and I don't think it's ever crossed his mind to take that way out.'

'Oh, Patrick…' His stricken face was more than she could bear and she put her arms about his neck and her head against his, sobbing unrestrainedly. 'You don't have to be brave for me…big boys can cry, too!'

He said tightly. 'This one already has.' Then held her against him until her sobs subsided and she leaned, desolate and spent on his shoulder.

He continued to hold her and they sat quietly for a while. Eventually she sat up, wiping her eyes on her handkerchief. He straightened her cap, giving a wry smile. 'God knows what all this looks like to some casual passer-by…Not many old men reeking of whisky get to hug a beautiful young woman like you in public, particularly in a churchyard!'

She gave a pale grin.

'Not many young women get the chance to be hugged by a handsome old man like *you*…drunk or sober, in or out of a churchyard.' She was silent for a moment then said, 'I think I had a premonition about this. It sounds stupid, but I feel better now you've told me.'

'It was probably my thought waves coming out to you – and things are always better once the worst has been faced.' He leaned his elbows on his knees, staring out into the gathering dusk. He said huskily, 'I wish I'd told him, that last leave. I should have. Charlie wanted me to; he said he had a right to know, but I wouldn't take the chance. Being told suddenly you've an old queen for a father isn't the best bit of news to take with you into war, is it?'

'I don't believe that would be as important to him as knowing he has a father who cares about him.' She told him about their conversation in the café and he heard her out before pulling his mouth down and shaking his head.

'Perhaps as that aspect of my life hasn't mattered to him he might forgive my young man's confusion; much harder though to forgive me for being the cause of his mother's death.'

'That wasn't your fault. Even if you'd known and been there, nothing you could have done would have prevented *that*.'

'No? Ever heard of a broken heart – or of life becoming so unbearable that one simply loses the will to live?' He shook his head again, saying bitterly. 'Don't you see? It wasn't so much what I did then, but the abandonment that followed. I made it damned clear that I couldn't, *wouldn't*, play any further part in her life…I doubt she'd have wanted me to anyway, having read my letter and discovered the kind of man she'd given herself to.' His hand was so tightly clenched about a wooden slat of the bench that the knuckles showed white against the tanned skin. 'Imagine what it must have been like in those days to be left pregnant and disgraced in a small village community. How can I feel anything else but responsible and how could Asa possibly forgive any man, let alone me, on whom he looks as a friend, for doing such a thing?'

'When he comes back, you can tell him and I know he'll understand.' Now she was the comforter, putting her arm about his bowed shoulders. 'And he will come back…I'd *know* if he was no longer alive.' She put her hand against her breast. 'I'd feel it. Here.'

206

'If you have that much faith, how can I have less?' He rose, drawing her to her feet. 'I'm so sorry to have brought you this news and not been able to stay with you but I must go now. I'm flying out tonight and I have a car waiting at your HQ to take me back. Walk with me and that will give me time to sober up a little more before I return to duty!'

She gave the ghost of a smile. 'You know, Patrick, you *are* alike, you and Asa.' For a moment she stood looking up into his eyes then stood on tiptoe and whispered, 'Don't tell Charlie, but I think perhaps the reason I fell in love with Asa is because I've always been just a little bit in love with you!'

'I rather think Charlie knows that already!" He smiled and laid his hand against her cheek. "I may not have realised I had a son, but for the past ten years I've certainly felt that I've had a daughter.' Drawing her arm through his he turned and together they began to walk along the path towards the Abbey and the inexorable road back to duty, to the pain and reality of war.

Just before he stepped into the waiting car he bent his head to hers. Keeping his voice low, he said softly. ''Shan't see you for a while…but I'll be giving his Holiness a wave as I pass by…'

She smiled mistily. 'Then *arrivederci*…and take care, I need you.'

He kissed her forehead. 'Don't worry. You are right. He will be back, and so shall I.'

*   *   *

ROME, ITALY

June 8th, 1944 – 14.00 hrs

Félix stood at the top of the Spanish steps, watching as a group of American GIs distributed chocolates and gum to a hoard of clamouring Italian children.

After all the air attacks and bombardment that had seen the German defences around the city crumble, the practically bloodless, almost farcical occupation of only a few days before had left the advancing troops bemused, while even the enthusiasm of the welcoming Italians had been at first slightly muted with shock at the sight of American tanks rolling unchallenged along the Apian Way. Now, observing the eager, begging little hands outstretched, Félix thought that like kids everywhere these were more interested in what cigarettes and candy the liberators of their city had, rather than the fact that their own war at least, was over. They also appeared to know instinctively which uniforms to latch onto. The British he imagined would have few such goodies in *their* pockets!

Observing the children he thought with unaccustomed sentimentality of Maria and the child soon to be born to them both, and of the undoubted, if somewhat restricting pleasures of the marriage bed.

Confronted by his colonel and an inflexibly firm Spanish Vice-Counsel whose daughter he had finally managed to compromise, Félix knew when he had met his match and had acceded, more or less gracefully, to a marriage celebrated with a full nuptial mass witnessed by all her relations. Throughout which ordeal and the merrymaking that followed, he'd had the distinct impression that God was laughing at him.

Six months later the title of husband still sat somewhat uneasily upon his shoulders, and at this distance and without the eagle eye of Maria's papa upon him he was again beginning to feel restless. To compound his feeling of being ill-used, some silly sod of a British Colonel's aide had managed to get himself trodden on by a mule and he, Félix, had been bundled onto a 'plane and transported from Alexandria to Rome at short notice, leaving all home comforts behind.

A girl in a scarlet dirndl and delectably low-cut blouse sauntered slowly past, casting a glance back at him over her shoulder as his eyes followed her ripe inviting form. He glanced at his watch and sighed. There was no time for that now. He had to go and find his new boss, whoever he might be. Smoothing down his uniform, he resumed his tardy journey towards Intelligence HQ and what would hopefully turn out to be a peaceful and relaxed few weeks in the Eternal City.

There were times, he thought morosely, and this was one of them, when he wished he'd kept his several languages to himself. They had proved a useful tool in the newspaper business but a most inconvenient one in a world war. Now he'd probably find himself dancing attendance on some fat old fart who might even require him to do some actual work. An unpleasant prospect for him to contemplate with any feeling of equanimity.

He showed his papers to the sentry at the gate and walked up the short drive, manoeuvring his way delicately through the chaos of packing cases, filing cabinets and Army issue furniture being unloaded from a half-dozen heavy vehicles parked in the forecourt of the large villa. In the midst of this chaos a British sergeant, holding a savagely poised pencil above a clipboard, directed in stentorian tones and execrable Italian hoards of the local soldiery, all of them falling over each other in their efforts to obey his incomprehensible commands. Inside, where a British corporal reigned from behind a probably priceless antique desk the scene was only minimally less frantic.

The corporal studied Félix's papers then with curled lip afforded him a quick derisive glance up and down. 'The Colonel expected you several hours ago...*Sir*!'

Félix pushed his *kepi* up with one lazy forefinger and put his hands in his pockets. Leaning against the wall he inquired with weary sarcasm, 'So what do you think he's going to do about it? Shoot me?'

As the corporal opened his mouth to reply a man entered the hall from an adjoining room. Catching sight of him the corporal leaped to his feet and Félix winced at the crash of a British soldier coming to attention, while even the scurrying Italians began to walk more sedately and the noise level dropped several decibels.

'Sir! Your aide has arrived.'

'So I see.' The newcomer, wearing the badges of a Lieutenant Colonel walked unhurriedly across the floor; ignoring Félix he addressed the corporal. 'Spill one drop of ink or scratch one line of *graffiti* on that desk, Hennessy, and I'll have your balls on toast!'

'Sir!'

Félix winced again. The newcomer turned and gave him a long, leisurely appraisal, from his hand made shoes to his black and gold *kepi*. After one glance at the steely eyes levelled at him, Félix stopped lounging against the wall, clicked his heels and saluted. He knew menace when he saw it; a light sweat broke out on his brow. On the whole, he thought he'd have preferred the fat old fart.

'I apologise for having been er...unavoidably detained. I am Lieutenant Félix Gallimard.'

'Yes, I know.' The eyes if possible became even more chilling. 'And *I* am Lieutenant Colonel Patrick Farrell!' He turned on his heel. 'Follow me, *Mister* Gallimard!'

Holy God! There couldn't be two of them, could there? With a dry mouth and his heart swooping around the region of his elegantly shod feet, Lieutenant Gallimard followed Lieutenant Colonel Farrell with all the gloom and despair of a man being led to his execution.

*   *   *

Closing the door Patrick seated himself at another equally priceless antique desk. Casting a sardonic eye over the figure before him he asked, 'Do you possess battledress as well as full dress uniform, Lieutenant?'

'Er, yes...Somewhere. I think.'

'Yes, *Sir,*'

The prompt came with a silky menace; for the third time Félix flinched. 'Yes, *Sir.*'

'Then kindly find it and wear it. We don't want you to be mistaken for a hotel doorman, do we? All those shiny buttons, braids and lanyards, appropriate as they may be for Embassy functions and attractive as they undoubtedly are to the opposite sex, are inappropriate for the work we do in this section. So is that...' he hesitated, 'that *hat.* One of your fellow officers will no doubt be able to replace it temporarily with something more fitting and workmanlike!'

He made a dismissive gesture with what looked to Félix suspiciously like two fingers. 'If you would just see to the little matter of uniform and return here within not more than half-an-hour, I shall then be ready to discuss other rather more important business.' He treated him to another glacial stare. 'As you are inexcusably late we have a great deal of hard work to do to make up for lost time.'

Distinctly hot about the collar and swearing fluently in several languages, Félix hurried to locate the kit he'd sent ahead that morning before making his unofficial sightseeing tour of the city. After a frantic search through his three pigskin suitcases he found the necessary garments then had to bribe an orderly an indecent number of *lire* to press them into some semblance of order. Regretfully he folded his beautifully cut uniform into the bottom of his case, then dressed in the despised battle dress and wearing a beret borrowed from a grinning French Canadian Captain, made his reluctant way back again to the implacably hostile face and cold grey eyes of Anna's guardian.

What shitty luck, he mourned sadly, and wouldn't *she* just laugh herself sick to hear what had happened to him? Married, soon to be a father and now *corps de chien* to Lieutenant Colonel Patrick bloody Farrell!

Well, fuck him he thought as he knocked on the Colonel's door, at least I never left Anna any memento of my visits. Not that that is likely to stop him having *my* balls on the toast...his knees buckled slightly. *Mon Dieu,* what wouldn't I give to be back in Alexandria with Maria now!

*   *   *

But with commendable restraint, Patrick managed to spend the remainder of the afternoon briefing his new aide on his duties, which, Félix noted with growing dismay and downright terror, were many and time consuming and most of them to be performed in the company of this stern-faced man.

Inwardly Patrick was fuming. Vittorio Delgardo had been with him since Lisbon and it had been an efficient and pleasant working relationship. Now Vittorio would be at least a month, if not longer off duty with that crushed foot, and he'd had foisted upon him just about the last person he'd want to meet, let alone spend practically every working minute with.

His restrained but menacing call to London that morning had been met with some sympathy and the promise to "do something about it, but not just now, old boy as things are hotting up you-know-where...this chap can definitely be spared and his Italian is absolutely top-hole..."

'I don't care if he's won medals for his sodding Italian – and I promise you things will bloody hot up over here as well if you don't get the bastard off my back pretty damn' quick,' Patrick had ground through gritted teeth and slammed the 'phone down with unusual violence.

*　　*　　*

He paced his room before going down to dine that night. 'So much for Anna's Don Juan!' he cast his eyes heavenward. 'If he carries on quivering beside me like a frightened virgin I'll end up cutting my own throat...'

He stopped pacing and leaned against the window to look down onto the remembered soft blue shadows of a Roman evening, his mind in turmoil. Whatever I feel about the little shit, he thought despairingly, I'll have to let him know that his mother's still around...and that Asa isn't, nor likely to be...Oh, bloody hell, but I need your wise old head tonight, Charlie. He hunched his shoulders and stood gazing out over the rooftops until the gong sounded for dinner, then left the room quoting sadly, "'*I do not like my state of mind; I'm bitter, querulous, unkind...*'"

*　　*　　*

He caught up with Félix in the mess after dinner, where he stood gazing morosely down into his empty glass. Patrick placed a full glass of wine in his hand and said, 'Come outside away from this crowd. I want to talk to you.'

Holding his glass like the Holy Grail Félix walked stiffly behind him as he led the way through the gardens and sat on the wide stone parapet of a large fishpond.

'I think we must have a talk – off the record.' Patrick put down his own glass and offered his cigarette case, snapping his lighter for them both. He said tersely, 'In the past you have caused Anna, and those who love her, a great deal of unhappiness and anxiety. Happily, she has now recovered her senses so I think we can say that particular episode, disgraceful and prolonged though it was, is now safely laid to rest.'

Félix blinked, moistened his lips and said, 'Yes, sir.'

Patrick sighed. 'If this is going to be a two-way conversation, you're going to have to do better than that!' He drew hard on his cigarette. 'I have some good...and some bad news for you. The good is that your mother appears to be alive and well. It's been reported to me that some American flyers escaping from France into Spain discovered that she and a companion were running a safe house for any Allied hikers lost in the Pyrenees.' He gave a thin smile. 'I can't think of anything more likely for that lady to be doing in a war, can you?'

Relief flooded through Félix. 'I was told she had left Paris, but since then...nothing.' He spread his hands. 'Thank you, this means much to me. I hope the bad news is not too bad...' He looked up and for a second caught a fleeting, but unmistakable expression of suffering in the grey eyes fixed unwaveringly on his, and fell silent.

'Your brother, Asa, has been missing in France for over a month.'

Félix was bewildered. 'Then why haven't I already been told? I don't understand...what do you mean by "missing"?'

'He hasn't been with a regular fighting unit since nineteen-forty, but engaged in top secret work as an *agent provocateur* in France and Holland with the British SOE.' He explained the circumstances of Asa's disappearance as emotionlessly as he could, then paused and added quietly. 'A rumour that he was taken by the Gestapo was confirmed a fortnight ago. As none of his contacts have been arrested over these past weeks we must assume that he has told his interrogators nothing; in which case his continued survival is unlikely. I'm truly sorry that I've had to be the bearer of such news.'

Félix pressed his hands down onto the cold surface at the pond's edge. He said dully, 'If only one could know when it is the last time of meeting. When we last spoke together we fought...about Anna; for the second time.' He fixed his eyes on the moonlit water as a fish turned, ruffling the surface and flashing fire. He asked, 'Does she know?'

'Yes. I told her before I left for Italy.'

'Poor Anna.' Emotions he didn't know he possessed washed over him: of the great loss of Asa and of sadness and compassion for Anna. He raised his eyes again to his companion's watchful face. 'I am so very sorry to have treated her as I did and glad she found happiness with Asa.'

For a moment Patrick caught sight of an expression on that handsome but dissolute young face that went deeper than hedonistic self-indulgence. It might even be that of charity and understanding: perhaps the beginning of a genuine feeling for the pain and suffering of others. He looked down at his own wavering reflection in the pool.

You weren't so clever yourself at his age. After all, you'd seduced a girl not much older than Anna was then...and just where do you think you'd *have ended up without Charlie?'*

He gave an inaudible sigh and straightened his shoulders.

'You need to know everything your brother has done for his country, because when your mother returns home *you* will be the one who has to tell her.' He paused again then added. 'Asa and I were quite close in the way men are in war. Although we didn't see a great deal of each other, I think I can tell you quite a lot about him.'

Félix was silent for a moment then smiled faintly. 'Please. I should like that, but I shall not have to tell Maman,' he shook his head. 'Asa will be back even if only to make sure that *I* stay away from Anna!'

Patrick answered dryly, 'Then that makes two of you keeping the faith, although for quite different reasons. With you and Anna so sure he'll return, I really think the opinions of those who might disagree with you both are hardly worth the hearing.'

*   *   *

We are settling down together, Patrick wrote to Anna a week or so later. *Although I doubt we shall ever be bosom friends I am beginning quite to like him...I think I can even see why you found him so attractive for so long. At present he is still rather frightened of me, which is no bad thing as it concentrates his mind wonderfully on his work. Something, I fear, of which he has had little previous experience...*

213

Anna laughed loud and long on reading this, joining her Colonel at breakfast with a smile still on her face so that he asked, 'Who's got you going this morning? The ghost of Radley Grange shown up under your bed has he?'

'No, sir, just the news that an all too real gentleman of my acquaintance appears to have got his comeuppance at last!'

She refused to be drawn further, suppressing the minor explosions of mirth that threatened whenever she thought about Félix and his Spanish maiden. What simply appalling luck at having been foisted upon Patrick, of all people! For a time the news almost chased away the constant nagging pain that thinking about Asa brought to her heart.

With the successful launching of Overlord she had clung to some faint hope that despite the news of his capture, he might have escaped and be in hiding somewhere along the coast. But as the days became weeks and no news came, her pain settled into the constant dull ache of despair, and she threw herself feverishly into her work in a futile effort to assuage her fears. No one needed to tell her what would happen to him if he'd fallen into Gestapo hands. News of other captured agents filtered through from time to time and she had no illusions about what his fate might be.

She found herself making bargains with God. *Just let him be alive and I'll really believe in you as Patrick does...Bring him back tomorrow, even if he's horribly wounded and I'll go to mass every week, I promise...Just let me see him again and I'll never blaspheme or take your name in vain again as long as I live.*

But either God didn't make bargains or was busy elsewhere, because Asa didn't return.

22

MAZOWICZ, POLAND

August, 1944

Asa didn't know where the train was headed when it happened, none of them did. He had no concept of time; of how long they had been on the journey, aware only of the pressing bodies, the filthy floor of the jolting truck, the relentless gnawing pain of his hands and face and the broken ribs that made every breath an agony.

He realised something had changed when he came to consciousness to feel freezing ground instead of a wooden floor beneath his body, and something soft and cold falling on his face. He groaned aloud and a man's voice spoke commandingly in an unknown language. There were other voices, a sudden flurry of movement, then someone lifted his head and splashed icy water over his swollen face.

Slowly he opened his eyes to look up into a ring of impassive bearded faces. He struggled ineffectually to sit, muttering thickly. '*Deutscher*?'

The big man kneeling at his side and holding a tin cup spat on the ground and growled ferociously. Asa focused on the red star pinned to his black woollen hat. Still speaking in German he asked faintly, 'Not bloody Russians?'

One of the men in the circle spoke. '*Nei, nei...Pulaski!*'

He struggled to understand. Where the hell *was* he? They must be Polish Communist partisans, but how were they here and why? He turned his head slowly and felt blood gush down his cheek. All about him was strewn splintered wood and broken glass; a few yards away the remains of a cattle truck reared iron wheels to the sky. Somewhere close at hand there was the sound of repeated shots and an occasional scream. He decided to try English and asked, 'What's happening?'

The man with the tin mug grinned and answered in heavily accented but passable English.

'Germans...*Wehrmacht*' He put a significant finger to his temple and pulled an imaginary trigger. 'Bang! No more!'

'*Jesus*!' In sudden panic Asa struggled to rise again. Pointing a finger at his own chest he gasped, 'English ...not German!'

The effort made him cry out in pain and the man stood, then bent

215

and scooped him effortlessly into his arms and set off, striding over shattered glass and wood as though they were no more than pieces of crumpled paper. There was a sudden cacophony of shouts and screams and the stutter of machine gun fire, but Asa was beyond caring. The pain of his abused body reached a crescendo of agony as he sagged unconscious in his rescuer's arms and was borne swiftly away from the carnage of the wrecked train.

*   *   *

He came to consciousness again slowly, feeling the bandages on his hands, the comfort and relief of strapping around the wrenching pain of his ribs, the weight of cold wet linen on his forehead. Pain seared his eyeballs as he made to open his bruised lids. Narrowing them to slits he peered up into the face of a small, gnome-like man leaning over him. Seeing his eyes open the gnome spoke in the same thickly accented English as the first man's. 'Avake now?'

Asa made a brief motion of his head and the man continued, 'I do what I am able with your chest while you unconscious. They were old breaks so difficult. We have no anaesthetics so it is better then.' He gave a ghoulish chuckle. 'Not so much screaming, *tak*?'

Asa passed his tongue over his lips. 'Doctor?' he asked.

'*Tak*...Kristoff Kovak.' The gnome gestured at his bandaged hands. 'Gestapo tricks, yes?'

'Yes.' Asa risked opening his eyes a little wider. Turning his head cautiously he looked around.

They were in some kind of large underground chamber. He was raised a few feet above the brick floor, lying on what must be a wooden door, because he could feel a handle and a lock beneath his right arm. A single bare light bulb blazed above his head and in the shadows beyond the harsh pool of light he could see other, blanketed forms huddled on the floor along one wall, from which came movement and occasional groans.

'Your fellow prisoners...what is left!' the gnome stretched his lips in a gap-toothed smile. 'We blew up the wrong train; now Stanilaus goes further down on the tracks making welcome again for the right one!'

Asa remembered the trucks crowded with bodies. 'What happened to the others?'

'Some few we bring here, the rest dead...but better than the death camps, yes?'

'What death camps?'

The gnome looked at him curiously. 'You are not Jew?'

'No, a British agent in France; I was caught...I don't know how long ago. I was at Gestapo headquarters.' He wrinkled his brow, trying to think clearly. 'Then a prison before the train. Days, perhaps weeks...I don't know.'

'Better to have taken your pill, yes?'

He mumbled, 'I'm a lousy Catholic, but not that lousy...and I have a woman waiting for me!'

'Such a woman for which you would have your face and ribs smashed and lose your fingernails?'

He closed his eyes again. 'Such a woman as I would willingly lose my life for, but not to any little blue pill!'

*   *   *

Drifting in and out of consciousness, or sleep, he wasn't sure which, Asa huddled along the wall amongst the pitifully small remnants of his two or three hundred fellow prisoners from the cattle trucks, his pain dulled by a fair quantity of some raw fiery spirit that had been poured down his throat before his removal from the makeshift operating table.

As time passed he listened to the talk around him and began gradually to sort out something of the unfamiliar language spoken by his rescuers, at first trying the words out silently to himself. While not having Félix's gift he had an acute ear and soon picked out some repeated phrases.

A young woman came round morning and evening with thin, watery soup. Spooning it between his lips she wiped his mouth with her skirt, asking, '*Dobry, tak?*' He nodded, pretending to understand, but between her third and fourth visit had learned to say, '*Dziekuje, bardzo tak*'...'Thank you, very good,' at which she put her hand to her mouth, giggling and making some comment which had the comrades playing cards nearby laugh and poke each other in the ribs.

'What did she say?' he asked Stanislaus, who stood watching. The big man's teeth flashed briefly in his black beard.

'That you must have been pretty before the Gestapo had you and she would like to keep you warm at night!'

*   *   *

Despite his injuries and the lack of any food other than the thin vegetable soup and slices of heavy, bitter tasting black bread, he was soon impatient with lying idle. With his broken ribs skilfully set and bound by the gnome, and face and hands healing slowly, natural resilience and a hard, well-disciplined body enabled him to drag himself from his blankets within a few days.

His long experience in packing explosives and setting fuses was welcomed by the Poles, who appeared to wage a ceaseless underground war on their invaders. There was plenty of such work to occupy his time and in the process he soon learned enough Polish to be able to communicate reasonably well with his rescuers.

His fellow prisoners from the train proved to be a motley crew. A few Polish, a dozen or more Czechoslovakians, a brace of intellectual Frenchman who had failed to toe the party line and a score of Italian Jews. Like him some had been first in Gestapo hands others simply dragged from their homes or places of work and bundled onto the train headed for what they told him was a concentration camp. All, like him, owed their survival to being in the last carriage of the derailed train.

The cellar that served the partisans as home, explosives stores and occasional hospital was one of a warren of such places under the remains of a village, razed in the first wave of the German advance and left abandoned as winter advanced. The principle cellar in which they ate and slept had been beneath a school, and an ancient carefully tended generator gave light for part of the time, but most of their days and nights were spent in darkness or semi-darkness. Songs were sung and tales told in the long hours without light. The walls echoing sometimes with the sound of Italian love songs, or Slovakian laments. At others voices would tell tales of the ghosts of long dead heroes, or stories of sacrifice and love and war.

At these times of quiet and nostalgia, Asa sat with his back against the damp wall and felt again Anna's arms around him and her voice in his ear.

'...Even if this is all there ever is to life, all I'll ever have, I'll always be glad I had it with you...'

Then he would promise silently, 'I'm coming back, my love; I don't know how or when, but I'm coming back.'

*   *   *

Southampton, Hampshire. August 2nd, 1944 – 20.30 hrs.

Anna collected the documents from the plotting room at Combined Operation Headquarters then began walking towards the main road in search of a taxi. Five minutes later a bright smile and a judiciously heightened skirt brought one swerving to an abrupt stop beside her.

'Where to, Miss?'

'The station, please…but there's no rush. I've plenty of time.' She smiled. 'I'm having a lazy day out and it's not my money!'

'Righty-O!'

As they began to pass the common she could hear the dreaded thrum of an approaching buzz bomb and felt her stomach first lurch then contract into a hard, tight ball. The cabby said chattily, 'Them bugger's is busy today…that's eight I've counted so far…I thought the R.A.F was supposed to be poppin' 'em off over the channel!'

'I suppose they can't get them all.'

She tried hard to keep her teeth from chattering. The buzz bombs rattled her in a way the Blitz seldom had. Even when she'd stayed at Stratton Place through nights of incessant bombing she had never felt gripped by such fear. *I'm tired of all this.* She clutched tight to her briefcase. *We all are. Even Sir is jumpy as a cat when these bloody things come over. It's because they're so sodding impersonal*!

The cabby slowed to a crawl then stopped and they waited in tense silence for the engine of the flying bomb to cut out; Anna dug her nails into her palms as they both counted aloud: 'One, two, three, four, five, six…*Shit!*' They ducked at the explosion then came slowly upright again to exchange embarrassed grins.

'Reckon that was right close to The Dell…buggered up the pitch a treat I shouldn't wonder.' The Cabby fired the engine, began whistling '*There'll always be an England*' and picked up speed. Anna wiped her sweating palms on her handkerchief and leaned back shakily against the cracked leather seat, admiring the driver's aplomb and hoping she didn't look as jittery as she felt.

As they approached what had been the commercial heart of the city she looked out of the cab window at a scene of almost total devastation; the few buildings left standing were all damaged, either by high explosives or incendiaries. The long street Above Bar, once home to a shopping centre built around green parks and gardens lay in ruins. The beautiful Sailor's church now just broken walls with shattered stained glass lying amid the rapidly encroaching weeds. It was surreal to see people still walking the streets and going about their affairs, as though living amid razed buildings and walking broken pavements was a natural part of their lives.

I'm a coward, she thought, because at this precise moment I'm alone…no Patrick, no Charlie, not even St-John sodding Travers. Worst of all, no Asa….

'Where are you?' she asked the unresponsive heavens. 'Come

back to me, Asa. Please, come back to me.'

*   *   *

'Had a good journey?' Travers looked up as she laid the folder on his desk.

'Yes, thank you, sir.'

'Any trouble?'

'No, sir, only the usual pieces of pie falling from the sky…and the big Yank brass hat at COHQ couldn't decipher your margin notes; nothing out of the ordinary, sir.'

She smiled but her voice was brittle. Watching her back as she crossed the room to her own desk he could feel the tension coming from her in waves. Had it just been a particularly bad day, he wondered, or was she beginning to reach the point when she'd accept that her chap was never coming home to her again. If and when that happened, he thought compassionately, she might just simply fall apart, then what the hell would he do without his strong right hand?

*   *   *

SAN MARINO, ITALY

August 26th, 1944 – 09.30 hrs

'*Avez-vous quelque chose contre un gueule de bois?*' asked Félix plaintively, sprawling across his desk and holding his head in his hands.

Patrick looked at him with a jaundiced eye.

'No I haven't, and if you can't hold it, don't drink it. I could hear you giving your all most of the night.'

'How else but with wine should I celebrate the liberation of Paris?'

'How else indeed, but half the amount would have been sufficient.'

'*Ah-ah…Mon Dieu! Mon Dieu!*' Félix raised pitiful eyes. '*Je ne suis pas très bien, m'sieur…une aspirin, s'il vous plait!*'

Not for the first time, Patrick wondered what on earth had possessed him to keep this feckless idiot around when it became clear that Delgardo would be invalided out of the Army. Perhaps it was the link with Asa that had made him keep Félix at his side. Sometimes in a laugh, or the turn of his head he could catch a tantalising glimpse of

220

that other young Gallimard. He sighed and reached for his cap. 'Get up and make the rounds with me. Fresh air is what you need, not aspirin or the hair of the dog.'

'*Nom de Dieu*, but I must survive until this week-end and my leave!' Félix followed Patrick's stiffly disapproving back from the room. Fishing into his breast pocket he asked ingratiatingly, 'Did I show you the latest *photographie* of the little Carlos, sir?'

'You did,' Patrick threw him a grim look, 'I know him like a son. Now shut up and concentrate on your work or so help me, you'll never father another!'

'Yes, *Sir.*'

Like Anna before him, Félix had quickly learned how far he could go with M'sieur Patrick Farrell.

23

WHITEHALL, LONDON

September 9th 1944 – 16.20 hrs

'I'm getting fed up to the teeth with this view…I'd hoped someone might have sent us somewhere decent by now: Paris, for instance!' Anna leaned from their open office window and looked down on the drab greys and blacks of the home-going crowds surging along Queen's Gate. 'The last time I was *there* was in the spring of 'thirty-seven. Hitler was ranting and raving in Munich but in Paris it was still just one big party.'

'And you danced in the moonlight and fell in love with your chap!' observed Travers, with a grin.

'Danced in the moonlight, yes…but I didn't fall in love with him then; I was still too busy doing that with his brother.' She turned and regarded him with her direct look. 'You don't believe he's coming back, do you?'

'After all this time?' he shook his head. 'Sorry, no; I don't believe it likely.'

'I do. Against all the odds, I really do.'

'I hope you are right.' He looked up at the clock. 'Time those walla's downstairs were rustling up some tea – give them a shout, will you, Anna?'

'No, sir,' she detached herself from the window and began walking towards the door, 'but I shall go down and ask very nicely if we – '

There was a great roar like that of an express train racing through a tunnel, closely followed by a massive, deafening explosion. The window out of which she'd just been leaning crashed from its frame onto the street below as files fell from the shelves and plaster showered from the ceiling.

'Bloody *hell*!' Travers staggered across to where a dazed Anna was cowering against the door and helped her to her feet. 'What the *fuck* was that?'

She smothered a hysterical giggle, 'An exploding tea urn?'

'Ha!' He made his way gingerly to what was left of the window and peered out. 'There's a bloody great column of smoke going up

Chiswick way...' He turned incredulous eyes on her. 'How in hell can a bomb dropped that far away cause this sort of blast?'

Anna cleared rubble off her chair and sat down, clasping her shaking hands tight between her knees. 'There wasn't a warning, was there? I didn't hear any planes, did you?'

'No, it was quiet as a bloody tomb.' His cap had been blown under the desk and he stooped and picked it up. Banging it against his leg to remove the dust he said, 'Come on, we'll go down and see if we can find out what's happened...Tell you what,' he paused and pulled his mouth down in a grim smile. 'I shouldn't be at all surprised if that wasn't the first of those You-Know-What's we've been expecting. If so, I'd say we're going to be in for one hell of a noisy time!'

*   *   *

LONDON

November 22nd, 1944 – 10.00hrs

The V2 rockets continued to arrive unheralded, devastating in their power and destructiveness. 'Give me an old-fashioned Dornier laying eggs any day of the week, rather than buzz bombs and rockets,' remarked Anna as they once more began to pack all the files and papers, preparatory to their move out of the capital. 'At least you could shake a fist at *them* and yell 'Bastard!' when they dropped one on you.' Methodically she stacked files into boxes, grumbling, 'I can't think why we're even bothering to move, most of what we're doing now is pure routine, and it wouldn't matter all that much if everything did all go up in smoke. Anyway, seeing that the ruddy things are landing all over the place nowhere is safe.'

'They're beginning to target them better and London, as usual, seems to be a favourite,' he reminded. 'We'll be safe enough where we're going.'

'Shattered though my nerves may be it seems a pity to leave just as all the lights are going up.' Anna looked wistful. 'I walked around Piccadilly last night and apart from the fact that it was jammed with uniforms and an equal number of tarts and you couldn't get a decent gin, it was just as it always was. The shop windows lit and "Guinness is Good for You" foaming all over the corner of Shaftsbury Avenue.'

'You go on walking around Piccadilly at night and you may get more excitement than you bargained for...and there are more things in life, Lieutenant, than gin.'

'Tell me about them,' she said gloomily, 'but I really don't want to be buried in some bloody country village, just when Charlie is making noises about moving back to Stratton Place.'

He was reproving. 'Winston wouldn't like it if all our hard work did go up in smoke – and if I were Charlie I'd stay where he is a little longer, particularly as he'll be getting some company.'

'Would you mind explaining that remark, sir?'

He grinned. 'We are headed for a little hamlet near Albury, just a few short miles from your friend Charlie. *Now*, will you be a good girl and get on with the packing?

*　　　*　　　*

DOVE HOUSE, TRING

Christmas 1944

Anna stretched her stocking feet to the fire and gave a contented sigh. 'My first Christmas dinner here with you since the war started!' She smiled up at Charlie as he handed her a brimming glass. 'What's this…Rhubarb?'

'Certainly not; elderberry…and I've been saving it for a special occasion. It's been maturing for two years and has a kick like a mule!'

'I was hoping Patrick might be here this time as well.'

'No, he's still in Germany and working the flitter mouse's backside off, but they're expecting to move on into France very soon.'

She laughed and raised her glass. 'Here's to them both. I never believed they'd last that long.' She tasted the wine, 'umm. I bet our St-John isn't drinking anything as good as this.'

'No. I daresay he'll be surrounded by children and dogs and toys and sipping on a dram of blended whisky by now – if he's lucky.'

He sat beside her on the couch and she curled her fingers around his hand. 'I love you, Charlie. Do you know that?'

He smiled. 'I hope that's not the drink talking.'

Anna's fingers tightened. 'Keep another bottle of this for when Asa comes home.'

Her voice was not quite steady. He put down his glass and clasped her hand in both of his. 'When did you last have a damned good bawl?'

'Not since the day Patrick told me;' she confessed, her mouth twisting into a painful smile. 'I dare not when there's no one around to pick up the pieces.'

'Well I'm here now, so just for once why don't you stop being such a bloody stoic and let go with a damned good cry?'

Her face crumpled and she turned her head into the cushions; weeping away the sorrow and pain of her loss; finding a kind of healing in the release of long pent-up emotions and clinging to his hand as if it were her anchor in a stormy sea. Afterwards, when she was quiet he fetched a rug and tucked her up on the couch, then sat beside her until she closed her swollen eyes and drifted into an exhausted sleep. Only when he was sure she slept deeply did he leave her and seat himself in Patrick's chair by the dying fire, to settle back and wait patiently for when she would wake and need him again.

Frankie jumped onto his knees and ran a sympathetic tongue over his hand. He stroked the rough brown head and sighed.

'Why can't we take somebody else's pain and make it ours, Frankie? And what can we do for our bonny lass if she's wrong and Asa *doesn't* come back?'

*   *   *

GOSHESSAN, GERMANY

Christmas 1944

Patrick walked the silent streets, his footsteps crunching over the hard-packed snow. All about him was ruin and desolation; great twisted girders and broken walls rose skeletal and menacing against a leaden sky, the mounds of concrete and rubble beneath mercifully cloaked in a blanket of white.

He would have felt pity for those who huddled in cellars deep under the ruins or in makeshift shelters of wood and tarpaulin, if he'd been able to banish from his mind the remembrance of what had happened in places just like this; on *Kristallnacht* when the killing and looting began, the systematic 'cleansing' of the Warsaw ghetto and the obscenities of Hitler's 'Final Solution' of the Jews. Pity for the displaced and murdered left little to spare for the people of this brutalised country's bombed and ruined cities.

And yet it was Christmas.

This time last year he had knelt in a Spanish church and celebrated the birth of a child born to save and forgive the sinner. Now he was walking these ravaged streets without compassion or charity in his heart for the remnants of humanity that they sheltered.

Something moved in the shadows and he turned swiftly, his heart thumping, then gave an audible sigh of relief when he saw it was only a child who came slithering towards him over the icy ruins. She held out a filthy hand. '*Sie haben nahrung, herrn?*' she said then when he shook his head put her fingers to her mouth, '*Zigarette?*'

He smiled. '*Nien. Nichts nahrung – nichts zigarette!*'

Her feet were in boy's boots without laces; she wore no stockings and her legs were blotched blue and purple with cold. He guessed she was no more than twelve, if that. He began to unbutton his greatcoat to reach his wallet and she came nearer, lifting her thin cotton skirt to her waist with a sickening parody of a coquettish smile. '*Wie hätten Sie es gerne?*' she asked.

It wasn't the first time he'd received a like invitation in this place, but not from such a child. He crouched down in the snow and took her hands from her skirt, then pushed the wet hair back from her grubby forehead. '*Nien*' he said gently. He took out all the money he had in his wallet and folded her hand over it. '*Nimm das hier und geh Heim.*' He gestured towards the ruins. '*Jetzt! ...Schnell!*'

She scuttled away, back to wherever her home was beneath those ruins and he stood brushing the snow from his coat, feeling as though he'd been afforded a window into hell. Glad that he had sent Félix away from this bottomless pit of suffering and shame to spend his Christmas at home with his wife and child.

Soon would begin again the task of seeing how many pitiless, guilty men and women he and his men could ferret out from amid the greater herd of those who were guilty only of playing a deadly form of follow-my-leader. This was a shameful way, he thought as he made his way back to his quarters, for any man to celebrate the birth of Christ.

*　　　*　　　*

ALEXANDRIA

Christmas 1944

Maria lay with her hair spread in a dark cloud across his chest. Relaxed and half-dozing, Félix luxuriated in the slip of her silk nightdress against his skin. After all the cold, lonely nights in Germany it was a blessed relief to feel so warm and content.

He still had a sense of disbelief that he could so enjoy returning again to the same woman. Only two women had ever continued to draw him back to them like this, no matter how unwillingly: one the woman who now lay in his arms, the other, Anna Farrell.

Maria trailed a finger across his shoulder. 'You are happy to be here and making love with me?'

'Yes.'

'And have you been faithful?'

'Of course!'

A fine chance to be anything else, he thought, with Anna's old man on my back. Although that wasn't entirely true. There had been a couple of occasions when Patrick Farrell had diplomatically looked the other way, allowing him the opportunity to spend a very discreet hour or so away from his all-seeing eye.

She laughed and stretched like a contented cat. 'Look at me and say how you have made such a reformation, you bad boy.'

'I don't know,' he grinned. 'Yes I do – I have a slave driver for a boss and he leaves me no time to do anything but work.'

'Is that the only reason?'

'No. I like coming back to you.'

I can't believe I said that. He gave an inward smile. *Merde*, he even *meant* it! Thoughtfully he gazed into her eyes. When a woman had looked at him like that before it had always been the signal for him to get up and leave …and stay left. Now, he didn't have the slightest desire to do anything but remain in this bed and make love to his wife again.

Hoist with my own petard he thought, and began to laugh aloud. So this was what love was really all about! Still laughing he slipped the straps of her nightdress from her shoulders and closed his mouth on her creamy breast.

A thin wail sounded from the adjoining room, growing quickly into a full-lunged howl. Maria smiled and taking her husband's head between her hands shook it gently. 'Not yet,' she said, 'not now that you have been so noisily laughing that you have awoken Carlos!'

He growled, 'I will go,' and slid out of bed. She watched his slender back appreciatively as he padded naked across the room. Such a beautiful man! He would stray, she knew, but not for long. He was changing. Slowly, of course, but he *was* changing, she could tell. Perhaps there would be times when he was unable to resist temptation, but now she was sure he would always return to her and their child. She listened to the sounds coming from the nursery, then smiled again and settled herself for sleep. Carlos was already learning how to wind his father around his tiny fingers; it would be a long time before Félix returned to their bed…

In the nursery Félix lifted the baby and laid him against his

227

shoulder. He was warm and grizzly…and very wet, also not so fragrant. '*Nom de Dieu!*' He held his son in both hands at the full length of his arms and looked sternly into the tearful liquid brown eyes. '*Tu a un monstre gros, n'est-ce pas?*' He shook his head. 'Now your papa must hold the nose and change *le couche*, then do the walk around the room while your mama slumbers – ah, that I, Félix Gallimard, should have come to this!'

*   *   *

'I should like to know more about this man who works you so hard and keeps you faithful!' Maria smiled at him as she sat brushing her hair before the mirror the next morning.

'He is an ogre…you would hate him.' Félix buttoned the cuffs of his shirt and scowled. 'He keeps me away from *you*!'

'No. It is the war keeps you away. That cannot be helped – and you are nicer for being no longer with your fat colonel who let you drink too much and make love with too many girls.'

'No chance with this one,' he grunted disparagingly. 'The only time I got drunk he wouldn't even give me an aspirin, and he doesn't allow any camp followers.'

She laughed. 'I must write and thank him for sending me back such a reformed character.'

'He'd probably like that. He has a whiff of the Jesuit about him.' He grinned suddenly. 'I think that like the good brothers he is not himself very interested in women.'

She was amused. 'What a terrible thing for you to be with such a virtuous man.'

'Indeed. He is like a very stern papa.'

'And he does not like women at all?'

'Oh, I think he likes them all right; he just doesn't seem go to bed with them!'

'You men,' she put down her brush and shook her head, 'is going to bed *all* you ever think about? I simply do not understand any of you.'

He leaned and kissed her shoulder.

'That, *ma belle chérie*, is as it should be. Men understand men. Women understand women – but that one should understand the other? Oh, la, la, la! *That* would be disaster…for men!'

24

MAZOWICZ, POLAND

January 1945

It was cold in the cellar, a deep aching cold that penetrated through flesh and bone. Asa suffered torment with his hands; although the raw ends to his fingers had healed the crushed knuckles were permanently swollen and inflamed by the cold.

At Christmas the girl Irana had brought in a branch of fir and he'd helped her decorate it with paper stars. It stood in the corner still, brittle and brown and with the stars curling. Asa teased her about it but she refused to let him throw it away; it was a symbol, she said, of the last Christmas the Germans would spend on Polish soil.

Inevitably they were drawn together; both much the same age and enduring the same hardships they became close. Sometimes too close, he realised when in unguarded moments he would find himself wondering what might be found beneath her bulky jacket and heavy trousers. If she were small and slim; had a beautiful body like Anna, or was perhaps plump with thick legs...

There were more men than women amongst the comrades and while some of them had regular partners, others appeared to sleep with various others; and not a few with those of their own sex. There was little privacy in the cellars and much ribald talk and laughter some mornings when the generator was started and unlikely couples emerged into the light from under the same coverings. Félix, Asa remembered had come back from Spain ready to relate at length his experiences of Free Love with the female comrades but this was the first time Asa had seen it in action. He was aroused but also slightly shocked when Irana snuggled up to him in the dark one night, pressing her body against his, rubbing his crotch and saying: 'This is nice, yes? But better with no clothes!'

She was completely uninhibited and made no secret of sleeping with whom she wished or of wanting to do the same with him, laughing when he told her seriously that the girl he was going to marry was in England waiting for him. 'But England is so far and you have been away so long,' she'd answered, 'when you return she will have another lover, for what woman can wait so long when she has already known a man?'

He tried not to think about that. Even the perpetual cold and his aching wounds hadn't subdued his libido sufficiently to stop him tormenting himself with the memory of holding Anna in his arms. Of how she would wake in the mornings and turn to him, soft and warm from sleep, yielding readily to his hands and lips. That she might be feeling the same and perhaps thinking about another man as he found himself thinking increasingly about Irana, caused him many painful sleepless hours.

In this strange barren country and speaking a strange tongue, he had never felt further from his love, or more despairing of ever seeing her again.

*   *   *

Half-asleep and allowing thoughts of Anna to have full reign over his senses, he huddled into a far corner of the cellar where some faint warmth from the generator still lingered on the packed earth; only dragged back to partial wakefulness and away from his erotic imaginings by a breathless laugh and Irana's whisper in his ear. 'Do you know what Stanis took from that last train wreck? A sleeping bag! Feel...' she chuckled and catching his hand moved it over a mound of soft wool. 'Is it not large? It must have belonged to a very fat officer who had it made for sharing!' Thrusting his hand down into the bag she breathed, 'In this no clothes are necessary...'

She was naked; her hand pressed his into the heat between her thighs while with the other she began pulling urgently at the fastenings of his jacket whispering, 'Quickly, quickly!'

Already aroused, suffused with thoughts of Anna, Asa had no defence against the tide of desire now racing through him. Stripping swiftly he wriggled down into the warmth of the bag. Dragging Irana beneath him he thrust her legs apart; with an equal ruthless directness she responded and as the heat of her body closed about him all reason was swept aside by a rampant unstoppable tide of lust. It was a coupling without tenderness, violent hard and swift. Swearing he fought the confines of the bag, pounding towards the jagged edge of an agonised, tearing climax while she panted and cursed, raking him with nails and teeth, arching and bucking beneath him like a wild thing, and when he collapsed, drenched in sweat, every muscle aching, she gripped his buttocks tight, her body still throbbing and shuddering in the dying cadences of passion.

Suddenly he was overcome with guilt and self-disgust; he had never before used a woman in that way, wouldn't have believed he was capable of such violence – and it had not been Irana but Anna who'd filled his thoughts and arms; Anna's body he had penetrated in a frenzy of lust; Anna's the name he called silently into the night as he took her with a vehement bruising passion. Ashamed he made to leave her body but she dug her fingers deeper, holding him to her. 'Good, that was good. You do not go yet. We sleep like this, yes?'

Too weary and spent to resist he lay passive, cocooned in her heat, his face pressed into the hollow of her neck. 'Yes,' he said, 'now we sleep…'

*   *   *

Stanislaus crashed down into the darkness of the cellar, waking the sleepers, bringing forth a barrage of curses for this rude arousal from the dozens of huddled bodies packed tightly together for warmth.

'*Szybko, Szybko*! wake up, wake up…the Comrades are here!'

A babble of voices broke out, questioning and exclaiming, but his voice rose above them.

'Quick, quick…up, all of you!' his great laugh bellowed around the cellar. 'The Red Army has arrived! They have food…*food*!'

Asa tugged at the fastenings of the sleeping bag and tumbled out, the shock of icy cold air on his naked body bringing him rudely to life. Scrambling into his clothes and leaving Irana groping for her own garments he leapt up the cellar steps, following his companions out onto the bitter cold of the grey, crimson-shot early morning light.

All about them tough, wiry horses stamped and swirled, on their backs men wearing the hammer and sickle of Russia on their fur hats, their broad Mongolian features pinched into smiles at the exuberant welcome, while across the plain, moving towards them in a long line from the east, tanks, lorries and guns cut a wide dark swathe through the frozen snow. Asa's knees buckled. The Russians were here! The retreating Panzers, he realised, must have passed close to them during the night.

He began to shake with excitement and cold, thinking wildly that somehow he would go out with them. If they'd let him he would fight with them all the way to the German border and beyond …and if they wouldn't take him he'd bloody well walk behind them until he dropped.

'I've beaten you, you bastards!' He shouted the words aloud, flinging them from him across the acres of frozen snow. Grabbing Stanislaus in a bear-like hug he yelled wildly, 'Stanis, I've beaten

231

them and I'm going home!'

Stanislaus roared with laughter and wrapping his own arms about him lifted Asa off his feet. 'If those hands can still fire a gun, little brother, we shall see what we can do. For a man who can beat the Gestapo, Stanis will do much.'

'I don't want much.' Moisture froze on Asa's cheeks. 'I just want to see my woman again.'

*   *   *

There was some argument with the Cossacks, but Stanislaus was persuasive. He and several dozen of his men and the Czechs from the train, all of them experienced soldiers and partisans fighters, would be going forward with the main Russian army. He argued fiercely that the Englishman was a soldier and a saboteur and could fight as well as any other man. A doctor came from an artillery column and looked at his hands, touched his scars and gave a wry smile, then grunted and nodded. Stanislaus beamed, clapping Asa on the shoulder and he knew he would go with them. But he didn't doubt that if these tough, impassive men found him less than useful they would dump him by the wayside and leave him behind without a second thought.

They were in a hurry and in no mood to waste time. Those who were leaving made hasty and emotional farewells. Irana pulled Asa into a corner and holding his head between her hands, kissed his mouth passionately, then pushed him away: 'Go...go!' she demanded, then pulled him to her again, clasping him tightly for a moment before turning and walking away without a backward glance.

He looked for her before they left but couldn't find her amongst those clustered in the road to watch them leave. As he climbed into a waiting truck he looked back again, searching the crowd once more for a glimpse of her, but in vain.

*   *   *

Packed shoulder to shoulder, seated on boxes of ammunition, they laughed and talked together. For the first time since his capture more than six months before, Asa had a full belly, his body warm in thick, kapok-lined Red Army coat and trousers, stout boots on his feet and a hat with flaps that could be brought down over his ears. He leaned on the rifle clasped between his hands and wondered if his eye would be as keen and straight along the sights as before and if his damaged fingers would obey his commands, but if he wasn't so good with a rifle now he could still use a machine gun or mortar, or lob a straight grenade.

The men gradually fell silent; a few snores sounded as some slept, but Asa stayed awake, thinking about Irana as with every jolt of the truck his aching body reminded him of the night just passed.

He wondered if Anna thought him dead and if some other man had put his arms about *her* and used her roughly as he had used Irana. His gut twisted painfully at the image that arose in his mind.

He thought about Charlie, and Patrick who had been like a father to him.

He wondered if Maman was alive and well and if Félix still lived.

It was very peaceful. The driver hummed softly: *"Stenka Razin"* in a deep, rolling bass and the whole world seemed hushed. And then, as yet far off, came the rumble and flash of heavy guns and Asa knew his war was about to begin again.

*   *   *

DOVE HOUSE, TRING

10th February, 1945

Anna watched Patrick across the dining table while they ate. He looked harder, older, leaner, with the lines etched more deeply on his face, and he was wearing a closed, 'I don't want to talk yet' expression. He caught her look and gave his sardonic smile. 'Don't try to count the grey hairs,' he advised. 'That would take more time than you have leave!'

Only when they were seated around the table with their coffee did he relax and begin to talk.

'Félix is getting himself into a stew because Dorothy hasn't yet returned to her Paris apartment.' He lit a second cigarette from the first and leaned back in his chair. 'It's beginning to dawn on him that if she were alive and well she would be back by now, but there's no sign of her. I've pulled all the strings I can...' his mouth went down and he shrugged. 'An ex-guide I hired has found the place where she was living in the mountains but it was by then deserted. So far as we know, the last people to see her were a couple of escaping Canadian Air Force chaps who were hiking it into Spain. They'd been shot down and captured after D-Day, but that was towards the end of August last year.'

Anna tried to visualise where else but Paris the redoubtable

233

Dorothy might have gone. 'Was she all right when the Canadians left?'

'Apparently.' He looked sombre, pulling at his lower lip. 'However, one man died on the way over the mountains, the other only just survived. He was found in time and taken to a Spanish hospital where they discovered he had pharyngeal diphtheria. It's highly contagious so there's a possibility the infection was passed on to Dorothy and her companion.'

They were silent for a moment, then Charlie asked, 'What about hospitals where they might have been taken? Have you tried those?'

'Yes. I've got a chap checking on both sides of the border – Gaston Tatarin, a Breton I knew in Lisbon. If anyone's likely to succeed, it will be him. He's a bit of a rogue but has a nose like a ferret. If she's alive, he'll find her.'

'It isn't necessarily a killer, is it – diphtheria, I mean?' Anna was thoughtful. 'I remember there was an awful panic at school once when one of the senior girls caught it. She was shot off to hospital and none of us were allowed out for about a month. She was ill for ages but recovered and came back to school.'

'Umm, but she wasn't stuck up a ruddy great mountain miles from anywhere, was she?'

She smiled briefly then sobered again. 'Poor old Félix, he must feel terribly alone.'

'Now he's finally grasped that something's gone badly wrong, it's hit him very hard ...you know Félix, he's the eternal optimist. All along he's been saying airily "Oh, no-one ever gets the better of Maman; she will turn up when she's ready!" Unfortunately, his confidence hasn't been rewarded.'

'Marriage and fatherhood haven't changed him all that much then?'

'Not having known him before Rome I can't say, although eyeing up every attractive woman he sees has certainly taken a nose dive of late. However, *you* still have something in common with him, because he's also convinced that Asa is alive somewhere.' Patrick's mouth twitched. 'He says Asa would fight his way back from hell to make sure you didn't go to bed with *him* again!'

Anna blushed. 'I'd no idea you two had got pally enough to discuss with whom Asa might think I would go to bed.'

'You'd be surprised,' he answered, pithily, 'at how pally we are.'

*   *   *

234

Later, when they had done what had become their customary walk to the Rose and Crown and back again, he said, 'I gather your department is staying put at Albury for while. That's rather a pity as I'm taking some leave in a month or so to move everything back to the gallery. Charlie's finally had enough of it here anyway and now the Home Guard's been disbanded he's bored to death.'

'That's all right,' she returned amiably. 'Now I no longer have to worry about expecting every moment to be my last I'm more than happy to spend any future leaves in the Great Metropolis. '

Charlie grunted. 'That's always supposing I'm willing to put up with you.'

She blew him a kiss. 'If you're very, *very* nice to me, my man, I'll buy you a new apron to celebrate your return!'

*   *   *

GOSHESSAN, GERMANY

15th February 1945 – 17.00 hrs

Félix arrived back from his leave an hour before Patrick and spent the time waiting for his return in wandering restlessly between the mess and the office.

'Have you any news?' he asked when Patrick finally appeared, brushing snow from his coat and swearing at the cold.

He shook his head. 'Not yet. I phoned from London. Gaston thinks he's wasting his time looking along the border and wants to extend his inquiries further into Spain. I said I'd ask you.'

'Whatever you think, sir.' He stood at the window frowning down onto the trampled snow. 'I told Maria what a mess the Germans had made of the apartment and she thinks she should leave Carlos with his grand-mère for a week or two and get it cleaned up and ready for maman.'

'That might be a good idea.' Patrick hung up his greatcoat and cap. 'In any event, whether, or whenever, your mother returns, this war will be over well before the end of the year. Then if you intend to stay in France *you* will need somewhere to go. I imagine good apartments will be at a premium by then.'

Félix sat down; resting his elbows on his knees and pushing his hands through his hair. 'This isn't how I imagined it would be to go home…I thought she would be back, you see. Sometimes I was not a good son and I wanted perhaps to make things better between us. Now it may be too late.'

'Don't give up yet. We know she was all right up until the autumn. Now we must trust to Gaston's nose to find her.' Patrick was suddenly brisk. 'Don't sit there like a wet week in Glasgow...Come along and I'll stand you a whisky.'

'I think it's time that I stood you one, m'sieur.' Félix broke into a smile. 'If I keep on your right side you may give me a few week-end leaves in Paris when Maria comes!'

'Ever the opportunist, aren't you?' Patrick gestured towards the door. 'Out, and buy me that drink before I take pity on your wife and have you posted to Burma.'

25

CONVENT OF ST-IGNATIUS LOYOLA

CALASONA, SPAIN

25th March 1945

Dorothy reached the bench and stood for a few moments, gripping the wooden back hard with both hands. It was the first time she'd been able to walk this far unaided and she sat down slowly, sparing a wry smile for all the times in the past that she had climbed the mountain paths, not even needing to pause for breath.

She turned her face full into the sun, luxuriating in the peace and beauty of the morning; breathing as deeply as her damaged lungs allowed. Down in the valley spread acres of vineyards, with tiny colourful figures moving between the greenery. Only the busy murmur of children's voices from the building behind her, and the occasional faint bleating of Sister Theresa's goats tethered somewhere on the hillside disturbed the silence.

Soon, she thought, she must take up once more the broken threads of her life. Now that France was liberated, the war almost at an end and her strength returning, she must leave this safe haven, even if only for a little while and take steps to put her affairs in order. If spared, Félix would be back soon, and Asa sure to at least visit before settling for good in the country of his birth and where he felt most at home. He had, she thought with amused tolerance, certainly shown the pull of his English heritage to be stronger than his French upbringing.

Footsteps sounded behind her and she turned to smile at the young man walking towards her with swift, purposeful strides.

'Good morning, doctor. Have you come to make sure I don't fall off the edge and tumble into the valley?'

'I have no fear that you will do that.' He sat beside her and taking off his straw hat let the faint morning breeze stir his dark hair. 'Reverend Mother tells me you are become restless and speak of leaving soon,' he shook his head, 'foolish talk, Señora Gallimard.'

'I'm getting stronger with every day that passes and I have to go back to Paris, to my apartment. If my sons have lived through this war they will look for me there – '

He interrupted her gently. 'Señora, you will never be strong enough to return and live in France, you know that. You will need always the pure air of these mountains that have made you whole again. You would never survive an autumn, let alone a winter in Paris.'

'But it is not yet autumn,' she smiled again, putting a hand over his. 'Let me leave when I am able and I promise to return before the winter, when you may continue to watch over me see that I do as I'm told.'

'You seldom do as I tell you,' he was disapproving. 'We shall see Señora…all in good time, but not just yet.'

'It's hard, you know.' She was suddenly wistful. 'For so long I was in charge, not only of my life but also the lives of others. It isn't easy to accept I shall never again do as I wish, when I wish.' She gave a sudden ironic smile. 'If Mother Veronica were listening now she'd tell me that it was good for my soul to be humbled and come to this state, but I wasn't born into her faith and am abysmally bad at offering up my suffering as a form of penance.'

'It shows!' he smiled and stood, offering his arm. 'Come, it is time you walked back and rested on your bed…' he held up a hand as she made to protest. 'Señora, do as your doctor orders or he will not allow you to go to Paris as you wish.'

*   *   *

She lay in the plain white room that had been her home for so many months and let it begin to work its familiar healing balm. A peaceful haven this place had proved after the crowded hospital ward in which she had first awakened, desperately ill and frightened and with Louise Garnier lying still and white in the next bed, Louise, who had been such a staunch friend and brave companion through all the years of war, who had taken her to the chalet and later never hesitated to give shelter to any of the young men they found fleeing to safety over the mountains.

But Dorothy had fought her way back through the delirium of her disease only to find that Louise was dead, and herself left friendless and penniless alone in Spain.

Illness and the privations of war, she remembered now with shame, had not cured, but rather exacerbated her arrogance and impatience. When her slow recovery from the diphtheria had been halted by pneumonia the harassed doctors and nurses in the overcrowded old hospital had been grateful to have the sisters of St-

238

Ignatius take her off their hands. Here, in this quiet place during all the long and painful months of her recovery, she had at last gained some humility from the nuns devoted care of an obdurate and often ungrateful patient. Latterly, she had tried to make amends by teaching for a few hours each week in the small school adjoining the convent, gaining an unexpected pleasure from her attentive class of small girls.

'You have a gift for teaching,' Mother Veronica had said on one visit to the classroom. 'Perhaps God has sent you here that you might find happiness in staying with us and helping these little ones grow and find pleasure in learning from such a teacher.'

Very different she thought now, with a grim smile, from the way she had once been viewed by one young pupil in particular! Down the years she could still hear that clear impassioned young voice raised in defence of those she loved. See the rebellious tilt of the head and the scornful, grey eyes as she faced her, defiant and refusing to be cowed...Anna Farrell, who had made her own spirited stand against intolerance and injustice and won hand's down.

What had become of her, Dorothy wondered? Had adulthood and the vicissitudes of war changed *her*? And did she still have that fiercely uncompromising loyalty to her beloved Patrick?

She turned her head and stared hard at the white wall, summoning the vision she'd shut for so long from her mind: A young man, whose stern good looks could break so easily into a smile and grey eyes that sparked into sudden laughter. The head of dark, curling hair that she had so wanted to push her fingers through, but never dared...Patrick Farrell, who had seemed to promise so much, but ended by breaking both Cecelia's heart and her own.

After all this time she was able think back calmly, without that immediate rush of anger that the remembrance of him had for so long aroused; only in recent months had she come to acknowledge that he had not been alone in causing Cecelia's tragic decline; admitting, reluctantly at first, her own part in the death of her young sister.

The line between love and hate had been very thin. She had been inflexible and intolerant in her condemnation of Patrick, poisoning Cecelia's mind against him. By the time the child was born she had made her sister as bitter and angry as herself and in the process sapped the young girl's strength, and eventually even her will to live.

Consumed with unendurable jealousy by Patrick's rejection of herself, and his very real affection for Cecelia, even after her death she had kept from him the knowledge that he had a son. Perhaps that alone had made hers the greater sin.

Now it was too late for recompense.

CALASONA, SPAIN

2nd April 1944

Determinedly, the nun barred the doorway, her arms folded into her sleeves and a forbidding expression on her plump face.

'Señor, You cannot just walk into a Convent as you wish...did your mother not teach you such things, or are you perhaps a heathen who has been taught nothing?'

'Do I demand an entrance? Or have a sword in my hand?' Gaston spread his arms wide and gave his villainous, broken toothed smile, so that the nun recoiled slightly. 'I come only to make inquiries...the Hospital at Logrono sent me here.'

She frowned. 'To me you do not look in need of care from us!'

'No, madame, I am not ill. I look for a lady...an Englishwoman: Madame Gallimard?' He looked hopeful. 'She is here?'

'Perhaps; what is your business with her?'

'A friend has been trying to find her – for her son, you understand, who is now returned to France.'

Looking askance at this unprepossessing male the nun hesitated, then closed the door on him firmly, instructing, 'Wait there. I will inquire of Mother Veronica.'

Gaston waited, leaning against the wall and exploring his teeth with the silver toothpick he had taken from the German officer whose throat had so unfortunately come into close contact with his knife. He thought with satisfaction that his friend the colonel would be pleased that he had found his way here so soon and reward him well, though why the handsome M'sieur Farrell should go to such lengths and spend so much money to find one sick, useless old woman when there were thousands of young and healthy ones left in the world to enjoy was a mystery. He shrugged. The crazy English: they were not like other men.

*   *   *

GOSHESSEN, GERMANY

3rd April 1945 – 08.00hrs

'Sorry, sir,' Pettigrew was apologetic, 'but there's a telephone call come through for you from Spain. I said to put it through to your office.'

Patrick stopped on his way to the mess and turned back towards the staircase. 'Thank you – find Captain Gallimard and send him to me, will you? He's probably at breakfast.'

'Right away, sir.'

Good or bad, news, thought Patrick, Félix had better be on hand to hear it. He reached his office as the 'phone began to buzz and lifted the receiver. 'Colonel Farrell here...'

Félix arrived to hear Patrick say 'Do nothing else...I shall see you in Andorra as soon as possible...*merci beaucoup...que vous avez fait bien, Gaston mon ami...à bientôt.*' He put down the receiver and turned to Félix. 'He's found her...in a convent up in the mountains in the Cantabria region.'

'Is she well?'

Patrick hesitated. 'She's been very ill and as she's not yet recovered enough to leave, you will have to travel to Spain. Gaston hasn't seen her; the sisters didn't want her disturbed. Apparently she's been anxious to return to Paris and they feel if they let her know you're so close to home she'll just take off, which would be most unwise. You can fly from Frankfurt. I'll drive you this evening when I've made all the arrangements. They should be able to get you there by tomorrow morning.'

Félix was silent for a moment then asked, 'How ill is she?'

'I'm not sure. Only that she should stay in the mountains and is never likely to be able to return to Paris and live.'

'I see. Are you coming also?'

Again, Patrick hesitated. 'That might not be a good idea.'

Félix frowned. 'You have to see Gaston in Andorra, I heard you say. So why might it not be a good idea, m'sieur, to come to Calasonsa first? Maman, I am sure would want to thank you.'

'Of all the people your mother is unlikely to want to see, let alone thank, I probably head the list!' Patrick answered rashly, and cursed his carelessness as Félix's eyes immediately sharpened.

'Why should that be, sir?'

'Believe me, you don't want to know,' he was brusque. 'Don't argue; just do as I say.'

'I'm sorry.' Félix flushed but held his ground. 'I have been most curious for almost ten years why my seeing Anna was enough to send Maman into a rage and why she threw the plates at Asa when she knew he had visited her in your home!' He gave a scornful laugh. 'I suspected from the beginning that it was not Anna, but her family that provoked such fury, and m'sieur, I will *not* face my mother again until

I know why.'

'My family history is none of your business.' Patrick was tight-lipped. 'I've just given you an order; are you proposing to disobey it?''

More afraid of his mother's temper even than the threat in Patrick's voice, Félix threw caution to the winds. 'Sir, if you and my mother once had an *affaire* do not take it out on *me*!' he said recklessly, then quailed before the look turned on him. He backed towards the door, feeling behind him for the handle, 'Pardon, m'sieur. I will pack – '

'You'll stay where you are!'

He leaped aside as in two strides Patrick reached the door and flung it open. Bellowing, 'Pettigrew! Here – *Now*!' when the man appeared at a run he treated him to a tight smile. 'Pettigrew; will you pack my small valise please – I shall be gone only a day or two.'

As the batman left he turned again to Félix and pointed a threatening finger. 'One more slanderous flight of fancy from you and I bloody well *will* see you posted to Burma. Do I make myself clear?'

'Yes, m'sieur!'

'Go and see to your kit. Damned if I trust you to go alone to see your mother without stirring a further load of mischief. We'll leave immediately after dinner this evening.'

He watched the younger man out of sight before slamming the door then seating himself behind his desk. Sod the whole bloody clan of them, he thought sourly, they'd haunted him for over half his life and now here was this little puppy snapping at his heels and forcing him into a situation that would make a showdown almost inevitable.

'Well, it's been a long time coming,' he mused aloud, 'so brace yourself Farrell and be prepared to grovel. Because if Dorothy Gallimard gets one whiff that you have been playing *pater familiaris* to not only Asa but Félix as well she will undoubtedly be looking for rather more than a mere pound of flesh...'

*   *   *

SPAIN

4th April, 1945 – 08.30hrs

There was a jeep waiting for them at the airfield; not for the first time Félix wondered at the authority of this man, whom it appeared need only raise a finger to have people and things made ready for him. In

242

all the months he'd spent at Patrick's side he'd never seen him refused anything he requested.

Now the latter threw his case into the back of the vehicle and climbed into the passenger seat saying curtly, 'You drive, I'll direct and for Christ's sake don't go over more potholes than you can help.' Taking a map from his pocket he unfolded it across his knees and perused it in silence for a minute or two. Félix slid behind the wheel and waited, stealing a sideways look, noting the grey face and the sheen of sweat on the forehead and wondered if his boss was ill. He'd looked like that since they'd taken off; surely he wasn't scared of flying? He glanced at the treble rows of ribbons from two wars on the immaculately pressed battledress jacket and judged that wasn't a very likely fear in a man who'd managed to collect all those.

Patrick folded the map and leaned back in his seat. 'Turn right outside the gates,' he directed, 'follow the road to Valunza and even you can't get it wrong. It's about a two-hour drive, so we should arrive in time for coffee!'

He lay back and tipping his cap over his eyes appeared to settle himself for a nap. Félix sighed and pulled the starter. It was going to be a long two hours.

It was a silent drive as it had been a silent flight, with Patrick remaining comatose but not sleeping. Félix knew he was still in the dog house and likely to remain so after the previous day's *contretemps*, and waited in vain for the slightest indication that another abject apology from him might clear the air.

After an hour's driving and without any warning his companion suddenly jack-knifed swiftly into life, causing Félix to jump and swerve dangerously. Ignoring their near collision with a goat tethered by a roadside *casita*, Patrick pointed to a small shrine set within a grove of trees. 'Pull over just here. You may be the biggest pain in the arse since time began but I think it only fair I should put the record straight before you see your mother.'

Félix stopped the engine and sat waiting, his shaking hands gripping the wheel and heart thumping from the near miss with the goat. Patrick took out his cigarette case and offered it, then sat for a minute, tapping the flat Turkish cigarette on the lid before lighting first Félix's then his own. Eventually, he said, 'Should Asa return and you meet again, I want your word that you'll repeat nothing of this conversation until I've had the chance to speak with him first. Is that understood?'

'Yes, sir.'

'All right,' he drew deeply on his cigarette. 'You are aware, of

243

course that Asa is not your brother but your cousin, and that his mother was Cecelia, your mother's unmarried younger sister who died shortly after his birth.'

'Yes. I heard it as gossip and Papa told Asa, but our mother would never allow it to be discussed openly. Asa and I talked a little about it though when we were older.'

'And his father, were either of you told anything about him?'

'Never, although papa said once that he thought he was almost surely an Englishman.'

Patrick expelled a long breath. 'Have you *any* idea, Félix, why your mother always hated the thought of you knowing Anna...and precisely why she was so angry to hear that Asa knew *me*?'

Félix sat for several minutes deep in thought then turned to look at him with dawning comprehension. 'You?' he said, '*you* are the one who got her pregnant then disappeared?' his eyes widened, 'Holy Jesus!' he shook his head and a grin began to steal across his face. 'Anna knew, didn't she? The little vixen...no wonder there was such an explosion and Maman returned to France in such a hurry!'

'Yes, Anna knew about Cecelia because I told her – years ago while she was still at school and after your mother had pretty comprehensively let the cat out of the bag. It was only later that she put two and two together after *you* told her Asa was Cecelia's child. But she wouldn't tell me, and it took a great deal longer for me to work it out for myself. I'd had absolutely no idea that Cecelia had borne a child, or that she was no longer alive.'

Félix sat back, taking off his cap to scratch his head. 'But why such a fuss even if you – if you –' he snapped his fingers, 'how is it – screwed and did the bunk?'

He looked genuinely bewildered. Obviously, Patrick thought with some exasperation, screwing and doing a bunk had little importance in his world.

'It wasn't quite like that.' Much as he had done with Anna years before, Patrick put his companion in the picture about his life before and after Charlie and when he finished swivelled round, pining Félix with his direct gaze. 'Now that you know everything: from my rejection of your mother, the seduction and desertion of her sister and the small matter that I am, in the eyes of the law a criminal, and in your parlance, a poof – do you *still* think it's a good idea for me to be making this journey?'

Félix could scarcely repress his mirth. 'I think it is absolutely vital, m'sieur.' His voice shook. 'What a hornet's nest I might have walked into, alone and unprepared!'

Patrick was caustic. 'You still might. I suggest you take that stupid grin off your face and start driving again!'

'Yes, *sir*,' he turned the engine, 'but really, such a fuss about so little...and after so long!'

Patrick sat back and took a long look at the much too handsome profile, then asked pleasantly, 'Have you always been such an amoral little shit, Gallimard?'

Félix lifted his shoulders in mournful, quasi-penitential sorrow.

'I fear so...but Maria says I'm improving so we must hope she may be right.'

'Indeed we must.' Patrick couldn't quite hide his amusement. 'All right, drive on – and don't forget, there is always Burma if the improvement starts to slip.'

*   *   *

'If you will just wait here, señors, I will go and prepare Madame Gallimard for your visit.' Mother Veronica held up a warning hand. 'We must not let the sight of you both to come as a shock. You understand?'

As she moved towards the door Patrick rose to his feet saying quickly, 'Only Madame's son will visit, *Madre*. There's no need to let her know that *I* am here.'

'As you wish; please be seated again and wait a little. Madame is teaching this morning. I shall release her class and take her where she and her son can speak without disturbance.'

Félix paced up and down the small office his face set and lips tightly compressed. Minutes passed. In the distance children's voices sounded quietly, then louder as a door was opened; there was the sound of laughter and running feet in the corridor outside. A woman's voice called softly to quell the noise and once the children had passed whispering and giggling, there was silence again.

'*Mon Dieu...*' Félix was sweating. 'I would rather this was not happening, I do not know how to behave or what to say when we are once more alone and face to face.' Shaking, he took out a handkerchief to wipe his forehead and palms.

Patrick laid a calming hand on his shoulder. 'Don't think about what you should say and do...just speak and act as you feel.'

'If I do that I shall make a fool of myself.'

He smiled. 'You'd be much less of a man if you didn't!'

Félix was almost wringing his hands. 'I can't lie convincingly enough to Maman to cover all these last months. I shall have to tell her about you.'

'You must act as you think right; only be sure to do it gently.'

He shuddered. 'I'll try...but she's scared the shit out of me since I was a little boy. You don't understand; you have never seen my mother in a rage.'

Patrick looked down and smothered a smile. 'Oh, yes I have,' he said, 'but fortunately I was on my knees in a church at the time, and apparently even she wasn't prepared to do battle under those circumstances!'

Moments later the door re-opened and a plump little nun crooked a beckoning finger. Throwing one last desperate look at Patrick, Félix followed her from the room.

Two minutes later he was clasped in his mother's arms and weeping like a child.

*   *   *

When after twenty minutes neither the Reverend Mother nor Félix had returned, Patrick left his uncomfortably hard chair in the austere little room to walk along the corridor and step through an open door into the gardens. The grass sloped gently up towards a line of firs, through which he could glimpse a range of snow-capped peaks. The convent was built high on a plateau on the mountainside, the air of a purity that momentarily made his head swim. He walked slowly towards the trees, breathing deeply and enjoying the light-headed, euphoric sense of wellbeing it brought him.

Beyond the firs was a wooden bench, a low iron fence near the edge to stop any further progress to where the ground sloped away into the valley. He sat down and taking off his cap placed it beside him and ran a hand through his hair. Leaning back he closed his eyes and let the sun warm his face.

Strange, he thought, that the volatile Dorothy should have ended up in such a peaceful place – and teaching again. He thought of Anna and her flight from Dorothy to him. How angry and cruel he had been that night: hounding her until she'd all but collapsed and turned from him to Charlie's gentler arms. Had he been able to lay his hands on Félix then, he thought with a grim, inward smile, he'd have beaten the little swine until he begged for mercy...

A shadow fell between him and the sun. He opened his eyes and looked without recognition at the woman before him; snatching up his cap he rose to his feet, exclaiming in Spanish. 'Your pardon, senora; I have taken your place?'

She answered in English, 'No. I was looking for you.' She sat down composedly, letting her gaze travel slowly over his face. Then she gave a faint, ironic smile and he recognised his old antagonist.

Distressingly thin, with greying hair and a lined face that spoke of suffering and much pain, she bore little resemblance to the imperious, handsome young woman he remembered. He stood, disconcerted and hesitant until she held out her hand, saying gravely, 'I think that after almost thirty years and two world wars it is time for *our* hostilities to cease don't you?'

He took the hand offered, felt it tremble in his and knew what an effort that sign of peace had cost her. 'A generosity I don't think I deserve.'

'You brought my son back to me, after I had kept your son from you. *That* is generosity.' She touched the seat beside her. 'Please sit down; when we are a little more comfortable with each other I should like to talk about Cecelia and explain my own part in her death. But first will you tell me what you know may have happened to Asa?'

He sat silent for a few moments, turning his cap in his hands and looking out across the valley, before he said gently, 'There is little enough to tell about what may have happened after he was captured, but one must not give up hope. He has intelligence and great courage and if alive will find a way to escape from wherever he is – and he will come back.' He gave her a sideways glance and smiled 'Anna says he will, and Anna is usually right!'

'Then she hasn't changed.'

'No, not in her loyalty to and faith in those she loves.' He was silent for a few moments then said, 'I don't know how much Félix has told you, so I think I'd better start at the beginning and explain how Asa became a part of our lives, and with what courage he has fought his particular war...'

247

26

PARIS, 22 Rue de la St-Denis
10th April 1945

Anna paid off the cab and approached the tall building with some trepidation. Now she'd arrived she was beginning to wish Travers hadn't needed her in Paris for these meetings. Knowing that Patrick was stationed at St-Germaine he'd generously sent her off for the weekend, telling her to come back refreshed and ready for work on Monday.

She'd telephoned Patrick to find herself invited to spend the time with him in Madame's Parisian apartment, fortunately not with Madam in residence but with the even more disturbing company of Félix. The memory of their last encounter was still uncomfortably clear in her mind and quite how Félix would view such a meeting she didn't care to think. He might still bear her a grudge, or even worse take the opportunity to make at least one pass at some time during the next forty-eight hours.

Entering the hallway she rapped on the window of the concierge's lair, summoning a placatory smile as a hand resembling the claw of a large bird of prey dragged back the glass.

'*Pardon, Madame, pouvez-vous me dire ou se trouve l'appartement de Madame Gallimard?*'

The concierge folded her arms across a skinny bosom and examined Anna's uniformed figure minutely and with a suspicious eye before grudgingly directing her to the second floor.

*Well, this is par for the course...*Anna groaned with the effort needed to heave shut the gates of the lift cage, then pressed the button, rewarded after several second's delay by a constipated grinding of gears and a snail-like progression upwards. Obviously the Occupation had not frightened away the witch-like characters that had always guarded a Frenchman's castle with such tenacity of purpose, nor improved the efficiency of the lifts.

The scars left by impatient jackboots were evident on the lower panels of the door to Madame's apartment and the brass knocker hung askew. Anna rapped it gingerly thinking it would be just her luck if it dropped off and fractured her toe.

248

It was Félix who answered her knock and for a long moment she stared at him, letting her gaze travel from the close-cropped hair down over the sober army uniform to his well worn, but shining shoes. It was more than three years since their last meeting and the over-confident; egotistical dandy who lived on in her memory had somehow metamorphosed into just another man in khaki.

Then he grinned and winked and suddenly there he was, the old, unmistakable Félix. As he leaned to kiss her cheek, Anna smiled, observing amiably, 'Hello, you bastard...you haven't changed all that much, have you?'

'And you are still the sweet-natured girl I remember!' he returned, then stood aside as Patrick appeared behind him, Félix watching with a tinge of envy how Anna's face lit up as he hugged and kissed her warmly.

'I am afraid there is much to do before we restore the elegance of Maman's home.' Félix led the way into a large, well-furnished sitting room. 'Maria was here for a short while and managed to find decorators for this room and purchased new furniture. She will move here with Carlos in a week or so and then have time to remove all trace of the occupation.'

'It's a beautiful apartment and I love being back in Paris.' Anna was struggling with the vision conjured by Félix as a family man. She shot a quick look at Patrick that spelled HELP in letters a foot high and he didn't let her down.

'Perhaps we could all go out to lunch now that you've arrived... Félix knows where we can get a decent bit of horse!' He smiled and took her arm. 'Come along. I think conversation will flow more easily on neutral ground.'

*   *   *

They'd finished their meal, walked around the city and returned to the apartment to drink the best part of a bottle of Dubonnet and exchange all their news. Anna, conscious of looking her best since changing for the evening into a midnight blue silk dress and high-heeled shoes, was feeling pleasantly relaxed, and when Félix suggested they should all go conclude the evening with a visit to a nightclub she agreed with enthusiasm.

'You can count me out.' Patrick was decisive. 'I don't have the resilience of youth on my side and I've brought some papers with me I need to work on. Go on and make a night of it...Just don't wake me up if you come back too long after midnight.'

'We shall be like the mice, sir.'

Patrick looked up sharply. 'Not too late, mind...and look after her.'

Félix spread his hands. 'But of course...but I think perhaps *I* might be the one who needs that. Anna can be very fierce.'

She kicked him under the table then gave Patrick a beatific smile.

'Cluck-cluck...you're getting to be as bad as Charlie,' she said, and blew him a kiss.

*   *   *

No city had ever recovered itself so swiftly from the misfortune of war as Paris. Everywhere was light and laughter, and despite the prevalence of every shade of khaki, with a sprinkling here and there of navy and light blue, the crowds and the feeling that everyone was bent on pleasure were much the same as she remembered.

'When I was last here it was spring and Asa and I went dancing,' she offered, hugging Félix's arm as together they strolled leisurely alongside the Seine. 'That was the night sex reared its head between us for the first time and we almost got carried away. Then he got drunk as a skunk and I ended up having the most *awful* row with Patrick. He was so furious when I called him a fucking sadist in the middle of the hotel lobby full of people that I thought he was going to hit me...I went roaring up to my room and left him standing there looking a prize prat!' She laughed then pulled a face. 'I had practically to crawl to him on all fours the next morning. That was the very last time I ever swore at Patrick.'

'That I can imagine,' he answered with feeling, then grinned and took her hand. 'Now you and I will dance tonight in Paris and you can pretend that I am Asa.' He saw the fleeting spasm of pain that crossed her face; cursing himself for the careless remark he squeezed her hand. She recovered swiftly and gave him a mischievous, sideways glance. 'Do you realise that this is the first time you and I have ever walked together...or talked so much? That it's the *only* time you've ever suggested we go dancing.' She stopped suddenly and turned to face him. 'Félix, in all those years we never did *anything* but have sex!'

He gave a shout of laughter. 'Do not look so appalled; we always had a very good time doing it...much better than dancing.'

'Well, dancing's all you're getting tonight, Félix Gallimard, so you can just wipe that look off your face,' she swung his hand, 'but while I'm in the mood you can lead me to a night club, buy me a very large Vermouth and we'll do an exhibition tango that will make the barman's eyes pop!'

*   *   *

At midnight they were almost the last couple left on the dance floor. In the long months since Asa had left, she'd danced with many men and managed to remain detached, even with the attractive and sexy St-John Travers. But she hadn't reckoned on the powerful effect of being in Paris again, nor how much the closeness of Félix would flood her whole mind and being with an unbearable and overwhelming desire and need to make love again. She had spent so many months dreaming of Asa, of feeling his mouth on hers, his hands caressing her...

She tried to be rational. To bring her mind to bear on this problem as she would any other, knowing it was Asa she wanted, not Félix, but somehow her brain refused to follow its usual logical pattern. Félix simply wasn't there, she was seventeen again and dancing with Asa, feeling that first stirring of passion and helpless to break the spell.

Félix's heart was pounding against hers, she felt him draw a deep breath. When he spoke his voice was crisp, but held an underlying note of panic. 'Anna, will you please do something about this? I am trying very hard to think of my wife and you are being no help at all!'

She came back to the present with a rush. 'Oh, hell – I'm sorry.' Her face flamed and she pulled away from him, 'but just for a few minutes...' The tears started to her eyes. 'Oh, Félix, I miss him and want him so much I can hardly bear it...'

'It's all right. I know it isn't me you want.' Gently he touched her burning cheek. 'Once, I would not have stopped, would have taken advantage as I did that last night – and for that, Anna, I am so sorry...But now,' he smiled, 'now I have Maria and Carlos and soon you will have Asa again.'

'Don't...I feel such a fool; letting myself get carried away like that.' She took the handkerchief he handed her and pressed it to her eyes. 'It's this damned city; it seems to have a very bad effect on me!'

'I will find us a taxi.'

'No. Let's walk. I don't want Patrick to see me just yet.'

'Then we shall walk slowly that you may recover, or he will blame me for making you upset so that you weep!'

She gave a shaky laugh at his apprehensive expression. 'Why, Félix! After all this time you're still frightened of him!'

He drew her arm through his as they stepped out into the street.

251

'Not so much now, but because he has stopped savaging my ankles at every turn doesn't mean that I go looking for trouble.'

'No need to play the hero and take the blame Félix, it was my fault.'

'It was nobody's fault. *C'est la guerre!*' he said then pulled his mouth down. 'But Patrick, he has the sharp eyes. He will see through us both.'

'It's all right.' She was recovered now and gave him a teasing glance. 'He'll only skin you alive! No, honestly, he will understand. You don't know Patrick as I do; he can be such a stuffed shirt sometimes, but nobody ever knew better than him when *not* to notice what's going on.'

Félix was thoughtful. 'That is true, he can, as you say, turn the blind eye.'

She gave a disbelieving snort. 'You louse, he's already done that for you, hasn't he?'

For the first time she saw Félix looking abashed. 'Only once or twice: at the very beginning,' he ventured. 'I think he knew how hard it was for me to be away from my wife for so long!'

'How did I ever manage to fall in love all those years ago with a bastard like you?' She began to laugh. 'No more dancing for you and me Félix Gallimard; you go back to your Maria unsullied and free from sin.'

'In future when we meet she will be with me and I shall be very correct.' He squeezed her hand, 'and you...*you* will have Asa...'

'Yes, I shall have Asa, and I expect we will all smile and shake hands and talk about the weather.'

He sighed. 'I know now that I did love you, Anna.'

'I believe you did...just a little.'

He leaned to very briefly kiss her lips. 'Quite a lot, but – no more comforts for the troops!'

She shook her head decisively. 'No more comforts at all, Captain Gallimard ...except from your wife.' She searched his eyes her own clouded and suddenly unsure. 'He will come back, won't he, Félix?'

'Of course he will...if only to give me another bloody nose for dancing with his woman!'

*   *   *

'Have you enough francs for the taxi?'

'Yes, Patrick.'

'Ticket, identity papers, leave pass?'

'Yes Patrick, and a clean handkerchief.' She smiled. 'In a minute you'll be telling me to be a good girl this term.'

He pulled his brows together. '*That* would be a waste of time, judging by last night's little *contretemps*.'

She blushed. 'Please, don't give Félix a bad time. He was terribly noble about it all and you frighten him enough as it is.'

'I know perfectly well which one of you got carried away; it was written all over your face when you came back.' His mouth twitched, 'and I won't frighten him; at least not any more than usual. But it's good for him you know – keeps him on the straight and narrow. He needs to have the fear of God put into him from time to time!'

'Umm, and you're just the one to do it, aren't you?'

The cab drew up beside them. He put his hands on her shoulders. 'Just make sure you don't have *too* much to confess when that man of yours comes home.'

'Well, there are one or two things...' she gave him her brilliant smile, 'but go on looking after his little brother and tell him I won't let Asa bully him again. That wouldn't be fair, would it? Not with you doing such a good job in his absence.'

27

BERLIN

4th May, 1945

Asa made his way through the unfamiliar streets. He felt lost without the comrades with whom he had travelled so long and fought so many hard battles, but knew he must reach the British HQ as soon as possible.

Moving slowly through the devastated city he found himself in a section that appeared to be inhabited mainly by large, healthy-looking Americans in well-cut uniforms, who walked confidently through rubble strewn streets empty of all but cautious men, wary-eyed women and ragged children. At one corner he came across a group of GIs distributing what looked like half the contents of their PX Stores amongst a throng of half-starving urchins, while a crowd of sullen youths stood at a distance, looking on, spitting ostentatiously and muttering amongst themselves. Catching sight of Asa, one of the Americans hailed him loudly.

'Hi-ya, Ruskie ...want some cigarettes?'

He shook his head. 'No thanks. Actually I've given up!'

The GI gave a bellow of laughter, 'Say, whatcha doin' in that get-up Limey...goin' to a fancy-dress party?' he left the group and walked over to Asa. 'I met up with the Ruskies at Torgau – did we have a party; I was bushed for days.'

'I believe you. I was there.'

'You fought with them?'

'I did; all the way from Poland.'

'This I gotta hear,' he held out his hand. 'The name's Colleano... Sergeant Pete Colleano.'

'Asa Gallimard.'

They shook hands and Pete grinned, 'Sounds more Frog than Brit!' He clapped his shoulder. 'C'mon, lets go find a beer...not in any German bar though, even if there was one left. One look at that outfit you're wearin' and the *Gastwiert* would crap himself!'

'With good reason,' Asa was terse. 'What we found on the way here didn't exactly incline us to love our enemies.' He fell into step beside the American. 'I'm on my way to Spandau – to the barracks; I must report to the British Army HQ there – and I need to get a message to England to my girl, God knows where *she* is now. Then I must go to Paris and see if I can find my mother and brother. But I guess I can make a small detour...I haven't tasted beer since nineteen forty-three!'

'What was your outfit and how d'ya get in with the Russians?' Pete asked when they were seated in the sergeant's mess, with a line of beer cans between them. When Asa explained he whistled and looked closely at the scarred hands with their misshapen half-grown nails. 'Jeez, but I bet you'd like to catch up with the Kraut who did that!'

'I have dreams about doing so,' he answered shortly, then raised his beer can with a sardonic smile. '*Prost*! God rot all who ever wore Gestapo uniform, may they fry in hell!'

Put at ease by his welcome Asa drank more than was wise for his lean and temperate stomach.

He had fought his way across countries ruined and laid waste, the retreating German army leaving little but scorched earth and dead cattle in its wake. Not all the surviving Poles in the villages and towns they passed through had welcomed the Russians. If they had food they kept it well hidden unless they were Communist sympathisers and the army had lived for months off iron rations, supplemented from time to time by supplies of meat and canned vegetables from the U.S. With a constitution accustomed only to survival rations and little alcohol, a large number of cans of beer consumed in the steamy heat of the mess soon had his head spinning.

Hours later he staggered to his feet. Squinting at the wall clock he laid an affectionate arm on Pete's shoulder, slurring, 'Gotta go now...Nesh time I'll stand *you* the beersh...'

'You're stoned – better stay here, pal. We can find you a bed for the night.'

'No. 'S'all right. Mush report I'm not dead n'get some proper clothes...can't walk about in this get-up mush longer – s'got a lot of crawlies in it!'

Escorted outside and launched into the night by a dozen willing, if not entirely sober pairs of hands, he walked with exaggerated care along the dark, deserted streets, humming softly to himself. Tonight, he thought, he would sleep in a proper bed and tomorrow get a haircut and shave and a decent uniform that didn't have lice in every seam and then...and then he would find Anna.

He sang aloud in a melancholy tenor.

'*Goodnight, sweetheart, now the day is dawning,*

Good night sweetheart, see you in the morning.'

He didn't hear the stealthy rush of feet behind him, nor cry out at the blow to the back of his head. Just fell silently, and lay, arms flung wide, his face in the dust and grit of the road.

A young voice said: '*Russisch arschloch*!' Hands searched his pockets, found only a few coins. '*Schwein-Scheilse*!' A boot drove into his ribs and someone spat. Then there was the roar of an engine as a jeep turned the corner and drove erratically towards the group, the driver yelling and swearing vigorously and they scattered, melting away into the ruins and leaving the still figure of Asa Gallimard sprawled in the dirt.

* * *

STRATTON PLACE, BLOOMSBURY

7th May 1945

When the 'phone rang Charlie left off polishing his shoes to answer it, glancing at his watch as he did so and hoping it wasn't Anna ringing to say she couldn't make it today.

'Charlie.' It was Patrick, his speech clipped and strained. 'Is Anna with you yet?'

'No. She's coming after lunch. How did you know she was due here today?'

'I phoned Travers; he thinks she might have gone to the V&A first. Can you go and look for her? If you find her grab a taxi and take, don't send, her straight to Travers. He knows what's happened.'

'Which is more than I do,' Charlie cut in crisply. 'Speak up, Patrick. This is a lousy line and you're not making sense.'

'Asa's been found. He turned up unconscious in an American hospital at Landsfürt, wearing Red Army uniform but fortunately still with his ID disc, so they were able to trace Félix. He's with him now and I'm leaving in an hour to fetch Dorothy.' He was speaking carefully, measuring out his words, and Charlie who knew him so well could sense the effort it was taking to stay calm. 'I can't tell you much, only that he was attacked last night in Berlin after spending the evening boozing with some American servicemen. How he got to Berlin and where the hell he's been all this time I've no idea…I might know more when I've spoken to the chaps he was with before it happened.'

Charlie asked quietly, 'How bad is he?'

256

'Pretty bad.'

'Are you all right?'

'I am while I have something to do.' There was a pause; he said, 'I need you. I wish you were here.'

'Shall I come?'

'Later, not yet; it's hell here. If he doesn't regain consciousness soon we'll try to get him to Paris – or even better, to London. I can stay here for a couple of days then I have to go back to France. Better if you come then if necessary...' He broke off briefly as someone spoke to him then came back on the line. 'I have to leave now. Find Anna for me, Charlie and break it to her gently. Travers is pulling strings and tying to make arrangements for her to fly out from Northolt, so the sooner you can get her to him, the better. Try the Victoria & Albert first; if you draw a blank there, see if she's visiting her old boss at Lorenzo's.'

'I'm on my way.'

Charlie put down the receiver then squatted to pat an inquisitive Frankie.

'Hold the fort, old boy while I break the news to a lady that her man is back from the dead, although if I'm reading *my* man right, it could be touch and go whether he makes it for much longer.'

*   *   *

BERLIN

8th May, 1945

'I'd like to know how Captain Asa Gallimard is and where I can find him. I've been travelling all night so please don't say I can't.'

The white-coated doctor eyed the wild looking young woman confronting him and shook his head. 'He is still unconscious, Lootenant.'

'What's that got to do with anything? I didn't bloody ask if he could see *me*, did I?'

The doctor made a swift clinical appraisal of this truculent female and thought she looked as though a bed in a quiet ward might be the right place for *her*. It was a long time since he'd seen anyone look that ill and still able to stand on her own two feet, let alone fire off a double salvo like that. He cleared his throat.

'Are you all right, Lootenant? You look kinda sick yourself.'

Anna stared back at him with hostile eyes. *Of course I'm bloody all right...and what the hell is a 'Lootenant' when it's at home? Bloody idiot!* Aloud, she said very carefully and clearly, 'I should like to see *Left*-tenant Colonel Farrell, please. Going by appearances so far he's probably the only one around here with marginally more sense than a headless chicken. The moron who met me at the airport and brought me here couldn't tell me anything, nor could that fat bastard of a porter I found downstairs. If you won't either I'll need to speak to someone I know who *doesn't* keep his brain in his bloody trousers!' She closed her eyes for a moment then opened them to ask apologetically, 'I'm sorry, did I say that?'

He smiled nervously. 'If you'd just like to follow me...'

Since Charlie had found her in the museum Anna felt she'd shifted gear; possibly even landed on a different planet. She was pretty sure she was walking and at least thinking normally, but all along had a nasty feeling that she might be speaking some of her thoughts aloud. She made a tremendous effort now to focus properly on the doctor. He wore enormous horn-rimmed spectacles, looked about sixteen and must have shaved in a hurry because there was a piece of tissue stuck under his chin...

'This way, Lootenant,' he was waving his arms invitingly and she tagged on behind as he led the way down a long corridor and into an over-bright room with wooden chairs upholstered in orange, the windows hung with lime green curtains.

A grey-haired woman and a man in army uniform were seated by the window engaged in earnest conversation, but both looked up then rose to their feet at the sound of the opening door. The woman took a step towards her. 'Anna...'

Anna looked at her blankly, then at the man. She said, 'Sir?' then uncertainly 'Patrick?' before everything changed gear again, there was a rushing sound in her head and then she was hurtling down a long dark tunnel into oblivion.

*   *   *

She was lying on a narrow bed and the light was too bright. From behind her closed lids she could see it, hot and red. She said, 'It hurts. Put it out!' Someone moved and almost immediately the glare was dimmed to a soft glow. Slowly she opened her eyes and said sleepily, 'Hello, Patrick.'

'Hello.' His face creased in a smile. 'Back to normal, are we? You quite frightened that young doctor...he thought, as he put it so succinctly, that you'd 'flipped'!'

'I think I had.' Hazily, she passed a hand over her forehead. 'Did I swear at him?'

'Only moderately.'

'Oh, shit! I thought I might have,' she rubbed her eyes. 'I got a bit pissed-off when he kept calling me 'Lootenant' and looking as if I'd come from Mars...I had to find you, you see, because no one would talk about Asa and I had to know.'

'It's all right. The night staffs were just changing over, that's why no-one was looking out for you.'

'Can I see him now?'

'You can in a minute, when you are quite awake.'

She pushed the blanket away and sat up. 'I'm OK. I feel a prat lying here. Is Félix around?'

'Yes. He's catching up on his sleep.' He looked at her with compassion, asking, 'When did *you* last do that?'

Her brow wrinkled. 'I don't remember. It doesn't matter.'

'It does to me' He stroked the hair back from her temples. 'You did get yourself into a state, didn't you?'

'I'm all right now.' She wanted to curl up and be cosseted but it was time for her *alter ego* of balanced, competent woman to re-emerge. She swung her legs off the bed and sat on the edge, rubbing briskly at her hair. 'You wouldn't have a comb, would you? Damned if I'll let Asa see me looking this messed up.'

'He's unlikely to see you at all.' he warned. 'They think he's over the worst, but he still hasn't regained full consciousness yet. His night nurse reported a slight improvement and whilst you were out for the count Dorothy said his eyes flickered and half opened.'

'Oh my God,' Anna was horrified. 'It *was* her, wasn't it? When I came in she was with you – she isn't still here, is she?'

'She most certainly is.' He showed his amusement at her reaction. 'There's no need to look quite so panic-stricken. She is not the monster you remember but a perfectly normal human being!'

She said '*Oh, yeah,*' under her breath and stood up, automatically smoothing down the creases in her uniform.

Patrick gave her a severe look and handed her a comb. 'Are you going to behave yourself?'

'I think so, although I wouldn't bet on it.'

'No,' he said dryly, 'neither would I.'

*   *   *

She stood motionless and silent by the bed, looking down at Asa's ravaged face. A long deep scar ran from one eyebrow to join the old one across his scalp, hidden now beneath a streak of white hair. There were other healed scars on his cheeks and jaw, while the once beautiful tapered fingers were misshapen, with something akin to transparent cracked mica in place of nails.

Battling with the emotion that threatened to overwhelm her, she sat down on the edge of the bed and lifted one of his hands, smoothing it gently between her own then leaned forward and put her lips against his ear.

'Wake up, you *imposteur sanglant* and get yourself home!' she breathed unsteadily. '*Ce lit n'est pas assez grand pour nous deux*!'

For a long minute nothing happened then one corner of his mouth went up and stayed there for a few seconds and his lips parted, but so briefly that she wondered if she had imagined the slight movement.

The young doctor, who was stood behind her said quickly, 'That's the second response in an hour…what did you say?'

Anna blushed, 'Nothing that I'm telling *you*.'

'Well go on saying it!' The eyes behind his spectacles shone with suppressed excitement. 'The guy grinned and damn' near said something. If he's your guy you know what to do to get him going, so do it.'

'Oh, very clinical and professional; stop breathing down my neck, you voyeur and I'll do my best,' she gave him a scathing glance, 'and my best is pretty damn' good.'

Patrick inclined his head towards the door, suggesting mildly, 'If you want more response from *him*, without getting an awful lot more from *her*, I think you should leave them alone. Believe me, it could get worse.'

Anna didn't even notice them leave. With her head on the pillow beside Asa she talked him back through their times together in Paris and London, and all that had happened since they'd last said goodbye. Once, his fingers moved against hers and she could feel a muscle working in his jaw. Scarcely daring to move, she sat on while her legs went to sleep and her back ached and she said all the things she'd been storing during the long months apart.

*   *   *

Félix stood with his arm around his mother and watched through the round window of the door. 'She is pretty wonderful, is she not?'

A little worm of jealousy stirred in Dorothy, then as quickly died. 'Yes,' she agreed, 'pretty wonderful.'

Félix grinned and squeezed her shoulder, 'Quite wasted on Asa of course,' he said, 'but then, *viva l'amour,* eh, Maman – *viva l'amour!*'

*   *   *

It would be a long haul back, but by the time Anna was due to leave and return to duty, Asa was out of bed and walking and talking normally. The big American sergeant, Pete Colleano, who had followed him in his jeep and saved him from his attackers, came almost daily with his arms full of candy for the nurses and magazines of a somewhat dubious genre for Asa. Then just before Patrick and Félix returned to France, Charlie arrived to take their place with the invalid, narrowly missing Madame who had been borne off after a few days by her anxious Spanish doctor, much to Anna's relief. Although the animosity towards Patrick was apparently at an end and Dorothy had welcomed Anna's presence at Asa's bedside, the likelihood of Charlie ever being more than politely tolerated by her was, she thought, fairly remote.

'Just as well she's gone, then,' Charlie said comfortably, when Anna met him at the airport and voiced her thoughts. 'There are some people, my lass, whom one should *never* meet in this world and hopefully not in the next one either – if it exists, which despite all these years with Patrick I personally doubt.'

The day before Anna was to fly back to England he managed one of his diplomatic disappearing acts, leaving her alone with Asa.

They sat in long cane chairs at the end of the hospital garden, shut off from the outside world by high walls, and masked from the one storey building by an old willow tree. A lone bee buzzed around some early blossoms and the air was redolent with the subtle odours of spring. Anna held Asa's hand and wondered how anyone could look so sexy in drab hospital pyjamas and dressing gown. Though enjoying some very pleasurable sensations stirred by these thoughts, she knew if he was willing and she could find the courage to speak, there were other deeper matters to be faced before they could go down that road again.

Patrick had warned her before he returned to duty. 'You know what I have to tell him, but the medic's think I should wait. I've given them a letter for him to read as soon as they think he's well enough. He knows I'm on the end of a 'phone at any time, but if you're still here when he's read it I think you'll be the one he'll want to talk to first.' He gave a strained smile. 'You may, of course, be the *only* Farrell with whom he'll wish to speak ever again! I don't believe anything can spoil the future for you and Asa, but whether he'll want me as any part of that future, I'm not so sure.'

'There are a few things *I* have to tell him that I'm not too sure about,' she had replied gloomily. 'So it should be a jolly time all around!'

But sooner or later the contents of Patrick's letter which she knew Asa had read that morning, and her own past indiscretions with Félix must be faced. Accordingly she had engineered this time alone together when they could talk with no chance of being interrupted by hospital staff or friends.

Now in the peace and privacy of the garden she waited for Asa to make the first move, but he seemed in no hurry to talk. Eventually she took a sideways glance at his face and he met her eyes. Squeezing her fingers gently he broke the silence.

'I have been thinking: if you can put up with me we should get married as soon as I return, then after the war find a house a little away outside London. Somewhere on the river...' He was contemplative, his strong, dark face softened and shaded from the late afternoon sun by the trailing branches. He lay back, keeping hold of her hand, his head turned towards her, his mouth curved into a smile, 'where I shall return each day from the university and spend my evenings making love to you!'

She took his cue, playing the light-hearted game with him.

'And what shall *I* be doing with my time when not making love?'

'Oh, you will take your Fine Arts degree then help to run the gallery until Patrick is too old and doddery to do so, when he will retire and you will be the boss.'

'Huh, don't I get to do anything else but work and be made love to?'

He offered teasingly, 'There will be the babies to keep both of us busy.'

'I'm not too happy about the plural.' She wrinkled her nose. 'One little Gallimard would be nice, two would be tolerable, but I'm not at all sure about venturing further. It might be rather like playing Russian roulette, there could just be another Félix in the chamber if you spun the barrel too many times!'

'Hmm...'

He fell silent. Anna felt her heartbeat quicken. 'Is there anything else you want to say, or ask, before I leave tomorrow?'

He said 'Hmm,' again, then, 'One thing...I could hear before I could speak and move, you know,' he turned his head to stare into her eyes, 'Certainly enough to hear you tell me you'd slept with Félix

262

again. You really did say that, didn't you?'

She hedged. 'Well, I might have. I said a lot of things at that time, some of them pretty far-fetched and quite a lot of them downright disgusting. I was only trying to jolt you awake...I didn't know you were listening and storing every word.'

He said slowly and deliberately, 'Anna did you, or did you not go to bed with Félix after *we* had made love together?'

'Well, yes...' She stared into the lengthening shadows thrown by the tree. 'It didn't happen the way you're doubtless thinking. I thought I was handling it all so brilliantly until he caught me completely off guard. And you know Félix...'

'Tell me.'

She took a tighter grip on his hand. 'It was after you'd gone back from those few days we had alone at Stratton Place. I got a lift up to London that Christmas. I only had a forty-eight and the weather was too foul to travel to Tring...'

Not looking at him, but still keeping his hand clasped in hers, she went through the events of that night. When she had finished he sat without speaking, but he left his hand in hers and she took courage from that. 'I thought I'd cleared up...scoured every trace of him from the house. I didn't want to tell you; didn't want you to know I'd let him come between us to spoil all the lovely hours we'd spent together.' Absently she stroked his fingers, her brow puckered in a frown. 'Although Félix was really the most unprincipled louse, it wasn't altogether his fault; I *should* have just shoved him down the stairs and locked my bedroom door, but I was so desperate for you that I hadn't the moral strength to stop him. Then when you found that cigarette packet I panicked and lied. The first, the only time I ever lied to you. I'd often been what Charlie calls economical with the truth, but I never really lied.'

There was a very long silence. She looked at him again. He was watching her, on his face the kind of thoughtful, assessing expression she'd seen so often on Patrick's, when he was trying to make up his mind how high he was prepared to bid in the auction room. Under that steady gaze she blushed. 'I do understand if you're angry, all I ask is that you don't shout...when anyone does that it always brings out the worst in me!'

'You mean there's more than I've already seen and heard?' He looked away for a moment then turned to face her again. A smile began at the back of his eyes. 'If I also tell you something quite disgraceful, will you promise not to shout at *me*?'

'That depends; how disgraceful?'

He let his eyes travel down the length of her before looking out again across the garden. 'The night before I left with the Russians I was in our freezing cold cellar, having some *very* erotic thoughts about you that kept me from sleep. When a girl called Irana took off her clothes to proposition me in a sleeping bag, it was an offer I couldn't refuse – well,' he added honestly, 'I suppose I could have, but I didn't!'

'Oh!' She caught her lower lip between her teeth. 'Was she OK?'

'I'm not sure. She might have been.' He flushed and looked away again. 'At the time I wasn't fucking her, I was fucking you – that is, I pretended it was you: but I was rough – violent: I used her – no, I did more, I abused her, and through her, you. Afterwards I felt like a rapist.' He lifted his shoulders; tried to smile. 'So you see I have no grounds to censure your surrender to Félix.'

'I think it's time we left what each of us has done in the past.' She moved to sit on the edge of his chair, lifted his hand to her lips and kissed each scarred fingertip. 'Now we have got our murky sex lives out of the way perhaps we can talk about Patrick's letter that the Doc gave you this morning.'

He put his hand in the pocket of his dressing gown and handed the envelope to her. 'Read it,' he said, 'and you will see there are some things that are beyond discussion; even beyond words.'

Close to tears Anna read the beautifully phrased, uncompromisingly truthful letter that Patrick had left for his son. Restrained and deeply moving, his honesty and integrity shone through every word. When she finished reading she laid down the paper. 'Didn't you ever guess?'

'No. I knew there was a bond between us. I felt his concern for me and in return I liked and trusted him more than I had any man. It puzzled me, but that was all.'

'How do you feel now that you know everything?'

He leaned back, looking up into the gently stirring leaves in silence for a minute. At length he answered simply, 'When I speak to him in the morning, I shall tell him as I tell you now, that I feel...honoured.' He turned again to smile into her eyes. 'What a time you had keeping the truth from me for all those years!'

She answered him feelingly. 'My juggling act between you, Félix, Patrick and Charlie would have got me a passport into any circus.'

He put out his hand to grasp her wrist. 'This isn't very romantic. Why are we still sitting apart?' He pulled her into his arms. 'I didn't fight my way half across Europe just to sit and talk; I came to make love to you.'

Anna laced her hands behind his head. 'In less than two weeks you'll be home and we'll make full use of my lovely big bed at Stratton Place again.' She kissed his eyes. 'No air raids, no blackout and no more cloak and dagger for you. Just a nice quiet job behind a desk, haranguing the cookhouse, inspecting for athletes' foot and sorting out dying grandmothers until the war ends and they throw you out.'

With a familiar expertise he slid her down beside him and laying his lips against her throat murmured, 'Two weeks is a very long time, we could perhaps do with a little practice? Nothing too energetic, you understand.'

'Don't try to run before you can walk,' she admonished with a smile. 'The doctor says you must take one step at a time. If you have a relapse I won't be accountable for my actions.'

He grumbled, 'It was my head those thugs hit, the rest of me is still in perfect working order.'

'I had noticed.' She took his face in her hands and kissed his mouth. 'Patience, the war is as good as over. Soon we shall have all the time in the world.'

*　　　*　　　*

They lay quietly as light died from the sky and darkness closed around them. Anna's head was on his shoulder and his long arms wrapped around her. He browsed his lips slowly over her hair and down her cheek.

The night was very still; far off and to the east he could hear the rumble of trucks and wondered if he would ever see any of his Polish or Russian comrades again: it seemed unlikely. He thought about Patrick and what he would say to him when they spoke on the telephone in the morning. How he would feel, how they would both feel when they met again as father and son. Strange, probably a little awkward at first, but that would soon pass. He gave a little inward chuckle. Oh, to have been a fly on the wall at that meeting between Patrick and Maman! Félix, mischievous and insouciant as ever had likened it to the immovable object, his maman, giving way to the irrepressible force, Asa's papa ...ah, that brother of his; what a bad boy he had been; could he really be changed for the better?

It would be good to go back to Bloomsbury, he thought dreamily, to taste again Charlie's cooking; to sit with Anna and Patrick in the quiet garden and plan their future; hear Charlie's wise old Scots voice smoothing over troubles and sorting their silly lives into some kind of order.

But despite his light-hearted words about their future he wasn't fool enough to imagine that the first years of peace would be easy. For those returning from battle, and those who had stayed at home and kept the faith, the future was far from clear and not very bright.

Five years of war had changed everything; now they were different people returning to a different country from the one they had left in nineteen thirty-nine. A country which had been bludgeoned and brought almost to its knees would face a long convalescence before the wounds of war were healed – if ever...

Anna stirred and murmured in sleep; putting such melancholy thoughts aside he laid his lips against her hair. Anna, his dearest, awkward frequently wrong-headed, but always loyal Anna whom he loved above life itself...he felt a sudden upsurge of desire, sharp as a knife, then relaxed and let it fade.

I can wait, he thought. Anna is right. We have time now; we have all the time in the world.

By the same author

A Year Out of Time

A Year Out of Time is the story of one twelve year old girl from a "nice" middle-class background and a "nice" private school (where her mother hoped she might learn to be a lady) who, in the Autumn of 1940, finds herself pitched into the totally foreign environment of a small Worcestershire hamlet.

For the space of one year her life revolves around the village school and its manic headmaster; the friends she makes, notably Georgie Little the "bad influence"; the twee but useful fellow evacuees, Mavis and Mickey Harper, whose possession of an old pigsty proves the springboard to some surprising and sometimes hilarious happenings; and Mrs 'Arris, the vast and formidable landlady of The Green Dragon Inn.

In the company of Georgie Little she awakens to the joys of a new and exhilarating world: a secret world which excludes most adults and frequently verges on the lawless.

The year comes to an explosive end and she returns unwillingly to her former life – but the joyous, anarchic influence of the Forest and Georgie remains, and sixty years on is remembered with gratitude and love.

ISBN 978-0-9555778-0-2

Available from Sagittarius Publications
62 Jacklyns Lane, Alresford, Hampshire SO24 9LH

By the same author

And All Shall Be Well

And All Shall Be Well begins Francis Lindsey's journey through childhood to middle age; from a suddenly orphaned ten year old to a carefree adolescent; through the harsh expectations of becoming a man in a world caught in war.

Set mainly against the dramatic background of the Cornish Coast, it is a story about friendships and relationships, courage and weakness, guilt and reparation. — *The first book in a Cornish trilogy.*

ISBN 978-0-9555778-1-9

Chosen as the runner-up
to the Society of Authors 2003 Sagittarius Prize

"The author has succeeded to an extraordinary degree in bringing Francis to full masculine life. The storyline is always interesting and keeps the reader turning the pages. All in all it is a good novel that can be warmly recommended to anyone who enjoys a good read." – Michael Legat

"Seldom do I get a book that simply cannot be put down. The settings and characters are so believable, the shy falling in love for the first time and the passion of forbidden liaisons written with feeling. Many of the sequences left me with a smile on my face, others to wipe a tear from my eye." – Jenny Davidson, The Society of Women Writers and Journalists Book Review

"A beautifully written novel. Eve Phillips' writing is a pure joy to read and her wonderfully graphic descriptions of the Penzance area of the Cornish Coast made me yearn to be there." – Erica James, Author

Available from Sagittarius Publications
62 Jacklyns Lane, Alresford, Hampshire SO24 9LH

By the same author

Matthew's Daughter

Matthew's Daughter is the second book in a Cornish Trilogy and follows Caroline Penrose, as she returns from her wartime service in the WAAF to her father's flower farm in Cornwall. But once home she finds a number of obstacles and family conspiracies impeding her path to peace...

ISBN 978-0-9555778-2-6

The Changing Day

The Changing Day the final book in a Cornish Trilogy, begins in 1940, when a meeting between WREN Joanna Dunne and Navy Lieutenant Mark Eden is the start of a love affair that at first seems unlikely to stand the test of time. She is 22, single and an Oxford graduate; he is 36, married and in civilian life a country vet. She is attracted but not looking for romance, he is attracted but not looking for commitment and, as Joanna soon discovers, he is the black sheep of his family and has a very murky past.

ISBN 978-0-9555778-3-3

Available from Sagittarius Publications
62 Jacklyns Lane, Alresford, Hampshire SO24 9LH